HOLOHEAD

A NOVEL

T.D. HOLT

Novels also by T. D. Holt

Substrate

Oblique

www.tdholt.com

Library of Congress Cataloging-in-Publication Data
Holt, Thomas D (T. D. Holt)
HoloHead. A Novel / T. D. Holt
ISBN-13: 978-0692158234 (T.D. Holt)
ISBN-10: 0692158235
1. Romance. 2. Science fiction 3. Politics.

V1.7-08.08.18

Printed in the U.S.A.
Cover design: Marin Graphics
Cover: iStock Photo: 495607759-AGSANDREW

To Life—
filled with Innovation,
tempered by Wisdom
—graced by God.

Following the 2024 election, Mac, a war-torn veteran suffering from PTSD, stumbles across evidence that the President of the United States is not the woman elected. Targeted by a nation that has perfected the use of holograms, can Mac rescue the real President from that nation's lecherous leader to help her return to unite America?

The universe was a vast machine yesterday, it is a hologram today.
Who knows what intellectual rattle we'll be shaking tomorrow.
— R. D. Laing

If everything moves along and there are no major catastrophes
we're basically headed towards holograms.
— Martin Scorsese

Tell me and I forget. Teach me and I remember.
Involve me and I learn.
— Benjamin Franklin

Give me mass and I exist. Vector me and I go.
Release me and I control.
— Hoppy Hologram

...What If...?

Some questions, before the action.

Is this story a distortion of reality—a science fiction flower-child?

Science fiction? That's what folks thought of the musings of Galileo and Jules Verne: spacey notions from marginal believers.

Far-out bull, or insightful warning? That depends on a person's background, perspective, education, belief in God or not, and, imagination: the ability to grasp new ideas, to fathom innovation.

Innovation? It's the unveiling of science's secrets, the conversion of science fiction into reality, the unique blending of pre-existing ideas and technologies.

Has innovation been beneficial? Sure, there are plenty of examples: Shakespeare, Madame Curie, Henry Ford, Hedy Lamarr, George Washington Carver, and Elvis. Even Einstein, who brilliantly innovated the relation between energy (E) and mass (m) and light (c) as: $E = mc^2$. His equation suggested that mass and energy are the same. That energy derives from mass and that mass can be expressed as energy. All tied to the speed of light, which is considered a constant—essential to our reality take on the universe.

Reality? It's been extended by tech innovation. Virtual- (VR) and Augmented-Reality (AR) continue to invade our screens and sustain the mantra of brave new geeks everywhere. Virtual reality is the digital re-creation of a setting to provide a lifelike immersion. Augmented reality creates overlays to alter and enhance what is real. Within these realities, filmmakers, storytellers, and tech geeks have long imagined an android—a robot-like synthetic organism resembling a human. But such creations have existed solely in imaginations and altered realities of games, film, and books. Until, perhaps, now.

The reality is that some innovation is intended never to see the light of day. When kept secret, innovation's end game is *control*.

There are nations that hang their identity on the fertility of new ideas, on innovation. *What if* a nation has focused world attention elsewhere so that it could secretly innovate energy and light and mass in a way never before imagined: $m = E/c^2$?

At first glance, this flipping of Einstein's equation mimics ninth-grade algebra. Easy to imagine, to express on paper. The subtle trick, however, is that if the speed of light were *not* a constant, one could create and *alter* tangible mass.

What if this nation has devised a way to *create* mass by *reducing* the speed of light within optical interference patterns? Patterns that form holograms. The tactical aspects of this technology are less important than the strategic implications: this nation now has a way to create mass from light to yield free-standing life forms.

Hologram forms with self-sustaining space occupancy, light energy, behavior, touch, and *mass*. A human facsimile, a replica out of thin air, vectored by the nation's artificial intelligence (AI) backend.

What if...

CHAPTER 1

The President

And so it began in earnest: the kidnapping of POTUS—the newly-elected President of the United States. Yet, to fully understand the unlikely events leading up to this unnoticed crime requires patience and a full appreciation of humankind's propensity for innovation.

As you may remember, the outcome of the November 5, 2024 presidential election, resulting in the closest electoral results in U.S. history—chads and popular-vote stats aside—remained contentious. Until, on December 12, 2024, when the incumbent—blaming the loss on the systemic disease once referred to as fake news but now widely accepted as journalism-as-usual—finally conceded defeat. Regardless of confirmation of the incumbent's dereliction of duty: the *oblique* plot to hijack the government of America.

After the election and leading up to the inauguration, the president-elect was ardently resisting pressure to assign—once she took office—a special prosecutor to investigate what many considered the ex-president's most egregious violation of the nation's trust. Placards and cries of "Bring back the pillory. Send *him* to Gitmo!" erupted across America. Fortunately for the nation—especially the soon-to-be ex-president—the president-elect understood that her number-one priority was healing the long-divided country. To do so, she must also defuse the incendiary rhetoric of the headlines penned by the yet-to-be humbled media. Humbled? *That* will always be fake news.

On Monday, January 20, 2025, Margaret E. Perserve, the forty-eight-year-old farmer's daughter, took the oath of office of the President of the United States. She stood atop the inauguration platform on the western front of the U.S. Capitol, beautifully fashionable in a charcoal topcoat, her shoulder-length auburn hair tossed slightly in the chill, whimsical breeze. The sun's rays, filtered by threatening overcast, played off the single strand of pearls at her neck.

Moisture crept at the edges of her gray-blue eyes (historians would debate if from the wind or the moment; the less tolerant suggesting that, after all, she *is* a woman.) Her high cheekbones, offset by lush eyelashes and sensuous lips, lent a boundary of grace to her lingering, yet determined smile.

The enraptured crowd, a shimmering sea of enthusiasm estimated at more than two million, packed the Mall from the Capitol Building to the Lincoln Memorial. To engage the crowd in this momentous event, huge *iMe* augmented reality (AR) screens—alongside Dolby air-cushion speakers—were arrayed astride the gravel paths that framed the Mall. This was indeed a momentous event. The first inauguration of a woman president. It was also the first AR-immersive inauguration, where each person in the crowd, while wrapped in the sound pulsating from the speakers, could use their mobile device to embed themselves on the AR screens. For example, sitting there stolidly on the platform, next to the First Husband. A tug-of-war of sorts began between those wanting to augment the First Husband's bare head with a formal top hat and those wanting him adorned in a Senators baseball hat.

Others had themselves sitting next to that ancient Senator from California, the one oft-quoted as saying, between sips from an oxygen cylinder, "Immigration with limitation is the death knell of liberty!" Others, mostly women, embedded themselves next to that handsome, retired NFL quarterback, now a newly-minted representative from Massachusetts. The ripples of excitement, while members of the crowd pointed and pushed as their image splashed across the AR screens, drew attention from the final words of President Perserve: "So help me, God!"

The roar of the Salute Battery's 3-inch guns echoed across the Mall, startling many in the crowd, including two young girls held by their parents who were standing right below the inauguration stand. The girls' cries, rising above the cannon din, caused TV network directors to switch cameras onto the family: emblematic of a new era for women.

The girls' mother, standing proud and erect in her blue dress Marine captain's uniform, turned to her husband, whispering to his ear and planting a sweet kiss on his cheek. The cameras zoomed in, catching a tear on her cheek which she firmly wiped with the palm of her hand as she adjusted her daughter in her left arm.

The network commentator's voice-over carried the moment. "Have we, as a nation, *finally* come together? Is it possible? While I may not, and this I say in all humility, I do not believe in God, I must admit our nation's journey over the past sixteen years has been fraught with such disharmony and division that its peril seemed a foregone conclusion. But, and here again, out of character, I rejoice, as do we all, at the election of Ms. Perserve. Something, some spirit, is back among us. The spirit of America? Divine intervention?"

The captain's husband moved the daughter he was holding to his right arm and, standing at attention beside his wife, held her right hand tenderly in his left. The masses spread across the Mall absorbed this seminal moment playing on the screens.

A transient hush swept the crowd, no longer immersed in their own images upon the screens. From somewhere out of the stillness (TV pundits would argue over the exact location), a woman's voice rose softly from the Mall's huddled masses: "God bless… America…"

Muted at first, then with an accelerating, collective rush, the entire Mall erupted into song. The TV cameras swept across the faces of the crowd. Hardly a dry eye. Frowns of bewilderment, transitioning to tears, filled the screens.

The commentator, choking back his own residue of emotion, allowed, "Is this joy I hear? Can it be? Is it love for country, from all those in this diverse mass of citizenry? Oh, joy! A sound we have all so wished would return to our national dialogue. I am, along with my many journalist colleagues, thankful, and frankly quite amazed, at how, since the election just two short months ago, this woman, now our president, has won the hearts of most Americans. Especially those who supported our departed and hopefully forgotten ex-president. A true miracle! It may well be impossible to replicate this moment. To realize the potential before President Perserve and her message of unity."

After crinkling out a smile to her young daughter and son who sat arm-on-arm next to their father, the president cleared her throat. She took a deeply-drawn breath as she looked down at the pages of her acceptance speech fluttering in the breeze. An expression of humility—an acceptance of responsibility—flittered across her face. It was the same expression she'd had the first time she had driven a harvester combine across the wheat fields of her father's farm.

She smiled and nodded briefly to herself at the amazing journey she had made from those fields to this moment. She raised her eyes out towards the Washington Monument, envisioning its peak adorned by the words, "Laus Deo" (Praise be to God). She looked off to the right, taking in the facade of the Museum of African American History. It was emblematic of how far the country had come, yet, too, how much farther America had to go.

Gracefully dabbing her nose with a tissue taken from her coat pocket, she rotated back to look up at the American flags framing the Capitol Building. Nodding with determination and understanding, she turned slowly back to the microphones. None of this was lost on the audience—those on the Mall and those in front of their TVs—around the world. A moment of supreme hope surged across the globe.

For all, save the secret innovative team of a nation, thousands of kilometers away, laughing at the ironic accuracy of the commentator's use of the word *replicate*.

CHAPTER 2

The Nation

The inauguration video streamed live to Building 666, hidden deep within a remote complex: the headquarters of RID—the nation's Recursive Intelligence Directorate. Thick-necked to match her body, with dark eyes of penetrating fierceness framed by close-cropped black hair, Director Dong absently brushed her flushed cheek with an open palm. She was intent on studying the rapidly changing variations in the images of President Perserve suffused by the Directorate team.

Laughter carried across the secure room as some of the team augmented the motion of the First Husband's left hand—his right hand holding the *Bible*—to reach out and grope the president's increasingly AR-enhanced chest. One could work wonders with AR. In combination with heuristic robotic hacking, AR was a key tool in the nation's intelligence arsenal. An arsenal assembled by the nation's Leader— himself living testimony to Lord Acton's insights about power— without regard for his citizens' naturally peaceful inclinations, well-being, or levels of vitamin deficiency.

Ever since the nation had lost its basketball franchise and incurred devastating sanctions, the nation's Leader had pulled all stops—sparing no expense or citizen—to accelerate his singular goal of personal self-preservation.

A heavy clap by Dong, invoked via a rapid double-blink on her data glasses, echoed across the headsets of her team. All snapped to attention. All except Dr. Heraldo Juong who was absorbed in synchronizing his secret hologram-generating software to the images coming in from the D.C. inaugural platform. He was matching President Perserve's every nuanced move. His discrete nod conveyed to Director Dong that it was time to call the Leader. The hologram-generating system was ready!

She nodded, smiling at her team's cheers, raising her hand to her forehead at the memory of two years earlier—January, 2023.

—— . ——

On that cold January evening, she had had drinks with the nation's Leader in his Humbleness Garden. He had asked, "Comrade Director, why, again, do we want to perfect the application of holograms?"

She had replied, "As you know, dear Leader," bowing slightly, "a hologram is formed from the interference, ah, the combining of light beams." Her eyes had narrowed slightly to take in his right eyebrow as it folded into his forehead to form an unspoken, too often dangerous, question mark. "Yes, yes. I know," she continued, nervously stroking the air with her hand. "It seems old tech. Yes, companies in the decadent West did come out with what they called hologram-based virtual assistants and presenters. All have been static, not interactive. Even efforts by nations to enhance their opening Olympic ceremonies with the use of holograms—even those efforts have fallen short. Nothing like what we have developed with Cassidy."

"Cassidy?" The chairman had frowned, clearing his throat as he purposely looked away, counting the koi nibbling at the cracker crumbs he tossed. Cassidy? He knew all too well it was a name assigned by Dong—herself an addict to the untamed American West, circa 1880— as portrayed by her other love, Hollywood. His frown had transitioned to a smile. Knowledge was power, and he knew everything that happened within *his* country.

Encouraged by the chairman's pleasant demeanor, Dong had continued. "Cassidy is our ability to create and *deploy*," she whispered hesitantly, "free-standing holograms. Holograms that embody mass. We will be able to park and control human-like forms anywhere in the world, in any building regardless of security. This will be a most elegant achievement. It stems from our ability to manipulate the speed of light. An innovation that no *human* on earth thinks possible!"

Seeking to hide his astonishment, the chairman had continued nodding, silently working his lips around his teeth and squinting to contemplate how Dong's innovation might be used to terminate sanctions and his self-imposed threat of annihilation. How it could be used to *finally* establish his rightful legacy in the world.

His lip-smacking had transitioned to a self-congratulatory smirk, acknowledging his own genius of usurping the world's focus the past twelve years. Now an unnecessary strategy. Why threaten the world with his own self-destruction? Why not control the world by controlling the linchpin—the United States, those arrogant bastards—using a hologram-based manikin to replace their doofus American president. So that he, the chairman *himself,* controlled the linchpin?

"Tell me more," the chairman had asked Dong as he stroked his chin. "How many on your team? You say you can manipulate the speed of light? That *is* unimaginable! Are there other uses?"

"Oh, yes! Beloved Father! Doctor Juong and I are the two who know how to manipulate the speed of light. Besides holograms, we envision many uses. For example, a light-shield of sorts, thwarting any attempt by the West to attack us," Dong had replied, fearful the chairman might focus on her non-regulation, non-vynalon Western-style pants. Shrewd as well as brilliant, Dong knew the chairman preferred fire-plug bodies. She hoped her regulation, dog-fur-collared, squared-off coat would draw his eyes from her pants.

"Shield? Yes, yes. Indeed intriguing. But perhaps unnecessary, given the potential for your... ah...?"

"Cassidy!"

"Yes, your Cassidy. *That* potential is inspiring. I must commend you, Comrade Director, on your innovative thinking, and... your jeans."

Holding her breath, her heart in her mouth, waiting for the next move by the chairman, the director had almost fainted until the Dear Leader slapped her back and laughed like, well, like the dumb donkey that he was. She had joined in, cautiously bowing with a slight chuckle.

As he had smiled at the idea of riding Cassidy to world domination—unsure if Cassidy was the cowboy or the horse—the chairman had struggled to bite down his reoccurring bile re-visitation. A condition that all too often accompanied his recollection of that American president—the one who had called him the "goat of all time." Such pejorative language had kept the chairman up late at nights in spite of the many pretty and varied *treats* his loving toadies—such sycophants—had recruited, forcefully or otherwise. He was mildly aware that such love was hollow and merely the progeny of fear. Not something to dwell on. Instilling fear in his subjects, from the highest general to the lowest prison serf, was his primary skill set. Fear, too, in the West. But enough with the fear tactic. Cassidy could provide the platform for a new skill set: control through guise and grace. It would no longer be necessary to be known as the world's *forcebully*—that disgusting label ascribed to him by the now-deceased Norwegian journalist.

"Can you shape your hologram, your human, ah... replica, to the likeness of anyone?"

"Anyone? Indeed!" Dong had replied, choking as she caught herself almost admitting that anyone included anyone, *even* the chairman.

As he had sensed this dangerous potential, he stepped back to look more closely at this brilliant scientist. She was attractive, in a squared-off manner. He tried to imagine if she would be a good thump without her coat or her jeans. "Another time," he told himself.

"Anyone?" he had mused. "And from anywhere?"

"Yes, absolutely, Dear Leader."

He had stepped closer to Dong, raising his hand to her shoulder. "Let us consider the many possibilities, and yet, also, cautiously, the consequences, if anyone were to hack or hijack those possibilities."

"Yes, indeed. But please know that hacking will be impossible. We have developed an impervious, autonomous data transmission method."

"Wonderful, wonderful. And you say, 'anyone'? I'm curious. To whom might you consider applying your hologram technology?"

Dong had rubbed her forehead in quiet contemplation, thinking back, cautiously, to her desolate childhood in that state camp for orphans whose parents had not found favor with the nation's leader. A camp filled with pain, longing, and isolation. A camp she would not have survived had not another orphan shared with her the few moments of freedom he had experienced reading a *Hopalong Cassidy* comic book found in the waste bin he had been cleaning. The Cassidy stories had been the seed that, over the years, nurtured Dong's subconscious desire for letting right be done while the hardships she had endured fueled her innate propensity for technology and analytics.

She had struggled to recall the look in the eyes of a woman—said to be her mother—last seen on a frigid day when she was four years old. It was a look of love and grace framed within the hardened features of fear and starvation.

Standing in the garden with the Leader, watching crystalline waves of breath roll from her mouth—waves propelled by an accelerated beat of her heart—Dong had first sensed a vague hesitancy, a doubt about the innovation she was creating on behalf of the Leader. Created solely for the Leader. Not for her country or the myriad thousands languishing in the camps. All like the camp where she had learned to retreat inside her thoughts, to survive through artful cunning. The hardships she had endured forged in her an unyielding conviction of what it took to survive. Foremost were the belief in her own decisions and the will to push forward with a determination that bordered on righteousness. She had been fortunate. It had taken a coldness of will— a coldness she despised without realizing it.

As she had focused on the Leader's large nose protruding through the clouds of breath, furrows of doubt crept across her forehead. She had had to shake her head to formulate a cautious reply. She had answered, "I would start with a list of world leaders for whom we could substitute holoheads. Ones that would make policy in favor of our, ah, *your* nation… dear, wise Leader."

Dong had jumped back in shock as she absorbed the chairman's sudden, raucous shout. "I like it! Holoheads! Call the technology Cassidy, yes, but its output will be holoheads that *I* control. Yes, truly, I love it! You are a good military strategist as well as a superb scientist," the chairman had replied, lowering his hand farther to stroke the dog-fur collar of her squared-off coat. "Another time," he told himself.

"How confident are you, that our holohead can imitate the exact physical, intellectual, and even the spiritual nature, of the person it replaces?" he had asked.

Timing—the mimicking of expected responses—was essential. Dong had glanced at the koi as she said, with a coy smile, "A perfect physical match. On that, we have measured and are certain. And from a behavioral standpoint, our holohead has an intelligent backend…"

"An intelligent ass?" he had asked, narrowing his eyes as he gave further pause to consider Dong's tight-fitting jeans.

Closing her coat's fur collar as if to shield her body, Dong had replied with a slight bow and a humble tone, "No, no, dear Leader. A backend, meaning computers here in our building that create an artificial intelligence—AI for short—that will replicate, in absolute real-time, any of the behaviors and attitudes we want your holohead to display. Behaviors that reflect what we've observed from hundreds of hours of studying the target, with the added benefit of vectoring of all decisions in *your* favor."

The Leader had looked away, as if studying the Siberian fir and other coniferous trees ringing the garden. He walked along the cobbled path bordering the koi pod, noting the crystalline rocks arrayed along its edges and the overhanging mulberry trees. He turned back to Dong.

Sensing weakness in his understanding, Dong had continued, "But, spiritual, Dear Leader? I was not aware that such consideration was appropriate? Do you mean something like the soul that the Greeks imagined, the incorporeal essence of a human? Or do you mean, perhaps, the soul as viewed by some religions as living on in a state of heaven, united with God?"

"Of course not! You know what I mean, Comrade Director! How does a holohead deal with what the West would consider various types of ethical dilemmas? Does our holohead ponder? Does it struggle with the many serious decisions like the ones I am faced with? Without that sense of reflection or an occasional display of angst, its guise might be pierced, even revealed."

Angst? "You are so wise, dear Father! Yes. In appreciation of the myriad challenges that you so ably deal with, and in anticipation of your insight, we've developed an AI module. We call it SS—our Soul Simulator. It provides the holohead with an overlay of passion, of moral longing and conflicted thinking in the face of dilemmas. As you have so wonderfully taught us, we know that the essence of what might be called a soul is really *only* the firing of chemical synapses in the brain. Maps of which we have been able to derive based on MRI imaging. These maps reveal how firing patterns link memory with the prefrontal cortex of the brain regarding emotional regulation, judgment, and impulse control. We have translated these maps into our Soul Simulator."

The Leader nodded, his eyes narrowing to bypass the confounding technology and focus instead on the vision he imagined of himself at the vanguard of humanity. He lost concentration until Dong's words broke back into his consciousness.

With a loud outburst and her hands in the air which caused the front of her coat to open, she had exclaimed, "I laugh most sincerely at those dorky geeks in Silicon Valley who have long dreamed of androids. All the while admitting that androids can only be figments of one's imagination! Easy to imagine, yet impossible to deliver. Besides actual physical manifestation, the key reality component of an android that remains elusive is the *soul*. Our SS delivers the components of a soul. All aspects of a holohead's thoughts *and* its behaviors are controlled by our artificial intelligence modules and our Soul Simulator. Our holohead is nothing like those simplistic replicants portrayed in *Blade Runner*. Not at all!"

With a smirk to cover his wandering thoughts, the Leader had asked, "Runner? Components of the soul? What might those be? Regardless, well done, Comrade Director!"

Stepping closer, his hand moving down the open front of her coat, he had continued, "We can discuss your, ah, simulator at a later date..."

—— . ——

From that 2023 garden chat, Dong was given the strictest mandate to complete Cassidy in time for the 2025 inauguration in America. From Cassidy she was to create a holohead that could hop along, interacting in real life, as it were: drink tea, sign papers, ride horses, shake hands. Make love? Yes, just another cowboy: a hero, a fiction by which the duped audience—the world—could be led.

The inauguration would be perfect timing, of this, the Chairman had been beyond certain. He had interpreted his numerous dreams, often featuring pigs, as sufficient evidence that the United States would elect a new president at the end of 2024. A president with whom the American minion citizenry would not be familiar, and thus one whose persona his holohead could easily replace with minimum suspicion. True, there would be those close to this new president—intimate, even, if the behavior of past American presidents was any indication. But not an issue, his RID team had assured him. The Leader had reflected, momentarily, on the notion of stereotype: that all leaders had intimate diversions to temper their expression of power. All leaders in the West, and in the East.

———— . ————

Staring intently at his television screen as the inauguration scene unfolded, the Chairman—the Leader—hung up the phone, Dong's joyful words ringing in his ears. "Dear Leader, I am so pleased... I can report that Cassidy is ready!"

Watching the new American president babble on in her crude, foreign tongue, he imagined his holohead in her place. Her kidnapping would be a delicate challenge for his State Security Ministry, true. Timing would be critical. But once the replacement with the replica— the holohead—was complete, he would have accomplished an unimaginable achievement: unprecedented, secret innovation—*control.*

Stepping closer to the television, he pressed his lips against the warm glass, kissing the image of President Perserve—standing there so pristine. "*Latrudomio,*" he growled. After a moment of reflection, he nodded. Her non-squared-off body was, indeed, quite appealing. He scratched his pants as he considered that he would continue to subscribe to the stereotype of leaders with their intimate diversions. Only this time, his diversion would be, or would have been, the most powerful woman in the world. Making him the most powerful of all.

CHAPTER 3

Mac and Mindy

As Director Dong basked in the plaudits of her team and the Leader in his imaginings of the kidnapped president, near Boston, Massachusetts, video of the inauguration streamed into the dorm room of basketball star Gloria Reynolds where she stood transfixed, watching the television with her fellow screaming students. They were the cadre—the InnerTraction (IT) team—that had played such an essential role in exposing the truth: the ex-president's D37 plan for hijacking America. The students' yells were sparked by unbridled joy for the righting of their beloved country's ship of state under President Perserve. Yet, their yells were dampened somewhat by pain over the condition of their beloved professor, Lincoln "Mac" MacMahan.

Mac was the Army veteran—the wounded warrior—who had so ably taught them about communication and messaging. He had been their professor, their mentor on life. It had been his guidance and example, his sacrifice and love, that had nudged the students in pursuit of the truth in uncovering the D37 plan. For a brief period within that pursuit, the opposing forces of reason and human nature had played out as point-counterpoint on the international stage. With truth, distortion, and variations thereof spinning within the global news cycle like so much dirty laundry. Until the original values and intent of America's founders prevailed in a most unique expression of liberty: the outcome of the 2024 presidential election.

Lost within a spectrum of PTSD, Mac had sleuthed faith from confusion, had given his all to his students and his country. Ironically, he had been rewarded—as he sought his missing girlfriend Mindy— with a night stick swung by a NYC police officer. One who, to put it mildly, was having an exceptionally bad hair day.

More than two months had passed since Mac had been beaten by that NYC police officer. A painful period of devastating emotions had bridged Christmas and the welcoming of the new year: 2025.

The blow to Mac's head from the policeman's baton had caused severe injury, sending him to the emergency room. Mindy, still recovering from her car accident, had asked—more like insisted—that her friend Joanna find Mac. Along with boyfriend-doctor Santiago, Joanna had found Mac at Bellevue Hospital, in a coma. Further investigation had revealed that maverick medics using false IDs had tried to silence Mac and his revelation of the D37 conspiracy. They had injected him with an overdose of an untraceable drug, further complicating his head trauma. After a series of negotiations, Mac had been transferred to New York Presbyterian Hospital, the same hospital where Mindy was recovering. It had taken two weeks for the doctors to rid Mac's body of the drug. During that time, Mindy had stayed by his bedside, whispering words of love and encouragement into his seemingly-deaf ears.

Slowly—agonizingly slowly—Mac had regained consciousness. He would mumble only a few words, the most important being a warped sound which she took to be "Mindy," as his eyes reflected a love for her from the depth of a soul lost. He was fighting. Fighting to recover, to spend time with this vision before him: Mindy.

In early January, two weeks after Mindy had been released from the hospital, Mac was moved to a rehab center paid for by grateful citizens to acknowledge his role in steering America away from the D37 collusion of the ex-president. While the ex-president had avoided impeachment, several officials at the Pentagon and Veteran Affairs were fired for their participation in the campaign to discredit Mac.

Mac was alive. For that, Mindy thanked God. Alive, but in what form? On that, she too often consulted her demons of worry. So unlike her, but there it was. She'd wept over the doctors' words of caution that Mac might not fully recover from his brain trauma.

Now, as she sat by Mac's bed twirling her fingers through his hair, she excitedly watched the inauguration on TV. Smiles were all Mindy had for Mac. At least, attempted smiles. After barely surviving her own head-on crash last September, the plastic surgery to reconstruct her jaw had been a success. Her natural beauty was returning, her blue eyes drawing attention away from the slight bulge in her right cheek—also masked by her shoulder-length, wavy brown hair. Attempted smiles? Her heart—oscillating between an overwhelming desire to lie next to Mac to make up for time lost *and* his obvious pain—dismissed those smiles. She held his hand, following with her eyes the track of his empty stare out the window. Shaking her head in sad wonder, she mulled over the random, ironic events leading up to Mac's present condition.

Mindy hoped the restoration of his reputation might help heal Mac's emotional wounds and offset, somewhat, his PTSD. She worried about how much more he could take. She grimaced as she stroked his hand, at how, during his time in the Army, he had received three serious wounds. The worst from RPG shrapnel that had torn through his face, leaving a severe scar running from his right eye to his mouth.

"Are you there?" she asked as she leaned over the bed to kiss his scar. Her lips moved gently to the tip of his nose, then to his lips, which she moistened with a tender caress of her tongue. Her breasts pressed against his chest.

"I am now," Mac replied, his widening eyes struggling to form a smile. He squeezed her hand. Stronger than yesterday.

Mindy stared into his hazel-green eyes as they searched back and forth across her face, his pupils dilated, his breaths short and puffy, enveloping her. He moaned, and with their lips softly expressing love, she brought her right hand to stroke the left, unscarred side of his face. The moan was not one of pain, but longing. The doctors and nurses had cautioned Mindy, with titters and chuckles directed at themselves, to minimize physical contact and arousal. His brain would not benefit from the release of too much dopamine or phenethylamine. Not yet. Mindy had scowled at their inside joke. She was well past wanting to avoid getting herself or Mac excited, but she accepted the essence of the staff's message. She and Mac had much to talk about, much to share, and much to learn about each other. After all, it had seemed like love at first sight. And then her accident. And then his. Touch would come in time.

She moved her left hand around to the back of his head, raising it as she reached for a glass of water. She wondered if he would ever drink again without dribbling. The straw was a sad reminder of that question.

"Well, Mister... Professor... Sergeant MacMahan, I sure hope so! I'm getting tired of holding *just* your hand!" Her eyes moistened as she smiled. She couldn't pull her face away from his eyes. They penetrated straight to her soul, her womanhood. Taking a deep breath for both of them, she pulled back slightly, stroking his hair and nodding in unspoken understanding.

Mac reached out to her waist, running his fingers over the fabric of her blouse. "Tell me about our chance meeting on that back road. A meeting I play over and over again in my head. About the beautiful love that you've so tenderly expressed in caring for me. I know almost nothing about you. I want to know more about your life, the accident, your time in-country. You said you'd been there, right?"

"Yes, yes," Mindy acknowledged with a slight nod. "But... I'm not sure I want to talk about the accident."

"I don't mean the details about what happened..."

"You know I was hit head-on by a truck?"

"Yes, I do. I don't mean going back through that. No. I was wondering about during your recovery? Santiago said you were in the hospital for, what, about three months?" Mac whispered, shaking his head, imagining the courage it had taken even to want to recover from her massive injuries. Mac knew first hand that in the early stages of recovery the way forward could seem impossible. That it took a special asset of character: perseverance. He'd been there.

"I was in a coma for a short time. Not like you," she laughed, guardedly. "Don't remember any of that 'cause I was pretty well mangled..."

She paused, looking out the window, dwelling in her heart on the word *pretty*. She no longer felt pretty. She knew it was vanity that nurtured such feelings, but she couldn't avoid a sense of loss. What did Mac think? Was she no longer the beauty he'd first met? Her glance moved to the mirror on the wall, which was (fortunately, she thought) too high up to show her reflection.

"There was a long time, a really long time, when I couldn't talk. My mouth was wired shut, you know. I couldn't see very well. I had a bunch of broken facial bones. My ribs were crushed. The pain was close to impossible. What kept me going was thinking that you'd find me…" Mindy choked, her cheeks shimmering as her tears fell onto Mac's chest.

He squeezed her hand as hard as he could.

"Stronger, you *are* getting stronger. Just…just like my love for you!" she wailed, wrapping her arms around Mac in a firm, yet gentle, embrace.

"It's more than mutual! Oh, Mindy! How can we feel these things when we hardly know each other. How?" He didn't want to hear they were being foolish. "And how about, you know, in-country? I got the impression you spent time in the Middle East?"

"I told you, if you think back to our time in the ditch," she laughed, wiping her tears, "that yes, I've been in war zones, 'in-country,' as you put it."

"What branch, and where, when?"

"I told you what I am. Think back."

"I'm not able to think about much other than how warm your body is…through your blouse. I ah…"

"At ease, Sergeant!" Mindy shook her head in mock anger. "I was and still am a photo journalist! I took an assignment in Iraq back in 2019. I wore flack jackets and helmets but never got near a fire fight. Even so, I saw what war does."

Mac nodded. He'd been there. Moving his hand to her cheek, he asked, "Are we acting like a couple of teenagers, talking love? How'd we get here? Not that I want anything else but being here with you."

"Some things just happen. Timing. Random. I don't know. But I do know that what kept me going though all my recovery were dreams of you and your embrace. Imagining that you loved me," she whispered, as she took a tissue to wipe her eyes.

"Me, too," Mac blinked.

Mindy laughed with release, hope beaming from her eyes. She dabbed Mac's eyes, caressing away his tears with a tender touch that could be conjured only by a woman devotedly in love. "Anyway, I wondered where you were. I thought I must have misread your signals. That I was a one-ditch-stand?"

They both sputtered, gulping the air between their tears, thinking back to that lonely back road, their near collision, and the ditch.

"It's the darndest thing, but I was thinking the exact same. I had no idea, zero inkling, about why you never answered your phone. I could only think you'd forgotten me. That feeling didn't mesh well with my, well, my PTSD."

"Hardly, Mister!" She looked at the tissue, then kissed his tears.

"Well…I'm so damn thankful that we found each other again!"

"Me too!" Mindy paused, then added, "I thank God." She looked intently into Mac's eyes, trying to read a reaction.

"God, huh?"

"That's part of me. Something you don't know, but need to know. To find out."

"God. Hmm? Along those lines, I've been touched by people—well mainly my family—well, mainly my brother, Sam. He knew God in a way that guided his life. He seemed to be best friends with Jesus. I don't know how someone gets to that point?"

"By faith. A simple, not complex frame of mind based on knowledge, like through the Bible. And… helped by the Holy Spirit."

"Ha! I've studied all the major religions. I just don't know if religion is like belonging to a political party. Something you choose, or what?"

"Faith is an individual thing. Like I said, a journey. Love, that's God's domain. So if we talk love, we're standing in His space… that is, if it's real love. We can make that journey together, maybe, huh?"

Mac pulled back his arms to raise himself in the bed. "I feel like a kid again. All the knowledge and studies I've encountered don't explain what I feel. There are no words. Just a confused kid."

"It's called love, Mister Kid," Mindy shot back, followed by a more forceful kiss that pushed Mac into the bed. She felt his warmth.

"Better keep your distance, Miss," he sputtered with a mock scowl.

"Right. So back to story-telling. You know I missed you. Dreamed about you. Do you remember what I told you about me, back on the road? Seems so long ago," she sighed.

"I think I do, yes."

"Well, we'll have plenty of time to catch up, to share. I think I've overstayed my visit. I see the Doc coming. I'll tell him you're stronger today, and more, ah, excitable," she laughed.

"Better keep that between ourselves," Mac replied as he reached up to touch her hair. "And I'll tell you more about me, about my life, and my time in-country."

"I already know a bit about that."

"How?"

"Elinor, your friend from the university, shared things with me. And, um... Blake and Devon shared your letter to your brothers with me. Wait!" she exclaimed as Mac grimaced, bringing his hand to his forehead. "Before you react, you gotta know!" her voice wobbling. "They, like the rest of us, were told you might never recover from that cop's hit, and they wanted me to know the real you... the intimate side of you." Mindy started crying again. "I hope you understand, I really hope you do, because if you don't, then maybe, well..."

"Maybe there's a gap we haven't seen?"

"Something like that."

"I guess I see that, too. But..."

"No buts! Those guys love you. You just don't know. Think of how close that letter to your brothers brought me to you! It showed a side of you that so wonderfully complements the, ah...chemistry I felt looking at you out there in the ditch."

"You," Mac mimicked a fake stutter, "you mean, I turned you on?"

Mindy reached out and squeezed Mac's lips shut. Giving him an impassioned look of outrage, she kissed him hard, the word "Yes" squeaking out of her compressed lips.

"They love you. I love you. There's a lot of us who love you. So behave, and don't disappoint your fans!" she growled, rising from his bed as the doctor entered the room.

"So, how's our American hero?" the doctor asked, a tinge of envy shrouding his question, more for Mindy's obvious doting head-over-heels for this guy than for Mac's reputation as a mentor, warrior, and patriot—a hero in the truest sense of devotion and sacrifice.

"Getting better, Doc. Thanks." Mac answered, his eyes following Mindy as she waved goodbye from the door. Mac had been told that his IT team students—Devon, Blake, Gloria, and Justin—had visited his bedside often. That they had regaled the doctors and nurses with colorful accounts of Mac's ruggedness, manly shyness, and unflinching dedication to their welfare and safety. And, his faith and perseverance against so many odds. Odds magnified by his PTSD.

The inauguration celebration in Gloria's dorm room paused. She turned to her teammates, her dark eyes glinting, her fist pumping the air. Their celebrating hit a new high as Gloria related the call she had just received from Mindy. That Mac was getting stronger—that the doctor said Mac would be released sometime soon to Mindy's care.

As she clicked off her iPhone, laughing at the joy in Gloria's voice, Mindy turned to the mural hanging in the hallway. "Will we be lovers?" she asked the mural self-consciously, looking back down the hall to Mac's room. Her thoughts drifted to the future, to a family with Mac. "Will we have children, I wonder?" she asked again. Her eyes moved to her reflection in the glass covering the mural. She smiled at herself, acknowledging her warm thoughts of young children—thoughts subconsciously enhanced by the reassuring voice of President Perserve coming from a television in an adjacent room.

CHAPTER 4

The Early Years

Floating on an amber sea! For as far as her eyes could see, she felt as though she was floating on amber waves of grain that rolled and fanned in the gentle breeze, lapping at the edges of the bordering fence.

Ten-year-old Margie Perserve leapt from the fence railing, careful not to trample a single stalk of the beautiful turkey red wheat that blanketed four sections of her family's Kansas farm. Careful, too, not to choke—as she landed hard on the furrowed soil—on the stalk of wheat that dangled from her lips. Dangled in a manner that mimicked the cigarettes she had seen hanging from her brother's lips when she spied on Eddie and the Butcher boys smoking behind the barn. Smoking while sitting in drifts of hay and grain. Such idiots!

In mock disgust, Margie bit off a piece of the stalk and spit it to the ground. The boys knew the fire danger! Her love for her big brother had been his guarantee that she remained mute on the subject. Until now. Margie sensed a tangle between the fun thoughts that always seemed to bounce from her heart and the notes of caution that now rode the crest of her mind. She was becoming increasingly aware of what her mother had called her conscience, as Sunday-school lessons were gaining traction with her adventuresome, innocent outlook on life.

She leaned back, rubbing her shoulder blades against the fence railing. "Darn!" she muttered, taking in the beauty of how the sun, setting low in the sky behind whispery clouds, magnified the rhythmic sensation of the waves rolling directly at her. Tilting her head ever so slightly, she listened to the caressing rush of the heavy grains as they brushed together in the wind. Margie closed her eyes, allowing the rush in her ears to create a vision of breakers on the ocean. Her eyes popped open in wonder as a brief gust tossed her long, amber hair. Hair that, her father claimed, in a most embarrassing attempt at poetry, covered a brain as rich as the soil beneath his wheat. Oh, boy! And now he was fretting that her amber hair was molting to auburn. Auburn did not match healthy red wheat. She smirked at the foolish superstition her father sometimes displayed. Farming was challenging in the best of times, subject to the whims of nature. But superstition did not make sense nor have a place in her way of thinking. Still, she knew she was just a ten-year-old.

Margie was the only daughter of Pierce and Mary Perserve, descendants of Karl Perserovich, a Mennonite immigrant from the Ukraine. She was proud that it was her ancestors who had brought the heritage grain—turkey red—to America. It was a rust-resistant hard winter wheat that had replaced the less hearty soft spring wheat originally grown by most Kansas and Central Plains farmers.

Funny, she thought as she gazed at the sea before her, that names can be so funny. Like 'turkey red'. Where did that come from? And how about her last name: Perserve. The kids at school teased her, especially Roy ("RoyBoy") Butcher, who, foolish in his awkward crush on her, claimed that a name like Perserve meant that she was soft like jelly. The fact that he couldn't spell, and that she could out run, out ride, and was smarter than all the boys in her class, including RoyBoy himself, was somehow lost in the fog of affection that surrounded his private musings. Roy was not alone. Most of the boys at Tabor Elementary had the same thoughts. It was hard to ignore Margie with her soft gray-blue eyes, full dark eyebrows, and a face that charmed by virtue of its innocent beauty and grace.

———   .   ———

As she grew into a teenager, the onset of acne did not blemish her outlook on life, for Margie remembered what her mother had told her. That beauty on the inside, in one's soul, far outweighed perceived beauty on the outside. Margie took to heart the lessons from Sunday School about God's love and grace and Christ's sacrifice. She had no reason for doubt. Her family was an example of love: nurturing, caring, encouraging, hospitable, and creating enduring relationships.

On her sixteenth birthday she pestered her father, once again, about getting her driver's license. He replied that if she could first master driving one of his wheat-harvesting combines—safely and with confidence—that would champion her argument for a driver's license. Not one to shrink from a challenge, Margie announced—with a rare display of hubris—that, as Margaret, she would drive the combine as well as Eddie had before he went west to UCLA for college.

Somehow, perhaps through the church grapevine, word of Margie, (now "Margaret") driving the Perserve Farm's old John Deere S590 spread like a wildfire through the Tabor community. On a cool Saturday morning in mid-April, the sky's gray-dull veneer torn by threatening clouds, Pierce drove the S590 to the edge of Section Two. A crowd of about one hundred had gathered, leaning on the fence railings, watching Margaret climb into the combine's cab.

"You can do it, girl!" RoyBoy shouted, followed by claps and yells from the others. Margie's mom stood behind the crowd, her hands clasped in silent prayer, her heart bursting with pride, her eyes moist with love. "Sure," Mary Perserve said to herself. "Sure, Margie's been towing the small harvester behind the tractor since she was twelve. But driving this huge combine in a straight line with 400 horsepower awaiting your every touch and the conveyor-blower lurching off to the side? Well, this is no small harvester! Yes, *you* go girl!"

Margaret pulled the cab door shut, looking down at the confusing dashboard her father had carefully explained the night before. She looked out at the crowd. She couldn't hear them, nor they her, but they were all waving: hands, hats, smiles. She saw RoyBoy, perched on a post, hat in hand, nodding. It was like watching a silent movie. She strapped in and, giving the crowd, especially Roy, a thumbs-up with her left hand, she leaned forward across the steering column with her right hand and hit the ignition button. The roar and vibrations were startling. She adjusted the ear protectors, disengaged the emergency release, aimed the wheel, and released the gear. The combine lurched and sputtered, moving slowly to reap the rich turkey red held so dear by her father. (Pierce, desiring to maintain his family's pure strain of the best wheat God had granted, refused to consider the use of hybrid seed.) His daughter shared this love for red and was determined to make a perfect run.

With no mirror inside the cab, there was no way of knowing if the surge of joy—the sensation of independent accomplishment that enveloped her—was evident on her face. She was all business. That she knew from the set of her teeth. In the right side-view alignment mirror she could see the crowd well behind her and the swath she had cut in perfect straight-line alignment with the mirror's grid. Margaret kept steady pressure on the throttle, her strong arms on the steering wheel absorbing most of the machine's lurching. Now came the hard part: avoiding the end-of-field marker looming up as she made the turn back. Braking hard on the left-side pedal, easing on the throttle and straining hard against the steering wheel, she maneuvered the combine in a perfect, albeit somewhat wide, semicircle. As the front cab window of the combine came around, she could see the cheering crowd from afar. Margaret allowed herself the briefest of smiles as she re-focused on the alignment grid to minimize overlap—what her father called "kerf loss."

"Here I come!" Margaret shouted above the machine's din. Shouted to the mute crowd far away, to the driver's license that waited.

Later that evening, friends and family gathered on the patio behind her family's yellow clapboard farmhouse to celebrate her achievement. RoyBoy said, "Margie-girl, you looked so confident, so determined, so purposeful up there in that big, old machine. You didn't see us, focused like you were, but we were shouting and cheering like you can't believe. It was like you were leading, bringing in the sheaves."

She reached out to take his hand. "It was such a thrill, a sense of responsibility. Of needing to maintain control. Oh, Roy, I loved it! Something welled up in my heart. Something so big I can't describe. A purpose I have yet to find, waiting for me."

Roy's thumb played against her fingers. "I bet Eddie would be so proud of you. I know I am," he muttered, looking down at the ground.

"Are you? Really? I mean, all these years growing up together, ever since we were kids, you've always been on my case. Like... always giving me a hard time."

Roy threw his lips out in a pout. He released her hand and brushed back his rich black hair. "Is that how you see it... me?"

"How else?"

"We're not little kids anymore. Why do you think a guy makes a fool of himself over a girl? What do you think?"

Margie the teenager, beamed. "Because he likes her and doesn't know how to tell her?"

"Shoot!" Roy pulled at the gingham tablecloth, smoothing down the ridges.

Margie reach out to take his hand, her gray-blue eyes turning incandescent blue, aflame in the glow of the fire. "I love you Roy Butcher," she whispered. "I always have!"

Shocked, his eyebrows warped in bewilderment, Roy stood, rubbed his hands down his jean legs, turned and walked away without a word.

"Wait! Roy?"

He shuffled to the side of the house and, once out of sight, ran to his car. Margie ran after him in close pursuit.

"Wait, you RoyBoy!" she yelled.

He turned to meet her angry face as he opened his car door.

"What in the world?"

"Love? What's a kid like you know of love, huh?" he gasped. "All these years I've dreamed of nothing other than loving you. And here all the time you felt the same. But we're just kids. You can't even drive. So please don't torment me! It's not possible."

Margie's face softened. She held out her right hand, then her left, and softly, gently settled into Roy's outstretched arms.

"We, we can't do this," he moaned. "I'm off to West Point this summer, and you're just going to be, what, a high school sophomore? We've been friends and enemies all these years, up close. And secret lovers, I guess you can say, always at a distance."

"So? So we can wait."

"Margie... Margaret Perserve. My bowl of jam..."

"Don't you start! Don't you ruin this moment" she yelled, pushing back from Roy.

"I meant to say, my sweet, gray-eyed bowl of jam. So beautiful. So fun. So serious?" he smiled. "Yes. We can wait. It will be hard, you know. But, yes, we can wait. I'm in shock. Happily so! But not sure my folks will be keen on us."

"You mean my family being Mennonite and yours Baptist?"

"Probably that. I know Eddie talked about how it would break your parents' hearts if he joined the Army after UCLA. If there was a war, he'd sign up. That would probably make your parents disown Eddie. And me? I'm no pacifist. I'm Army! They'll never approve of me."

"That's my parents, not me," she whispered, reaching out to take hold of Roy's hands. "My faith in Jesus is the same faith as my parents... as yours. Oh, Roy! They do care for you. I think they know deep down that our generation is different, more pragmatic, given the state of our world, all the conflict. Oh... I love peace, I pray for it! But I'm realistic that there is evil, and in spite of the courage and faith and peaceful resistance of people like Dr. King, we need to be prepared."

"You're worldly-wise for your sixteen years... Margaret," Roy said, caressing her hair as he leaned over her waiting lips.

"Maybe so," she whispered. "We're both young. Lots of living to do. But I'll wait for you, *my* RoyBoy. Here, I'll seal that with my kiss!"

—— . ——

Beaming with pride, waving from afar at Margaret as she walked across to the podium, Mary Perserve sat with Pierce behind rows of black mortar boards at Harvard's 347th commencement. Mary leaned on Pierce's shoulder, recounting—in a voice seeped in emotion yet strident in amazement—all that their daughter had accomplished since graduating top of her class from Tabor High School. That she had secured a full scholarship to Harvard where she studied International Relations. That she had studied in Belgium and was now graduating with honors. All this by their farm girl. *Amazed* was too mild a word.

Mary began fidgeting in her chair, looking back and forth—across the sea of faces—to the entrances leading into Tercentenary Theatre. "Will he make it?" she asked of no one, squinting hard against the late-morning sun and the numerous crimson banners fluttering beneath the honey locust trees. Mary paused to take note of the joy on the many faces of families and friends gathered to celebrate their graduate's rite of passage. "Such an accomplished mosaic of humanity," she pondered, pushing against Pierce's shoulder to look far to the left. "There he is!" she exclaimed.

Pierce's eyes misted as he removed his coat from the aisle chair that he had been reserving for Captain Roy Butcher, U.S. Army.

"Sorry I'm late. Traffic at Logan," Roy offered, his voice full of emotion.

"Oh! Dear Roy, welcome home, back to the States! We're *just* so thankful that you made it, and right on time!" Mary replied, her voice bursting with love. Pointing to the stage, "Margie's about to speak," she said as she moved in front of Pierce to give Roy a lengthy hug. "How are you? How's your deployment been? And thank you for the letters!"

"Shh! Here she goes," Pierce said, motioning Mary back to her seat.

After acknowledging the applause, Margaret spoke softly through the microphone. "Thank you, Dean Rasmussen, for those kind words. And thank you, my fellow graduates, for honoring me with this opportunity to speak to you. Please everyone, be seated. It's going to be a fantastic day," she laughed, drawing brief cheers from the several thousand graduating students in the front rows. Pausing as folks adjusted themselves, she noticed a small group still standing behind the students, a braided hat held high. Taking in a breath, her squeak audible through the microphone, she had many in the audience following her joy-filled stare.

——— · ———

"The Assistant Secretary said, in no uncertain terms, that he thought you should stay and work here in D.C. at State," Margaret's roommate Brianna said as she arranged the flowers on the windowsill. "He went on to say that for someone just two years out of college, your work as an intern, you know, and especially your research on policy continuity, has caught the attention of the Secretary herself."

In spite of her sorrow, Margaret laughed at Brianna's always-on, rah-rah approach to life's challenges. "That would be a dream job, but…"

"I know, I know," Brianna replied, her voice quivering. "Or at least I can try to understand, to empathize. We're all so devastated by your loss. We know how much you loved your father and how important he was in your life!"

Margaret nodded, pulling back the window drapes, looking down at the geraniums and the brick walkway beneath their Georgetown apartment. She ran her hand down the window's molding, then putting her arm around Brianna, they hugged.

"How lucky one is to be loved by family. And how unlucky it is to lose that family. Yeah, devastated *is* right. But, I have my life ahead of me. Dad wants me to focus on that. He was only forty-eight, you know?"

Brianna nodded, wiping her eyes.

"Who'd have thought he'd die driving a harvester. Geez, just too darn shitty, huh?"

Brianna was at loss for words. She kissed Margaret's auburn hair and stepped back. "That letter from your mom was too dear for words. So caring, so strong in bearing her grief, and so beautifully expressing the vulnerability of life. You *are* lucky."

"Well," Margaret said, putting her hand to Brianna's cheek, "I don't wish my kind of luck, at least regarding my dad, on anyone!'

They hugged again. "We'll miss you, your can-do spirit, and your wisdom!" Brianna said as she walked with Margaret to the door.

"It'll be good to be home, to help my mom and Eddie run the farm. I'll miss everyone here, especially you."

Both sniffing, arms and hands extended to the other, Margaret stared intently into Brianna's dark eyes and nodded.

Brianna brought her hand to Margaret's cheek, wiping more tears.

Margaret stepped out in the street, closing the door. Kansas waited.

—— . ——

"Just look at that!" Eddie growled, standing alongside the fence and stamping his feet against the cold, surveying the dark auburn color of Section Three. "USDA is forecasting bad yields this year. And man! I forgot how cold Kansas can be. I'm missing the warm California sun!" He stood with Margaret, Mary, and the farm's foreman, Josh Henry.

"Low yields often mean better prices," Josh offered. "What a shame our wheat is suffering, too. The price per bushel may top four dollars, and here we'll reach just seventy percent of last year's yield!"

"It's not the end of the world, guys." Margaret replied. "Remember, we have fixed assets and variable costs. Sure, it's a bad crop, but that's farming. And we just won't know the harvest yield until this spring."

"Maybe, but your dad would be real sad to see how his red is suffering," Mary offered, her hand on Eddie's shoulder as they viewed the stiff stalks, seemingly frozen against the vivid, clear-blue December sky. Far in the background, gray, swirling smoke rose from the farmhouse chimney, drifting off and blowing east with the chill wind.

"Let's be good farmers and pray for the crop. 'Bout all we can do," Josh half-joked.

"Even with times looking tough, you, Margaret and you, Eddie, have run this farm better than Dad ever did," Mary said solemnly.

"I'll never believe that, Mom. But it does show what West Coast computer science can do when linked with East Coast international relations. Right, brother?" Margaret smiled, trying to lighten the mood.

"Seriously, You've done a wonderful job, both of you. Margaret, you would make Dad proud. Giving up your career for the family farm, and managing it so well," Mary added.

Eddie gave Margaret a loving shove. "Hmm, think so? Regardless, it'll be good to get 2002 behind us. It's been a strange year, all around, you know? What with all the reality TV crap. And Saddam heating things up in the Middle East," Eddie said to no one in particular. "What was it like when you were in Washington, when Gore lost to Bush? Musta been as bleak an outlook for the Dems then, huh?" he asked, reaching out to Margaret's arm.

She laughed in a knowing, frustrated way. "It was a crazy time, for sure. But nothing like we saw last year on September 11. Yeah, 9-11..."

The ensuing heavy silence was broken by the harsh caw of a crow flying in amidst the wheat.

"What does Roy think will happen, now that we've going after Al-Qaeda and making claims to the U.N. about Iraq's weapons of mass destruction?" Eddie asked.

"He sees war as inevitable. A given, he says."

"Oh, dear God, no!" Mary sighed.

"Mom, I've been wondering 'bout that. I need to talk with Roy. One thing I learned from my time in California is that there are too few Americans who are willing to stand up for our country. Reap the benefits, sure. But stand up, not so sure."

Mustering a stern look tempered by the need to cautiously apply motherly love to an adult child, Mary responded, "Eddie, you know we don't believe in war, in violence. We raised you that way."

"I know, Mom. But when I add things up, it's not right that just a few do the heavy lifting. Like, here on the farm, we all pitch in. We need to think that way about America, especially after 9-11. Times are different. It's not like Vietnam."

"That's a perfect example of why we don't believe in war. What *did* Vietnam accomplish, anyway? Just misery and death on both sides. Now we're almost friends with *that* country. Man's need for war is just plum wrong! You need to know that," Mary stated, her voice trembling with conviction.

"I agree about Vietnam. But this is different, now. We've been attacked on our own shores. We need to stop those religious madmen before we suffer another attack."

"Please, son, no more talk of war. We have a battle right here on the farm, getting a good harvest. What do you think, Margaret?"

Margaret took hold of her mother's hands. "I know that we need solid leadership in this country. Not partisanship. We've got to stop defining ourselves separately by gender, orientation, race, or even age. Separate, we fall. We must always seek compromise. Only in that way can we serve *all* the people. The threat from outside is real, sure. Eddie's right on that. Yet, there is also an internal threat—more insidious, less obvious. We have too much bias—generalization and polarization—in our dialogue, in the media. We must uphold and respect the laws of the land while—and this *is* key—accommodating the real needs of *all* our citizens. Yes, all citizens! As long as those needs uphold and remain within the law. And I mean real needs, not just wants or special interests. It's a tightrope, but we must be determined and vigilant, caring and embracing, and united! Unity through continuity of policy and based on our Founder's words, that's what we need!"

Pulling her left hand from her jeans pocket and waving out to the grain in an exaggerated appeal, Margaret spread her hand high for all to see.

"Wait! What's that on your finger?" Eddie burst out.

Margaret pirouetted in a circle. "Yes, yes! Roy got early leave. He sneaked over last night. Oh, Mom! We're engaged!"

Mary's hesitancy held her frown in place. Was she now to have two sons in the Army? "How could this happen?" she mumbled, finally releasing a smile to give Margaret a loving embrace as Eddie and Josh joined in.

"Major and Mrs. Butcher! Man! Who'd of thunk?" Eddie laughed as he gave Margaret another hug. "But hey, sis! What with your beaucoup talents and listening to you pontificate just now, it sounds more like 'President and Major Perserve.' Huh?"

Margaret smiled softly at the field of struggling wheat. The slight shirk of her shoulders suggested, "Who knows. Maybe it *is* time for a woman."

CHAPTER 5

The First Family

President Perserve waved to the crowd as the presidential limo, "The Beast," turned off Pennsylvania Avenue into the east gate of the White House. The fluttering inauguration flags reminded her of the waves of wheat on her father's farm. She chuckled once more at her amazing journey from those wheat fields to the current moment. She glanced up the drive to the North Portico, to the red carpet tumbling down the stairs and to the waiting staff and dignitaries bracketed within the huge columns.

"Is there really a shooting range in the basement?" her eight-year-old son, Todd, blurted with excitement.

Margaret blinked a loving smile to Todd, so innocent of the import that now fell upon her. As she stroked his check reassuringly, she said softly, "No, no. But there's a basketball court and a swimming pool."

"Really, Toddy!" his fourteen-year-old sister, Kari, exclaimed. "This is the White House! Our new home. You still don't get it?"

Retired Army Colonel Roy Martin Butcher, their father, sitting deep in the folds of the plush limo seat, looked up at the White House as the limo came to a halt. "This is our nation's house, guys. And we're working for them, now. No more farmhouse, at least for a while." His hand on Margaret's thigh, he gently squeezed out their secret code for "I love you." As she leaned over to brush her cheek against his, Roy whispered, "And I *always* will, Madam President."

Margaret's soft sigh belied her confident countenance. Searching his eyes as an aide opened the limo door, "Me too, my RoyBoy. Sealed with my kiss," she breathed.

Todd, his eyes reaching out the thick limo window to take in the high columns of the portico, had to be held back by his father to allow the president to exit first.

Kari let out a groan, leaning over to Todd. "Now that Mom is the president, I see I'll have to be in charge of you!"

Todd took her hand off his arm, holding it in his hand. "Mom's our mom. You're my sister," he replied. "We're probably the luckiest kids around, even if Mom wasn't president. Isn't that right, Dad?"

Roy tousled Todd's hair. "Pretty smart for an eight-year-old, mister. Yes, I would say you have a very special mother. I know this past year has been hard for you. For her and you both. What, with Mom away from home so much, off campaigning." Turning to take both children gently in his arms, the applause coming through the open car door from the portico, he added, "Mom has come a long ways, from managing agriculture and state government to be here... to be president. Kari, I know you're doing your best to appreciate the magnitude of her job, but none of us really can. So little of what she faces is predictable. But like you, she has faith and confidence, a virtuous conscience and solid fortitude. We must always pray for her and be her private support group here at the White House."

"But what about all the butlers, those guys?" Todd asked.

"They support Mom in keeping the house clean and proper, but they can't give her the quiet love that we can," Kari added with a knowing, big-sister smile.

"Because you two have what your Mom has—character—it's all going to be fine. Be yourselves, honest and reserved..."

"Dad means, be good," Kari interrupted.

"Yes, good. But in a special way. Many people will be watching you. I know if you're just yourselves, that will be more than good enough."

"I guess I get it," Todd answered, inching towards the door as the crescendo of applause grew. "Hey, look, Mom is waving back at us."

"Okay, let's go," Roy said with a loving smile. "Always remember that you represent the President of the United States and that she is your mother and God is her father."

The Chief Usher, a gray-haired woman of sixty standing at the side of the top step, discreetly used her elbow to nudge Donny Perkins, the Chief Butler, as Todd, somewhat off-balance, popped out of the limo door side-by-side with his father. Roy had to grab the car door to avoid stepping on the boy's foot.

"Not an auspicious start," Donny chuckled.

As the limo pulled away, the president waited at the top of the six steps leading into the White House vestibule, her hand out for Todd as he scampered up.

"And so much for decorum," the Chief Usher whispered.

"And what would you do if you were an excited eight-year-old?" Donny whispered back, chuckling in a low voice. "That is, if you can remember back that far."

Sharon Webster, the Chief Usher, subtly rotated her left shoe to tap Donny's shoe. "And who again, is your boss, *young* man?"

Donny smirked, almost laughing out loud. The entire household staff and operations personnel were ecstatic to have children, young children, once again in the White House. Especially this family, who, according to *People Magazine*, was the most grounded and loving family ever to occupy the national home. A claim apparently justified based on the size of the crowds now leaving the Mall.

President Perserve watched Roy climb the steps hand in hand with Kari. Together, all four, hand-in-hand, with the children between their parents, entered the vestibule. Todd shuffled his feet along the plush red carpet until Kari gave his hand a jerk. He looked up at the two Marine guards, standing at attention inside the vestibule entrance. His stare continued as he took in the high ceiling with its ornate carvings, the long red carpet leading into the Central Hall, and the crowd of officials and press standing to the right side of the carpet.

"Wow!" Todd almost shouted. The resulting laughter from the crowd broke the sense of stiff formality.

"Shh!" Kari whispered as she jerked his arm, this time harder.

Donny stepped forward. "Madam President, if I may, I would like to show the children their bedrooms upstairs: the Yellow and Blue rooms?"

"Thank you Mr. Perkins," the president replied as she turned to talk with the waiting vice president.

Todd let out a howl and raced off to the right towards the staircase he assumed went upstairs.

Donny looked over, smiling at the president. "It's going to be fun," he said, bowing slightly and in a more refined manner, held out his hand to Kari.

Forgetting that just seconds before she had been ready to strangle Todd, Kari responded with what she hoped was her most beguiling smile. She had read in *American Girl* that Donny was only twenty-eight years old, a wounded Marine and the youngest Chief Butler ever to serve at the White House. He was also way too handsome.

As Kari walked with pronounced grace, imagining herself to be Scarlett O'Hara allowing Donny to escort her up the staircase, the president turned to her Chief of Staff, Deshon Williams. "Is the list of Cabinet nominees ready?"

"Yes, ma'am."

Margaret put her hand gently on Deshon's arm, her gray-blue eyes expressing admiration and grace. She smiled at his Princeton bowtie. "I thought we agreed to call me President, or Margaret. And as I recall, there would be no collegiate references or adornments."

He put his hand on hers as they leaned in together, laughing. They were the best of friends. Deshon had been her highly effective staff coordinator during her years in Kansas government. "Yes. I've vetted the list with the vice president, your council of private advisors, and the colonel. Not only are you the first woman—and might I add destined to be the greatest—president, but you're clearly the most organized. You already have your team, a great team, ready. And your policies reflect compromise, the essence of unity… your handle," he added.

They both laughed with a sense of relief, acknowledging the value of preparation and planning. The president scanned the gathering of dignitaries, nodding in response to warm expressions and waves of congratulations.

"Yes. And our policy profile that we've improved throughout the campaign. Like, limited abortion while emphasizing the value of life, sovereign borders and immigration within the law. Even our approach to clearly explaining the need for deficit reduction while maintaining essential programs. All with a focus on national security! These have wide approval, at least according to the polls. Probably because I see *all* us citizens as *one*. One race, one nation, one national treasure."

Deshon squeezed her arm. He loved her like a sister. Her natural beauty paled next to her moral character and her strident effort to create continuity in policy. A continuity necessary to avoid the jerking back-and-forth of America's citizens and its global allies. Necessary to heal the polarization of the past sixteen years. Quietly, he said, "Margaret, ah, Madam President. Might I suggest we discuss all this in tomorrow's strategy meeting? This is your first day on the job. We have time. Say... from all the stares you're receiving, it's time to, ah, work the crowd..."

"You do know how I dislike that term?"

"Just trying to get you out and about, ma'am," Deshon whispered, as he stepped back and casually motioned Colonel Butcher to stand next to the president. The camera flashes pulsed against the vestibule's white walls.

One reporter, a tall, brown-haired woman from a morning television program, after making sure her cameraman was on cue, pushed herself closer to the president. "Madam President, if I may?" she started. "As one successful woman to another, how does it feel, taking steps no other woman has ever taken?"

Colonel Butcher quietly cleared his throat.

The president tilted her head—providing a sense of pondering the depth of the question—while actually wondering if the reporter knew the virtue of modesty. "Monumental," she replied.

The reporter, licking her lips and nodding knowingly, turned to make sure her profile was at optimal camera angle. 'Monumental' meant top of the mountain, with all the trimmings of a glorious ascent.

The president continued. "Monumental in terms of responsibility and in terms of addressing the overwhelming diversity and magnitude of needs of our citizens. Monumental in terms of making sure those needs come well before my own, before those in Congress, or..." turning and gesturing to Roy, "my family's."

The reporter frowned, not recognizing the language the president was using. "Pardon me?'

"Throughout my campaign we've advocated pragmatics and results. We've all heard the ways Washington has been described, from an old-boys' club to a swamp. It's been all the above. But to see my role as anything other than an opportunity to bring us all together would be a mistake. As you may know," absorbing the reporter's blank stare, "or maybe you don't or care not to? I'm not here to make America great again. Great? Against what standard? Global recognition and national pride, ego? No, that is not the standard we need to go by. I fully accept that America is a light upon the hill. That we are, and have been, a shining example of humankind's best in service to others... allowing the democratic process to flourish, regardless of what the yield is."

The reporter squinted, brushing back her hair, in spite of its glue.

The president continued, "In other words, regardless of who gets elected. That's the beauty of democracy. It's self-correcting. At least here in America with our institutions and our American spirit, the notion of equality and letting right be done. I'm aware that, as the first woman president, I have a unique role and responsibility. To show, to perform, to explain—and let me *emphasize* this so that gender becomes a *non-issue*—that it is the American character that I represent. I am not some token to womanhood. That may disappoint some, but if so, they are purveyors, like so many other special interests, of self-righteous justification. They allow themselves to ignore the needs of their neighbors. I am here as an American. I have to be. That is my sole role."

The reporter, unaware that the Secret Service was now using the moniker of *Unity* for the president, and unsure how to segue to a more comfortable topic, stood back in surprise at the solid applause that accompanied the president's words.

Colonel Roy Butcher, the "First Dude" as he had become known, moved closer to Margaret, the knuckle of his left hand's index finger, unnoticed at his side, tapping out their code of love on her right hip. She stiffened briefly, hoping the crowd didn't detect the amorous glint in her eye.

The formal atmosphere was shattered as Todd yelled down the staircase, "Hey, Mom! You gotta see the secret closet in my room!"

A yell followed, accompanied by a skirmish of sorts as Kari attempted to pull Todd back into the upstairs hall. "Donny... Mr. Perkins, please help me with my brother!" she shouted.

The crowd in the downstairs vestibule roared with laughter. And joy. A real family seemed to be at the helm. The helm of America.

——— · ———

"Well, how'd we do on our first day here in our new home? Do you think the neighborhood is going to accept us?" Margaret asked Roy as she slipped into the large, comfy bed in the President's Bedroom—the primary bedroom of the White House's master suite.

"Fine, just fine, Madam President," he replied, taking her tenderly in his arms. "Say, aren't I supposed to be sleeping in the second bedroom? You know, the First Lady's bedroom? What will the staff think if they find that bed unused and this one all tousled ?"

"They'll be happy that we're in love and behaving like any normal couple. There is the connecting passage to the First Lady's room in case a fast adjustment—decorum—is called for. Mostly, let's use that room as our private living room."

"Decorum? More like, *when* I need my beauty sleep," Roy laughed, his voice muffled as he exhaled in the smell of her lush auburn hair. "Just wondering, you know, what time is your first meeting tomorrow? Just wondering..."

"Breakfast at seven. Staff briefing begins at eight. We're off and running. Oh, Roy!"

As he turned out the light, he said, "I hope this room isn't bugged!"

Margaret giggled with innocent joy, just like that ten-year-old watching the sunset back, years ago, in Kansas.

Later that night, sixty feet down the second-floor Center Hall from the master suite, unnoticed by the President and the First Dude, a brief scuffle occurred as Marine sergeant Sandra Sanchez, on second-floor duty, checked the Clerk's Room. She was grasped by unseen arms, only to reappear moments later back in the Hall, a subtle halo momentarily illuminating her shadow cast upon the Hall's wall.

Thousands of kilometers from the Hall, applause and shouts filled the control room of Building 666. Director Dong calmly extinguished the celebration with a rapid double-blink on her data glasses.

"My comrades, attention! We have launched—embedded—our first holohead." She waited for the cheers to subside before continuing. "If Cassidy is able to control our replica of that toady female guard, we'll move to our second target: the president! But first, we must verify immersion of the lesser replica: the guard." Looking sternly at her team, some with heads downturned in respect, she continued. "Our methods of transmission currently support only two replicas. Doctor Juong. Please adjust the holohead rendering to rid that back glow. It's affecting shadows, as you can see."

"I'm on it, Comrade Director," Juong replied excitedly. "I've had to make timing adjustments in our autonomous transmission—our light speed derivatives—to compensate for some weird radio-frequency scanning by the White House. Yes. Two replicas are our current limit..."

"Damn..." he said to himself, aware that light-speed derivatives from more than two replicas might create a collision of ebundles. Might trigger a fusion event in their own backyard. Hiding his frustration in a smile of confidence to the team, he said, "New hurdles are always a part of innovation. So frustrating, but we'll soon break through those barriers to create an army of holoheads. Yes, iteration and patience are the grease of innovation."

After more cheers, an eager interruption came from the team of twenty gathered around the large vectoring screen. "When can we *do* the president? What happens to that, ah... guard?"

The Director casually smoothed the folds in the army-issued blouse that encased her ample chest. "The guard? Not your concern. She will be disposed of. After all, we are the RID team, yes?"

More laughter and shouts. Dong smiled, thinking, too, of the success the State Security Ministry had had at tunneling from the *Ole Ale Tavern*—across H Street from Lafayette Square—to Blair House, the president's guest house. Her chest swelled with pride at the ingenuity of her country's engineers. At how their tunnel design easily got past the inept Secret Service of America: such toads with all their partying and lack of focus. Her mind drifted to The Leader's request that all "reclaimed baggage," as he had called the guard and the president, be held at his private retreat, forty-five kilometers east of Building 666. So much for preferring squared-off bodies.

"Patience, my children. Patience," she continued. "Dear Leader, in his infinite wisdom, will know the right time to embed the president's replica. But soon, very soon. It must be well before that American president becomes established."

"Infinite wisdom?" she said to herself. "More like infantile warbling. Regardless," she concluded, "the Leader will serve our purpose. For the time being."

CHAPTER 6

The Lovers

A debate had erupted even before they started to leave his room at the rehab center. The doctor had insisted that Mac be taken out to Mindy's car in a wheelchair. An insurance issue. Devon and Blake, having just arrived from Boston, countered the doctor, suggesting that Mac was more than able to walk on his own. Mindy intervened. She thanked the medical team for all their effort, pulled Mac to a standing position and put his right arm around her shoulder as they walked off down the hall. Devon and Blake followed closely behind, ready to help. The doctor called after them, "Best of luck. Take care." Without turning back, Mac raised his free arm in thankful, victorious acknowledgement.

Mac was all smiles as he looked down the long, gray hall lined with wheelchairs and patients. He was finally escaping through the heavy glass doors to fresh air and the street! He felt flushed with a sense of joy for being with Mindy and for her assertiveness. He loved the warmth he felt in the exaggerated motion of her hips next to his. He was a little too excited, hoping no one noticed—glad that Blake and Devon were walking behind him.

"Did the Dean actually ask you to return to your teaching position, with full tenure?" Devon asked, as he scurried past Mindy and Mac to hold the doors. Blake came alongside, taking Mac's other shoulder in anticipation of crossing the sidewalk to Mindy's car. It was double parked, its emergency lights begging off any police ticketing attempts.

Mac stayed focused on walking, the front doors opening to a bright, sunny day at odds with the snow-covered sidewalk and street. He hesitated at the threshold, the noise of the city a shock.

Mindy held Mac's left hand in hers, supporting his elbow with her right hand. "Thanks, Blake. The sidewalk was slippery this morning."

"What a winter, huh? Looks like your snow removal here in the Big Apple sure lacks what we have in Boston," Blake laughed. "And yeah, what about your job, Professor? You taking it back? We'd love for you to be back on campus with the IT team."

"I vote no!" Mindy stated firmly as they cautiously navigated the snow-packed pavement. "And I've told Mac that many times. He needs time to sort things out. I want him here, with me, in New York!"

Mac halted, pulling back on her arm. "I'm still not sure what to do, to be honest. I really enjoyed teaching you kids, but…"

"Kids?" Devon asked, rotating to look at Mac and holding out his hand palm up in mock exasperation.

"Okay, you… *guys*," Mac continued. "But… there's that damn *but*—continuous uncertainty—that dominates my thinking and plays off my PTSD. I've still got issues with the university, the administration, how they handled the whole IT team thing: the D37 hijack. Not sure what to do next. Guess the one bright spot is our new president!"

"We're all agreed on that," Devon replied. "Funny, I remember Gloria telling that senator in D.C. that we weren't very keen on Perserve. But now, I gotta admit she is *exactly* what this country needs!"

"Amen!" Mindy injected.

"I've had plenty of time during rehab watching events unfold at the national level, at least after I woke up."

"What, since this morning?" Blake said, attempting some humor.

"Yeah, ha ha, yourself. No. The past couple of weeks, since the Dean called."

"And I'll say it one more time, to heck with the Dean! With the whole stupid university!" Mindy growled, rubbing her hips against Mac's for emphasis as they came to her car. "Yeah, I know you loved being a professor, helping the kids, as you call them. But there are other teaching positions. You've had offers, yes?" she prompted. "Maybe even outside of teaching? Okay, okay," she continued in response to Mac's frown. "How about something that combines your teaching, your military experience, and your athleticism?"

"Like what? And you're assuming I'll be able to get back in shape. The docs seemed iffy. At least that's my read," Mac responded.

"I've already got a trainer for you at my gym, right around the corner from our house, on West Eighth."

"*Our* house? I like that," Mac replied with more interest, looking back at the rehab building, its bland exterior and sterile checkerboard windows. Leaning against Mindy's car, he nudged Blake to help him rotate, looking past the few barren trees down Clarkson Street with its cars and people. Some of those people had turned on him when all he had tried to do was help America.

"What is it?" Mindy asked, her gloved hand at his cheek, the moisture from her eyes, wind-swept, running across her face.

Mac popped his lips, his wide-eyed stare at some distant thought giving her pause.

She removed her glove, blew on her fingertips, and caressed his cheek, his scar.

After a fragile minute, lingering inside his trance, Mac shook his head, exhaling heavily. Watching the moisture of his breath float off in the breeze, he tried his best to form a goofy smile—one in conflict with the PTSD-fueled memories projected in the tightness of his emerald-green eyes. Holding out his hands, he saw them shaking. He quickly placed them on the hood of Mindy's car. "Oh!" he said as he tried to step back, Blake catching him. "This is the same car your were driving when... it can't be? That one was totaled, right?" He turned his head to ask Mindy, her arm now around his waist.

"You fall off the horse, you do what, Sergeant?" she asked tenderly.

"You... you bought an identical replacement?"

"Call me superstitious, but I liked the color and model, so why not?"

Mac adjusted his feet for stability and, gently putting his hand behind her head, pulled her into a passionate kiss.

"Hey, hey! Professor, not in public!" Devon joked as Mindy wrapped her hands around Mac's shoulders for their first *real* kiss—one free from hospital beds and tubes and chiding staff.

"Back off, Private!" Mac exploded good-naturedly, smiling at Devon. He went back to the kiss.

"Guess you *kids* are fine on your own, huh?" Blake laughed, as he nodded to Devon to head back to their car.

"Remember, we're staying at my cousin's up on Amsterdam, near Ninety-Eighth," Devon said. "You've got my cell. Call if we can help in any way. How 'bout we get together, say, maybe tomorrow for dinner? We'll come down to the Village so Mac can stay close to... *home*."

"Thank you, guys, but I can handle Mac," Mindy cooed—thinking of how she would *handle* Mac once they got home—as she opened the SUV door for this man, this fragile warrior. Her soon-to-be lover. Her breath quickened.

Devon, watching her check the traffic as she walked around the back of the SUV to the driver's door, asked Blake quietly, "Do you think she can take care of Mac? He's still weighs a ton, even after months lying around in rehab. It'd be the shits if he fell, hit his head."

Blake watched the SUV start out, the tires spinning slightly on the icy pavement. "No idea. But my guess," Blake replied as he kicked the snow with his shoe to check how icy it really was, "they'll be okay. Imagine if you'd been holed up for two months with injuries and Jayla was all over you. Would you want me tagging along?"

"Shit, no! And speaking of Jayla, she said you and Gloria have a date at the jewelers when we get back to Boston. What's that all about?"

"Just a necklace. Yeah, a necklace." Blake answered with fading interest, watching Mindy's car pull out into traffic. He said a little prayer for their happiness and health—for lasting love. That thought took him back to Gloria. He grinned as he searched the dirty snow to fashion a snowball to aim at Devon, his D-Man.

Mindy looked back at Blake and Devon, thankful for their help and for their understanding that she and Mac needed to be alone. She noticed Mac's shoulder strap rubbing high on his neck. "Can you adjust your strap. Do you need help?" she asked softly.

Mac grimaced as he raised his right hand to pull the strap. "Still weak in my right shoulder. Doc said it'll pass." He took a breath. "Ah. The new car smell. I don't remember when I've ever had a new car."

"Elinor told us it was against your principles to buy new. That you were cheap... I mean thrifty," she laughed. "I'd like this to be our car. It reminds me of *the* ditch. Someday I hope we can visit that ditch again, and maybe relive how we lay together there at the bottom?" She laughed, looking up at the stoplight at Greenwich Street to make sure it wasn't going yellow. Hoping, too, to mask her longing.

Driving on snowy city streets had always made her nervous, especially streets within canyons of tall buildings that hid the sun, making for icy conditions. Extra cautious, the horrible memory of that truck coming at her head-on, she wondered briefly if she should have had Devon drive them to her place. She looked over at the car stopping to her right. Did it skid to a stop? Now she was worried, even if it was just a few more blocks to her house.

To still her worries, Mindy squinted out the window and thought about the good news: that she lived on the ground floor of her charming two-story brownstone. The doctor had cautioned that stairs and balance might remain a challenge for Mac. She had asked her friend Joanna to help clean the house, putting up a second bed in her bedroom—hopefully a bed they wouldn't need. She smiled at the thought of sleeping in with Mac on a quiet, snowy morning. With nothing on their minds but warmth, snug in the embrace of love.

"Ditch? What's that mean?" Mac asked, breaking into her thoughts.

Her mouth open, taking a deep, cleansing breath, Mindy replied, "Okay. Time for full disclosure."

"Come again?"

"That, too," Mindy sputtered, embarrassed at how her risqué musings were obviously foremost in her mind. She felt a little, what was that term? Horny? Maybe more than a little, she realized.

"I'd like that." He put his hand on her thigh, moving it with gentle strokes. "We could visit that ditch, *again*, and your aunt out on Bendix road. Yes?" He gave a tug on her thigh that ran chills down and up her spine. Mindy's breath came quickly, matching her rapid thoughts. Should she be driving? It was only a few more blocks. Damn the traffic!

Mac adjusted the heater control. "The heater isn't working."

"Here, let me," she scolded with mock frustration, pressing the Auto button for the heater. "That hit on your head did take its toll, that's for sure," she chuckled, trying to gloss over her anxious thoughts with a patina of humor. "We're almost there. It's too hot in here anyway," she said, reaching to flick off the Auto button, her hand landing on Mac's hand. She gently slid it farther up her leg.

————— . —————

"Where am I?" Mac asked, rolling to his side, facing the window Mindy had opened to let in the bright sunshine and chill breeze. "What's that smell?"

Mindy sat on the edge of the bed, caressing Mac's hair. "You were heavy in slumberland. Now, you're here with me." She smoothed out her jeans and adjusted her blouse, her bare feet on the cold floor.

Mac raised himself on his elbows, taking in the room with its rich wallpaper, antique furnishings, and Impressionist prints on the wall. "Oh, that feels good," he moaned, pushing his head farther into her hand. "Now I recognize where I am. California. But... who are you?"

"Me? I'm your babysitter. The one who tucked you in when we got home yesterday. The one who slept over on that rollaway because you were thrashing around in your sleep. The one who wants to marry you."

Mac, still groggy, gasped. "Marry? I like the smell of that!"

"You smell breakfast, dummy. It can wait. I'm serious! I want to marry you... and... give you some exercises to calm your thrashing. Do you *get* me, *Professor*?"

"Marriage? Yeah... yes! I accept, with *all* my heart!" Mac replied, wiping at the sleepiness that dripped from his eyes. In his softest, most sincere voice, he asked, "Mindy Bendix, will you marry me? Please, say yes!" With a quick nod, he held up the sheets as she crawled in next to him. "The Doc said to go slow," Mac cautioned, sighing as they snuggled. "The window, the neighbors?"

"Heck with them!" Mindy whispered, her cheek nuzzled in against his as she stared intently into his emerald-green eyes. "I love you, my dear, wounded, wonderful man! Yes, I will marry you! I long to have little Macs and Mindys... a family with you."

Mac caressed her cheek, brushing strands of hair from her sparkling blue eyes. He took her head gently in his hands, rubbing his nose to hers, connecting their souls with the intent look in his eyes.

"Believe it or not, this... is all new for me. Please, be gentle," Mindy whispered, her voice soft, her heart racing.

"What? New to you!" Mac gasped, leaning back, a vague pressure freezing his eyes. Was it his PTSD? "You mean you're a... Oh, man! Forgive me? Wow!" He looked down at his hands. "I'm no longer sure about this. It's like, I hold you up on a pedestal. You're *the* woman of my dreams. I mean, in the months I spent in combat and in recovery, I would fall asleep dreaming of a woman in my arms. Someone who actually loved old, mixed-up me. Someone just like you."

"Are you saying you're in love with a figment of your dreams? That I just happened to be here? Some kind of virtuous statue?" Her hand at her face, she started crying.

"Oh, no. No! Those dreams had no face. The woman was more like the essence of what I wanted life to be. Beauty and grace. Not the life I've seen too often, randomly lost in battle. My dreams are a composite of the goodness in life that I wanted for myself and my troops. A piece of the memory my brother, Sam, left for me: the *goodness* of people."

"So? Where do I fit in?" Mindy asked, pushing away.

"Damn! Wish I could explain better. Like I told that civie shrink, my emotions get hammered too easily! I can see the thoughts in my head as if I'm looking in at someone else's thinking. Can't explain it."

Mindy pulled back as he reached out to her shoulder. She sat up. "Oh, Mac! I'm so sad, so disappointed. Frustrated! Here I am, ready to give myself to you, my first lover, and you're *thinking* too much!"

"Don't you see, Mindy? I'm confused and hesitant *exactly* because I do love *you*!" He put his hand to her cheek. She didn't budge. "The one takeaway from my dreams is the sense of *cherish*. I do cherish you! It's beyond love. It's the desire to have our love represent all that is good. And hey, yeah! I'm so turned on right now. You can tell, right? But it would sadden me to make love not remembering something that Sam and I talked a lot about. That making love should be in the expression of making *life*. Otherwise, it's just sex. Maybe I sound crazy? Like, in today's world, having sex is a total *why-not*. A non-issue. You talk about little Macs and Mindys. That's what I want, too! I want our family. And I want to be able to look our kids in the eyes when they're old enough, and tell them that they were conceived out of love—within the embrace of God's love. Within our marriage. I see that now…"

Mindy was sobbing, quaking. "God? Are you… do you mean that you really *believe*?"

"Whatever has come over me, I can't describe. But it's a sudden clarity that's been lacking in my life. An acceptance because you've awakened me with your example of love. That the resistance I've mustered to keep God—Jesus—out of my thoughts, has really been because I've been unsure, thinking I already know so much. It's you who's helped me see what faith is. It's *you* I love. All of you! Like how you, adoringly, give me hope that dreams can come true. That my fears, my demons, are not what's real. That you, and God, are."

Mindy was smearing her tears against the sheets, nodding her head and gazing at Mac while sniffing with rapid breaths. For a fleeting moment she so wanted him to grab her. But then, no. "You'll never know, my gallant soldier, how hot I am for you right now. It's not sex. It's a heart bursting hot with a joy I've never before felt."

"Remember the ditch? I told you I've been around the block?"

Mindy pulled Mac closer, tears streaming down her face. "Yes. I *do* remember. I remember thinking you were not talking just about death and combat, but a war within your soul over having not lived quite the way you wanted. Feeling regret, shame?"

"Yeah, that's right. Wow, you do know me!" He paused. "Hot? I admit, I can feel your body heat. If we stay like this…?"

"I want to be married to you, right now!" she whispered.

Mac moaned, hesitated, then kissed her as tenderly as possible—a sweep of lips barely touching. "Soon, but we'll wait," he whispered, crawling out of bed. "This I do know," he choked. "That no one would ever believe this. They'd think me a total PTSD dumbshit! That I didn't tear off your clothes, take you in my arms, and make passionate love to you. Right now!"

"To heck with them! I believe it, 'cause I'm the one here with you. And I love you all the more for the *why*, for the cherish," Mindy said softly. Her eyes were moist, her heart racing, yet her soul was at peace. "It's time for breakfast. Dessert can wait."

CHAPTER 7

The Plan

Contemplating—with an absent focus of her dark eyes—what the future might look like, Director Dong flicked the cigarette ashes from her desk. "As you know, Doctor Juong, our Leader instructed me—given our successful test with the guard—to proceed with the American president. The Leader has selected the first day of April—Fool's Day in the West. A day he wants to fool the world—as the date, even though our State Security team is already in place in Washington and the tunnel extraction of the guard flawless." Using the finger-signal she had established with Juong to denote guarded conversation, she continued, "I have been told by other, unnamed sources, that what we're really waiting for is the Leader's dreams to convey the presence of *more* pigs."

"Forgive my hesitancy, Comrade Director," Juong scoffed, furrows of doubt warping the flawless skin of his forehead. Skin that Dong envied. "We are more than ready to do the president. The first of April is too far off. The American president has been in office already for two weeks. It's now early February. The longer we wait, the more she'll be established with her cabinet and her policies. Can we not proceed sooner?" Leaning in closer to the Director, his exhale of smoke drifting across her face, Juong looked out through the glass partition separating the Director's office from the RID team's cubicles. He mouthed, "What if we started next week, on the anniversary of our Leader's birthday? Would he not be pleased?"

"Pigs, my dear Comrade. It's all about pigs! Have you never noticed how his beam—belt size—equals the girth of those award-winning pigs at our nation's State Ag clinics? He is enamored by their omnivorous hooves, sparse bristly hair, and flat snouts. I think he secretly identifies with them. Not only in looks, but as being a source of wealth for his nation. Well, for a few of us, anyway."

"Caution, Comrade Director," Juong whispered, covering his mouth in an attempt to thwart the listening devices as he recalled the horror of the camps that Dong had described. Camps available to all who countered, in the slightest, the will of the Leader. "Forgive me, but I note sarcasm in your tone. You must be cautious. Does the ire in your voice have anything to do with our Leader's sampling of that reclaimed baggage, the guard?"

"How dare you, Juong," the Director whispered back, raising her arm as if to strike him and drawing stares from staff on the other side of the glass wall. "Not only do you impugn the behavior of our great Leader, but you suggest that I bare him affection? You know perfectly well that I love *only* my work, my Cassidy!"

"A thousand pardons, dear Director. Please forgive me! But… am I really so far from the truth?" Juong replied, his hand still at his mouth.

Dong's slowly broadening smile inflated her already plump cheeks. She turned away from the glass partition so none of the staff would notice. She reached out to pat Juong's hand. "You are observant, my dear friend. And trustworthy. Yes, we should launch earlier, I agree. But heads will roll, will fill his feeding trough, so to speak. Shh, shh," she cautioned as Juong took a deep breath, unable to avoid laughing. "If we guess wrong, much is at stake across the entire globe. We must discuss the implications. Wisely."

"There's always escape Mode Two, no?" Juong asked through his hand. He suddenly went ashen-faced as he absorbed the Director's angry frown, her fingernails piercing the skin of his knuckles.

Dong brought her mouth next to Juong's ear. "You must *never* mention that again! Only we know the origin of your innovation. It is essential that we never reveal our hand!"

"Again, ten thousand pardons!" Juong nodded with a downcast look of shame. "I understand. Please accept my humble submission."

"Enough, already, with the apologies," Director Dong whispered, somewhat disoriented as her favorite quotes from Hollywood seeped into her consciousness. "Now, here's the real question. If we were to launch our holohead president next week, do we first launch and *then* tell the Leader? Or, do we first provide reasons for requesting and justifying an early launch?"

Juong furrowed his forehead further. "I suggest we launch first, then tell. We can attribute the early launch to an expendable staff member who, so enamored with our Leader, mistakenly entered his birthday into the system as the launch date."

Dong stroked her chin, looking past the glass wall and wondering who the unlucky staff member would be. "Assuming the Leader bought this excuse, we'd be wise, regardless, to have documentation readily available. Some type of verifying analysis that suggested this mistaken, early launch is actually better."

"That could work," Juong replied, his eyes narrowing slightly and his lips compressed in serious contemplation.

Dong, nodding absently, deep in her own assessment of options, rubbed the skin on Juong's hand, then slapped it. "It *must* work. Have a re-assessment report prepared. Yes, excellent cover. And remind me again, how confident are you in the untraceable vector-control of our holohead president? Our replica guard was just a trial test, the president altogether different. Daily, there will be millions of eyes cast upon her, with millions of minds analyzing, parsing her every move."

"As you know, Comrade Director, our data transmission method is autonomous, involving a bundle-wrap method of teleporting photons of light. We isolate transmissions within a teleported *ebundle*."

"A what?" Dong responded, incredulously. "Don't try to snow me with your techno-talk, Doctor. You would do well to remember that I was manipulating photon particles when you were still a child."

Bowing slightly from his chair, Juong continued. "You're aware that we've perfected what the Chinese first attempted back a few years ago. I think it was 2017? We've gone light years beyond their technology, no pun intended," he laughed, cautiously. "Our ebundle is an encrypted bundle of light. That is to say, a quantum entanglement of photonic states that is impervious to any detection, interception, or interference. To put it in simple terms, it's a bundle of light-based data that we create here. Through teleporting, its *separated* state appears as the holohead. Both in appearance and behavior. In effect, creating an instantly-parallel light bundle at the destination without using known methods of transmission or wave frequencies. Teleporting directly into the second instance. The hologram president."

"Yes, fantastic! Do you realize how ingenious we are, Doctor? Absolutely *brilliant*... to use that antiquated British term. You're saying, then," Director Dong squealed, fully aroused and flushed-faced, "that the teleporting essentially percolates or creates the substance of the transmission directly at the receiving end? That it does so without filling the airspaces with waves of data that can be sniffed?"

"In a hazelnut, yes!"

"You mean, in a *nutshell*. Please, Doctor, remove your attempts to apply metaphors of the decadent West," the Director replied as a wave of uncontrollable laughter rolled over her normally dour countenance. She peered out the glass wall, noticing several of the staff staring at her.

Turning to follow her glance, "One of those will be the unlucky one with the Leader's birthday," Juong chuckled quietly. "I will proceed to have the team prepare to launch our holohead president next week. Our onsite intel team suggests we execute the launch late on a Friday. The president spends the weekends with her family at the White House. The fewer around her at the time of the switchover, the better."

"Perhaps?" Dong considered. "The timing does concern me. As we know, many agents and many eyes, surround the president. The switchover, as you call it, is the most crucial aspect of our endeavor. What if the president is being intimate with that husband of hers, the one they call the First Dude?" A scowl crossed her face. "First Dude? How crude and childish the West is in its societal acceptance. Disgusting is too mild a word for the American culture."

"Does that include Hollywood?" Juong asked, hoping to ride the earlier wave of Dong's laughter.

"Hollywood, Bollywood, *even* our friends in Hengdian," came Dong's tempered reply with a guttural chuckle. "You know I'm a fan of pioneers. Not just handsome cowboys, but Hollywood itself. It was the *first* to introduce film-based fantasy. All we've done is remove the need for the screen. With Cassidy, we can project—immerse—real-life characters into any setting. We've harnessed the ultimate expression of creativity, my dear Comrade Doctor. It may excite our Leader and play into his plans, but the credit, the innovation—the *control*—is ours!"

Juong rotated his chair away from Dong's desk. He considered the autographed photo of William Boyd hanging on the wall. He rubbed his hands down his pant legs, swiping at some imagined dust on his shoes. "Acting and timing, such as by your hero there," pointing to the photo, "is the essence of human nature that runs the world. Timing? We need to decide when to switchover the president."

"A delicate issue, yes," Director Dong replied, slipping back to reality as she shooed Boyd from her imagination. "How well do we see, get feedback, from our replica guard?"

"Real-time. Absolute. We see on our screens and the holographic simulator here, what the guard sees, hears, feels. Right as it happens. Directly from the guard's point of view, as if we were the guard."

"The wise choice, then, is to monitor the president's actions via the guard. From that view, we can best time the switch, no? Perhaps have the guard ask the president into a room by themselves?"

"My understanding is that guards at the White House are mute, not allowed to speak unless spoken to."

"Even in emergencies?"

"What! Create an emergency? That would be the foolish, drawing more attention to the president!" He looked back at the Director who was nodding to herself, her eyes black diamonds in a languid setting of thought. "What do you have in mind?" Juong queried, his tone subdued to match the curious squint in his eyes.

"A little-known corollary to methods advocated by Sun Tzu is to create a diversion in *plain* site. If there is some sort of emergency, we can presume the guard would be responsible for the president's safety. If our guard then announces she is isolating the president for safety, in that few moments we might have the time we need. The *key* is isolating the president!"

Juong used his feet against the floor to swivel back to the photograph of William Boyd—Hopalong Cassidy. It was positioned on the wall next to a poster for the movie *Hopalong Cassidy Returns.* "When was that?" he asked, pointing to the poster.

"Years ago. Last century, around nineteen fifty."

"I'm astounded at the non-existent level of technology back then," Juong whispered. "It's amazing, when you think about it. That your cowboy is returning in a form of technology that even the most advanced thinkers—way back then—could not have imagined."

Removing her glasses to avoid any errant transmission to her staff, Director Dong rubbed her hands in glee. "Yes, even today's most advanced thinkers cannot imagine the milestones we've achieved." She stood to walk around the desk, moving to the glass partition and smiling out at her staff. "We're on the verge... the beginning. A whole new era of existence. By we, I mean you and me, my dear Comrade."

"And of course, you mean our Dear Leader?" Juong asked, his hand no longer at his mouth

"Of course," Dong replied loudly, her unspoken scoff held in her throat to avoid detection by the sensors arrayed throughout Building 666. She went to her wall, stroking her chin as she considered the photo of Boyd, nodding absently as she adjusted its tilt. "Of course, my dear Doctor Juong, of course!" she spoke to the sensors, her certainty no longer certain.

CHAPTER 8

The Switch

President Perserve lay exhausted beneath the crumbled sheets, staring at the inlaid patterns of the crown molding high in the bedroom ceiling, her hand in her husband's.

"If only America could see us," she whispered as she rolled over, her right leg on his and her arm across his chest.

"That's the last thing on my mind," Roy replied, giving her a gentle squeeze. In the dim light cast by the embers in the fireplace—encased in its marble mantel, a gift from former Princess Elizabeth—Roy could barely make out the shadows of vases and antique clocks against the hand-painted 18th-century Chinese wallpaper. The reverie of the past moments clouding his thoughts, "I do like this room," he whispered. "Happy Valentine's Day, by the way," he added, kissing her ear.

"You mean you don't like the back-to-Abe's-log-cabin décor I was considering?" the president laughed into the folds of Roy's shoulder.

"Naw, I think keeping this room just as it is makes the most sense. Maintains tradition, and… the beauty and graciousness that is you."

"You've had your sweets for tonight, my RoyBoy. No need for soft-talking me," she said as she raised herself on her elbow to watch the fire. "You know the décor was done by some major designer, a darling of the Hollywood set?"

"Yeah, that's why logs don't seem quite the right motif. I mean, look at those paintings hanging there, by Cézanne and Peale. How the shadows from the fire, flickering across Cézanne's *Mont Sainte Victorie*, mimic our Kansas rolling waves of grain. Can't do that with logs."

"I'm glad my farm boy is getting some culture," the president joked as she laid back down, moving her leg farther across his.

"I thought you said no more sweets tonight," he laughed, catching his breath in her auburn hair.

"Complaining, Mister First Dude?" Her voice wavered in passion. "You've got three choices. Sweets, sleep, or talking policy. What's it to be at this late hour?"

Just as Roy was to say, "The first one…" there was a loud knock on the bedroom door as the red alarm rang on the bedside phone console.

"What the…!" Roy exclaimed.

"Madam President!" The guard's voice carried through the door. "I'm so sorry to disturb you, but there's a situation… an emergency!"

Listening with one ear to the guard while picking up the phone, the president, all seriousness as she moved off Roy, yelled, "What is it?"

The Assistant Chief of Staff, on the other end of the phone, his voice shaky, "There seems to be an intrusion."

The president cut him off. "The children!"

"No, ma'am," came the fast reply. "They're secure. The motion sensors picked up some movement on the balcony outside your bedroom. The guard, Sergeant Sanchez, is at your door. Please let her in. She'll escort you to the Clerk's Room—your safe room!"

Roy was already out of bed, grabbing the president's robe as he motioned her to the center of the Turkish rug, a Glock in his right hand. Holding her hand and pulling her in behind his back, he approached the bedroom door from the side. "Sergeant, is it clear?"

"Yes, sir. More Marines and agents are with me now, securing the hall. Please, sir, open the door, and I'll escort the president to the Clerk's Room while they search your room and the balcony."

"Can the children join me in the safe room?" the president yelled in a high pitch that Roy had never heard. He, too, was feeling panic. Moving the Glock to his left hand, standing to the left of the door, he pushed Margaret well behind him with his right arm.

Finished donning the robe, she whispered, "Okay."

"I'm opening the door, Sergeant," Roy yelled. "I'm armed. What about the children?"

"I understand that you're armed, sir," the guard replied. "The children are secure. I can hit the door's emergency release, but we'd prefer you to open the door from your side."

Looking back at Margaret, taking in her nod, Roy thought about turning the room lights on. Better to stay in the dark. "Are the hall lights fully on?" he yelled through the door.

"Yes, sir!" Roy heard additional voices and saw shadows in the light beneath the bottom of the door. He pulled the door open.

Behind Sergeant Sanchez, he recognized two of the White House Marine guards and four Secret Service members. Armed with MP5 submachine guns and Remington shotguns, they formed a phalanx around the sergeant standing at the door.

"Please, ma'am," the sergeant commanded, her hand extending into the dark bedroom. "We must hurry!" Pointing to the agents and Marines, she said, "They'll carry out the search. You must not be here."

"I'm coming, too," Roy stated, flatly,

"No, sir! No time for that, not procedure," one of the Secret Service agents said, motioning to Sergeant Sanchez to take the president while holding an arm against Roy. "Please, sir. We've practiced this many times. Just the president. We'll escort you to the children."

"Go, Roy!" Margaret said, determination and firmness in her voice.

As two of the agents motioned Roy towards Kari's yellow bedroom across the hall, the sergeant took the president's elbow and together they walked briskly to the Clerk's Room at the end of the hall.

Once inside the room, Sergeant Sanchez holstered her sidearm and closed the heavy door, engaging several switches to arm the door and activate monitoring and air-flow devices. Motioning the president to the Chippendale chair next to the 19th-century drum table, the sergeant said, "Please, ma'am, have a seat. We'll wait for the all clear."

Her hand on the butt of her holstered gun, the sergeant went to the closet door. Opening it slowly, she gave the briefest of nods to what she saw inside. Not closing the door completely, she turned to the president.

In Building 666, the RID team held their collective breath as they watched the large-screen display that showed the situation as seen directly from the guard's point of view.

"Now for the switchover," Doctor Juong said to no one in particular, beads of sweat forming on his forehead. "This is the most delicate, complex part. We must let our holohead, waiting there in closet, replace the president without raising alarms or being viewed by the two video monitors in that clerk room." Juong took a deep, relaxing breath.

The RID team heard Sergeant Sanchez say, "Please, if you will, ma'am, put on this Kevlar vest, here in the closet."

"Is that really necessary?"

"Please, ma'am. You're on my watch. Yes, it's standard procedure. We've not yet had time to drill you on this. Please, step over here," Sanchez said as she pulled the closet door open.

The RID team watched the president step into the closet in front of the guard, who carefully pulled the closet door shut just as a brief burst of light flashed from beneath the closet door. Listening via the guard, they heard a muffled scream.

Inside the closet, President Perserve gasped in fright as she raised her arms to fight the guard. The guard pinned the president's arms behind her. Margaret felt as if she were staring in a mirror. Before her stood herself with a strange light around the edges. "Sanchez! What is this, what *are* you doing!" she screamed as she felt a sharp prick in her neck. The mirror image started to wobble and fade as she passed out.

On a second screen next to the simulator, the RID team could see the guard from the president's point of view. Both the guard's and the holohead president's perspectives showed Margie, the real president, slumped to the floor of the closet. The guard was assisting the holohead president into the vest. "Let's move quickly," the guard said, flashing a finger-gesture—a signal to the RID team. So far, so good.

"What about the president's body?" one of Dong's team asked.

"It will remain covered in the back of the closet until tomorrow night. The guard—and this is another crucial part of the plan—will then carry the president to Blair House and our tunnel," Dong replied, irritated by having to disclose the details.

"Carry? Is that possible with all the security cameras?"

Dong replied curtly, "Yes." She now knew which unlucky team member would take the blame for the early launch of the plan.

The guard opened the heavily paneled door of the closet, backing out, her hand on the president's shoulder, guiding her back into the Clerk's Room. The Secret Service agent watching this from the security console in the White House basement, about to order the Marines to check out the Clerk's Room, gave a sigh of relief. "The is C-One," she said into her mic. "POTUS... ah, Unity is go! What are the results from the second-floor search?"

"Negative," came the lead agent's reply. "We've swept the entire floor, the balcony, and confirmed all windows secure. You just heard the outside team give the all clear. I'm having the president's husband return to their bedroom. Go ahead, have the guard escort the president back here."

"Roger. All units, clear!" said the agent at the security console.

Watching from the president's perspective, the RID team saw the guard motion the president to back away from the door. She pulled out her sidearm, slowly opening the Clerk's Room door just as standard procedure required. "Well done," Dong murmured.

The agent at the White House security console continued, "The guard is bringing the president out. Stand by!"

The president stumbled slightly as she walked out into the waiting circle of Marines and agents. She reached out to the arm of a Marine to steady her steps. Her cheeks were flushed, her eyes dilated—the AI backend at Building 666 was exceeding all computational limits in order to control the holohead's behavior.

"More nuance," Dong ordered, her hand on the back of Juong's chair as she looked over his shoulder.

"Apply affection, level seven," Juong spoke into his voice-activated control mic, accelerating the AI heuristics.

"Thank you, young man." The president smiled, squeezing the Marine's arm. Looking up, she said, "I thank all of you for your rapid response. Are the children... chil... safe?" she asked.

"Apply speech, pattern tightness, eleven," Juong said, further adjusting the AI heuristics.

"How much tweaking is required?" one of the RID team asked.

Another unlucky member, Dong noted. "Doctor Juong will have to make subtle, ah... tweaks, as you call them, over the next twelve hours. As you all know," she said turning to face her team, "our backend AI system is running on the fastest, most optimized computer." One, she thought to herself, that benefits from our ability to regulate and accelerate the speed of light. Her resulting warm smile, misinterpreted by her team, had them all bowing in respect.

A red light flashed on Juong's panel. "Problem!" His high-pitched voice echoed off the control room's walls.

"What?" Dong demanded.

"Okay! Okay... not critical. We had an ebundle anomaly. It self-corrected," Juong replied, the sheen of his forehead reflected in Dong's glasses.

"Invoke tertiary redundancy," Dong ordered. "We've come this far, we must *not* fail!"

"Done," Juong replied, wiping his forehead, his confidence waning. He loved Dong like an older sister—one who had replaced his two sisters. Both of whom, in beauty and grace, has exemplified all that was wonderful in life, only to have them killed in the nation's worst train wreck. A wreck that the Leader—as judge and executioner—had attributed to the entire Rail Committee. All of whom were dealt the same fate as his sisters. Regardless of the fact that the Leader's brother had been in charge of manufacturing the steel used for the defective trestle.

CHAPTER 9

The Outcome

The first thing Roy noticed was the clammy feel on the back of her neck as his put his arm around the president to walk back to their bedroom. "Are you sure you're okay? That was a real scare!"

The president slipped as she staggered across the carpet.

"Hold on!" Roy ordered.

The entire entourage of agents and Marines stopped in the middle of the hall, surrounding Roy and the president.

In Building 666, the director moved her hand from the back of Juong's chair and grabbed his neck. "What *is* this?" she demanded.

Juong, also noticing the stumbling nature of the president, adjusted some controls on his console and spoke into his mic, "Gross motor firmness, up four degrees. Muscle release, attitude eight."

The president stretched and smiled as she rubbed the back of her neck. She scraped her slippers across the carpet, testing the need for stability.

"Voice texture, intimate, up seven," Juong ordered. The RID team watched, spellbound. "The doctor is such a master," one of the female team members said softly, nudging her friend and wishing the Doctor would master her.

The president placed her hand on Roy's arm. Clearing her throat, she said, "Still just a…" her voice wavering, "bit shaky. Need to get to bed. Busy day tomorrow. Or, is it already tomorrow?" she laughed.

In spite of the surrounding phalanx, Roy embraced the president with a loving hug, stroking her hair and whispering. "We both knew this was going to be a challenge, you being president. But for sure, this is a rude awakening so early on." His hand on her neck, he gently squeezed out their love code. When the president did not respond, Roy felt a sudden pang of guilt. Should this precious woman—the love of his life, the one who has led and cared for so many others—have to be exposed to the same deadly threats he had encountered in his tours of duty? He knew it came with her job. But still, should he have encouraged her to run for office? Would fear change her? She already felt different.

The lead agent cleared his throat. "Sir?"

"You're sure the bedroom area is clear?"

"Yes, sir! None of the in-house detection devices show any evidence of motion or intrusion."

"Then, what the hell caused the alarm?" Roy demanded, his combat experience not accepting a pat answer.

"Unknown. We've arranged for Solidarity Two throughout the White House for the night. All is well, sir. We wish you and the president a sound sleep, sir!" the agent replied.

Roy scanned the bedroom as they entered. "Thank you," he answered, giving the Marines and agents a semi-salute. He closed the door, guided the president to their bed and helped her remove the heavy body armor. He held it high, gauging its heft. "*This* would not have made for a sound sleep, Madam President," he said, attempting humor. Receiving no response from the president, Roy returned the Glock to its bedside holster after helping the president remove her robe and crawl into bed.

The president pulled the covers up, rotating away from Roy without a smile. He stood looking down at her, again feeling guilt. He decided that from that moment on, he would be her closest guard in spite of the Secret Service and others.

Juong rotated his neck, hoping the Director would release her almost-stranglehold. "That was close. Way too close!"

"Indeed!" The word grated on the director's voice. The RID team, sensing that they had just witnessed a most crucial moment in the entire holohead enterprise, ambled back to their cubicles. Their comments and discrete murmurs blended in with the fan noise from the air conditioner.

"I could tell from that husband's look that he's going to be a problem," Juong offered.

"What look is that? You're an expert on love," the director scoffed.

"While our Dear Leader frowns on any display of affection, of succumbing to amorous thoughts other than those for him or our nation, I have read some books," Juong replied, whispering. "And then also, I have observed you and your cowboy there. I have seen the longing and concern in your eyes, Dear Director."

"Harumph!"

"Please don't deny it, if only to recognize that the husband, the Dude guy, is totally in love with his wife. That he'll insert himself in a way that could endanger our effort. I read once that love is naturally part of the human genome."

The director cleared her throat, accompanied with a dismissive gesture of her arm. "When do you anticipate our holohead capacity will exceed two?"

"A few months, maybe, but not soon enough. We could create a husband replica, but then we'd have to delete the guard."

"Poor options, at best. You must increase our holohead capacity sooner," Dong stated, rising from her chair to once again adjust the tilt on the photo of William Boyd. "Tell me, Doctor, could we have our president deliver some form of heart attack or poison to that husband?"

"We've run such a scenario through the simulator numerous times. The result was always one of extreme risk. The husband is in perfect health. His removal could raise suspicions pointed at our president. Totally counter-productive!"

Director Dong brushed her short bangs from her forehead, momentarily pausing as she felt the rough skin below. Her eyes focused on Juong and his forehead. She wondered if perhaps their Cassidy technology might be used, at some time in the future, to supplant body parts, even skin, as a form of body enhancement.

"It's been a long, stressful day, Doctor. I think we can assume the president will sleep through the night. We need our rest, too."

"I'll stay on watch, at least for a while," Juong replied. "We don't yet know how the president might respond to some world crisis that comes in during the night, or if the husband decides to exercise his marriage rights. Please rest well, Director. It has been an eventful day."

"Indeed. Eventful, and successful. Tomorrow is yet... new again."

———— . ————

The clock on the side table quietly chimed out reveille. Roy, sleeping back to back against the president, yawned and stretched his toes, awakening from a stressful dream where giant stalks of wheat were stalking Margaret. He blinked the tears from his eyes, momentarily unsure of where he was. He reached his hand over his back to caress the president's hip.

"Ugh!"

"You awake?" Roy asked, turning to spoon the president's backside. He glanced at the clock: quarter to six. Still early, enough time. "How did you sleep, my Margie-girl?"

"Poorly. Took a pill when you got up. What time was that, about three?" she replied, her back still to Roy.

"Were you warm enough? You feel cool," Roy asked, rubbing her hip and moving his hand to the front of her right leg.

"Just lying here thinking about my first day on the job. Lots to deal with. I hope Deshon is prepared."

"Is there time for some sweets?" Roy asked, remembering how their loving touch in the morning had always made for a sweeter day.

"Sweets?" the president asked, as she threw back the sheets to crawl out of bed, away from Roy.

"Sweets?" Juong said to the young female RID member who had just arrived with a cup of tea. "What does that mean?" Speaking into his mic, he asked the AI system, "Quickly, now. What might the term *sweets* mean between a man and a woman?" Instantly, across his screen came several suggestions, all dealing with Valentines Day and candy.

"Is that some kind of code?" the RID member asked.

"You forget, Comrade Assistant, that *our* president has no established code with that husband. All the nuances we observed of the real president are limited, at best. We have to assume the president and her husband had some intimate aspects of their relationship that we could not determine or sleuth out."

The RID member leaned against Doctor Juong, hoping he could sleuth out the warmth of her body through her squared-off coat.

Juong pushed back from his console to gaze into her eyes. He felt her warm breath on his cheek, the smell of honey mixing with the aroma of daechu-cha tea. He realized it was a sweet smell as he watched her close her eyes, waiting for his lips. Juong quickly glanced out the glass wall. The office was quiet, empty. "Another time," he told himself as he clapped his hands. "I have it! It means being intimate. I was wondering if the husband would get around to that," he laughed, gently pushing the member away as he rotated back to his console. "Update database," he spoke into his mic. "Sweets mean sex. Adjust arousal mode down to avoidance level three. Create bodily irritation level two in holohead to provide reason for avoidance."

The RID member stood, brushing Juong's shoulder with her hand. Somehow, the mechanical, methodical method of sex advocated by the Dear Leader seemed to be lacking. However, she knew that out of loyalty, she should not ponder such issues.

Juong looked up as Director Dong entered the control room, rushing past the bowing assistant.

"How was their night?"

"Without incident. And… we've learned how—more like when— to keep our president from amorous inclinations by that husband. It might even help us establish a way to remove the husband's influence. Overall, good."

"Wonderful!" Dong replied, anxiously rubbing her fingers beneath her eyes. "I had dreams that our transmission methods had run amuck. That somehow the Americans had uncovered the holohead and traced it back to us."

"Not possible," Juong replied. "Our transmission method makes the ebundles self-erasing, not traceable. If we encounter failure, the holohead simply evaporates, leaving no evidence who it was or by whom. We're safe in that regard."

"Excellent, my dear Doctor. Let us proceed with getting their president out of the closet and into the tunnel!"

———— · ————

Entering the White House breakfast room, the president smiled at the Marine guard standing at attention near the entrance. Gracefully smoothing her black fitted dress, she sat down at the chair Roy held for her. Her gold-braided necklace—suggested by her policy assistant so to enhance her credibility as president—sparkled, accentuating her beauty. Donny Perkins, the chief butler, stood admiringly near the hall door leading to the kitchen. His silent nods directed the staff as they served coffee and a yogurt-granola-blueberry parfait.

Upstairs in the Clerk's Room closet, face-down on her stomach and near suffocation beneath a heavy rug, Margie struggled with the bindings. She couldn't roll over, kick or move her legs. Her hands were zip-tied behind her to a pipe in the back of the closet. With her mouth heavily taped, she could make only the faintest murmur. The musty smell and dust from the rug clogged her nose with each increasingly panicky inhale.

"Why haven't they found me?" she tried to scream. Then she remembered, with a convulsive shiver, the apparition she had seen standing right before her—as if she were looking in a mirror—smiling with a heartless expression. "What is it?" she tried yelling, the sound from the bottom of her throat caught in the tape. "What's happening!"

CHAPTER 10

The Heft

A wave of claustrophobia slowly seeped into her consciousness. It began painfully over her left eyebrow, crawling to the back of her ear, and then up her neck to reach back across to pull against both eyebrows. A jumble of nerve endings fighting a void: fear. Try as she might, the President of the United States, Margaret Perserve, could not dispel—overcome—the feeling of being in a coffin. For all she could sense, she was. Her neck was strained from the many unsuccessful attempts to throw off the rug, her motion stilted by immovable restraints. She was stuck. Simply, wholly, stuck. With an increasingly frightening perception of defeat, her confidence—from years surmounting myriad challenges, of maintaining fortitude against all odds—was evaporating.

She started to weep. "I'm allowed to," she thought. "Where is this hell that I'm in? How did it happen? What about America, my family?" she cried. As the rug absorbed her tears, she thought back to Roy, to Kari and Todd. To her dad and mother. She recalled the last words her father had spoken to her right before she left for D.C. and the State Department. She had initially dismissed his words as part of his superstitious nature. Now she wasn't so sure. "My dear daughter," he had started. She recalled now, with a sense of guilt, how those words had played havoc with her awareness as an adult, as a woman. Now she found them comforting. "Life is a miracle. All life. That which we see and that which is unseen. All God-made. You, all of us, are born with skills—call them gifts. Some we see and some we can't yet see. I believe in you. I always have. How you care for others. That when you fight, you always fight fair. I believe that one's life is formed in a crucible of summons… events that shape us. That, if we allow, hone our gifts in ways we can only see when we look back. Remember that. That you're gifted. Not so much with lots of smarts," he had laughed, "but with character. What you do when no one is watching."

President Perserve had no idea if anyone was watching her now. But this, she told herself, was exactly what her father had been talking about. About reaching beyond the obvious, to embrace that which God had placed before her. No matter what!

Shaking her head, she struggled to take calming breaths through her dust-clogged nose. She thought not of the dust or the bindings that held her, but that she was alive, and therefore, that she was able. "I'll fight this!" Her thoughts surged with a cleansing sense of righteous anger. Flaring her nose, she felt conviction in her eyes: determination to fight until her last breath. It was her duty to harness God's gifts in service to America.

Wound tight in thoughts fueled, too, by anguish, it took her a moment to escape her reverie, to realize that she'd heard a door open and footsteps on the other side of the rug. In spite of her intense desire to push forward, to fight—was it like machismo, she wondered—an overwhelming sense of relief enveloped her. She tried to cry out, "Help!" but all that emanated was a hollow moan. She heard a step and felt a foot kick her. "Who are you?" she tried to scream through the tape.

"Still alive? Good," came the quiet voice.

The voice sounded like that guard, Sanchez. Awareness dawned. Margaret remembered that she had been taken into a closet in the Clerk's Room by that guard, where she had seen a horrible apparition of herself. That the guard had grabbed her. She could remember nothing else other than waking, bound inside the rug. She felt a surging warmth in her groin. Ignoring that she had just peed in her pajamas, the president wriggled as vigorously as she could, fighting the binding, aware that she was yelling out venom. That she was pissed. She laughed for an insane second at the briefest of thoughts: she truly was, literally and figuratively, pissed.

"Oh, oh," the guard said. "Mamá got a problem, do we?"

"It's Sanchez, for sure," Margaret thought. "Or at least sounds like her with a strange accent. A hint of something almost like Mandarin, but not quite. More singsongy. Polynesian? I wonder?"

"We're going on a little trip. Here's some sustenance," the voice said. A hand, a strong hand, grabbed the edge of the rug and tore it off the president. Sanchez was kneeling, holding a syringe. Margaret rapidly went though all the Pilates' core-blasting moves she knew, but to no avail. With a wicked smile, Sanchez leaned forward and drove the needle into the president's neck.

Watching from the other side of the globe, "Wonderful, wonderful," Dong whispered into the ear of Doctor Juong.

Juong ignored her. Now came the hard part. Moving the body, later that night, to the tunnel. Two hundred meters away under Blair House.

———— . ————

The president's Chief of Staff, Deshon Williams, was thanking Sharon Webster, the Chief Usher, as the president came down the stairs to the White House hall.

"Deshon? Why are you so late here, in our residence, where I sleep like a dog?" the president joked, as she gave Deshon a clammy hug.

Panic enveloped those watching from the RID headquarters. "Eliminate cross-references to Asian colloquialisms," Juong screamed into his mic. "Use *just* Webster's!" Turning to the RID team, ignoring the scorching look leveled by Director Dong, Juong demanded, "How did Li Ching-Yuen's expression get into the natural-language mix?" His severe glance settled on the tall analyst responsible for backloading all lexical elements in the database. As Juong cleared his voice, the analyst bowed and left the control room.

"You did not do enough simulations, Doctor!" Dong stated, angrily.

"Excuse me, Comrade Director, but even with the accelerated computational cycle-count of our computers, the needed number of simulation permutations exceeds that massive googolplex number. We had to take shortcuts given our Leader's tight timeline, so we ran a utility function to select the highest value, most frequent expressions."

While hesitant to embarrass Juong in front of her staff, yet determined to emphasize the critical nature of their mission—not to mention that the "Dear Leader" might end up considering her to be "excess baggage" if they failed—Dong exclaimed, "Don't feed us that ridiculous Western line where 'Perfection is the enemy of good enough.' There is only one outcome that is acceptable. Perfection!" She clapped her hands. The staff, all except Juong, bowed and rushed to the door.

Juong, shaking his head, typed on his console keyboard. He leaned forward to scan the English text painted on his screen. Struggling with the proper pronunciation, he said as he turned to Dong, "You one mother-forking son of a beach."

"Please, dear Doctor. Let the auto translator do the English," Dong replied, glancing out the glass wall to make sure none of the staff were watching as she gave Juong's shoulder a gentle tap. "We made our point," she laughed, pointing to where the staff had been standing.

Juong bit his lips. He was exhausted and frustrated.

Rubbing his back and shoulders with unusual tenderness, "Let's listen in," Dong suggested.

Deshon stepped back, a questioning look etched on his handsome face. "Why... don't you remember, Margaret?" he whispered. "You asked me to brief you this evening on our four key policy positions. I'm sorry if I misread your request. Is this a bad time?"

Juong recognized that the president was apparently struggling with some form of memory loss. "Restore activity memory from entire day," he said into his mic. He turned to Dong. "This is not going as we had planned. Too many human-based adjustments. I can only do so much!"

"Hang tough, cowboy," Dong offered.

Juong's curiosity surged. What was this suddenly-strange—almost jovial—mood of the director? She seemed too relaxed beyond what the situation required. Then again, he remembered, she had been in the bathroom for several minutes with her picture of that Boyd cowboy. He chewed down his panic. Was the director losing control? If so, that could mean the entire enterprise—the future of their project—would fall on his shoulders. Juong put his elbows on the console, his head in his hands. Responding to the Director's pokes—no longer rubs—at his shoulder, Juong spit into his mic, "Call it a night!"

The president, stretching with an exaggerated yawn, said, "Let's call it a night. I'm tired."

Deshon frowned, giving a brief nod. "Yes, ma'am. Please rest well."

"Let's hope the entire house rests well," Dong whispered, as if she were standing next to the president. In a more guarded tone, she added, "Now, for the guard lifting the president and hauling her to the tunnel."

Juong responded, "There's is no way she can carry a body that distance to Blair House without someone noticing. So, I've asked our programmers to increase the guard's strength to an enhanced photonic state. We've also devised a way for the guard to carry the president under her topcoat."

"Won't that be too obvious?"

"No," Juong replied. "We simulated the lighting in the hallways and walks from the Clerk's Room to Blair House. At this time of night, the shadows will mask any additional bulk—the heft—of the guard. It's all we can do."

Dong and Juong looked at each other, eyes arched in concern. It was time. Talking to the guard within their simulator, Juong said, "Make sure the president is not responsive. You have the overcoat?"

"Yes, sir," the guard replied via the simulator. "And the straps."

"Does she know what the straps are for?" Dong asked, perplexed.

Juong looked over his shoulder with a scolding stare—from anyone else a punishable act of supreme disrespect.

Dong, still somewhat basking in memories from the bathroom, revealed something bordering on empathy. "Please proceed Doctor Juong. I'm sorry for thinking you've fallen off the saddle."

A spasm shot through Juong's shoulders. *Saddle?* Confirmation that he *was* alone. He alone was in firm, pragmatic control. He paused, smiling inside his eyes. "You can see for yourself, Comrade Director," Juong intoned, "that our stimulated guard is already lifting and strapping the president to her back. Once done, just a matter of putting on the overcoat and walking briskly out of the closet."

Both Juong and the director jolted upright as a strange voice came from the simulator. "This package is heavy. As you sure I have the strength to carry it the distance?" the voice asked.

"Stand by!" Juong yelled at the simulator as he motioned the director to a corner of the control room.

"Who *is* that voice?" Dong asked, her eyes wide with fear. "It seems the guard is self-assessing. Is that possible?"

"Not sure, but I suspect our AI backend has inadvertently given the guard independent thought. We anticipated the possibility, but never believed it possible. Nonetheless, we have a safety cutoff for that. I'll invoke it immediately!"

"Immediately!" Dong snarled.

Returning to his console, Juong ran through a series of sequences, finally nodding to the director. "All set."

"When will these little crises stop?"

"When we either give up, stop innovating, or die," Juong replied, his eyes focused on the simulator screen as he continued typing.

Dong noticed his forehead was once again smooth, without a wrinkle or sign of concern. Her eyes narrowed in suspicion. Suspicion, she knew, was her nation's cultural climate akin to the neighborly love that had been offered by the East German Stasi. "Yes, yes. Have the guard proceed."

Knowing his interaction with the simulated guard was no different from his being next to the guard in the Cloak Room, Juong said, "Wait a few minutes after your shift ends. Take the back stairs."

Excited, close to victory, Director Dong motioned to the RID team to come back into the control room. "Watch this, my children!"

On the big screen, the guard waved good night to the incoming guard as she spoke into her shoulder mic, "C-One, I'm leaving the premises."

"Roger that, Sanchez. Safe drive home."

The RID team watched from Sanchez's point of view as she exited the back stairs of the White House. She walked slowly to Blair House and went down one level to the garage park, stopping momentarily to enter a basement storage room. A moment later she reappeared, looking much thinner.

The RID team cheered as confirmation came from their team in the Blair House tunnel: "The Leader's baggage has left the building."

Chapter 11

The Newlyweds

The ice at the font doorstep of Mindy's condo had resisted the effects of salt and sand. It was hard, clear, blue ice. In the shade all day, given the continual overcast and blizzard conditions that had kept New York City in the deep freeze for a record fifth straight week. This was not supposed to happen in the Big Apple. Not in mid-March.

Icicles hung outside each of the windows. Her alley remained pristine white, replenished daily with a new blanket of snow. If one discounted the effect on traffic and the difficulty walking without slipping, the city was tranquil and beautiful. Stilled into silence.

It was six in the morning on Sunday, the four-week anniversary of their marriage. Mac, barefoot and wearing a torn tee-shirt and saggy pajama bottoms, slowly opened the front door to check the conditions. He nudged the snow with his foot and blew his breath out into the chilly air. "It must still be close to zero," he yelled over his shoulder. He blew again, watching the vapors whirl and fade into the background of snow covering the alley, the trees and the windowsills across the way.

"Close the door, it's freezing!" Mindy yelled. "And come back to bed. I *need* you!"

After taking another look at the blanket of virgin snow, Mac sighed as he closed the door. He skipped back to the bedroom. "Let's go out now, before anyone tracks up the new snow. I bet Washington Square is empty. We could have it all to ourselves," he said softly as Mindy held open the sheets. She was no longer wearing her nightgown.

"No wonder you're cold," Mac laughed, as he nestled in next to his wife, her beauty more breathtaking than the cold air outside. "There's no place else that matters right now. Just being here with you!"

Mindy ran her fingers through his hair as she pulled him in for a tender kiss. "Mrs. Mindy Bendix MacMahan," she cooed. "Mrs. *Mac.* I love how that sounds. There's no name I'd rather have."

Mac's heavy breathing masked the sound of icicles breaking off the bedroom's warming window.

Absorbing Mindy's loving embrace, Mac thought back to the whirlwind of events that had consumed them ever since that first night when Mindy had brought him home from the rehab center. And the morning after, when they had *not* consummated their love, waiting instead to *cherish* it.

He exhaled again, thankful the wait had been short.

They had eloped. At least, that was how they first viewed it. With no family nearby—Mac's parents were in California and Mindy's aunt in Massachusetts—it was the right way to start their adventure through life. But eloping was not really what they had done. They were merely proceeding without hesitation or family or a formal gathering of friends. Mindy had wanted a church wedding with vows made before God. Mac had been all in agreement, stating he wished Sam could be a witness. Mindy's heart had burst, and after what was a record embrace, Mindy had called Joanna to be their witness. Joanna had mentioned her friend, an assistant pastor at Trinity Church down Broadway, not far from Mindy's house on MacDougal Alley. With City Hall on the way to the church, it had taken only one day to effect their consummation of love.

And now, they were man and wife! Lovers, adventurers, kindred spirits, and Christ-followers, of sorts. Opposites for sure, judging by the pile of Mac's clothes in a corner of Mindy's otherwise pristine bedroom. And also based on Mac's expressed desire to lounge around doing nothing—other than exercising—while Mindy said she was anxious to get back to her photography projects. But not too anxious. Especially on snowy Sunday mornings when the sounds of the city disappeared in a vacuum of snow.

Later that morning, over coffee and French toast, Mindy asked, "Did you return Blake's call?"

Mac's moved his lower lip back and forth over his teeth as he lapped up the remaining syrup with the last piece of toast. "Forgot," he sighed heavily. "It's hard to get back into the swing of things."

"You've had time."

"Hey, aren't we still on our honeymoon?" he asked, pointing to the bedroom.

"Yes, we are," Mindy replied as she cleared the table and gave the back of Mac's head a pat. "But that doesn't mean others have to be excluded. Blake sounded sincerely concerned when he called. He said the whole team was. They wanted to know how you were. Of course, I said that you were fine. Doing well."

"Yeah, I remember you blushing and covering the phone 'cause you heard Blake say to whoever was there with him, 'We know what that means. Ha ha…'"

"So? They can think what they want. I just know that our love, and our love-making, is the most wondrously private thing in my life. I don't want anyone making assumptions or casting it into the world's collective guffawing over how others treat relationships, or sex. Period!" She paused to see if Mac was listening. He seemed distant sometimes. "Anyway, give him a call. I think they're still hoping to get you back on campus, which, by the way, I am not!"

"There you have it. I'm out of work. My wife doesn't want me to go back to work. Therefore, *Mrs. Mac*, I lounge around, enjoying life… and you." Mac looked, once again, at the bedroom.

"Not on a stomach full of French toast, mister!" Mindy gave him a stern stare, belied by the slight shaking of her head and her rapid breathing.

Mac's emerald-green eyes sparkled. "Oh, Mindy, how I love you! And… the way you bark out orders," he laughed as he stood, wobbled a bit, grabbed the back of his chair, then shuffled to the sink.

"I saw that, Mac!" Mindy cried, her voice breaking.

Mac held onto the edge of the sink, staring, for a minute, out the window at the white canvas of Mindy's small backyard. "It's nothing. Just a little dizzy, sometimes."

"Sometimes? How often? Why haven't you told me. Oh, Mac! What is it?"

"Can I ask you a question?"

"Of course. Anything. Always. Oh, Mac!" Mindy said as she noticed tears welling in his eyes, his countenance suddenly downcast. Damn!

Moods, expressing love with words, could change just too damn fast. Was it his PTSD? She couldn't help herself with so much emotion building in her heart. Gently, she continued. "When we exchanged vows, we said *forever*. Before each other, and God. Intimacy is not just connecting our bodies as one, but sharing our intimate thoughts. Our fears, prayers and dreams. No matter what the question is, or what's on your heart or mind, I'm here for you! Now and forever. Please get that through your thick skull!" she exclaimed, her fear-filled voice edged by a tinge of joy in having found love with Mac. She prayed that he would trust her with his private-most thoughts and that his PTSD would not be a wedge between them.

"Most couples don't share everything. They have private aspects of their life they never share, right?" he asked, sitting back at the table, wiping his eyes and taking Mindy's hand in his.

Her eyebrows rose in a frown of sadness. "Of course not. But there's a difference between being open and honest and withholding private thoughts that don't need to be expressed. The most beautiful love, I imagine—maybe it's impossible—is one where the issues of trust and of fear in exposing one's self are laid open as an offering... like, a gift to the other. Doesn't sound practical, now that I think about it," she laughed, the sadness lifting from her eyes, "but fear of being intimate in thought should not prevent that intimacy. If that fear becomes justified, then it's the other's fault. In our case, that would be my fault. I promise you that won't ever happen."

Chewing the right corner of his lip, lost in thought, Mac quietly twirled the bottom of his coffee cup against the kitchen tabletop. After what seemed to Mindy a horribly long pause, Mac stretched back in his chair, its antique bones squeaking in protest. "Never happen? I learned in the Army, *never* to say never. Shit comes outta nowhere. And then you're left to pick up the pieces. To bury the dead."

Mindy moaned. "Oh, Mac! How did we go from a beautiful morning of making love, to breakfast? To now, this... this doubt? This confusion?"

Mac leaned back to the table, wiping his nose. He took both of Mindy's hands in his. "This feeling I just had, it comes and goes. Empty thoughts, just like those *Le Mis* chairs that will forever be empty. Please understand? I want to depend on you, but not be a burden."

Mindy shook her head in understanding, tears washing her cheeks. She leapt from her chair, rushing around the small kitchen table to embrace Mac. Her tears of love, of desire, mingled with his as she kept her mouth at his ear, repeating, softly, "I am yours, I will be forever! I promise! I want nothing else than to love you. And please, never mention the word *burden* again. Love carries all! So... there's no such thing as a burden. We've found each other. The word *other* means everything that we share: bodies, thoughts, fears, dreams—our souls. Please ask whatever, whenever!"

Mac kissed her cheek and cleared his throat. "Yeah, I guess. Okay, here's my question. More like, here's how my mind works at random times. I'm not sure how to say this. It's why I haven't shared it before." He wiped his eyes and for a moment stared at the coffee cup, tapping its rim with his finger. "Okay, here goes. At times, like just now looking out the window, I know I'm awake, but I can't *grab* a thought. It's like having an empty *shoebox* for a head. I mentally shake it, but I can't grab a thought. Yeah, that's what it's like. Trying to grab a thought. It's scary. Not so much like being crazy, whatever that is, but realizing from the periphery of my thoughts that there's a tangible hole. Like, a discernible vacuum where most of my thoughts are supposed to be. I knew I was at the sink. I knew you were here. But I couldn't grasp the next thought I should or could be having. My mind was yelling, 'What are you thinking, where's the next thought, the next word!' I just couldn't find it. Shit! I bet it's like Alzheimer's. So my question is, could I have it? You know, Alzheimer's?"

Mindy laid both her hands on the table, palms down. She blinked, trying to find a good answer. What did she know? She looked up at Mac, softly squinting her blue eyes as if trying to bore into his consciousness with as ardent an answer as she could muster. "Let me try this on you, though little do I know. My Aunt Abby, who at seventy-six is about twice your age, has her senior moments. Forgets things. Leaves the windows open. She jokes about going into the next room and forgetting why she did. What she was supposed to do. She's never really described it the way you do—questioned it, like not being able to *grab* a thought. Maybe it's because she accepts it, at her age. But I don't like what I hear you saying. I mean, I love that you're being so honest and open, but it *is* worrisome. Have you talked to the doctors?"

"Not really. Figured if I did, it'd guarantee me being labeled in a way that would follow me for life, not be beneficial. I know PTSD—stress from battle—plays subtle havoc with the mind, with emotions. And that those emotions can erupt at the slightest trigger. But this doesn't feel like emotion or stress. It's just... just like a mental hiccup. Sometimes a long one."

Mindy took his right cheek in her hand, leaning in to kiss his scar, ever so gently. "Oh, Mac. Here's what we can do. Let's start by you always sharing these moments with me, like waving your hand when it's happening."

Mac interrupted. "Sure, but if the thought I can't grab is that I'm supposed to wave at you, that won't work."

"But you know afterwards that you've had this... this thought vacuum. Right?"

"Uh-huh. That's right."

"Then tell me, and I'll tell you if you didn't wave. At least that's a start. Does that sound okay?"

Mac stood rapidly. "I'm just testing for dizziness. Don't feel it now." He walked to the sink. "So far, so good. Yeah, sure, let's do as you suggest. It *is* worrisome. Mainly, I'm worried about being a burden for you. I'm sorry I didn't reveal this before, you know, before we got married. I was just hoping it had gone away."

"I love you for being you. For your tenderness, your touch, how you've handled and expressed your loss of brothers, just all of you. And that you have a need that you've shared with me. We're in this together. Hear me, Sergeant?"

Mac sat, his elbows on the table, looking up to take in the kitchen, the window, and the skillet with left-over French toast. "I hear you, and I *thank* you," he sighed.

After more newlywed exercises in the bedroom and then a romp through Washington Square—where they contested with other locals in making angels in the snow—Mac and Mindy returned home exhausted.

They sat on her living room sofa in front of a crackling fire. Mac looked at the fireplace screen to make sure none of the sparking embers were jumping out to Mindy's beautiful Persian rug. He took in the fan rocking chair, the plush period wing chair, and the books stacked before them on the vintage European coffee table. The gray-blue walls with their white crown molding and wainscoting lent a feeling of colonial America. Mac imagined himself sitting with the founders of America, discussing the merits of the Bill of Rights and the Constitution. Merits he had carefully explored during his effort to unveil the D37 conspiracy of the ex-president.

Mindy was making little questioning noises about the article she was reading in the *Sunday Times*. Her murmurs finally broke into Mac's imagined dialog with Thomas Jefferson.

"Here's a twist," Mindy said, snapping the paper's pages.

"What is?" Mac responded, holding out his hand to keep the pages off his face.

"This Op-Ed article in today's *Times*. Written by some guy at the Hoover Institute, out in California. Seems strange, the *Times* providing space for a conservative's perspective. But ever since President Perserve took office, the *Times* does seem a bit more balanced. Hard to believe."

"What, the article or the inclusion of the opinion piece?"

"Both. Evidently the writer's son, a high school freshman, has written an app that lexically compares quotes from politicians. Not between politicians, but it tracks the consistency of messages and quotes from any one politician. Over time. Remember how consistency of policy was a big part of Perserve's platform?"

"Not really," Mac replied. "I was busy defending the Constitution."

"Ego, get thyself to a nunnery," Mindy laughed as she shook the paper at Mac. "This app sounds like a neat idea. But the gist of the article is the trend the kid's program has found in Perserve's positions."

"Like, on what?"

"Like, a subtle shift in the president's policy on individual rights. That it's not good economics to accommodate all rights. Like, for some countries—even our enemies—corporate or party rights need to come first. That America needs to accept this stance to get along with the world and not go bankrupt."

"When the hell did the president say that? I don't remember anything like that."

"Well, to be honest, you've been kind of out of the loop, I guess we can say..." Mindy teased, dropping the paper to the floor and leaning over to nibble Mac's ear.

"Seriously, do you remember her saying that?"

"No, but the article has links to the sources and timing of the quotes. We can go online to check it out."

Mac suddenly turned his head so Mindy was nibbling his lips. "I love being a newlywed. I want to check *you* out..." he murmured, his hand moving to her blouse.

"Hey, hey. Enough, already today," she whispered as she stood to guide Mac back to the bedroom.

"Yeah, enough worrying about the president," he said as he stopped to give Mindy a tender kiss. They raced down the hall, their laughter and joy-filled shouts causing more icicles to fall from outside the bedroom window.

CHAPTER 12

The Control

She sat at her desk, glancing rapidly back and forth between a translated report she had been reading and the picture of William Boyd on her wall. Exasperation apparent, Director Dong tossed the report's pages across the desk as she reached for another cigarette. She took a deep drag, blowing the smoke towards the ceiling light and wiping the spittle residue from her lips. "How did this happen?" she kept asking the picture. "Are we not in the right? It is only fair. *Only* fair!"

Her staff, on the other side of the office glass wall, stole quick looks, fearful of how her frustration might play out in their careers and their lives as they watched her sudden, jerky movements. They all turned as the outer office door opened and Doctor Juong entered. Shouting collectively, "Here he is!" they pointed at him. Dong quickly rose from her desk, rushing to open her office door.

"Did you see the translation of that article in the *New York Times*? The one about the kid tracking the president's policy shifts?" she yelled at Juong as she swept him into her office, her hand on his back. "Have you? Where have you been? Why have you not responded to your pager?"

"I was being held in isolation by goons from our State Security Ministry! Our Leader, too, has seen that article and had me collected for interrogation."

Dong leaned on her desk with both hands, shaking her head. She opened a desk drawer to find her pills. After chewing down three, she lowered herself slowly into her seat, whimpering. "Oh, dear Doctor. I am so sorry. I know how fearful it must have been for you. The word is, the Leader did go to the mountain two days ago. We're all on pins and pitchforks. We know what the mountain can mean."

"And you think I didn't know all that? I was in shock! The Leader needs us. Without me, the holohead evaporates and a world shit-storm results. And our nation ends up at the bottom of the dung heap! What *is* he thinking?"

Dong motioned him to a side chair, patting the seat for him to sit.

"He is thinking what I was thinking. That our holohead offered up confusing policy changes, all too rapidly. Our whole enterprise depends on subtle, progressive stealth. We can't have the holohead president behaving out of character. I recall, did not the real president actually care for her people?"

Juong nodded as he tucked his shirt into his pants.

Dong blinked several times as it dawned on her what may have happened. "They beat you on your bum? Those goons?" she whispered, startled.

"No, no. Thankfully no. But I must admit, I was so scared. I had to stop at the loo before I rushed back here."

"Say no more. I *am* sorry. I will report to the Leader on your loyalty. But back to more important matters. How did that change of policy come about?"

Juong rapidly bubbled his lips, wiping his brow. He leaned in close to the director. "I can only assume we have a pacing flaw in the AI system. It must have skipped or accelerated steps in the policy formation process. I know, firsthand, how hard we've worked to make sure the holohead's policies evolve slowly, over time. We want to give those American politicians time to sift through changes to determine how they might personally benefit," he chuckled. "Even in a democracy, a real one like America, the notion of altruism—of common good—is a farce beaten down by greed."

They both laughed heartily, drawing looks from across the glass wall. "The subtleties of the Western mind are, indeed, a challenge to grasp," Dong said. "How hard will it be to mend the flaw? And how do we get the holohead to back down a bit on her policy statements?"

"That will be easy," Juong replied. "In the English language, the obfuscation of meaning is easily accomplished by a stream of internally consistent, reciprocal words. I will have the holohead make a correction that will confuse even the most dedicated policy hawkeye. And I will double check our pacing code to make sure future policy changes are released in a timely manner."

Director Dong popped her lips in appreciation of Juong's brilliance. "Dear Doctor. For this, you'll receive the Order of Marjakovich. I am most certain!"

———— . ————

Two days later, the *ABC Nightly News* anchor broke the story. She spoke with a solemn tone, her hijab slightly askew, as images of the president standing at the White House podium played behind her. "President Perserve has issued an apology regarding the story that *we* first broke last week about individual rights. Here is her apology, which I quote: 'My fellow Americans, I apologize that the comments I made last week, relating to the rights of individuals, as American citizens, were apparently misconstrued. What I meant, and what my policy has been and always will be, going forward, is that the rights of our citizens are those rights that accrue to the individual by virtue of their right to be a citizen.' There you have it," the anchor continued, her eyes momentarily to the side, absorbing her producer's off-screen motions to straighten her hijab. She closed nervously, saying, "Individual unity remains at the forefront of our president's goals."

As the network went to commercial, the anchor's hijab went further askew as her producer, slapping his hand against his forehead, yelled out, "Individual unity? What the hell does that mean!"

———— . ————

Late the next day, the president motioned away the offered coffee as she sat hard on her chair in the Cabinet Room, her grunt catching stares from several of the Cabinet members. One staffer, about to leave the room, whispered to his colleague, "It must be the temperature in here. I heard the thermostat is broken. You can see everyone's sweating. And in the middle of winter. Crazy, huh?"

His colleague replied, "Naw. I think it's from the grief Margie's been taking for her policy shifts. It's about time these pillars of national fortitude felt the heat." Both snickered as they closed the door to what local water-cooler chatter was now calling the "Sauna."

The president, casually elegant in her wrap skirt and pinstriped jacket with a double strand of pearls, grabbed a sheaf of papers, tapping them on the table into a tight stack. The Secretary of State, sitting next to the president, watched absently as he wiped his forehead with his pocket handkerchief. His armpit sweat seeping into his shirt, he admiringly took note how refreshed the president appeared. Not the slightest perspiration on her brow. "One cool lady," he mused.

The president cleared her throat. "We need to be thinking of..." she said, jerking her right shoulder ever so slightly to toss back her auburn hair, "Secretary of Defense Cameron and her trip to the Asian Sphere Conference. Her main goal is to discuss continued sanctions and those lunatic death threats that each of you have received." Her comment was met by shifting in chairs and fingers pulling at shirt-neck collars. "Is it warm in here? Some of you look unduly uncomfortable."

The Secretary of Labor, scanning down and across the table at her fellow Cabinet members, responded, "Margie, I think we're all boiling. Maybe fuming is more accurate. Yes, it's hot in here. But, I for one, am concerned for my own welfare and that of my family. We all appreciate, I am sure, how cool—collected—you have remained. But our nation has never experienced such a barrage of threats directed at its leadership. I sometimes think foreign entities have a payola arrangement with our media. Like, those journalists, who give so much coverage to stories that fester issues that are, in reality, just distortions of national priorities."

The Secretary of State, nodding in agreement, narrowed his eyes as he discreetly sniffed the air. Staring at the president, he couldn't quite place the smell. A mixture of the *Minx* perfume she was known to wear, and some other hard-to-place smell. The smell slowly came to him— his recent visit to the dermatologist when he'd had a mole removed—of skin being cauterized. Burning flesh. He looked more closely at the president. Her neck was bright red. He momentarily lost his train of thought as he took in her beautiful profile, perfect nose, sensuous lips, and lush hair until the smell became overwhelming. That, and the redness of her neck. He was tempted to ask her if she felt all right, but realized he was the only one, given the angle of his seat next to her, who could see the back of her neck beneath her hair. He didn't want to embarrass her. They were, after all, long-time colleagues.

Reaching her hand back beneath her hair, the president uttered some expression as she jumped slightly in her seat.

The Secretary of State leaned forward. "Are you okay?" he asked, baffled. Her neck no longer red, the smell gone, he could have sworn her expression was spoken in Mandarin. Although he couldn't be sure.

"Yes, Chuck. I'm fine. Thanks. I think the heat in the room got to me for a second," she whispered as the Secretary of HUD started to explain the impact of the president's policy on housing development for the nation's inner cities.

Standing next to the simulator screen in Building 666, Director Dong was congratulating the RID team, her eyes benevolently on Juong. "You can see, from the way our AI backend *perfectly* controlled the president's momentarily spike in light—the excess photonic levels at her neck—that Doctor Juong will no longer need to monitor every nuance. We can now release our two holoheads to full autonomous control."

After acknowledging her team's applause and closing her office door as they returned to their side of the glass wall, Dong turned to Doctor Juong. "Control will remain a problem, yes?" she asked. "Do we dare truly release our holoheads to an independent, autonomous life? How can we regain control, if needed? Once his horse is out of the shed, the cowboy is without his spurs," she mumbled, rubbing the rough skin of her forehead and staring at the picture of Boyd. "An example that haunts me is… remember that strange, questioning voice we heard from our guard?"

"I do," Juong replied. He stared, lost in thought, out across the glass wall, his fingers tapping the keyboard. "There is no such thing as true autonomy. Such a state, in a human or machine, is not possible.

There are glitches. Always some minor weakness. We know that even the most advanced and tested operating system code has on average a homeostatic state of approximately seven hundred latent bugs. We see it in humans, too, in how they react unpredictably to the same repeated stimuli."

Dong moved closer to Juong, bringing her hand to her mouth. "Are you, by chance, including our Leader in your assessment of humans?"

Juong slowly nodded, grinding his teeth. Remembering, too, the Director's recent remark about falling off the *saddle*. "Yes," he thought to himself, his eyes focused afar on an unimaginable prize, "Yes, the Leader, and even *you*, dear Director."

CHAPTER 13

The Shift

The surround sound bathed the Family Sitting Room in Verdi as Roy leaned back, sinking into the soft pillows of the Wilbersmith sofa. He stretched his feet out on the ottoman. His rich, black hair rolled against the grey sofa fabric as he mimicked conducting *Rigoletto* with his head. He especially loved *La donna è mobile*. The finger of his right hand—the lesser baton—cast rhythmic shadows against the white paneling in this, his favorite room in the White House.

He came here for solitude: to think, to ponder, and to gain space to thank God for his family, for America. For Margie, now fifty days into her presidency; a presidency filled with acclaim from the nation and the world. Yet, one of increasing curiosity for him. Starting mid-February, Margie had stiffened and had refused to share her bed. She had become distant. He knew first-hand how in-country tours of service changed even the most hardened commanders. Margaret Perserve, his sweet Margie-girl, was a veteran of politics, but no veteran of war. What had happened to her? It baffled him. The few times they did embrace, there was a smooth coldness to her; a felt-cushion of flesh that suggested serious weight gain, while in appearance she was as beautiful and trim as when they were first married.

The sound system began the slow intro to Einaudi's *Nuvole bianche*, Roy's thoughts stacking within the building piano theme, then halting abruptly with Einaudi's pause. A pause, then a suspicion immediately denied. Roy took a deep breath, sorting and parsing potential causes. Even Kari had asked him why Margie didn't seem the same. Why she didn't have the same gentle caress, soft words, and reassuring hugs that she gave out so lovingly back in Kansas.

A knock pulled Roy from his thoughts. Deshon stood at the door, filling the door frame. "Colonel, do you have a minute?"

"Hey, Deshon! Always, for you," Roy replied, pulling himself from the sofa. "What's up?"

"I've got the breakdown of our HUD goals. One thing the president added when we had our planning session this morning with the Secretary was better accommodation for the homeless."

"So? Nothing new."

Deshon wiped the corner of his mouth as he moved into the room. "A while back, HUD used to provide homelessness assistance to grantee programs. As you know, that funding stream was moved over by the ex-president to be administered under Federal Aid to states. Part of the push to reduce federal bandwidth. Margie now wants to move that funding back under HUD to make it an all-out national-level effort for *all* those who are homeless. Especially veterans. I did some checking. She'll get a lot of support for this position, but…"

"But? It's who she is. You know that better than anyone, having worked with her these past years."

"Sure, no buts—that part *is* great. But, yeah, here's the issue. Not only does she now want to hand homelessness back to HUD…"

"Can't see why that's a problem," Roy interrupted, standing to turn off the sound system.

Deshon raised his voice, his exasperation evident, his arms raised to the ceiling. "She wants homelessness funding to be extended. Have it included as part of foreign aid."

"What the hell!"

"Right! She says it will promote global peace and security. However, here's the real catch. She wants that homeless aid to go to any country, regardless of our relationship with them. Just as long as they have a certain percentage of their population living below some arbitrary poverty level. Ever since the backlash a few weeks ago regarding individual rights, seems she's continued to overreact towards serving the under-served, regardless of nation. Besides being a non-starter for the Budget Committee, it's counter to our current foreign policy. Seems like a new pattern in her policy formation. It sure doesn't jive with her whole approach to continuity in policy… just between the two of us, that is."

"Come on, Deshon. What're you saying?"

"In the same discussion this morning, she went on and on about increasing corporate tax rates, again. You know we've worked together now for over twelve years. I want to think I know her pretty well. So call me foolish, but it's almost like she's acquiescing to some kind of counter-guidance. She's always maintained that consensus politics is not how to run things. That balance—ultimately facilitated by the executive—is key. Now? Seems she's leaning so hard to serving the downtrodden that she's jeopardizing balance. We need to serve our homeless, sure. But not the whole world. It's going out of kilter. Fast!"

Roy pushed the ottoman to the side and motioned Deshon to sit across from him in the white wing chair. "Don't you think you're a little anxious, over-analyzing things? Been only a couple of months. She's still getting her sea legs. Right?"

Deshon sat with a sigh, slowly adjusting his tie as he contemplated a reply. "Colonel, you know me. My role is to help assess and contour policy. I totally buy in to our approach of continuity. But look at some of the international press she's received this past week. You know, some of America's adversaries are usurping that news, basically ballyhooing that she—meaning America—is finally waking up to recognize the legitimacy and the needs of all regimes. I'm suggesting that Margie, our president, is not thinking like the Margie... excuse me... like our colleague who got elected. It's as if she's playing into the hands of some of the nations we have pegged as...ah..."

"As enemies?" Roy stated, smoothing the sofa cushions with hard strokes of his left hand. "Some of the rogue nations threatening us?"

"Yeah, absolutely. No other way to put it. And if this global homeless initiative... which quite frankly scares the hell out of me! If that got traction, there'd be no way of knowing that the funding didn't go to some weapon system pointed at us! Reminds me of what happened in Afghanistan back in the '80s." Deshon stood, his tall frame towering over Roy. "Maybe it's just my imagination. I don't know. But I needed to talk with someone about this. Call it a gut feeling, but something's different."

Roy stood, giving Deshon a hard look, his teeth clinched.

Deshon's eyes went wide as he sucked in a deep breath. "Forgive me, Colonel, but I gotta say it like I see it."

Roy blinked, his hand at his chin, for a fleeting moment back alone with Verdi. He reached out, patting Deshon's left arm. "Duly noted, Deshon. I *hear* you, man. Let me consider what you've said. Give it a couple of days. Our number one priority, for both of us, is to support Margie. It's not an easy, smooth road we're on. Heck, you know that better than me. Margie's bound to struggle with adjusting to—balancing—national and special-interest needs."

Deshon stepped back, his chin dropping, his lower lips curling around his teeth. He hesitated, then smiled back. "I know, yeah. She *is* our top priority. God bless her! At the end of the day, though, it can feel *so* like a no-win job."

"It's why you're here. What Margie and I have always loved—appreciated in you, Deshon—is your loyalty to her and the principles on which America was founded."

Roy's words resonated, reflected in the set of Deshon's jaw and the moisture at the edges of his dark eyes.

Roy continued, "You're expressing this concern because of that loyalty. And in the few months we've been in office, I've learned there is no such thing as winning. There's only adjusting and guiding our great nation in a manner that sustains our liberty and freedoms. That will *always* be an ongoing war. Yeah, it can seem like a no-win. But the victory is in keeping America within its founding principles, nurturing liberty and our time-honored institutions. Near-term battles may seem like a no-win. But the war we fight... that we *must* always fight, we fight to win! That's the war for the very essence and the survival of America. For all it offers. Its principles, traditions, institutions, values, and liberty!"

Deshon smiled briefly, putting his hand in his pants pocket. "Good pep-talk, Colonel. You sound just like my coach back at the Rose Bowl. He said we take each play as a separate, single battle. That only successive, successful battles create stepping stones to victory. I got that part. My concern is that, today, we can't afford to lose *any* battles in the minds of our citizens. Otherwise, the war you talk about gets obscured."

Roy reached out, grasping Deshon's right hand in a handshake.

Deshon continued, "On the brighter side, other than this homeless concern and her attack on the military-industrial complex, her policies have gained traction with the voters. Latest polls show."

"Yeah, lots to consider. Let's stay abreast of any other policy shifts. I'll try to talk with Margie about this homeless focus. See what's motivating her to include global care for all."

Deshon released his handshake, nodding vigorously. "Thanks for your time, Colonel. Oh, also, there's a message for you from the VA."

"Yeah, right. Thanks, I saw that. I've been asked to join a panel, next week, at the VA in New York City to talk about how vets I know have adjusted to living with PTSD."

Leaning back in her desk chair, her office filled with cigarette smoke, Director Dong was reviewing a log with Doctor Juong—a tracking log of the president's interactions. An audio recording of poetry by Yun Dong-ju played softly on her computer.

"I note our holohead's increased interest in world homelessness. Seems it—she—is tormented by the homeless. While you have her slowly bending in our direction, I wonder how it's possible that this homelessness is part of the policy vector generated by your AI control? We have no homeless here. Is this a shift in policy?"

Sensitive to Director Dong's harsh upbringing, Juong replied, "Correct, we don't have homeless. Our Great Leader provides everyone with a roof over their head, camp or otherwise. Yes, I'm as baffled as you. We've repeatedly squashed any inclinations of independent thought by the president."

"Independent thought remains a concern, then. Is it possible that those *latent* bugs that you mentioned still exist?" Dong asked, gently.

"Yes. However, I am inclined to think that such bugs would not manifest themselves in this manner," Juong said as he stood, walking to the wall to study the picture of William Boyd. He reached out, touching the frame, imagining what the American Wild West really had been like. "How is it that you're allowed to have this picture so prominently displayed in your office? Our Leader has often said that adornments of the West are superfluous to our destiny. Has he not seen this?"

"Indeed, he has. However, as I recall, he spent a good deal of time staring at that picture, studying the facial features of Hopalong. His comments, his musings, were something like, 'What do you suppose this cowboy was thinking when this picture was taken? Is not his smile beguiling, almost seductive? But it's *just* a picture. We cannot know his thoughts or how honest his smile is. It is like any of our thoughts. The human mind can be so deceptive, even self-deceptive in its own denial.'"

"How does this relate to the holohead's fixation on the homeless?"

"Our dear Leader, in his pondering, revealed a side I'd never seen. Almost as if he cared. Perhaps, caring is a natural inclination. Why is it that I care for you? That we care for each other? Mutual survival perhaps? Yet, more than that. Judging by the success of your Soul Simulator, intentional or not, its algorithms must have given the holohead inclination towards empathy and compassion—components of a soul—for the homeless. It's as if the holohead is creating a notion of caring beyond the stop limits in your simulator."

"We've provided no such inclination. Not possible," Juong replied.

Dong raised her hand in quiet contemplation. "Must a soul learn by being flexible, like the heuristic code in your AI backend? Learning requires iteration. I wonder. Can a soul's canned behavior, like from your SS, create actual caring? I suggest your team prepare a boundary detector to spot behavioral divergence from the vectors you feed the holohead. My guess is, our holohead will stray. It comes with learning. We just need to know when it happens. But… then again…" Dong said, thinking of her long-ago talk with the Leader, "I am not sure about the soul, if it even exists? But if it does, does it adapt? Or is it fixed at birth?"

"You *are* saying, then, that the primary behaviors—the decisions and inferences that we vector to the holohead—will not be affected by its caring? For this excessive concern for the world's homeless?"

"We can only hope." Her hand shook as she reached for a cigarette.

"…and, that we *all* don't fall off the saddle," Juong said to himself, finishing Dong's thought.

CHAPTER 14

The Shoebox

"Another week of bliss," Mindy whispered, rolling over to give Mac a good-morning hug, her head on his shoulder.

Though Mac's grunt did not match her amorous thoughts, he put his arm around her, kissing her lush brown hair. ""Uh-huh," he said, running his fingers through her hair, all the while his blank stare lost somewhere near the ceiling light fixture. "Uh-huh, yeah," he repeated.

"Well, good morning to you, too," she laughed, lifting her head to kiss Mac, starting with tender kisses on his facial scar. She looked into his eyes, recognizing the far-away look. "What is it?" she asked cautiously, compressing her lips in a sadness Mac did not see. She dropped her head back to his shoulder, waiting for a reply she knew might never come.

"It happened again this morning. When I woke up," he finally said, his fingers absently stroking her hair.

"What? The shoebox?"

"Uh-huh, yeah. Worse than ever. Took, I don't know, a couple of minutes for a word to form in my head. Like, I was gazing off in space and had no clue what I was seeing."

Mindy raised up on her elbow, pulling the covers higher against the chill air, wondering why Mac insisted on sleeping with the heater off. It was freezing in the bedroom. "Oh, Mac! We've talked about this. It's way past time for you to see a doctor!" she insisted.

"I keep thinking I can lick this," he replied. "I don't want to get labeled as some nutcase."

"That wouldn't happen."

"Maybe not if I saw another private shrink. But I'm not keen on seeing the VA—part of the military. I just don't know. Seems to me they'd have to report this across channels. It'd be part of my file, no matter where I ended up. Shit, suffering from PTSD is the new normal.

Plus, you know the way the VA totally mistreated me during the D37 fiasco. That's still stuck in my craw."

"That was bad people in the VA, not the VA. Those people have been canned."

"Regardless, having everyone know I suffer from PTSD is *not* the issue."

"What, then?" Mindy questioned, moving her mouth to Mac's ear, pulling him closer.

"It's the empty-head shoebox syndrome," he replied with a stilted laugh. "PTSD can be treated with therapy and drugs. With group sessions. But if no one's at home in my head, what's there to treat? Who'd want me to work for them, be around them, be a professor again?"

"Me!" Mindy said, with a deep sigh. She would follow Mac into hell, She'd told him often. But other than her love and devotion, she was ill-equipped to counter his point. It was as if he was more shell-shocked than anything else. A lost soul wandering around, AWOL inside his own head. She had read a variety of articles on the Web, including those on the *VA.gov* website, all dealing with post-traumatic issues. Some PTSD reactions manifested in sadness, trouble concentrating, agitation, helplessness, and even aggression. But none specifically reflected a vacuous mental state. Other than flashbacks and moods, Mac did not display the typical reactions. Although there was always a chance the policeman's baton had caused Mac's shoebox state—done isolated damage aside from his PTSD. She knew in her heart that, with the improved functioning of the VA these past few years, that it—the Veterans Administration—offered the best way forward.

She rolled out of the covers with a brief squeak of awareness, smoothing out her nightgown that she didn't realize she still had on. Sitting on the edge of the bed, debating if she should leave the conversation dangling to go down the hall to the heater dial, she said, "Please, Mac. Please do this for us! Go to the VA. Maybe it's PTSD, maybe something else? Maybe for all you know, the docs didn't get all the metal out of your head?"

"They did, for sure. All the scans show that."

"Well, maybe there was some damage to an artery, blood flow to your brain? You're the brave warrior we all know. Regardless of the outcome, of all people, I know you can face this. But, you *have* to face it, not let it go. Seems it may only get worse?" She turned to tuck the covers back around Mac, hesitated, ran down the hall to turn up the heater. She returned to snuggle next to Mac, pulling the covers up, more for protection of Mac from this unknown issue than the cold.

Later that morning, sitting at the kitchen table—its warm tablecloth of spring flowers offsetting the mood of winter—Mindy watched Mac sip his coffee. Her eyes followed his far-away, thousand-yard stare to the wall. She reached out to take his hand. "You there?" she asked softly.

Mac blinked, shaking his head. He spooned more sugar into his coffee. "I am," he answered. "Most definitely." He squeezed her hand. "I was just debating going to the VA. Ah, debating is not the right word. It *is* the wise thing to do, mainly because you see it as necessary, and I want, more than anything, to show my love by not being a burden."

Mindy hardened her grasp of his hand, shaking a finger of her free hand at Mac. "That word, burden, will *never* be spoken again in this house. You got that, Mac? That is a word you *can* forget."

"I can't help feeling like a burden, 'cause I love you! You're the last person in this world that I want to inflict this on, sharing my *condition*."

Mindy released his hand, tapping the tablecloth in frustration as she leaned back in her chair. "For a guy with a PhD who's been around the block and who's studied religions and philosophy, you can sure be dense to the real meaning of love. Unconditional love... like the love of Jesus."

"Yeah, maybe, but..."

"But, nothing!" Mindy said, her voice rising. "Look. We're still getting to know each other. We rushed into our marriage. But it wasn't some hormone thing. Or foolishness. I know you love me beyond my wildest hopes. I know it's a forever love. But, and here's the deal. *You* have to let that love in your heart dissuade... like, shut down... the overly-analytical thoughts and worries coming from your brain."

"When my brain is there, you mean?" Mac laughed. His eyes held a sad smile: she was right *and* he was right. That whatever his condition, it stood between them.

Mindy compressed her lips, shaking her head, her lush brown hair spilling to the side of her head. "You know something, Sergeant...?" She left the question dangling, hoping Mac knew what she was asking.

After another, prolonged sip of coffee and adding more sugar, Mac finally asked, "What?"

Tapping her teeth, her frustration evident, Mindy decided to move the conversation to a constructive conclusion. "You're calling the VA. Today. End of discussion!" she stated firmly, rising to clear the dishes.

After washing the dishes and feeling the jolt from a fourth cup of coffee slapping his brain, Mac sat at Mindy's desk—a large flat door laid on stylish workhorses—in her second bedroom that she used for her office. Offsetting the pulse of caffeine, Mozart's *Piano Sonata No. 12 in F Major* gently cloaked the room in peace, giving him pause. With a prolonged wipe of his tongue across his teeth to secure all coffee residuals, Mac exhaled heavily. He looked around the room, taking in the antique poster bed up against the wall and the array of colorful van Dael prints on one wall bracketed by the other two walls filled with Mindy's framed photographs. All seemed to complement the warm colors of her kitchen and the décor of her entire house. It was obvious she was a talented photographer and that she loved color. No black mood in her portfolio.

Mac shuffled through some of the prints stacked on her desk. His eyes went from photographs of him in the rehab center—some fun-filled and others chilling in how they revealed a profoundness of thought evident in his gaze—to the phone. His eyelids quivered with indecision. He let out a laugh, thinking back to the many firefights he had faced. Most without trepidation or hesitation. Now? Maybe it was just fatigue. Maybe he was just old. Or wiser. But taking this step to re-engage the VA seemed the riskiest of his life. He wondered where the call would lead. Did he really want to know if he had some unsolvable handicap? Where would he end up ten years from now? How would it affect Mindy? "Oh, Mindy!" he thought. "How blessed I am to have you in my life!" With that thought and encouraged by the pace of Mozart's third sonata-allegro movement, he dialed.

"Sergeant Lincoln MacMahan. Army, disability, retired," he replied to the questioning voice on the VA's New York Health Care line. "I'd like to make an appointment, preferably with a doctor, to discuss my PTSD." After providing more ID and briefly explaining his concerns, Mac was connected to a counselor—a Major Evans. She introduced herself as a fellow Afghanistan veteran.

"Let's see..." the major began with a warmth that instantly thawed the cold hand of fear gripping Mac's heart. "The note I just received, before I took your call, is that you want to discuss PTSD? I'm available in the afternoon, tomorrow. Would that work, Sergeant? "

Mac coughed, thinking this must be the new VA he'd heard about. It seemed nothing like the 'hurry-up-and-wait-forever' process when he'd joined the Army.

"Say," the major continued in her warm Southern accent, "there's a panel in the morning. The president's husband, Colonel Butcher will be on it. The subject will be 'Life Beyond PTSD'. I see from your record that you also received a recent head injury?"

"Ah... yes, correct."

"A blow from a police officer's baton?"

"Right, again. I wasn't doing anything wrong, though," Mac offered, not sure what implication, if any, the Major was making, and amazed at how thorough the VA's records were.

"I see that, yes," she responded immediately. "I remember reading about you before the election. Thinking how unfair—with all your service to our nation, all your wounds—that you had to endure that cop's strike."

"Also affirmative, ma'am."

Mac could hear the major sighing. He imagined her nodding, with a warm smile. After a pause, she said, "Sergeant, let's consider CTE."

"Excuse me? Say again."

"CTE. Chronic traumatic encephalopathy. For the past five to six years—well after you mustered out—it finally became a recognized issue with those who've received head trauma. IED survivors, car crash victims, even football players. Perhaps, in your case, from that blow of the baton. How's about we attend the panel and then, after lunch, we have a private session?"

"Man, ah... Yes, ma'am! That would be great," Mac answered, wondering why he had waited so long to contact the VA. He sure didn't remember any officers sounding so sincere.

——— . ———

"I should be back for dinner," Roy said, leaning over to kiss the president's cheek. "You know Margie, I sure miss our quiet family time, together with the kids around the farmhouse kitchen table. Yeah, with the aroma of your leek soup steaming up the house."

"We should have that again, sometime," the president replied. "Is leek your favorite? I forget."

"Forget? How's that? You made it almost every week in winter."

"Oh, Roy, you know how horribly busy I've been," the president implored. "I must dig my well before I'm thirsty."

"What the... what's that mean?" Roy asked, looking intently into the president's eyes. He noticed her pupils were enlarged, even in the brightness of the hallway. Had she just repeated some ancient proverb? It sure wasn't Mark Twain.

"Just that I need to be prepared. Deshon has a heavy schedule planned. Where are you off to?"

Roy raised his thick eyebrows, looking down the hall, watching through the window the waiting limo's exhaust swirling in the cold wind. "I'm late for the helicopter at Andrews. I'll be in New York just for the day. A conference for veterans." His hand fell from the back of her auburn hair to her neck. Still clammy.

Nodding to the Marine holding the limo door, Roy looked back at the side entrance to the Executive Residence. He pulled down the collar of his overcoat, wondering about his Margie-girl. "Where is she? Where did my Margie go?" he thought. "More like, *who* is she?" as he ducked into the warm interior of the limo.

CHAPTER 15

The Connection

Flying far out to the eastern side of Manhattan in order to come in downwind on the approach, Roy's helicopter pilot had struggled against swirling crosswinds as he landed at the Manhattan Heliport near Wall Street. Other than the turbulent landing, the helo ride from Joint Base Andrews had been smooth. It had reminded Roy of some of his rides in Black Hawks in Iraq and Afghanistan. The pilot, inviting Roy to sit in the left pilot seat, had talked about his own experience during three tours in the Middle East.

By the time they landed in Manhattan, Roy felt a bursting pride—a reminder of the sacrifice and dedication of the men and women who serve, those who had served, and those who had died serving. He had missed the intimacy of his fellow soldiers the past few years, focused as he had been on getting Margaret elected. But now, he felt he was back home and prepared for the upcoming panel on post-traumatic issues.

Roy exited the military limo under the portico at the East Twenty-Third Street entrance to the VA Health Care Center. In spite of the cold wind there were several men and women in civilian clothes sitting at the blue benches adjacent to the entrance. He smiled at two women whose warm jackets had 'proud to be wearing combat boots' emblazoned on the front. One of the younger women, holding a cane, stared at Roy, gasping as she offered a slight wave. He returned it with a crisp salute. She grabbed the arm of her friend, pointing with amazement to Roy as she said loudly, "Hey, is it him?"

Roy was escorted by two aides down the Hall of Eagles, asking to stop for a moment so he could take in the colorful murals. The heavy handrail—also a wheelchair buffer along the hall beneath the murals—stood as testimony to the sacrifice portrayed in the murals. After a moment of reflection, they took the elevator to a third floor conference room.

Folding chairs for the audience were arranged in front of a table for the panel, at which sat two women and two men, each wearing sweaters with the same slogan about 'combat boots.' They all rose to greet Roy. The Center administrator, a Dr. Anderson, motioned Roy to his chair as he introduced the others on the panel: three doctors and a healthcare professional working at the Center. A sweater, with the 'boot' motto on it, was draped over the back of Roy's chair. Sitting in the audience were about a dozen Center staff, several media types, and dozens of veterans. Some in bathrobes, but most in civies.

In the back of the room a video camera was set up, a soldier working the controls with his prosthetic hands. Roy took off his heavy overcoat, handed it to an aide, and proceeded to put on the sweater. Several of the veterans applauded as Roy sheepishly tried to smooth out his dark hair. "I'm one of you," he replied, nodding, his voice catching for a moment as he looked into their eyes. His jaw set firmly with a sense of pride mingled with thanksgiving for these men and women, he walked down the aisle, taking handshakes from hands: real and those prosthetic.

As he turned back to the panel, he noticed an attractive officer—a woman, a major—walking in with a man whose face Roy instantly recognized. Not just the facial scar, but the emerald-green eyes that seemed to wander nervously across the faces in the audience. Roy recognized Mac as the ex-solider—the university professor. The one who had revealed the D37 plot; a revelation that had made Margie's victory possible. The major guided Mac to a chair near the back of the room. Roy racked his memory for that soldier's name.

Dr. Anderson opened the panel by thanking everyone for attending and Roy for making the time. The discussion began with definitions of PTSD: its symptoms, manifestations, and what progress had been made in the past few years regarding mitigation. Various panel members broadened Dr. Anderson's description until a Marine in the audience, sitting in her wheelchair, brought down the house in response to ideas on mitigation. She yelled, "Oorah!" followed by "Hooah" and "Hooyah" from the soldiers and sailors in the room.

Roy struggled to hold back his tears, his thoughts turning to memories of his own company and its officers, noncoms, and soldiers. Such wonderfully valiant men and women. Some gone. Others in VA rehab programs somewhere. With the curious changes in his wife these past few weeks, he felt more at home amongst these fellow veterans. He felt a shared bond of dedication and sacrifice running deep.

After testimony by a few soldiers and Marines, the panel discussion segued to how to better prevent and treat PTSD in future wars. The panel members admitted that from the First World War through Gulf War I, PTSD had been misdiagnosed, if not fully ignored. And that its victims had often been unfairly labeled and ostracized.

At the back of the audience, Mac leaned against the major. "My point exactly!" he whispered. "The PTSD label will be a permanent part of our records, and it will be a disadvantage. Maybe not so much for me, but for the Joe-average grunt who doesn't have a lot going for him, or her. Hard to admit, but it's true."

The major brought her hand to her mouth, whispering back, "You're wrong, Sergeant. If anything, with what we know today, those suffering from PTSD move to the head of the class, so to speak."

Mac turned to look her into the eyes, a doubting wrinkle warping his eyebrows.

"What I mean," she continued, shrugging her shoulders in slight irritation, "is simply that those with PTSD, even PTSD-like symptoms, are a priority. Did you consider how long it took you to get an appointment?"

Mac rolled his lower lip between his quivering teeth, as if chewing on reality. "Yes, ma'am. Understood," he said finally. "But as we discussed this morning, my issue may be more CTE, not PTSD. What if you determine that my CTE is from the cop's baton? Will the VA still give me treatment?"

"You're a vet, Sergeant. You'll get service and treatment for the rest of your life, regardless of what ailment or the cause. We owe you." Major Evans cleared her throat, paused, and brought her right hand to her chest. "America owes *us*. We'll get a fix on your CTE, I promise.

What you call your shoebox syndrome," she replied with a sweet southern tone, the sincerity of which calmed Mac. She patted his knee.

As the panel broke for lunch, Roy wandered through the audience, shaking hands, clapping backs, and giving hugs as he inched towards the major. The ex-soldier in civies, the one next to her, was sitting with his head down. Roy couldn't tell if he was asleep or praying.

"Thank you, Colonel Butcher, for attending," the major began, extending her hand. "I'm Major Evans, a clinical psychologist here at the Center."

"It's my honor to be here," Roy replied, taking in the major's sincere look, firm handshake, and pleasant demeanor accented by Givenchy perfume. "It's a shame we didn't have a larger audience."

"My understanding," the major replied, "is that this is a pilot. From it we'll develop a script for a more formal panel. One we can videotape and play throughout centers across the country. It's part of the immersion approach we're hoping will develop continuity across programs. Continuity, just like..." she laughed as she stepped back so Roy could move next to Mac, who continued to stare at the floor.

"Like my wife's approach to policy, right?" Roy said, smiling back.

"Yes, sir! Speaking of the president," Major Evans responded, gesturing towards Mac with her open hand. "Sir, perhaps you know of Sergeant MacMahan? There was much written about him before the election."

"Indeed, I do!" Roy replied, extending his hand down to Mac.

"Sergeant?" the major nudged.

Mac came out of his trance, standing and bracing. He took Roy's hand. "My pleasure, sir."

"On the contrary, soldier. It's my pleasure. The president and I had talked about sending you a note. But... the election..."

"And, all..." Mac offered.

"Right, but no excuse," Roy continued, noting Mac's wandering eyes. "This is a real bonus to being here, having a chance to meet you, and Major Evans."

Mac offered a vague smile, blinking, trying to find a word. Damn the shoebox!

"The sergeant is here because he's been diagnosed with PTSD. And there are some other issues of concern," the major added, careful not to violate confidentiality.

"Sergeant? Did you find the panel helpful?" Roy asked.

Mac brought his hand to his brow, then absently, ran his fingers down his scar. "Ah, no, not really," he replied slowly.

The major moved next to Mac, her hand at his shoulder.

"I mean, sure, yes... sir!" Mac added, the shoebox finally filling with thoughts. He straightened up. He was eye-to-eye as tall as Roy.

"There's a 'but' in there, right?" Roy suggested.

"Sir, I think we've taken enough of your time," the major said to Roy as she started to motion Mac away.

"No, no. Wait!" Mac said, his voice forlorn. "I don't mean to dump on you, sir. But, it's more than PTSD. The doctor here," pointing to the major, "thinks it might be CTE."

"Hold on!" the major said. "Let's not bother the colonel with this."

Roy clasped his hands together, staring at the wall, then moving to put a hand on Mac's other shoulder. "Major, I'm kind of an ornament at the White House these days. Sure, I talk a bit on policy and offer the president advice and support, but I've been disconnected from those I served with. Today has brought it all back to me. I know it's not standard procedure, but given what the sergeant had done for the president, for his country, I want to be more helpful. For him, specifically."

"Call me Mac, sir," Mac injected.

The major coughed, licking her lips. Sensuous lips, Roy noted.

She sighed. "Yes, sir. How about you join us for lunch?"

"If it's not too far out of bounds, I'd like to have lunch with the sergeant, alone. Please forgive me, Major. Something I need to do."

"Excuse me, sir. In terms of combat, sir, I've been there. Two purple hearts. Army Award for Valor," the major retorted. "I hope you aren't excluding me because you think combat-talk only happens between guys... sir?"

"Duly reprimanded, Major. I apologize." Roy smiled, offering his hand. "This is more about what Mac has suffered since his service.

What he did with D37. I want to learn more about his PTSD, his CTE. What it's like. It's personal, not combat, I assure you. Do you mind?"

The major looked at her watch. "The sergeant's CTE issue, if any, is confidential, sir. Not sure you should be talking about it. It's not a formal diagnosis at this juncture." She brought her hand to her chin. "Regardless, the sergeant and I have a session planned for 1300 today. The remainder of my schedule today is full. Have lunch, but please return him to me by 1300. A deal?"

Roy reached out, gently placing a hand on the major's shoulder, aware he was being somewhat forward. "Forgive me for reaching out, Major. My heart is heavy right now. For Mac, for *your* service, for all of you," he said as he motioned across the room. "Then, and now. So, yes! A deal." He gave her shoulder a slight squeeze. Somewhere the thought flashed, "A real shoulder." It remind him of how strong his Margie-girl had been. After taking a deep breath, Roy smiled, shaking his head to clear those thoughts.

CHAPTER 16

The Lunch

As they left the cafeteria line, Roy laughed at Mac's tray filled with six slices of bread and two bowls of soup. "What's with all the soup?" he asked.

"Not sure. Guess being here, back among fellow soldiers. Reminds me of eating with my own squads. Had a sudden craving for MREs. I actually loved the potato and cheddar with bacon," Mac answered wistfully. "And we never, ever, got fresh bread!"

"Miss it, do you? I mean, serving?"

Mac took a deep breath, his eyes misting. His thoughts filled with memories of his brother Sam and his brothers-in-arms. He sniffed, turning his head to the wall, his jaw locked with clinched teeth. "No, sir, Colonel. Not the serving. But, yeah. Missing those I served with. You probably know, right? It's something that gets etched into you. At least some of us. At least those of us who've led, or tried to, through the damn fog of war. An ongoing consciousness that you're not conscious of." Mac laughed, mainly at the circular vagueness of his reply.

"With you on that, Sergeant!" Roy said, emptying the contents of his tray onto the table and holding the empty tray in the air until an orderly came by to pick it up. He noticed Mac's look. "One of the perks of being an officer, probably," he muttered.

"Yes, sir. Or, being the First Husband."

Roy's laugh filled their corner of the cafeteria, bringing out smiles from those nearby. Roy and Mac were the center of attention, and it wasn't just Roy. Mac had his own admirers. Fellow warriors who knew and bore similar scars.

Mac kept his eyes downward, nervous, taking large bites of bread soaked in the soup. He smiled, thinking Mindy would not believe that he'd actually had lunch with the president's husband.

"Sir, if I may ask. What'd you want to talk about?"

"A couple of things, Sergeant."

"If you don't mind, sir, please call me Mac. It'd be easier to answer your questions if they're of a personal nature."

"How about I call you Professor?" Roy suggested with a warm smile, hoping to convey the respect he felt for Mac. Mac, the professor. A veteran who had served lower in the ranks while probably more than capable of leading the ranks as an officer.

Mac looked Roy directly in the eyes. "I'm no longer a professor, sir."

"All right. Let's go with Roy and Mac. Okay?"

After shifting in his chair, Mac soaked up more soup with the bread, being careful to wipe his mouth on a napkin. "If that works for you, fine by me," he replied. "What's on your mind... sir?"

Roy slid his plate to the side of the table, laying his hands out in front of him. "Maybe a bit of guilt that we never thanked you, and then..."

"No need to go there, sir."

"Please, Mac, let me finish."

"Sir?"

"And chill the *sir*, okay?" Roy answered quietly, rubbing his hands across the table surface, his eyes squinting out care and respect. A vision flashed of the time he had asked Margie's father for her hand. How nervous he had been, then. And how he had repeatedly said, "Yes, sir!" to every one of Pierce's good-natured questions.

Roy smiled—holding out his hand to fist bump Mac's—blinking in recognition. Here sat a wounded warrior. A special man. An exceptionally rare guy. Roy mused, sorting through mental images of some of the thousands of people he had encountered: from the fields of Kansas, to the Army, to the lobbyists who clamored for Congress's attention. From the most humble to the most biased and greedy. Here, before him, sat a soldier with emerald eyes that displayed zero bias. Who seemed to exude only fairness, humility, and pragmatics. Yet, also, a sensitivity. Roy knew from his own encounter with prejudice and fear, throughout his life, that all too often, one could not reveal innermost thoughts. That one had to buck up and be tough, deflecting the vicious barbs thrown by the ignorant. He also recognized a confusion in Mac, like how one squints when looking directly into a sunset when the sun is still too bright. Blinded by the beauty of light in the pursuit of life. A revelation of confusion, right below the surface.

"Yes, sir. Sorry, it's second nature." Mac laughed, for the first time. Roy did seem a regular guy.

Roy nodded, pondering the sanctity of life in good men. Men like Mac. "Fair enough. Understood. I won't dwell on how remiss we've been in our thanks. I ask your forgiveness, and we'll leave it at that."

"Roger that. Your questions, then?"

Roy made an oval with his lips, biting his lower lip, not sure where to begin. "The panel today got me thinking. I've had troops with PTSD, sure. Many with serious concussions. Probably CTE. I want to ask you what it's like. What you feel?" Roy asked, knowing he could not reveal his real reason: trying to figure out where Margie had gone. He didn't dare consult any of the White House doctors or staff. At least, not yet.

"How do you mean?"

"Ah, well. What does it feel like? Is there pain? Not sure how to ask the question. But obviously you've talked this over with Major Evans. There must be some symptoms. Some feelings apart from feeling normal?"

"What's normal, after three tours?" Mac joked.

"Got me on that," Roy laughed back. "I just want to know what you feel. What you think at the times you think the CTE is there. Or, is it always there?"

"I don't really know anything about CTE. Still have to talk with the Major on that. My guess is, it's not the CTE that comes and goes, but the symptoms. So no, not always. The effects, or whatever, come and go," Mac replied. "Okay, here's the best way to describe it. What I've told my wife and the major. When it hits, it's like your thoughts—the vague ones you're able to muster—are on the outside of your brain. Like, they're looking in trying to find a cogent thought—a word— inside your brain. It's what I call my 'empty shoebox syndrome.'"

"Do you lose thoughts altogether?"

"No. My mind just goes blank. But the crappiest part is being aware, again at the periphery, that my mind is blank. I struggle to find a

thought, a word. That's what's so scary. Being aware that you're not capable of what to think next."

"Maybe like being drunk. Just not coherent thoughts?"

"No. Not that. You're totally sober and aware, but empty. Don't know how else to describe it," Mac responded, his right hand waving in the air to accompany his exasperation. "If you don't mind, Colonel, why the interest? You have some troops suffering like that?"

Roy leaned back in his chair, wiping his mouth before folding his napkin and placing it on the table. "No, just curious," he answered casually.

Mac didn't appreciate that answer. And he felt like the shoebox was on the verge of returning. He blinked heavily. "Don't buy that, sir. FYI, the shoebox is 'bout to hit me. Sorry if I'm testy. I don't know, but seems you're scouting for something about your own situation? You ever get hit?"

"No, I didn't. Was lucky there. I apologize for seeming insincere. My questions do relate to someone I know," Roy offered hesitantly, staring at Mac to gauge recognition.

Mac laughed loudly, waving his hand in the air to blow off the joke he was about to make. "Like, who? The president?"

Roy laughed along, quietly. His mouth closed, his eyes alert with assessment. How could Mac have guessed? Or was it just a fanciful quip? He was, after all, married to the president. They both were all too often the targets of jokes: the acquirers of abnormal, funny, even atrocious attributes imagined by the press and others. It came with the territory. But such jest was rarely spoken directly to one's face.

"Sergeant," Roy continued laughing, trying to deflect by dismissal, "that's no way to talk about *your* Commander in Chief."

Mac's shoebox remained full. He took a long drink of water. "Sorry, Colonel. No disrespect meant. Was just too opportune a chance to joke with you. I'm thinking how much my wife won't believe that I had lunch with you. That we talked about personal things."

Roy glanced at his watch. "It's been my pleasure. An honor, Mac. Please tell your wife that. Have you been married long? Kids?"

"Just a few weeks. Still on our honeymoon, sort of. Working on the kids."

They both laughed hard, drawing stares. Mac made as if he was looking into the soup bowls to make sure they were empty.

"One more thing, if you have a second?" Roy inquired, sliding his chair back from the table and leaning forward with both elbows crowding the dishes. "When you have your, what, call them episodes? When you have them, does your body feel different?"

"Like how?" Mac asked, his forehead furrowed.

"Maybe something like lost muscle tone."

"I've felt none of that. My wife either, I think."

"How about train of thought? Mood? Forgive me for asking, but does this—your shoebox thing—lessen your newlywed inclinations?"

"Are we talking about what I think you're asking?" Mac responded, moving his chair closer to the table so he could reply in whispers.

Roy nodded, his eyes reflecting recognition.

"The only mood shift is getting frustrated. My wife picks up on it right away. Like, almost a signal, an advance warning. But, no. No other moods shifts, I think."

"How about train of thought? Staying on topic? Being consistent? Not swinging from topic one to two without reason?"

"That's not a symptom. No. Remember, in the shoebox, I have no thoughts." Mac's eyes popped open wide. "Say..."

Roy realized that Mac was connecting the dots. Damn! He should never have used the word *consistent*. Best to cut and run. Roy rose from his chair.

Mac stood. Moving closer to Roy, he said, "Say, Colonel? I saw it in your eyes just now. Maybe I've had too much psych-time dealing with the guys in my squads, with their terrors. I got pretty good at reading minds. So, what about your questions? Is this... I mean...?"

"At ease, Sergeant. I was just asking. No implications. Understood?"

Mac looked intently at Roy. He could tell when there were other issues that needed to be discussed. He could also gauge the character of a man. In Roy he saw a good man, a very good man. A man with serious questions. Mac put his hand on Roy's arm, once again, the mentor, the counselor. "Colonel, I think the world of your wife. My wife does, too. Hell, most of us. She's brought America back from the brink. To be honest, I gotta admit that when I was talking with my wife last weekend, we did joke about how the president seems to randomly switch her policies. Like, being less consistent. Forgive me for saying, but the president did build her campaign, evidently, on the continuity of policy. Am I mistaken?"

Hoping to dispel, to redirect the discussion from any conclusions Mac might be drawing, Roy asked, "Evidently? You don't know?"

"I was in the hospital the last days of her campaign."

Roy exhaled, looking around the cafeteria. "Sergeant, there is more I'd like to discuss. But you're late for your appointment. I'll be in touch. I'll expect you to treat what we've been discussing as *extremely* confidential. Am I clear on that?"

"I'll need to share some of this with my wife, sir. She'd pick up immediately if I avoid her questions. But she's totally reliable. I'll tell her."

"Then what we've discussed, and any implications, are between just the three of us. And don't jump to conclusions without recon. You know the exercise, right? Do I have your utmost word on that? As an American, as a soldier, and as a friend?"

"You do! Yes, sir, Colonel... Roy."

"Hooah," Roy responded, his left hand at Mac's shoulder, his right firmly gasping Mac's handshake.

"Brothers," Mac replied to the unspoken question. "Hooah!"

Roy blinked out his most caring smile and handed Mac his card with his private phone number.

Wondering all the while if his wife, his Margie, could be in some sort of declining mental state. In some sort of danger.

CHAPTER 17

The Arrival

The sun's rays washed through the layers of heavy cloud cover, bathing the massive rock outcropping in warmth. The two large front windows of the pagoda—the Leader's private retreat built below the rock—sparkled in the sunshine. Lush ivy, shaded by mature, shaped maple trees, grew against the rock. The quiet warbling of several Daurian redstarts rose from a nearby pond. Ancient stone steps led from the gravel parking area to the arched front entry.

The Leader stood at the heavily carved front door, sipping tea as he watched Director Dong climb the steps. He found her labored effort less appealing than memory provided. "Perhaps," he chuckled, "my preferences are changing?" He laughed out loud, in part to the glorious morning and mountain scenery surrounding his retreat. But mostly he laughed in gleeful anticipation of the pending arrival of President Perserve—*his* reclaimed baggage: soon-to-be at his service.

"Dear Leader!" Dong breathed out between gasps. She stopped one step below the Leader, bowing slightly. "It is a most beautiful morning. It is my extreme pleasure to be here."

The Leader murmured his assent, his jaw extended in firmness. "Hello, Director. You are late. What word do you have on the shipment due from America?"

They stood alone. Armed guards were off aways, screened by the dense mountain ferns and vegetation.

Dong wondered why the Leader still used indirect references to the captured President of the United States. There was no need for added secrecy. "The latest word from State Security is two more days…"

"Two days! Why the delay? What could possibly be the issue?"

"We had to *retrain* several on the transfer team while en route. As you have wisely advised, we can *not* permit any word, any inkling of who we have as our captive, to leak out."

"Perhaps so," the Leader sputtered, drops of spittle hitting his tea and causing small ripples that he studied. "Regardless, I am anxious to have her."

Dong bowed slightly. "It would be an honor to meet such an accomplished woman, even as a detainee."

"Detainee? You have that wrong. Just as with my ancestors, the worthy founders of this, my nation, I must have available, at all times, those who will attend to my every need. I will make this woman one of my secret courtesans."

Dong caught the grumble before it left her throat. "Dear Leader... this is not something you need share with me. We all are your subjects, as you so often graciously remind us."

"That is well enough. But still, I am frustrated at the delay," he replied, motioning to a servant hiding behind the pagoda's front door to refill his tea cup. After a deep breath, allowing the coolness of the morning mountain air to calm his thoughts, he continued. "Perhaps I am ahead of myself. As always, I will sacrifice my needs for the greater good of our nation. My needs can wait. I'm thinking of the intelligence coup possible by interrogating the... baggage."

Dong cautiously put her foot on the top step of the stairs, looking up at the Leader. "Again, very wise. Getting intelligence out of her will be a gold mine, as Hopalong would say..."

The Leader shook his head, smiling. "You and your cowboys. As long as your holohead stays on course, ride all the cowboys you want!" He laughed heartily at his own joke.

"What do you think the president knows? Surely not nuclear codes?" Dong asked.

"Of course not! But think how much our friends will pay for knowledge of America's strategic plans," the Leader answered, waving off over the mountains to imagined legions of fans and devotees. "I have heard from my privates sources that our holohead—*your* president—has recently not had timely access to the Security Council. How and why is unknown. But that means the intel and insight that we gather directly from *your* holohead might be limited," he added with a tone of distrust.

"But, dear Leader. Excuse me. We can't, we must *not,* reveal anything that would suggest you have some access to the real president. How else would you explain the intel coup you would claim to have?"

The Leader tossed what tea remained in his cup onto the steps, splashing Director Dong's sandals. He motioned for the servant to take his cup as he gazed out across the grandeur of the mountains, absorbing the majesty he believed he alone had created. He withdrew his hand from the coat pocket of his fitted grey suit to ply his fingers at his nose. "Is this magnificence lost on you, Dong?" he asked, pointedly.

"Leader?"

"Would you think I would expose our most secret secrets?"

"Of course not…"

"Of course not! That *is* the correct—the only—answer, you fool! Were you not such a valued scientist, I would consider sending you straightaway to the guards' barracks. Although…" he chuckled, stroking his cheek as his coarse laugh sent several redstarts into flight, "they might well reject you," His laughter unceasing, he looked at Dong, expecting her to join in, insensitive to the grotesque hurt of his words.

Knowing it was wise to acquiesce, without leaning down to brush the tea from her legs, Dong gently tapped her sandals against the stone stairs. "Dear Leader," she began, her tone soaked with humility. "It is a stroke of genius, your idea of plying the hostage—your courtesan—for information before you… well… before you fully engage her services. This would most definitely help us verify the behavioral mapping of our holohead and gather key intelligence before you did anything that might alter the hostage's natural behavior."

"Change my baggage's behavior? Do you not imagine that has already happened? That she is not traumatized? I know I would be greatly affected if anyone were to kidnap me."

"If, only," Dong thought, bowing slightly at the ridiculous notion. Ridiculously worthwhile and necessary. "Another time," she mused, while nodding in lockstep to the Leader's laughter.

"If that is the case, then might I suggest, dear Leader, that you allow me to initially interrogate this woman. I can engage her on a woman-to-woman level. Appeal to her female instincts. In your presence, she might be intimidated, awed, and thus less revealing. Might you allow me a first go at extracting information?"

The Leader stepped down to Dong's level. He sucked his lips, again wiping his nose, this time on the sleeve of his grey suit coat. "You have a good point, Director. I can see that she would, indeed, be awed!" he announced to the vista. He jerked both hands out the sleeves of his suit and adjusted his shoulders to fill his massive self-image. "And, might I add... I see the wisdom in your thinking. And your loyalty. It is not for me to apologize, but perhaps my comment about the guards' barracks was uncalled for?" He looked intently into Dong's dark eyes, detecting nothing other than a slight stiffening of her shoulders as he slid his hand down her dog-fur collar. "Then again, a trip to the barracks might be just what you need," he roared.

Dong stepped back. Leadership was one thing, cruelty altogether another. She nodded at the realization that she herself had often dealt out cruelty. Now she understood how demeaning a terror it could be. Her heart tore at the thought that she had been more like the Leader than her mother: a face framed in warmth and love. She drew in a deep breath through her nose, wondering if she was slowly developing enmity with the Leader. "This cannot be!" the voice behind her eyes screamed. "I am loyal, forever loyal," it insisted. But still, she wondered, "Loyal to whom, and for what?"

——— . ———

The helicopter landed in the clearing on the other side of the gravel parking area. The limbs on the maple trees bent back against the wash from the spinning rotors. Three guards ducked and rushed across the clearing to the stairs unfolding beneath the opening door. The Leader stood alone high above the clearing, ogling from his pagoda's large front window. He wiped his face excitedly—almost drooling—as his "reclaimed baggage" was helped down the stairs to the waiting guards. Although her legs were shackled and a sack covered her head, she was taller than he imagined. The helicopter lifted off immediately, the guards and the baggage cowering in the dust and flying debris. The

Leader watched closely as the guards dragged the sack to a waiting golf cart. For a moment his eyes were on the cart as it proceeded out of sight around a grove of camphor and camellia trees. The next moment they were on the helicopter as it cleared the ridge of the ravine one mile away. He hummed a few notes from his favorite song, "If Only My Love," as he watched the helicopter grow smaller against the horizon of green forests. He gave a slight nod over his left shoulder. The small image expanded, soundlessly, into a red flash. "Secrets must remain secrets," he muttered to the beautiful porcelain dragon jar and its mate bracketing the window.

Director Dong heard the approach of the golf cart. She sat in a chair on a large, circular bamboo mat in the center of the hut that attended the Leader's Tranquility Pool. The hut's door and windows were barred, the only furniture the chair occupied by the director. The tissue in her hands was soiled and damp. Her forehead perspiring. She wondered what she could really accomplish. Would she have any tidbits for the Leader? Would the president be responsive and cooperate? Dong had spent the past day studying details of the president's life, including the psychological profile developed by the RID team. She had called Juong for guidance, using their cloaked wording to hide detection. She was sure the Leader would be watching the interrogation via the several cameras hidden in the arched doorways. Her one possible strategy was to obscure the essence of her interrogation within the slow, tender removal of the sack and the re-clothing of the president. A strategy that might work given the salacious propensity of the Leader—like most male leaders throughout history. Including, she reluctantly admitted, the scions of Hollywood.

The smell of the president arrived first. Dong brought the tissue to her nose as the door opened and the guards dragged the sack to the mat, dropping it like so much soiled wash. The sack let out a scream. The guards bowed, dropping a key on the mat and leaving the Director to the smell and the bits of sound and whimpers emanating from the sack.

Dong reached to the stack of towels next to her chair. In her stilted English, she whispered, "You are with a friend."

The sack went quiet, motionless. After what Dong considered an unnecessarily long wait, "Who are you?" the president asked cautiously, her voice angry and warped through the sack.

"A friend," Dong replied. "I must help you from your bindings. Here, kneel if you can, and I will remove the sack." She rose from the chair, grabbing the president's shoulders.

"Let me first remove the shackles," Dong said, gently stroking the president's shoulder. She took the key and removed the leg restraints. She noticed the bloody wounds on the president's ankles. Dong took a damp towel and gingerly wiped the ankles, repeating, "Oh, my poor dear. We will make this right. Yes, we will."

The president groaned, almost collapsing under the tender graces of Dong's touch—the first caring human contact in what seemed like an eternity.

In his private room, viewing the feed from the hidden cameras, the Leader groaned, imagining himself in the restraints with the president tending to him. "Soon," he reminded himself. "Very soon!"

Dong said, "I will remove the sack now. Try to remain upright." With the president still kneeling, Dong stood and gently pulled the sack up around her shoulders and off her head.

"Oh!" the president yelled, breathing in fresh air for the first time in over a week. "Oh!" she cried, dropping back into a deep kneel, her body shaking in sobs.

The Leader's eyes were glazed as he let his imagination hijack the president's moans. "Oh, oh," he echoed.

Director Dong came around to stand in front of the president. She knelt, wiping the president's tears with a gentleness she never knew she had. Her thoughts flashed to that beautiful woman from long ago and words of love and tenderness from a starving face. "There, there," Dong said, realizing it was exactly what she would say to her own children. Her own? A notion she had always rejected. Until now.

The Leader was also feeling Dong's touch as he watched the video. He found himself reconsidering. "Two birds are always better than one," if he recalled that ancient rhyme correctly. He grabbed the arms of his chair, his agitation and arousal overwhelming.

Director Dong put her left hand beneath the president's chin with a lightness she imagined bordering on love. She didn't know what that might really feel like as she looked directly into the president's bloodshot, yet beautiful gray-blue eyes. She imagined them to be eyes like William Boyd's. "Ma'am," she said, ever so quietly, "my name is Dong. I am here to help you."

"Can..." Margie stuttered, finding her voice. "Can you help me escape?"

"No, no," Dong replied. Moving her mouth to the president's ear, wiping away the grime, she whispered quietly, "At least, not yet."

Beyond agitation, the Leader left for a cold shower. As tempted as he was, he did not want to interrupt Dong. Her intelligence coup was worth the wait. And regardless, there were always treats on standby.

Dong took new towels and began wiping the president's neck and arms. "What shall I call you?" she asked, finally. Timing was everything.

"Margie. Please call me Margie," the president replied, lost in Dong's tender touch, aware only that she was somewhere far from home. Perhaps in some Asian country if Dong's appearance was representative. Or so she surmised.

"Margie, you're in some type of strange clothing, yes?"

"These are, or were, my pajamas."

When Dong furrowed her eyebrows in question, Margie added, "My sleeping garments. I was taken when I was... I can't remember. I must have been sleeping?" She shook her head to recall what memories she could.

"I have a clean robe for you. Here, I will turn my back. Please remove your old clothes and put on this robe."

Dong turned as Margie changed. The Leader returned from his shower just as Margie tightened her robe. His expletive woke the guard at his door. Then he remembered that all the video was being recorded. "Later," he said, sighing in relief.

Dong pointed to a bowl of rice and to a pile of blankets. "Margie, you are exhausted. Eat and rest. Then I will tell you where you are. How things are and all that has happened to you."

"You have no idea..." Margie began, between sobs.

CHAPTER 18

The Danger

"Margie?" Dong whispered, gently shaking the president who was curled in a ball around the empty bowl, the blankets askew on her back.

Margie slowly opened her eyes, one at a time. She jumped, yelling out, "No! No!" before she finally recognized Dong. Lifting herself up on one elbow, she surveyed the inside of the hut, noting the barred door and windows.

"You've been sleeping for almost twenty hours."

"Am I a prisoner? Where am I? Do you know *who* I am?" Margie blurted out.

"All I've been told is that you are an American that I must treat with care and respect."

"American? Absolutely! I *am* the President of the United States!" Margie screamed. "I must be put in immediate contact with our embassy! I demand to be freed."

"Please, Margie, that is not possible."

"So, I *am* a prisoner?"

Dong felt a tug on her heart. She wondered if she did, in fact, have a heart, a soul. "Are such thoughts," she wondered, "tied to the image of that starving woman, when I was a child? My mother. My mother's face filled with a mother's love, sacrifice, and concern."

"That is not for me to say, at least not yet," Dong answered Margie as she gathered the blankets. "Please, we have a small bathroom with a shower." She pointed to a corner of the room. "Let us start by giving you a chance to clean up from your travels and ordeal." She helped Margie to her feet, her hand around Margie's waist. "Such a beautiful child," Dong thought, knowing such thoughts were not allowed. She escorted Margie into the bathroom. As Dong left to close the door, she hung a towel over the camera in the corner of the door frame.

Across the retreat, in the main pagoda, the Leader howled his rage, kicking his video monitor. "You will pay for this, Dong!" he shouted. More at himself for accepting Dong's approach that delayed his sampling of his baggage.

Dong sat patiently in her chair at the center of the mat. She could hear the president's coughing above the sound of the shower. She wondered how the State Security goons had treated this woman, this child. "Child?" she asked herself. "Where does that thinking originate?" Dong stretched out her feet, noting the stains of tea on her sandals. "A man can no more accurately imagine loving a child as a mother does, than a donkey can imagine itself a thoroughbred horse," she pondered, stroking her chin and fighting a curiosity forming in her mind. "What is the end game of all this?" she wondered. "Other than allowing one mere human to control and reek havoc, what are we doing?"

Dong extended her legs, clapping her sandals together. She gazed out the window at the billowing clouds framing the distant mountain tops. She was aware that the Leader might be watching. Or at the very least, one of his goons. She heard the president humming a tune, something familiar, but not allowed.

"Loyalty?" Dong asked herself. "Loyalty to a human, or to humanity?" Dong rose quickly from her chair, walking to a window, grabbing the bars. "Treasonous, dangerous thoughts," she realized, squinting into the sunlight, seeing the vista with the clarity of a mother's love. "So be it," she concluded as Margie opened the bathroom door, her hair spun in a towel and a fresh robe complementing her smile.

Dong pointed to her chair. "Please, Margie, sit. I will tell you all I can. It is complex. I must walk as I say it."

"Dong, I realize I am a prisoner. I have seen the bars, the locks. I must warn you that I am a strong woman. I see no guards."

"Please, Margie. Do not threaten me with your strength. You are younger, yes. I have studied you carefully—your entire life I know. You possess none of the marital arts skills that I have. Threats will harm you and your position. I am your only friend here. And if you persist in threats to me, I could lay you flat in the blink of a gnat's ass."

Watching the video feed, the Leader wondered if Dong was going too far. How would he win the favors of his baggage if Dong continued to make such threats of harm and isolation?

Dong turned to face Margie. "You have been taken by force. Correct. You define that as being a prisoner. But the alternative is death. For you, and your family."

"Are you...!"

"I am not making threats in return. No. I am merely stating the reality. Whether that reality is of my own choosing is not the issue. What is important here is trust. You have a binary choice. View yourself a prisoner and resist all you can, which will lead nowhere but to death. Or... by trusting me, you may be able to exert a constructive force. A force for good. Just one not delivered from your office." Dong hoped the Leader was not reading between the lines as he listened in.

"You mean, be a traitor to America!"

"Not at all," Dong replied. "You have not allowed me to explain what I mean by force. Consider this. No one on Earth, other than those of us at this remote compound, knows where you are. In a blink, you can be liquidated, disposed of. And in a manner, the prelude to which, might involve torture... or worse. I am but one member of our team. A team led by men, if you get my meaning. At least in terms of *worse*?"

Margie laughed vigorously, her face fierce in determination, the towel around her hair falling to the floor. "Dong? Do you imagine I don't see through your veiled threats? I *am* the President of the United States. Stop this lunacy! I can bring the full power and fury of American might upon you, directly on this team of yours, whoever you are. So let's not beat around the bush. You do understand that colloquialism?"

"Indeed, I do. I studied for three years at one of your famous universities. Under fake papers, of course. All part of your country's foolish H1-B worker policy. The net result has opened the door for people like me, thank you very much! It's a new world, Margie. One where bleeding hearts, bless them, have no grasp of reality."

Dong paused, feeling a spasm in her own heart. "Well, anyway. Now, as to the American power and might you just cited, please understand that no one knows where you are. Nor are they looking.

Why? Because you have been replaced by an exact replica. One which we control."

"You... you mean the image in the closet?" Margie screamed.

"Quite so," Dong replied, patiently.

Margie leaned over, picking up the towel and absently drying her hair. She was lost in a reality that she could not, would not... but *must*, accept. She smoothed out her robe, a feign to distract Dong. She calculated the distance she would have to cover to charge, to tackle Dong. Then again, Dong did look solid with a bulldog's body. Margie tapped the arms of the chair, acknowledging that she was still weak from her ordeal. She had lost track of how long it had been.

"I can see you are weighing alternatives, Margie. Unwise, at best. Were you to get past me, there are numerous guards surrounding this hut, monitoring your every move by hidden cameras. Then, beyond the guards, there is the mountainous terrain. Almost a jungle. It's many miles to the nearest village. And if you got that far, you'd be subjected to a mob of filthy, ignorant men. Laborers, miners."

Margie squinted out a window, trying to resolve the intel Dong had just provided with a possible location. She took a stab. "Given your accent and access to our universities, and the terrain I see out the window... is not your country, *China*... concerned about possible retaliation?"

Dong laughed hard. "You miss the mark on that one. No, we are not China. I imagine China would most seriously frown were they to know what we have accomplished. Like America, they would be wise to fear us. To remember that from a small spark comes a great fire."

Dong came close to the president's chair, sitting on the pile of towels and looking up at Margie. "I will tell you this. Unless you trust me, you are in danger. Grave danger. I have mentioned various types. I do not want to repeat myself. If you will talk with me and cooperate, then the danger to you and America will be lessened."

"Why should I even start to believe that?" Margie scoffed.

"One simple reason. We control your replacement. The replica has and *is* learning all there is to know about your nation's security and intelligence systems. Your defenses. We can, at any time, exploit that knowledge. Even manipulate the way our replacement handles your *football*, you know…"

"You're making this all up, Dong!" Margie yelled, jumping from the chair, rushing to a window and pulling on the bars. "What you describe is impossible. Some unbalanced madness!"

Dong moved to the chair, crossing her ample legs. "It's the simple truth, Margie," Dong sighed. "What evidence do you want? Shall you give us a prompt or a behavior that we can have our replacement follow to prove our capabilities?"

"That would mean nothing. You'd manipulate the news and the intel you'd feed me. No, you're more than insane!" Margie gasped in sudden realization. "Is this, what did you call it, replica? Does it think for itself? Is it aware that it's *just* a replica? Or does it imagine itself to be a real person? Which is impossible, pure science fiction! Only God can create a human with a heart… with a soul."

"Perhaps. I will not say more. However, I can say this much. Its awareness and behaviors are created and controlled entirely by us and our computers. It does not need intrinsic self-awareness. We have a way to give it the soul that you imagine is formed by your God."

"That's not possible! A complete fairytale!" Margie screamed. "You're not God. Do what you must to me. America will defend itself!"

Dong nodded, clapping her hands, laughing. "Do what we must to you? Shall I call you Nathan Hale?" she roared, her laughter catching Margie off guard. "No one will know of your sacrifice. It will never make it into your children's school books. Never!"

Margie came alongside Dong's chair. "It doesn't matter what happens to me. It's the way our system is built. With redundancy."

"You forget the one key element. That *you* are still at work, albeit in facsimile form. The replica? Yes, you have your hierarchy of who fills whose shoes. But your country has no way of dealing with a Trojan Horse disguised as you. In that case, none of the safeguards designed into your system will be activated. We will have complete control. As I said, you can trust me and be a force for good, or die."

Watching the video, his dark eyes beady pinpoints, the Leader was beside himself. He did not understand the tactic that Dong was using. "Force for good?" he asked the reedy prints on the wall.

Dong reached out to Margie's shoulder, gently pulling their heads together. "There is a solution, one I can't reveal right now. But you must resist, on your life, advances by the males on our team. You must!" she whispered.

"I would die, first!"

"They can use drugs and coercion. There are ways." Dong knew she had to maintain the Leader's hard line. But for whatever reason, she was drawn to Margie as she might be to her own daughter.

"I appeal to you as a fellow human, please help me!" Margie implored. "What is your role? Why are you doing this?"

"First, I have my own questions," Dong inserted, changing the subject. "About your children, Kari and Todd. What is it like, to be a mother? To give birth. To endure the pain of childbirth?"

"How is it you know so much about me?" Margie queried, drawn to Dong's sincere manner, but aware it could all be just a ploy. If another person had somehow been substituted for her, wouldn't her family notice? Wouldn't Roy miss the intimate details of their love? Would her staff notice? Deshon would have to notice. They were like brother and sister.

"We have studied you for the past eight months, noting every detail, from your childhood in Kansas to your state government positions to the nuances of love with your husband." Ignoring Margie's gasp, Dong continued. "We know how you react to policy, what foods you like, which Hollywood actors..." Dong paused in brief homage to her idols, "...you like. How else could we have successfully replaced you?"

"I don't believe any of it," Margie retorted. "It's a crazy, bad dream. Nothing else!"

"You may consider it as you will. No hair off my eyebrow. However, I would like to know you better, to help you further. For example, I would like to know about what you call your religion. I saw plenty of it being bandied about during my three years in the States. But none of it ever really made sense. Seemed like just people letting their human nature argue in support of their form of God, or gods."

Hoping for more intel, Margie asked, "Perhaps, yes. The *notion* of religion in America is a catch-all. Don't you have religion, here in your country? Maybe Buddha or a Hindu god?"

Dong studied her fingernails. "One thing is evident. You did *not* come into politics as a lawyer."

"How's that?"

Dong laughed. "Your questions are too direct. Not subtle or cagey as a district attorney might make them. Perhaps, though, that is part of your success and your charm. No?"

"What about my religion, as you call it? If you know me so well, what do you think?"

"We know you believe in the Christian God. That you cast yourself as a Christ-follower to distance yourself from the many other varieties, even charlatans, of Christianity. Do you really believe in this Christ? The whole story seems a fairytale—bad dream as you put it—to some."

"I can give you the standard reply about God and Jesus Christ, the Holy Spirit. Sure. What the Bible teaches. But it's one's own personal story, like mine, that means the most. How we see and know God. If the listener's heart is cold to the notion of Christ as God, then any such a story, my explanation, would not mean much. Your soul is the essence of your human being. God-formed. It's up to each of us to decide how to fill our soul. With good or with evil."

"You said only your God can create a human with a heart. With a soul. You really believe we each have a soul?" Dong asked guardedly, unaware why she could not let go of the notion of a soul. For a brief moment, her eyes focused on the vision of her mother who had one hand at her heart, the other reaching out to her daughter, A-Yeon Dong. As a scientist, Dong knew only that which could be observed or proved by evidence. Perplexed as never before, she continued, "What is the soul? Does it exist? Is it changeable, adaptable? Or is it a core in each of us, unchanged from birth? What can you tell me of your soul?"

Margie took Dong's hand, searching her eyes. "Why are you asking this? You keep changing the questions. Is this part of your interrogation technique? You ask about the soul. Do you know of Blaise Pascal, the theologian?"

"You mean, Pascal the mathematician?" Dong snorted.

Margie nodded, her eyes reflecting recognition.

"Of course I do!" Dong responded. "Our technology considers all of mankind's limited scientific and mathematical thinking."

"Well, then you must know that Pascal said something like, 'If we wager God exists and we are right, we win. If we wager God exists and are wrong, we lose nothing. That we know the truth not only by reason, but also by the heart.'"

Dong smiled, patting Margie's hand. She rose from the chair and paced around the hut, touching the wall and talking quietly to herself. She felt like a melting icicle, a strange release flowing out from her fingertips. Like a butterfly, emerging from its cocoon, blinking in the dazzling sunlight. Dong grabbed the bars for support, closing her eyes to avoid the dizziness overcoming her. The Leader must *not* see the swaying weakness she felt. She let out a gasp. What did all her questions mean? Why was she such a stooge for the Leader? The Leader—like so many men—was caught in an orgy of narcissism. It was not just testosterone. It was a vicious blend of ego and possession. Of a temporal view of life. Missing the beauty, the exquisiteness of life. Lost within an aura of invincibleness, power. Power over others to define one's self. An aura not real. Imagined.

Dong opened her eyes, catching the sun's rays piercing the swirling clouds with a beauty no man could create. Was there, indeed, a God? Was Pascal right? Was Margie's faith real? Dong knew that people wanted to ascribe the natural beauty of the world to some form of a god. All the sunrises, the rivers cascading over rocks, the magnificent animals of the forests and the seas. But could such consideration explain the love in a mother's eyes?

"Ugh!" Dong yelled as she turned angrily towards Margie. "This cannot be!" Dong's dazed look—her eyes wide and seeming to fill her face—caused Margie to cry out.

Myriad questions surged through Margie's thoughts. This was all too crazy. A horrible dream. Was Dong a friend? More likely a cagey foe. Did these people really have a substitute in her place? What was the danger for herself, for America? Who were these men that Dong mentioned? What country was this? Was it a country, or some fiction— a runaway James Bond-type global enemy?

Margie's sobs changed to a howling growl. "Yes, I will!" she yelled back at Dong. She would fight with her life to thwart whatever evil lay ahead.

CHAPTER 19

The Cue

Mindy passed a glass of wine to Mac as he sat, smug and snug, on their living room couch. "So, Mr. Big Shot. Looks like you and the president's husband are now best good buddies, huh?" she laughed.

Mac swirled the pinot, the glass in his right hand. He moved the rim beneath his nose, not sure if he was supposed to be smelling aroma or bouquet. Mindy sat at the other end of the couch, her legs tucked beneath her. She smiled lovingly at Mac—a twinkle in her eyes that he took as snobbish confirmation: he was a wine dunce.

"What am I supposed to be smelling?" he asked, piqued by the mirth evident in her eyes dancing over the rim of her glass. "Am I smelling oak, or peaches, or lavender?"

"Not with pinot," Mindy laughed softly. She shook her head, unable to control her glee at Mac's naïve sweetness—his innocence— on certain issues of life. Probably the less important issues. His purity— courage and caring, strong mind and body—represented to her a most amazingly authentic man. Her laughter was one of joy.

Mac exhaled heavily, leaning forward to put his glass on the coffee table. "What, then?" he asked.

"With pinot, you'd find the smell of fruits. Maybe berries. It usually has less tannin and is lighter than a burgundy. Both have tannin. You might be able to pick up a notion of that smell."

"Just tastes like wine to me. Though my tongue does have a dry feeling. Guess I'm really a beer guy. Just like Roy..."

"Your best new buddy?"

"Uh-huh. Yeah, so? Can you try getting off on something else besides giving me a hard time about Roy?" he laughed, leaning back to nudge her knee with his foot.

"Something else? You know, Mac, you're so cute when you get cornered. How about I get off on you?" Mindy teased as she looked down the hall towards the bedroom.

"You've got a one-track mind, Mrs. Mac!" he replied, grabbing her foot to drag her off the couch.

"Whoa, mister," Mindy yelped, grasping his hand from her foot to pull herself into his arms. "Let's finish our wine first."

"If you make me wait too long, I'll switch back to beer. And as you know, that makes me sleepy. Is that what you want?"

"I want you, Professor! But first, I want to finish my wine and hear more about your lunch with your bud, Roy."

Mac stood, stretched in a manner not lost on Mindy, turned to the couch to rearrange the pillows, and plopped himself down next to her.

"I could use a beer," he yawned.

Mindy gave a sharp elbow to his side. "Roy?" she added.

"Okay. I already told you about the conference topics. Interesting, and maybe helpful. But not much was said about CTE when talking with the colonel..." Mac caught Mindy's raised eyebrow. "Okay... with Roy. Dr. Evans discussed CTE with me in detail after Roy left."

"I want to hear about that, too."

"If you're denying me a beer, then only one topic, tonight. What's it to be?" Mac responded, his hand on her thigh.

"Okay, then. The colonel. What's he like? Is he as handsome in person as he is on TV?"

Mac sighed. "Yes, I guess. Actually, I didn't really notice. What I did notice—where we bonded—was in our profile of army experiences. Not sure how much action he saw. We bonded 'cause we've both walked that bridge of sighs... lost comrades. Those are easy words to say, but mean nothing unless you've been there. I could see the strain in his eyes. Not from being 'First Husband,' though I imagine that's a tough role. No, what I saw in his eyes was a lasting concern. A shadow in his soul. A wound for those who have served and suffered. Can't really explain it."

"I think I get it. I hope I do," Mindy whispered, taking Mac's hand.

"I'd call him a good officer, a gentleman. Probably tough as nails, but sensitive, too."

"Yeah, must be a tough job, being First Husband?"

Mac paused, reaching out to stroke Mindy's hair. He glanced out the window to the snow-filled alley. Such a peaceful scene. Unlike what he had sensed in talking with the colonel.

"Uh-huh. There was one thing we talked about, briefly. Actually, just a tangential reference. Roy tensed when he realized I'd connected the dots from what he'd said."

"What do you mean?"

"We were talking about his wife, the president. I mentioned that you and I..."

"You mentioned me!" Mindy interrupted with what Mac, by the extended roll of his eyes, obviously considered too much enthusiasm.

Mac continued, his index finger raised in the air. "Roy had given some vague hints that the president was somehow different. I told him that you and I had thought the same. At that, he clammed right up. Told me, basically on my oath as a solider, not to discuss or think about this issue. I did mention you," Mac said, the left side of his face raised in grimace as Mindy gave a little yelp. "Listen, you! I promised Roy that this was just between us three. He sees it as a serious issue. I have no idea what it is. But his manner was grave, *very* grave." Mac pointed his finger directly at Mindy. "No fooling around on this. There's something up. Just doesn't feel right. Like, I wonder if anyone else has picked up on this. I told you that Roy and I bonded, as soldiers, together. Whatever he's fighting or concerned about, I want to help him!"

Mindy's face went ashen. She nodded, realizing the significance. Maybe the president *was* having mental issues. "Oh, Mac. I love you for your sensitivity. For your dedication. But don't you think that Roy, as the First Husband, has a ton of staff to help him deal with whatever he's concerned about?"

"There was a vibration—unspoken between us—that suggested this whole issue, whatever it might be, is very private to Roy. Like, he has his suspicions, but nowhere to turn."

"So you expect him to call you?" Mindy joked.

"Damn it, Mindy. This is not funny!" Mac shouted, waving a fist towards the wall.

"Oh, Mac. Why are you so suddenly upset? Is the shoebox back? You're... you're scaring me. Not by your actions, but that you would have such a rapid reaction to something we hardly understand. Maybe you're just imagining things?"

"Remember that kid's app that tracked politicians' consistency?"

"Yeah, why?"

"Because the kid picked up on something. Evidently no one, not anywhere, thought it was more than the president changing her mind. Having a bad hair day. Whatever. Now, I wonder. You and I joked about President Perserve's behavior. I mean, it's still a swamp she has to deal with. What *else* can we expect out of D.C.?" Mac's stilted yell brought tears to Mindy's eyes. Was Mac having a breakdown?

Oblivious to Mindy's growing concern, he continued, "If you stand back and analyze our observations and that kid's app, there's nothing to suspect. But—and here's the kicker—when you add Roy's concern into the mix, you've got something really serious. I think."

Mindy moved closer to Mac, reaching out to gently run her fingers through his hair. "Mac, there's a lot of 'buts' in your thinking. Listen. We're familiar with the president's background. Solid. She's straight as they come. A Midwest classic. What could you possibly be imagining?"

"Dunno. But... and hey, screw the buts," he blurted.

Mindy stood, alarmed at Mac's outburst. "Let's change the subject. You're ruining the mood."

"For what?"

"For me! For us, you jackass! You're all wound up over nothing that makes sense. Leave it to Roy and the White House medical team. Leave it so there's room, right now, for us. Our love. Don't get spacey on me." She walked to the kitchen, not waiting for a reply.

Mac sunk in the couch, fearing an onset of the shoebox.

"Didn't the VA doc have some meds for you?" Mindy yelled out from the kitchen as she put pots and pans back into the cabinets.

Mac gazed out the window, seeing what was now just a barren landscape. He heard the slamming of cabinet doors. He felt like crying. Was it the damn PTSD, or CTE, that shifted his moods so suddenly? Was it worth it? Poor Mindy. Mac rose from the couch and ambled into the kitchen, leaning against the wall.

"See! Just like I told you. I'm a burden. My issues will never go away. They'll just get worse and make our lives—your life—worse."

He jumped back in alarm as Mindy threw a pan at him. "Listen, buddy-boy," she growled. "We're just having a... ah... a tiff. Okay? It happens. I need the right to explode once in a while. It's good for any of us. You're not the only one with stress and worry." She laughed sadly at Mac, standing flat against the wall, his arms raised against the prospect of more flying objects. "Look at you, Mac. The great warrior, the brilliant professor. But a real chickenshit when it comes to dealing with my outbursts, which are rare. Dealing with issues. And for the last time, damn it! See how you got me swearing?" She reached for another pan. Mac moved towards the door.

Mindy raised the pan, waving it at Mac like a hatchet. "Hold it, Sergeant! At ease. Now! This is the *last* time, got it! No more burden-talk, or you're getting this right between the... the eyes," she cried. She dropped the pan to the floor as she rushed to embrace her Mac, her warrior. The chickenshit who was hovering within himself, hugging the wall. She could feel his chest heaving in silent sobs. She held him, hard. They stood there in each other's arms, rocking back and forth.

Mac pushed Mindy away. His eyes—beseeching forgiveness—reflected like emeralds through his tears. "What are we to do?" he asked.

Mindy held his eyes in the love extending from her own. "Do? About what?" she said, as she kissed away his tears.

"About what just happened?"

"It happens, like I said. I know you're suffering. I need to be more patient. And you? You need to know, for the thousandth time, that you are *not* a burden. I'm here for you, forever! Evidently, your head's too thick to grasp that concept, but it's called 'undying, unflinching love.' Now, I'm taking you to our bedroom. Dinner can wait," she whispered, putting a finger to Mac's lips as he started to protest. Her finger went to his scar. "We all have scars. Yours are mine, and vise-versa. Come with me," she whispered as she pulled Mac down the hall.

Four hours later, well past midnight, Mac happily moaned, "Wow. I can live forever on this diet. No dinner. Just continuous love-making."

"No dinner, just a night-long dessert," Mindy murmured back, her head nestled on Mac's shoulder, her body draped against his.

Mac took a deep breath, listening to Mindy's soft breathing against the sound of a siren carried across the spaces out somewhere beyond Washington Square.

Mindy reached down to scratch her thigh. "Need help?" Mac asked, the warmth of their bodies arresting any desire for sleep.

"Yes," Mindy breathed, adding to the warmth Mac was soaking in.

"I love you, Mindy," Mac said, quietly. Moving to the side and up on an elbow, he looked intently into her eyes. "I am blessed to have you by my side. Not just now," he paused, "but always and forever, and for dealing with all the nutcase antics I do, or am."

"You *are* a nutcase, sometimes. Aren't we all, in one way or another? It's just that some of us, like you, have magnifiers—this PTSD—that puts a shine on things. No, not a shine. More like a dullness. Can't be helped. It's part of you, so it's part of me. We can deal with it. I'll learn more and try to be more patient. Shoebox or not, you're stuck with me!" she said, pulling Mac down for a prolonged kiss.

"I'm just about out of dessert," Mac exclaimed, coming up for air.

"Short-hitter," Mindy teased. "Thought you warriors were studs?"

"I'm a professor, remember? Intellectual type…"

Mindy sputtered a laugh, giving Mac a jab under the blankets.

"It's why my brain gets most of my blood, so ease up a bit, huh?"

"Okay, Professor. We'll take a brief recess. What a wuss," she joked. "And I mean, *brief* recess. While there, maybe you can tell me more about what concerned Roy. You know, regarding the president?"

"Not exactly pillow talk."

"Just speak slowly. Don't tax yourself. And don't use your brain too much. We'll soon need your blood elsewhere. So… lover," she cooed, "exactly what was it that concerned Roy?"

"For someone so new to sex, you can be kinda... wild, at times," Mac laughed back, wondering how to cue up the questions he had about Roy. In a manner that prolonged the recess. He *really* was beat.

CHAPTER 20

The Awakening

Mac lay on their bed, spread out facedown, his face in a pillow to prevent hyperventilating. His thoughts were a stream of flashbacks to elementary school where, he recalled, recesses were never long enough. And it remained so, married to Mindy, he concluded with a goofy, sated smile into the pillow.

Mindy was gently rubbing his back. "You okay? Not a heart-attack, I hope? Lover boy? You fell asleep during recess so I had to arouse you."

"Arouse? Webster would agree that you succeeded—in *all* possible meanings of *that* word," Mac mumbled as he rolled over and gently brought Mindy's head to his shoulder.

She put her arm across his chest, her hand on his heart. "Still beating. Fast," she whispered.

"Not surprised," he choked. "So? Where were we?"

"Where were we? You repeated the word 'Roy' three or four times before you conked out. That's where!"

Mac took a deep breath, clearing his throat. "Not satisfied?"

Mindy gave him a quick kiss on his cheek. "What'd you think? To bring you back on topic, you were about to tell me why you were concerned for Roy."

Mac stared at the ceiling fixture before looking over at some of Mindy's photos on the wall. He continued staring, considering how to best begin, until Mindy prompted, "You've gone quiet on me. Please, not the shoebox?"

"Naw, no. No. I'm just trying to sort through how to explain things to you. First of all, as I said—and I mean this in all seriousness—this is just between us, you and me. And Roy, if I ever talk with him again."

Mindy gave a quiet, "Uh-huh."

Mac could tell by the hurt in her voice that it was unnecessary to mention confidentiality. He let it pass.

"Mac?"

"Okay. It's hard to recall, exactly. Roy was trying to find out what it was like to go off the rails. To have a personality change, like mentally AWOL. Eventually we talked about the idea of continuity. He meant mental continuity. I shouldn't have, but I joked that maybe his concern was with the president. You know? Her policy on continuity, and all. He got real serious, all of a sudden. Tried to switch to another subject. But in the end, he sensed that I'd figured out that he was concerned about the president, her state of mind. That's why he swore me to secrecy. My guess is he's seen some intimate change in the president that's given him a reason to be concerned. Probably so intimate that he can't go to the White House doctors. At least not yet."

"You told him you'd discuss this with me?"

"Had to. Because I knew you'd sleuth it out of me, one way or the other. Maybe, too, I knew I couldn't keep this to myself, you being the only person I'd trust to share this with."

Mindy hugged him. "I like that last reason. And you're right to share it with me. We are one, in all ways. I wouldn't want some secret you were keeping to bring on the shoebox. Whoa!" she shouted as Mac took her in his arms and rolled over on top of her. "And no changing the subject, Professor! You don't get off that easy," Mindy laughed. "At least from talking about Roy, but maybe from getting off me!" She squeezed out from under Mac.

They lay side by side, staring at the ceiling, thinking the exact same thoughts. How blissful it was to be in love, to make love. Yet, also, what was the issue with Roy and his concern regarding the president?

"Where you going?" Mac asked as Mindy suddenly pushed out of the covers, grabbing her robe. "It's what, four o'clock in the morning?"

"My mind is spinning. You've got me thinking. Can't sleep. I'm curious if the president is exhibiting weird behavior. Something we don't see, like the tree in the forest."

"Listen to you. You're zonked. What you mean is, the forest for the trees. Right?"

"Whatever, you weenie. Go back and get your beauty sleep," she said over her shoulder as she walked down the hall, adjusted the heater thermostat and went into her office. She searched online for pictures of President Perserve and recent quotes. After saving several dozen facial images to a desktop folder and copying out an equal number of quotes, Mindy quietly went back down the hall to their bedroom. Mac did not stir as she pulled the covers over him and gently kissed his hair. "Talk about zonked," she chuckled.

Back at her computer, not really knowing what she was doing or looking for—merely following an inspired thought—Mindy brought up that kid's blog that tracked politicians' comments. She arranged the saved images and quotes by date in columns of a Word document and pasted in comments from the blog, synched to the same dates. She thought about using that hot, new facial-matching app *InYourFace* which found people across the Web whose face almost perfectly matched a submitted image. But she knew such apps were really only good for comparing facial-feature differences. She brushed back her hair and shook her head in irritation at how the tech world—enamored as it was with AI and myriad cool geeky apps—thought it could replace human instinct and pure intellect. Mindy was more confident in her own photographer's eye to spot changes in President Perserve's facial expressions. Some subtle aspect like pupils dilating, eyebrows shifting, cheeks folding differently. For each of the quotes in the date-sequenced column next to the images, she used keywords to summarize the reason for the change in facial expression. She mapped the keywords to the comments from the kid's app.

It was almost six in the morning. In the background of her mind the morning sounds of the city were growing more apparent. Regardless, Mindy was hooked, her excitement hard to contain. She was sure she saw one fundamental relationship. That for every keyword shift, in effect change in policy, there was a corresponding excessive dilation in the president's eyes. The president's facial contrast—her complexion—was always the same for similar keywords: in color tone, in eyebrow lift, and in cheek folds and position.

Mindy leaned back in her chair, rubbing her shoulders against its fabric. It dawned on her that she had proved nothing. That a similar study of any person might show similar—unchanging—aspects in their facial patterns based on context or situation. She looked at the clock, yawning. Without turning off the light, she walked down the hall and crawled in next to Mac, whispering, "Mac? Have I found it?"

Mindy yawned again, unable to silence her noisy exhale of air. "Oh, well, I'll get him up with the sun," she sighed, spooning in next to his warm back, her breath and heart calming. She was home with her Mac. Soon, with Mindy's quiet breath washing over the back of Mac's neck, their chests gently rose and contracted in quiet, peaceful unison. It was, her dream told her, a peace that surpassed all understanding.

After sleeping in, showering together, and sharing morning coffee, Mindy was at the kitchen table eating a grapefruit. Looking over at Mac, she said, "I studied the president's words and images while you slept. Did it all by myself. Didn't need my weenie, at least for a few hours," she teased. "Had me thinking about the photos I took in the Middle East. How the same photo could bring out different emotions based on context. For example, a GI on a stretcher. You can conclude she's mortally wounded in the context of the men, your brothers, that you've lost. Someone else might think, 'Thank goodness for the medevac capabilities in today's army. She'll make it.'"

"What're you saying?" Mac asked, his nose over the edge of his coffee cup, his mind somewhere off in conversation with Juan Valdez.

"That context is everything. Okay, if you were to look at the president's words in the same context, a standard frame of reference, you'd be able to more easily detect any variance or drift in her thoughts. Like in the modifiers, the adjectives and their targets, the nouns. My gut says you should be able to associate changes in her demeanor, her facial expression, with changes in her policies."

"Come on. How's that insight? We all probably have the same expression, or repeat our expression, in the same context or emotion."

Mindy poured herself more coffee. Mac noticed she added two extra teaspoons of sugar. "I'm telling you, if you'd listen," she said with a bit more exasperation than Mac thought necessary. "Okay... two things. Number one, the president's policies have shifted. And, number two, with each shift, her look is exactly the same. In other words, with each change in policy, her facial expression is the same."

"Still don't get what you're saying," Mac responded, getting up to butter more toast.

Mindy squinted her blue eyes until they were just dazzling slits. "Last night you were all huffy about how important this could be. Now, when I find what I think is some evidence, you dismiss me."

Mac looked over from the counter, turning to lean back on it. "You're serious, aren't you?"

"Yes, I am! Look, I'm saying that instead of a range of emotional expressions—the details, not just a smile versus a scowl—the president has no range. Each point of change in policy evokes the same eyebrow position, the same flush ballooning of cheeks, the same flatness of lips."

Mac walked to the back of Mindy's chair. He put his hands on her shoulders and leaned over to kiss her cheek. "Again, I still don't get it."

"Is the shoebox back?" Mindy asked, disconcertedly.

"Nope. Please, pass it by me once more."

"Maybe you need more coffee?" Mindy suggested with a bit of edge.

When Mac moved back to his chair, he put his elbows on the table and stared at her, begging with his look, that she continue.

"Here's the deal, in a nutshell that even you can understand."

Mac sensed she meant, "Even you, with your PTSD." He let it pass.

"The president, our dear Ms. Perserve, is like an automaton. In other words, in how she expresses emotions, she's perfectly consistent. More than I'd say is humanly possible."

Mac shook his head, laughing. "All this conclusion while I was sleeping?"

"Yes, and I can prove it. Let me show you the document I made. You can see for yourself."

After a half hour of Mindy explaining her findings and showing Mac the images, he said, "You're one hell of a sleuth, Mrs. Mac. Truly impressive. No idea what it means or if we all don't show the same consistency of expression. But seriously, it has me wondering if this is what Roy detected. He asked about making love. I mean indirectly…"

Mindy raised her hands in question.

"What he must have meant is that the intimate side of his wife was different. Something only he would pick up on. They've been married, what, almost twenty years? He'd pick up on changes. Yeah, I'm sure!"

"Okay, say she's different. What's that mean? She's on drugs?"

"No idea. But I'd like to talk with Roy about this."

"Mac, I think we're on thin ice. Wouldn't you be totally pissed if some guy you didn't know told you I was different, like weird?"

"Yeah, sure. However, Roy and I have a bond. Hard to describe. I think that bond would make my inquiry acceptable to him. After all, he was the one who started this whole line of inquiry."

Mindy bared her teeth, shaking her head in doubt. "I don't know. I just don't think it's right. Isn't there some other way to test what I found, what we're thinking? Before you talk with Roy."

Mac got up from the table, going back to the sink and looking out the window at the backyard, still covered in snow. He rinsed some of the dishes, then turned to Mindy. "There's a kid up at school. Justin. He was the IT team's geek. I heard he's developed a fake news detection algorithm based on simple lexical analysis."

"What?"

"On word use and frequency. It's really about pattern recognition. I wonder if Justin could write a program that repeated your process, but on many, even hundreds, of images of the president. Synched with her speeches. This would go way beyond that kid's app and give us a better, statistically speaking, sample to share with Roy."

"I guess, maybe," Mindy answered, moving to stand next to Mac as he stared out at the cold morning.

CHAPTER 21

The Analysis

"Professor! It's great to hear from you. I was wondering how you're doing," Justin began, putting down the book he was reading.

"School going well this quarter?" Mac asked, trying to follow a natural line of inquiry. Ever since Justin's overly zealous effort had almost tanked the D37 effort, Mac had remained somewhat suspicious of Justin's forthrightness. "You see Gloria, Blake, the others?"

"Yeah. We usually get together every now and then for a beer. Usually end up talking about D37 and the time you were here."

"For sure. That was an exceptional experience for all of us."

"You recovered? I mean from your head wound. Blake says you're almost back to normal," Justin asked.

"Almost," Mac laughed. "Thanks for asking. Just wanted to check in and find out how're you doing. I heard you've developed some cool new software."

"You mean my fake news app?"

"Yes, that. Does it really work?" Mac asked, cautiously.

"It does. Yeah, works great. Funny thing is, not too many users care one way or the other. What I've learned is that if you claim you've found fake news, you get a whole slew of people who rag at you and claim *you're* the fake news!"

Mac couldn't help laughing. "Sorry. Didn't mean to blow off what you've accomplished. It was a sad laugh. Just meant, it's to be expected. How polarized things got."

"They *are* still polarized," Justin retorted. He continued, "Sorry, Mac. I'm just sensitive about the mess that's politics."

"Sounds like you're getting wise in your old age," Mac joked.

"Maybe. But the whole D37 project. You know, all that we did. It's got me realizing that even with the unity efforts of our new president, gaps still exist. Embedded attitudes just *don't* change."

"Yeah, when you get to my age, the reality you describe is real."

Justin exhaled. "Yeah, you're old, Professor."

They both laughed, hard.

"Speaking of the president," Mac began. "What's your take on her?"

Justin thought for a minute. "She's a breath of fresh air, for sure. Yeah, but what's happening to her just proves how impossible it is to lead America. She's already changing in ways that I find troublesome."

"Like, what?" Mac asked.

"A couple of policy flip-flops. Just a gut feeling."

Mac looked around Mindy's office, taping his fingers, trying to find the best way to broach what he wanted to discuss. He decided that a direct, honest approach was best.

"Justin, there's another reason I'm calling. Interestingly, it has to do with your new app and our new president."

"What? She's fake news?"

Mac laughed, thinking that the dots seemed too easy to connect. Just as he had with Roy.

"No, nothing like that. I was wondering if you could write an app that does what my wife…"

"Oh, Mac! Sorry, man. I forgot to congratulate you. You're now an old married man, huh?"

"Thanks. Yeah, being married to Mindy is, well, more special than I thought possible."

"I've seen her picture. Blake showed me. You're one lucky guy."

Mac nodded as he glanced at some of the photos piled on Mindy's desk. "True, yeah. She is beautiful, inside and out." After a pause, "About the app I had in mind."

"Sure," Justin replied, his thoughts still occupied by Mindy.

"First off, and I really have to emphasize this, I need your solemn promise to keep this totally confidential. Agreed?"

Justin hesitated. "Are we talking something serious, like D37?"

"Could be. Not sure. But what Mindy has done manually is synch some of the president's speeches with her facial expressions. We were hoping you can do the same thing by writing a program."

"You mean, how her expression matches the message? And, yes. I promise to keep all this between just us. My word."

"Good, good. Thanks for that, man. Yeah, exactly. I told Mindy you'd get it," Mac answered, niggled by his memory of how Justin has previously gone ahead on his own, ahead of the team's D37 plan.

"Do you want to email me a detailed description, so I get it right?"

Mac was inclined to agree. Getting it right was crucial. "Yeah, sure, I can do that. Just not sure how to best describe what we have in mind."

"Mac, there's an old saying amongst us software-types: 'You can't define it, I can't program it.'"

Mac realized he was nodding in agreement. "Understood. By the way, this is something I want to keep private. Email is only so good. Not really secure. Let me give you a verbal outline. We want to analyze the density and type of words in her speeches. Like modifiers, adjectives and adverbs, and their targets, the subject and object. Effectively, the *what* and the *how* in her messages. Just like I used to teach."

"I remember well," Justin, interrupted. "Very effective diagnostic approach, to parse things in that framework. Why private?"

"Right," Mac replied, feeling a surge of excitement. "Your app would parse the what and how from a speech, and then, using photos of her during that speech, map the patterns of her facial expression. What we're looking for is a link between the words and whether her facial features are the same for the same words. Make sense?"

Justin repeated back to Mac what he understood was required of the app. "The bottom line is, for each set of words tied to a policy announcement, you want to see if the basic elements of her expression are the same. Right? And why are you thinking private? You've seen all the news relating to changes in her policies? Even that kid's app that tracks changes in her comments."

Mac smiled at Mindy as she walked into the room. He replied, "Private? Because what we're curious about is a total shot in the dark. You were there. You know the whole D37 effort. I got screwed pretty bad. Mainly, want to avoid anything that's political."

Mindy nodded her agreement as she sat on the corner of the desk, almost squashing some photos. "Oops," she yelped.

"Pardon?" Justin asked, hearing Mindy's voice.

Mac answered, "Mindy just came in. Say 'Hi' you two."

Mindy took the phone from Mac. "Hi Justin. I've heard a lot about you from Mac. We really appreciate your help on this little project."

Justin's memory called up the picture Blake had shown him.

"Hi, Mindy. Good to meet the woman who's finally grounded Mac," Justin blurted, rolling his eyeballs at himself, not sure what he'd meant.

"I try," Mindy replied, arching her eyebrows at Mac.

Mac nodded to her as he took back the phone. "Do you have enough to go on?" he asked Justin.

"Let me give it a shot. I'll call to let you know. And we can use a secure FTP site I have to exchange any results. No email. Sound good?"

"Perfect, Justin. I'm glad we're working together again, you know…"

"I am, too," Justin interrupted. "And please know, Professor, that I'll stay inbounds this go-around. No freelancing. I learned my lesson."

"Thanks, man. For your last comment. Means a lot," Mac said as he started to hang up.

"Thanks, Justin!" Mindy yelled at the phone.

—— . ——

Three days later, having worked almost straight through, Justin had finished the program. He had gathered more than three hundred facial images of the president and her accompanying comments as part of the database to feed his program. He wasn't exactly sure what he was looking for, but he wanted to please Mac and he'd grown curious as he studied the many images. By casual glance alone, he felt the president's look had a certain fixed quality. He grew even more excited when he fed in the data and found that her baseline facial expression was almost exactly the same when discussing similar aspects of policy. Especially points reflecting empathy towards a certain foreign country. He ran the database four times. The results were all the same. The president, in spite of her attractiveness and passion, was, under the microscope of his program, like a stone statue. The subtle details of her expressions were unchanging for the same keywords.

It was late Tuesday night, the city-sounds of Boston still slumbering under a blanket of cold overcast. Justin looked around his fraternity-house room. No two ways about it, it was a dump. Clothes were strewn on the floor and furniture, partially eaten takeout food moldered on paper plates, empty soda cans were stacked on shelves. He yawned heavily, feeling he was on a sleepless bender of brilliant creativity and that he could no longer keep his findings to himself. He figured it was too late to call Mac, the newlywed. It took a minute to regain his focus. 'Newlywed' with 'Mindy' had his thoughts elsewhere.

After an exhausting self-debate, he decided to call Blake. At least waking a fellow student and a member of the IT team at this ungodly hour was better and more considerate than waking the Professor. Again, the image of Mindy—in bed—flashed into his mind. Justin set down the Coke can, telling it, "I do need a woman." He dialed.

"Hello...this better be good," came Blake's sleep-deprived voice.

"Did I wake you, man? It's Justin. Tell Gloria I'm sorry to call so late," Justin chuckled, hoping Blake understood why he was aksing about Gloria.

"What the hell, Justin? Any idea of the time?"

"Sorry, Blake."

After a series of prolonged grunts, Blake asked, "So what's up?"

"The past few days, I've been working on a project for Mac..."

"What? The Professor?"

"Yeah, right. It's crazy interesting. Has to do with the president. I'll contact Mac tomorrow to let him know what I've found. Couldn't contain myself. Had to tell someone like you, who's close to Mac."

"Why, for God's sake? Can't it wait until tomorrow? That urgent?"

"I'm not sure. I've been on a bender. Had to talk with someone."

"You want me to come over?" Blake asked cautiously, recalling that Justin could be flakey. Yet also, that he, Blake, had learned from Mac and Gloria the need to care for and support others.

"No, guess not," Justin responded, hesitantly. "Can you come over tomorrow sometime? I want to show it to you."

"Would Mac mind showing me?" Blake asked. "And FYI, Gloria's not here. Don't' worry, she's looking, but still hasn't found a date for you."

They both laughed at the sad truth that Justin was not exactly a babe-magnet.

"I don't think so. You're as close to him as anyone. He does want it kept private, though."

"Tell you what. Gloria and I will come by around... Wait! Is your room still the same pigsty?"

"Yeah, so?"

"How 'bout instead you come over to my place right before dinner? We'll call Mac together. You can eat here with Gloria and me."

"I'd like that," Justin replied, relieved.

"Get some sleep. Don't tell anyone else. Mac, for sure, would be pissed. See you around, say five?"

"Thanks, Blake. Seriously!" Justin hung up, eyeing his bed and imagining someone like Mindy, waiting there for him. "Just you," he sighed to his pillow.

——— . ———

Late the next afternoon, the three IT team members were gathered in Blake's room. "Hey, Mac. It's Blake. I'm here with Justin and Gloria."

"Hey, Blake. What's up? Justin?"

Justin took the phone. "Hi, Mac. I've found some amazing results using the program you wanted. Wait!" Justin's voice went shrill as he heard Mac groan in exasperation. "Wait. I've shown them nothing. To be honest, it's been a real slog, all alone. I needed someone here with me when I tell you. The results are crazy startling. I figured you trust Blake and Gloria more than me. I hope it's okay if I describe what I've found, and show Blake and Gloria as I go?"

Mac took another deep breath. "Justin, did you tell Blake and Gloria what we're looking for?"

"Not yet."

Mac asked Justin to put them on the speakerphone. Mac said, "As I emphasized to Justin, this is private. If what Justin says is true, there could be implications. So before we go any further, I need you all to agree to confidentiality. I trust you, yeah, but you need to understand this could be something serious."

"Another D37?" Gloria asked, her voice conveying concern.

"Who knows. Maybe," Mac replied.

Blake and Justin, in unison, answered, "Yes!"

Gloria added, "Secret, for sure!"

Mac replied, "Great! I'm here with Mindy. Justin, is there any way you can share your screen and the results of your app with us here in New York, in a secure manner?"

"Yeah, easy, man. I'll email you an app. Install it on your computer to create a secure channel we can use to share screens and data. It'll also let us talk using our computers—like a secure speakerphone."

"Just what we need," Mac said, relieved.

"I want to see what you've found," Mindy said into the phone, her voice filled with excitement that her observations might be confirmed.

Once the channel had been established, Justin brought up a spreadsheet on his screen. "I've made seven columns. They're sorted by Perserve's keywords in column one. Column two is the date of the speech or image, and columns three, four, five, and six show her lips, eye dilation, eyebrows, and the folds in her cheeks against her nose. Column seven shows the image variance, the difference or delta, from the image in the prior keyword-sequenced row, sorted by column one. Basically, I overlaid in column seven, for each ascending row, the image from the prior row. You can see that there is almost no change in column seven for the same keywords. Almost a perfect overlay. No change at all. It's not possible. That's why I got so excited and had to share this with Blake and Gloria. Mac, I have no idea what you and Mindy discovered. But one thing for sure, this *is* crazy."

Mac was not sure he believed what he was seeing on Justin's shared screen. Doubt evident in his tone, he asked, "Justin, you sure you aren't comparing the same image against itself? Seems impossible that there is little to no change—delta as you call it. I felt the same way when Mindy made her suggestion. I doubted it. That's why we got you involved."

"Mac, I ran the data four times. No way the images are duplicated. It's for real. So... what's it mean? Hey, Mindy, what did you suspect?" Justin asked, his voice tinged slightly with the joy of having others appreciate his work.

"I'm not sure, honestly, what to make of it. Thought maybe the president is on drugs or something," Mindy replied. "But what you've found, Justin, goes way beyond what I was imagining."

"Hey, Mac," Blake asked, still amazed as Justin's revelation. "Why did you and Mindy even think to look at Perserve this way? Is there more to the story?"

Mac answered, "Can't say for now, Blake. I need to confirm some things. You guys can see why this needs to be kept quiet. Right?"

"For sure. Scary," Gloria injected.

Justin was biting his fingernails, lost in nervous thought.

"You okay, man?" Blake asked.

"There's more..." Justin moaned. "I'm hesitant to say what, even though we're on a secure line. Yeah, it involves Perserve, but I went one step further. I applied concentric math modeling which shows an effect I can't even start to explain. Mac, I gotta show you this in person. I can take the Acela train down tomorrow."

Mac turned to Mindy. "How's your schedule tomorrow?"

Mindy spoke up, "As you guys may know, Mac doesn't have a job, yet. Yeah, tomorrow works for both of us."

"Wait," Mac responded. "I have a meeting in the morning at the VA with Major Evans. Justin, how urgent is this?"

"It's got me not sleeping. Put it that way. It's crazy, like I said."

Mac took Mindy's hand. He whispered, "What'd you think?"

Mindy leaned over, "I don't know Justin, but he seems really upset. I say he comes down here ASAP."

Mac, feeling a familiar stress behind his eyes, said, "Justin, come down tomorrow, first thing. To Mindy's. Blake has her address. I'll be out for a few hours, so begin by showing Mindy what you have."

Blake asked, "Mac? Gloria and I'd like to be involved. That okay with you? We can catch the noon train, right after classes."

"Yeah, sure," Mac replied hesitantly, sensing echoes in the shoebox.

CHAPTER 22

The Loss

After thanking the Uber driver, Justin walked gingerly through the snow down the alley to Mindy's house. His teeth were chattering more from nerves—the prospect of meeting Mindy—than the arctic blast that had paralyzed the East Coast for the seventh straight week.

Before Justin could ring her doorbell, Mindy opened the door, startling him. He had to catch himself from slipping on the ice. She was more beautiful than her picture.

"Hey, Justin!" Mindy yelped, grabbing his arm to keep him from falling. "I'd hate to see you land on your laptop," she laughed, trying to warm her welcome of this gangly young man whose long hair, deep-set brown eyes, and acne scars seemed to highlight his awkwardness. She pulled him inside, closing the door.

Justin stamped his feet on her threshold rug, looking down at the pile of snow left from his boots. "Oh, oh! Sorry 'bout the snow," he stuttered. He could still see his breath in the warm air of her house. He pulled off his laptop bag and removed his coat.

"Here," Mindy said, reaching out to hang his heavy black coat on a nearby antique rack. "Not much of a mud room in these condos," she joked. Putting her hand on his shoulder to move him aside, she opened the door, brushing the snow outside with a small broom. She turned to face Justin who was still considering the rug and how to look at Mindy. "You made good time coming down from Boston. How was the train ride?"

"It was good. I slept most of the way."

"I bet you needed it. Sounds like you built a really neat program. And there's more, you said?"

"Yeah, there's more. Actually, I really didn't sleep much on the train. Not much since we talked yesterday. Is Mac here? He won't believe what I've found. Not sure I do!"

"He's at the VA. He'll be home in an hour or two. Can I get you some coffee or hot chocolate?"

"Coffee would be great. Black. Thank you," Justin replied, reaching down to untie his boots.

Mindy watched him with appreciation. Awkward, but considerate. He wobbled as he tugged on the laces of his right boot, his left arm splaying in the air. Mindy moved fast to take hold of his left elbow. "Slipping on the ice outside is one thing, but here in my front hall? Not allowed."

They both laughed. Justin moved his free hand to squeeze Mindy's hand. He hunched his shoulders in mockery to his poor balance. "Sleep deprived and cold. Coffee?"

Mindy led Justin into the kitchen. He gulped in the warm air as his soul soaked in the warm colors and the loving atmosphere of the house. It was like the home he had always longed for.

He closed his eyes, sipping the coffee, savoring the feeling of family. At least this was how he imagined an intact family's home felt. He opened his eyes, taking in the image of Mindy in her blue-and-white checked wrap blouse, her lovely brown hair, and her piercing blue eyes. He thought he was in love.

Mindy went to the counter. "More coffee?" she asked as she pulled the pot from the coffeemaker. She was standing in silhouette, backlit by the kitchen window.

Justin choked, blinking his eyes several times to shed the dream he was having. "Yes, please," he whispered. Clearing his throat, and also he hoped, his mind, he added, "When did you say Mac would be back? I'm anxious to show you guys what I have."

"Why not start with me? Mac's a fast study on this tech stuff. It'll give me a head start," Mindy answered with such genuine warmth that Justin had to fight down his imaginings once again.

Walking gingerly in his socks so as not to slip on the kitchen floor, Justin retrieved his laptop from the hall coat rack. He set it up on the antique coffee table in her living room, sat on the sofa and looked up as Mindy brought in the coffee. He moved slightly to the side so they both could view the laptop's screen.

"Yeah, this is a good idea," he said, turning to watch Mindy sit next to him. She sank into the plush cushions, bringing their hips together. Some voice in the back of his head was yelling, "What the hell are you doing, idiot?"

Mustering all his willpower, Justin began. "Let me start with what we covered yesterday." He brought up the spreadsheet and, pointing at the screen, explained the comparative data. He focused on column seven which showed how the president's expressions were identical for the same key words. "So, you've seen this. Looks suspicious, right?" he continued, turning to look at Mindy and trying to forget how close she was to him.

"Yeah. So far, so good," she answered with an enthusiasm that Justin soaked in, causing a few typos as he brought up the next screen.

"Now for the really disturbing stuff!" Putting his finger to the center of the screen, he said, "This looks like just a jumble of circles, right? What it is, is a portrait—call it a display—of President Perserve's life. Like, for the past thirty years. I created the data set for this display by summarizing information from *Wikipedia* and other sources I used on the Web to get her pics and videos. The videos were an aside to what you and Mac wanted me to analyze. I thought that capturing them in datasets, for whatever reason, might somehow be helpful. And boy! What it ended up revealing is totally bizarre!"

Mindy put her hand on Justin's arm to calm him. "Tell me."

"I mentioned it yesterday. Didn't want to say more over the phone. The concentric math model has been used by only a few in research. It's still a new concept for studying patterns. It goes well beyond the types of data structures and queries used to mine big data."

"You're starting to lose me, a bit," Mindy offered softly.

"Okay. Not important, other than to say that big data experts have not embraced concentric math. It seems too elementary and simple. And simple doesn't justify big budgets," Justin said, his awkwardness gone. He was in his element.

"Let's look at the results. I used concentric math to plot behavior points of the president over time, from Kansas politics to her campaign and her first two months as president."

"What's the purpose? I mean, I'm sure there's already a ton of presidential historians trying to tie together the influences in her life."

"Right," Justin responded. "But those are basic patterns at the macro level. What concentric reveals is the density of patterns at the micro level."

Mindy's hand went to the screen. A gesture of confusion.

Justin, anxious to impress Mindy, leaned back in the sofa, playing with his shirt collar. She was leaning into the laptop as he put his hand on her shoulder. "Concentric allows us to slow things down, to see what you might call the rhythms of her life. It's analogous to the rings in trees. You know, when they do tree-ring dating."

"It tracks the president's age?"

"No, no," Justin answered, frustrated that he was not being cogent.

"Forgive me, Justin, but her age isn't any great insight. Aside from this project, though, I had a flash. I wonder if your concentric math could be used to find patterns in photographs?"

"I hadn't thought about that, but yeah, that's possible. Here's why. Light is what lets you see anything, like photographs. Light travels in waves—call them patterns. For example, light from the sun or from a flashlight. Colors are just light at different wavelengths—a different unique pattern. I know this all sounds techie, but even holograms are created by the combining patterns of light. This ties into what I've found studying the images, using concentric math."

Mindy turned to Justin, putting her hand on his knee in innocent amazement. "Holograms? Is what you've discovered have to do with…"

The door of her condo slammed open as Mac came in, followed by a heavy gust of wind. "Man! It's like… freezing out there!" he exclaimed. Looking into the living room, he saw Mindy and Justin on the couch, seemingly shocked by his entry, her hand leaving Justin's knee.

After a long stare, the cold air filling the house, Mac closed the door. He'd noticed Mindy discreetly moving away from Justin.

"What're you guys up to?" he asked, pointedly.

Justin, oblivious to the implication made by Mac and feeling just the warmth of being with Mac and Mindy in their house, said, "I was showing Mindy what I came to show you."

"Mindy?" Mac asked, his face growing angry, ignoring Justin. "You guys... cozy? I come home and find you two..."

Mindy stood, taking in a deep breath, her eyes ablaze. Her mind was burning with the meaning of love and trust. "Cozy? What's that mean?" She turned, pointing to Justin who sat frozen on the sofa. "You barge in here and instantly throw a jealous fit? That's ridiculous. Your distrust is hurting me! More than you can possibly know. I'm your wife, for God's sake. Yeah, and with God's blessing. Of *all* the things you might imagine or think, my faithfulness to you, to our marriage under God, is sacrosanct! You're being an ass!"

She stood, bumping the coffee table hard. Justin reached to grab his laptop and coffee cup. Scrambling around the table, she stood before Mac, her voice raised, "What's with you? I'm your wife. Justin's your friend. Oh, Mac, darn you for even thinking what you're implying!"

Giving Mac a shove, she turned and ran down the hall to the bedroom, slamming the door. Throwing herself on the bed, she buried her face in a pillow, its smell of Mac overcoming her strength to think. Her work as a photographer had exposed her to the many burrs and barbs in relationships: in families, with boyfriends, and with fellow workers on projects. And yes, Mac at his core, was a most wonderful man. But, he had baggage. Baggage not apparent at the outset. How could this wonderful husband be such a fool? How could she deal with his issues—the ghosts that roamed and the doubts that filled his mind.

She felt the dampness in the pillow, blinking against its fabric, sensing the tears pooling. Her chest heaved with sobs she tried to silence deep within the pillow. Had she not always treated others with love and sought not to judge or gossip. Done what she imagined God asked of her? Where was the fairness? Mindy rolled over, brushing back her lush brown hair and wiping her eyes. She stared—her eyes narrowing—at the ceiling. Just like Mac, lost in thought. Her eyes went to the Impressionist paintings on her bedroom wall, settling on the print of Cailleboote's *Floor Scrapers*. She raised up on her elbows, admiring Cailleboote's ability to create an almost photo-like reality: the lines of the floor enhancing the dedication and effort of the workers. It reminded Mindy of her mother, cleaning the kitchen floor. Daily. Of her father renovating the rooms in their house. All labors of love. All labors in addition to raising a family and dealing with their own relationship issues. How, throughout her childhood, her mother had always been the calming force. A force, she realized, not for reasons of ego, but simply with steadfast dedication. "Dedication," Mindy thought. "Grace and dedication. Qualities in short supply these days." Even so, she seethed that Mac had allowed the ogre of doubt and jealously into their marriage. She rose from the bed, determined to set Mac straight.

Mac stared at Justin shrinking into the sofa. Justin had said he would stay inbounds this time. In-bounds, where? Mac was spent. He was not sure what questions he was asking Mindy or himself. He stood like an ice sculpture with shoes shedding snow. He looked down at the mess he was making on the rug, so much like the mess melting in his mind. His session with Major Evans had not gone well. She had confirmed his CTE. She had tried to comfort Mac, to reassure him that his was a mild case and that it would not affect his life expectancy or his ability to lead a productive life. And now, when he comes home to seek reassurance from the one person he trusts, he depends on, he finds her with another man. Not even a man. A grubby geek.

Mindy's crying from the bedroom etched his soul. He turned to the hall mirror, its antique gold frame bracketing his image. What he saw as a lost cause. He understood it was the end of the road. That he had to finally come to grips with the loss of his brother Sam, his band of brothers, his reputation, his job, his health, and now his wife.

And, with CTE—the shoebox—probably himself.

CHAPTER 23

The Shadow

Just as suddenly as the front door had burst open with Mac and that gust of wind, the bedroom door flung open as Mindy ran at Mac. She slapped him hard across the face. "This is your last chance, dumb shit!" She turned, pointing to Justin. "Look at him! Look at me! What could you possibly be thinking?"

Almost in tears, Justin closed his laptop and stood to leave. "Mac, I…" Justin started, before Mac's hand shot up for silence.

Mac, the decorated warrior, the hero of the D37 plot, the love of Mindy's life, sank to the floor, his knees collapsing, his chin in his chest.

Mindy, her chin up, her sniffing giving way to resolve, turned to Justin. "Could you please leave. I'm sorry you had to see this."

Justin sat back on the sofa, his head in his hands, quiet sobs leaking out between his fingers.

Mac, too, was quietly crying, his spirit broken. He'd endured too much. He'd been given so much, but he'd lost even more. He'd always tried, but missed gaining hold of that elusive brass ring. Now he was falling, failing. The shoebox his final destination.

Or so allowed the self-pity that, for the first time in his life, he was embracing. "She slapped my scar. Shit! How she must hate me?" he thought in shame as his emotions swam ahead of his courage. "What courage?" he wondered. He opened his eyes. Less than a foot away in front of him were Mindy's legs. Mac was tormented. Oh, how he wanted to reach out to her calves, her ankles. To kiss her feet. To hold on for dear life. To shake them back into allowing his caresses and his love. What had Mindy yelled? "Last chance!" Oh, such misery, to be inches away from the legs he loved, the person he loved and the heart he loved and cherished. That word, *cherish*. Wasn't it a cornerstone of their love? Didn't he cherish and need Mindy? Hadn't he come home to lean on her strength? Why couldn't he control his mind better? Why couldn't he simply outgrow the damn shoebox? Why couldn't he buck up from the doctor's diagnosis? He'd been to hell and back, sure. That meant he was able. Why didn't he see the fullness of Mindy's love, her devotion? He was able. So why didn't he?

"Mac, oh Mac. Please! You're hurting my legs," Mindy whispered as she leaned down to pull Mac up. "Yes, you *are* able!"

Mac realized that his plea—his questions—had been spoken aloud. Mindy had heard his ranting, his cry. He had been embracing her legs.

"I'm going. Sorry I came," Justin's voice broke as he reached for his coat.

Mac stood, leaning on Mindy. His hand went to his eyes, his tears, just as hers went to his scar. His burning scar. "Oh, Mac, my Mac," she repeated. "What will we do with you?" She reached out, grabbing Justin's arm. She took a deep breath, grinding her teeth.

Wiping his eyes, Justin put his laptop back on the table.

"So, Mac?" Mindy began. "Let's say I walk in and see you two on the sofa together. What am I to think? A couple of gay guys playing solitaire? Come on, Mac, think about it. Think about our love, our words. Think about our confessing our love before God. Think about the joy it brings me to care for you. Do you really *not* get it?"

"It's my fault..." Justin began.

"No way!" Mindy responded. "Mac walks in, assumes the worst—without thinking—and throws a fit. A totally stupid fit. We need to deal with this, here and now!"

"Mindy... I don't think that's the way it happened. I can see Mac's point," Justin moaned, pausing to gather his thoughts. He sighed heavily, his eyes wide. "All right. I admit to you Mac, as someone I totally respect, and to you, Mindy—someone I've dreamed of knowing—that I let my attraction to you," he pointed at Mindy, "keep me from keeping my distance. I welcomed your touch. It was so kind and friendly. And well, given my shitty life, I just didn't want it to stop. Mac? Mindy was just being warm and caring. She was excited about what I was showing her. It's my fault. I didn't stay in-bounds. When I realized, just now, how wanting to be part of your lives caused such a problem, I was ready to bolt out the door. Like, forever. But, *no*! I see that what I have to show you is *too* important. I *must* show you!"

Mindy released Mac, gently pushing him away and cocking her head slightly as she gave him a stern look, her eyebrows raised. "Mac? Do you see how you made a mountain out of nothing? Did you stop to think that Justin, in his classic geek mode, was... forgive me, Justin..." She walked to the sofa and put her hand on his shoulder. "Lonely?"

Mac stood on the entrance rug, his wet shoes squeaking as he rocked back and forth, his head on his chin, his lips tight. "I'm a mess," he began. "I had a hard time at the VA and I was looking for your support. Not looking for what I saw with you two on the couch."

"What you saw was something in your imagination, nothing more. I'm sorry for slapping you, but as I lay crying on our bed, I was overcome with pain—a hole in my heart so huge I didn't think was possible. How your doubt in me is *ruining* the preciousness of our love. I was angry and beyond mad. I know you're fragile at times," she said as she moved back to Mac, taking his hands in hers. She put her arms around him, rocking him to get a reaction.

Mac closed his eyes, holding her tight. He bit his lip as he looked out at Justin, sitting on the sofa, so forlorn.

"I've been so wrong these past couple of times," Mac whispered, his chin over Mindy's shoulder. "I'm such an unknown quantity. Not predictable. I won't use the b-word, but it's who I am."

Mindy kissed his cheek and then his scar, pulling back to look up into his eyes. Her lips curled into the slightest smile as she recalled when she had first seen those emerald eyes, there in the ditch. Eyes filled with such uncertainty, yet soulful beauty. Without mentally dwelling on each point in their lives since, she knew that even with Mac's confusion, he was the only man she had ever wanted, or would ever want. The only issue before them was how to help him understand his condition. She briefly wondered if he'd had uncertainty when leading his troops. Maybe civilian life was not for him? Maybe he was strongest when absorbed—lost in the life and death challenges of the battlefield? She let out a sad whimper, acknowledging for the Nth time that his PTSD and CTE issues were not going away.

And neither was she. "This storm, too, will pass," she whispered back. "We'll find better times. Even when we go through these episodes—and there will be more—we'll survive. This, if you will always remember it, *is* my promise to you."

Justin had been fiddling with his laptop, trying not to be part of Mac and Mindy's private moment. Mindy turned to the sounds of his keystroking. "Guess you see that life can be shitty for all of us, huh?" she laughed, weakly.

Justin let out a croak, his chin snapping to the side, hoping to stop the tears. After stilling his hands on the keyboard, he gazed intently at the fireplace, its embers gone cold. Leaning back with a cleansing breath, he replied, "At least you guys don't yell at each other."

Mac's hand went to his scar as his mind went to her slap. And Mindy's words. "Not, usually," he mumbled.

He walked over to Justin and, pulling him up from the couch, wrapped him in a manly embrace. Through her own tears, Mindy looked with sympathy at Justin's face resting on Mac's shoulder, his eyes wide as more tears flowed.

Mac stepped back, clapping his hands. "I ask, for what seems the millionth time, Mindy, for your forgiveness. With your continued love and patience, we *will* get through this."

Turning back to Justin, he said, "Man, you too. I apologize! Things just piled up, and with this little project being all too important, my mind got sidetracked, thinking you were hustling Mindy," he said, croaking out the laugh of an embarrassed fool. Mac went to the fireplace mantel and paused. "Why, man, did you say your life is shitty? How? Is it classes, your future?"

Justin sat back on the sofa, his legs intertwined under the table. "It's harder than that. My parents yell all the time. Shit! They're getting a divorce. To top that, I've never had a real girlfriend or a good family life. You two seem to, well, have a good life together as a family."

Mindy realized the mood was descending into an unnecessary downer. "We can be your family, Justin. We'd like that. For sure. So now, I'd like to get back to what you were showing me." She sat next to Justin, patting the sofa for Mac to sit on the other side of her. "Justin was telling me about concentric math. How it could reveal patterns in light. Like, in holograms."

Justin reached around Mindy to tap Mac's shoulder. "Want me to review the math or the holograms?" he asked.

Mac answered, "No. I know about holograms. The Army was considering using holograms as decoys. Didn't get very far. Not sure about the math," he shrugged, "but continue. I'll stop you if I get lost."

Justin sat up straight. He felt warmer, more intimate with both Mac and Mindy. They were real. Like him, they had problems. And they could be his family. He opened a new window on his laptop. "When I was preparing the results of my program to see if the president's expressions were, like, set in stone, I decided to also analyze a video of her. I got it off *ABC*. It was taken last week, when she was leaving the Kennedy Center. I wanted to see what her facial expressions were like in a video. Did they vary when she looked at the crowd. This is where I applied a concentric math filter. It effectively slows the motion to fractions of frames per second. Normal video runs about 30 fps... frames per second. With my filter, I was able to parse each frame into inter-looping pixel patterns of a fiftieth, then a hundredth. You know, a thousandth and so on. As I slowed things down more, I noticed pixel-ripples in her movement. These seemed to emanate from what appeared to be a hidden shadow. It was weird, but I thought maybe it was typical. So I ran other videos through the same filter. Videos of other politicians, even the president during her inauguration. None of those had any shadow effect. No ripples whatsoever."

"What's it mean?" Mindy asked quietly.

"Couldn't it be some optical illusion?" Mac wondered. "Maybe it has to do with the bandwidth limitation of your laptop. Like, it can't keep up with the display speed?"

"No. The exact opposite is true. We're not trying to shovel more data through the computer's processor. We're isolating fractions. So it's not bandwidth. I searched the Web a couple hours before our call yesterday. Studied all kinds of posts on optical distortion. The causes and effects. Nothing like what I saw with her video. Let me show you."

Justin reran the video, applying the concentric math filter. He stopped at each incremental fraction as the speed slowed, the subtle ripples and the weird shadow becoming more prominent.

They were dumbfounded, intently focused on the screen, when a loud knock on the door caused them to jump.

"What the…" Mac started.

Justin looked at his watch. "Might be Gloria and Blake. They'd be getting in around now."

Mindy said, "Mac, get the door. And wipe up the rug, could you?"

Mac raised his arm in question. "We going to share this with them? Justin, maybe you should shut down?"

On her way to the kitchen, Mindy responded over her shoulder, "No, leave it on. They're part of your IT team. We need all the brainpower we can muster to understand what we're seeing. To decide what to do next."

With the continued knocking, Mac yelled, "Coming!" He pulled a towel from the hall closet, laying it on the entrance rug. Mac opened the door to find Blake and Gloria huddled together, using the recessed entrance as a shield from the wind.

"Mac! We're freezing. Thank goodness you're home," Blake blurted, pushing Gloria into the hall. Justin rearranged the chairs around the coffee table as Mindy brought in more coffee

"Whew," Blake shivered, his hair flecked with flakes. "Great to be warm again."

"Your house is warm *and* lovely," Gloria said, smiling at Mindy.

Holding their coffee mugs to warm their hands, Blake and Gloria took a minute to catch their breath. Blake leaned to the side to brush flakes from his hair.

"Blake!" Gloria growled. "Not on the rug!"

They all laughed, exchanging nods and smiles of friendship. Happy that they were all together. Blake looked over at the fireplace. "No Boy Scouts in the building, huh? Mind?" he asked Mindy.

"Please, yes. Mac was out early this morning at the VA Center."

"How's that going? I mean," Gloria asked, pausing to find the right words. "Are they helping?"

Mindy and Justin stole quick glances.

Mac sipped his coffee, watching Blake build the fire. "Going pretty good, I'd say. Still some issues, but I'm thankful for what they offer." He nodded at Mindy, who smiled back.

With the fire crackling, Blake made sure the screen was in place before returning to his chair. "So what's up? Any further insight into the big mystery of the president?" Looking at the others' long faces, he asked, "What?"

Mindy, sitting on the sofa between Justin and Mac, said, "There's been an unforeseen development. Something Justin has unearthed. Brilliantly, I should add." She patted Justin's knee.

Mac responded, on cue. "More than brilliant. Before we go further, I gotta tell you, Blake, Gloria, that this project has gone from serious to mysterious. It's top secret, in terms of our IT team bond. No more need be said in that regard," he continued to the nods of Blake and Gloria. "In a nutshell, Justin has discovered an anomaly in the..."

"Patterns of light comprising the images of the president," Justin finished for Mac.

"Right. Thanks, Justin. What's more, it seems to happen only in the most recent videos of the president. What we're going to show you will blow your mind. There's also a shadow that seems to follow the president's image."

"Show us," Blake said. "Maybe it's a new protective security? I don't know, like a Secret Service aura they've created to surround her?" He laughed at his own imagination.

"Anything's possible, sure," Mac concluded. "See for yourself. It's a shadow with ripples. I have concerns I can't share right now." He looked at Mindy, who frowned back. "I don't think it's anything the president, her family, or her security detail knows about."

Blake and Gloria traded places with Mac and Mindy. After viewing the video twice, Blake rose to warm his hands by the fire. "Can't believe it! Totally weird. And what's with that shadow? Is that the real president?" he exclaimed.

"What should we do?" Gloria asked. "Contact the FBI?"

Mindy cleared her throat, looking at Mac. "Roy?"

CHAPTER 24

The Sway

The ridges of the distant mountains, gray in the flat morning light, blended seamlessly with the overcast sky, matching Margie's mood. Dong had left her to her sobs which had continued through the night. With heavy clouds screening the sun, Margie rose to tug, once more, on the bars of the windows. She tugged more in frustration at the unknown than in an attempt to escape. Although escape was foremost in her mind. Almost. Her thoughts drifted to memories of family and dear friends like Brianna from her days interning at the State Department. To memories of overcoming challenges while striving for unity among the many varied people that comprised the citizenry of America and the world. She pictured Kari and Todd, perhaps bowling or swimming with Roy at the White House. Roy? How could he not have detected something different in this replica that Dong claimed to have created? It was impossible to think he didn't. Didn't the kids notice? More importantly, didn't America? It was being misled. Dangerously so. All these thoughts intersected at one conclusion: she must escape! She must live to escape. She must warn the world of the technology that Dong had unleashed. That was all that mattered now.

Her thoughts pinned her hands to the bars. The urgency. The dire consequences. She searched through the windows for signs of guards. She saw none. Focused as she was, she did not hear Dong enter the hut.

"Good morning, Margie," Dong said, her voice even sweeter than before.

Margie turned, scowling. "There is nothing good about it as long as I am in here and that creation of yours is loose!"

Dong sat on the mat, motioning Margie to take the chair next to her. "I see from the redness of your hands, that you have been struggling with the bars. And... from the red furrows in your brow, with your situation."

Margie scoffed. "What do you expect. Otherwise?"

"The video cameras that we have monitoring these rooms," Dong swept her right arm in a wide arc, hoping Margie took note, "show you crying during the night. I watched, mesmerized. Your anguish seemed so true and honest. Did you not hear me yesterday when I said, 'it cannot be'? Do you think no one else has anguish? I, too, lay awake. Your anguish is my anguish. Almost the entire night, I thought, too, of our conversation yesterday. About religion. About the soul. Please, come with me to the bathroom."

The Leader, back in the pagoda, up early and glued to the video feed, frowned, unsure of the tactic Dong was using.

"I'm fine where I am," Margie retorted. "You may control me as you try, but I am not your prisoner. I am the *President* of the United States. I am... God's child!"

Although he knew nothing of her strange language, the strident urgency in Margie's voice had the Leader salivating with imagination. His dreams last night, featuring many pigs, had him high in anticipation.

Dong rose, approached Margie and ran Margie' hair through her hands as if to study its texture. Dong leaned over, whispering, "I told you to trust me. I did not order it. Trust cannot be ordered or inflicted. That is what I struggled with last night. So, please. In the bathroom we can talk more openly."

Margie took a deep breath, her loud sigh creating a murmur in the Leader's groin.

Margie followed Dong into the bathroom. "Why here?"

Dong rolled her eyes to the door frame. "Here, let me wash your hair." She turned on the water. The gurgling water, as it hit the drain, filled the room with background sound.

"What the..." Margie watched as Dong, with her back to the door frame, rolled her eyes to the ceiling. For the first time in weeks— however long she had been captive—Margie felt a shock: not of pain, but of hope.

As she washed Margie's hair, Dong tapped out some sort of signal on Margie's scalp. Was it the rhythm of a lullaby? Dong left the water running as she brought a towel to Margie's head, drying her hair in gentle strokes.

The Leader's hands, as he watched the video, moved with similar strokes, his breathing rapid. "Any minute now, I will take over," he said to the reedy prints on the wall.

Knowing the sound of the running water would interfere with the audio of the Leader's video, lowering her voice Dong asked, "In your American culture, is trust the opposite of enmity?"

Margie shook her shoulders ever so slightly, hoping Dong took that as a signal.

Dong patted Margie's shoulder, adding, "I understand."

Margie almost caught the sob bubbling up from her heart. The shudder of her body. Almost.

"I understand," Dong repeated, gently stilling Margie's head—for the briefest moment—in her hands, as if she were holding a newborn.

Margie suddenly held up her arms. She wanted Dong to stop. She imagined she was being hoodwinked by Dong, who, this morning, was playing the good, caring cop. A fresh start to the interrogation. Margie rose, turning to Dong. "Please stop this charade! Do you understand that word, Dong?" As she sought to have her look of anger and distain burn a hole through Dong, Margie noticed tears welling at the edges of Dong's eyes.

Dong choked, working her mouth, her lips warped in torment. "Is this how your God feels when you reject him?" Dong asked, wiping her own face with the towel and thinking, "The Leader must not see this foolish emotion I am showing. But to hell with him! I feel something inside me. As if I am one of those humans free to have a soul."

Dong pushed Margie back into the chair facing the sink, away from the doorframe's video camera. She leaned into the back of Margie's head as she continued drying her hair. Dong asked, in a whisper, "Is trust the opposite of doubt, so that doubt and enmity are the same?"

Margie's shoulders sagged. She was subdued by doubt. Doubt that she could trust Dong. Doubt that she would escape. Yet, there was no doubt that Dong's caresses were, as Margie imagined, how she had caressed Todd and Kari as infants. How she had caressed Roy after an afternoon of sweets. A caress of pure, enduring, human-to-human love. A touch of safety.

"Dong," Margie answered. "Trust might have elements of doubt. But trust is not what you feel when you have enmity towards someone. I do not know if I trust you. I doubt you and your motives. I feel enmity towards all that you have done and are trying to accomplish!"

"I understand," Dong replied quietly. "And I agree with all you just said." She squeezed Margie's shoulder hard to emphasize her point. "You have no reason to trust me. I understand. However, that thinking leaves no room for a person to change." Lowering her mouth to Margie's ear, Dong said, "I have seen the light, as you Christians like to say. No, no..." she continued, pushing Margie's head back away from the cameras. "No, I am only speaking by example. The anguish I felt last night and the fear I feel right now in your rejection of me, is for you, my child. For you and all that you have given birth to. I can't explain it. But I now see that... as you put it, 'what we are trying to accomplish' as an investment solely in the ego of one man. When so many suffer as the price for that ego. Do I make myself clear?"

"Words, Dong. Only words. How do I know you mean well?"

"How do I get you to trust me? That is the question, and the answer to your survival." Dong took a firm hold of the back of Margie's shoulders. "Perhaps you need not trust me, but instead, trust the reason why I have had this revelation. A softening of my heart that was so hard that it stood as stone to all the pleas and cries of those, my victims. Why I am vacillating. It is a matter of loyalty. I have been loyal to a cause comprised of one man's thirst for power. His greed! Your resolve and your answers to my questions have caused me to question my loyalty. I see now that a loyalty to one other human, man or woman, who injects pain and suffering in others, does not reflect a soul. God-made or otherwise. I see that. Truly, I have been swayed by something"

Margie pulled away from Dong's grasp, turning to face her tormentor. All she saw were large, dark eyes filled with quiet tears of hurt. Tears of suffering and sorrow. And guilt.

"Oh, Dong!" Margie started.

"Enough!" Dong yelled over the sound of the water as she pushed Margie back around so they were both facing away from the cameras. She took firm hold of Margie's shoulders, screaming, "Enough, enough!" She leaned in to Margie's ear, whispering, "Enough doubt. Please, on my life! We *must* make my interrogation look authentic. The Leader is watching. Please know, my child, that I will help you escape. You must play along. I must make this look like hard interrogation."

"Dong?"

"Enough," Dong whispered again. Pushing Margie hard against the sink, Dong screamed, "You must tell me! You resist my efforts. I was trying to help you. Now, I must turn you over to other sources. Ones that will learn what you know!" She slapped the back of Margie's head.

"Ow! Dong?"

The Leader felt the slap, smiling that he, too, would soon be slapping *his* baggage. He jumped from his chair. Dong had failed. He would deal with her as she deserved: the barracks. And with this foreign woman, slaps and all.

Dong dragged Margie back into the main room of the hut. Pinning her to the mat, Dong whispered, "They will be coming shortly. For you and for me. We have little time. Listen carefully, for I will tell you how to escape. And know, that our Leader has freaky sexual fantasies. I wish them upon no woman, especially you… my child."

Margie choked, "Dong, do I trust you?" She struggled to break the hold.

"You have no choice. Not now. Here is the plan. You *must* follow it. Our Leader will have you brought to his room under guard escort. His fantasies will be in your favor. He loves foreplay. You must go along. He drinks, but not well. He does not speak English. So you must gesture to him that while you will prepare for his pleasure, you are more amorous with drink. You must get him drunk. You must play the game well. It is your only choice."

Margie gasped, fear and doubt warping her face.

"It is the only way. Please! Wait for him to doze. Time it well. It is risky, yes. But it's your *only* option. If you can get him to sleep, there is a door behind the drapes next to the bed. It leads to a high-walled private garden. As with the entire compound, security cameras are everywhere. To make it through the garden undetected, find and wear layers of the Leader's clothes—coat, pants. Also, a hat. The cold of the night can be fierce. Hunch down as you walk through the garden. Do not rush. At the back of the garden is a tall security gate that opens to the edge of the forest. The gate code is six-six-six-six-nine-one. Be sure to take water and fruit from the bedroom table. Beyond the forest edge, I cannot tell you. It is dense and impenetrable. The mountains fierce. But you can do this! You have come far in your life. You have a faith that will guide you. Keep heading in the direction of the sunrise, towards the east. Let mountains peaks be your daytime guides. East takes you to the sea, where there can be safety. More for you I cannot do, other than... what is it you do? Pray?"

As Dong released her hold, Margie immediately hugged Dong, who pushed her away, shaking her head in caution.

Margie whispered, "We are God's creation. Most people are good. Dong, you are good, I can see your soul." She hugged Dong again.

"I have a soul?" Dong asked, her voice breaking. "The Leader is human, but does *he* have a soul?"

"All humans do," Margie replied rapidly, standing as she heard guards at the hut's door. Her father's words, 'You have skills from God,' sparked conviction in her eyes. She would use those skills to return to her family and lead America. She would!

"Humans?" Dong asked herself as she was pushed forcefully to her knees by the guards. She looked back at Margie. Their eyes met in an exchange of understanding, gratitude, and love.

Margie, struggling with the guards, seeing Dong on her knees with her hands folded, yelled out, "God bless you... Mother."

CHAPTER 25

The Escape

The Leader sat at his vanity mirror, preening, making sure his long, black hair was neatly tied, his cologne pungent. Satisfied, he jumped up, walking around his Napoleonesque bedchamber, noting stains in the rug here, dust in the corner there. He bit his lip. Heads would roll.

Although she was mere baggage, he knew this American president would be an exceptional treat. His appearance, and that of the room, must put him on par with the great wealth of *America*, causing her to succumb to his power... his size. He would appear a great leader. A hero. He laughed, thinking of Dong's hero, Cassidy. "Yes! I will ride this baggage better than Cassidy might," he bellowed.

Sounds of trucks and yelling from guards trickled in through the open windows. He adjusted the room's sound system, raising the volume to mask the harsh outside sounds of reality.

"Where are they?" he yelled at the reedy prints on the wall. He tugged at the sash on his robe, pulling it tight, girdle-like. He was about to sample, for the first time, a non-fireplug body. His must be of similar form. He inhaled deeply, pulling again on the sash. He was beyond excited. "Calm, calm," he repeated. "Let the moment evolve, uniting my ampleness with the mystery of this woman."

Finally, a knock on the door. "Enter," he commanded. He stood at an angle to the bedpost he was holding. He imagined himself a fearsome admiral gripping the mast of his ship, sailing into victory.

The diminutive, fear-filled face of his translator came into view between the massive, yawning double doors. "Dear Leader? May I be of service in directing this woman?" He stood aside to gesture towards the president standing behind him, her gray-blue eyes afire as she struggled with the guards.

Brusquely extending his hand, the Leader dismissed the translator and any notion that help was needed with the intimate language between a man and his woman. Or, more accurately, between *the* Man and his "reclaimed" baggage. The Leader gave another command. The guards, shoving Margie into the Leader's bedchamber, bowed heavily, clicking their heels as they closed the doors.

Margie instantly recognized this man, and now she knew the nation, the geography, and the wisdom of Dong pointing her to the sea beyond the mountains. From Intelligence Community (IC) briefings, she knew his personality and penchants. In person, his face was broader, his skin smoother. His dark eyes danced. His hair was pulled back in a long ponytail. His beam was broad, to say the least. He stood a few inches below her height. He kept taking short, seemingly constrained breaths. She had never been in this type of circumstance. Not on dates with cads. Never! However, now the advantage had turned slightly in her favor. She had Dong's insights and those from the IC. She inhaled deeply, nodding to the Leader.

He pointed to a chair. Margie stood defiantly, studying, from the corner of her eyes, the layout of the room. There were drapes next to the bed. She prayed that Dong had been truthful. Before she realized it, she knew it was true. That escape was possible. She bowed slightly, awarding the Leader her most seductive smile.

He spun to face the wall, his fists clinched, the anticipation too much to bear. "Calm, calm," he reminded himself, as he turned back to Margie. He bowed slightly as she went to the chair.

Clearing his throat, the Leader sat on the edge of his bed, his hands absently patting its quilt. He fought to control his lust, though he felt it was not sexual lust, but more a lust for conquering—in the form of this rather skinny woman—America, and thus the West. He must go slowly, bringing the West to her knees. He nodded, remembering that with the holohead, he already had America in his control. Perhaps then, it was sexual lust. True, it was to men—the few like himself—that *all* women must bow. But enough thinking! Time to begin. His hands quivered and his heart raced. The hours watching video of her in the hut were coalescing into an urgency he struggled to control.

Grunting, he slapped his knees and shuffled to a table bracketed by exquisite tapestries that depicted worshipping mortals being destroyed by a fierce god. The table was filled with an extensive array of bottles and food. He gestured to the bottles. Attempting to apply his phonetic English talents and, remembering what hearty Russians drank, he said, "wo'ka," pointing to a bottle that Margie took to be vodka.

It was now or never. All or nothing. She could fight, if necessary, to try to kill this monster. However, Dong's strategy seemed wiser. She must play along. Margie smoothed out the wrinkled pants she had been given by Dong. She rose and walked slowly to the Leader, standing next to him. She let out a soft "Ha-hmm" sound as she raised first one finger, then two, then three on her right hand, pointing with her left hand to the vodka bottle. She smiled warmly, or at least with what she hoped was a seductive smile, as she fought to keep the bile of disgust low in her throat. The circumstances were beyond imagination: to be kidnapped by a rogue nation and directed to serve this evil monster.

The Leader seized the bottle, frowning as he pantomimed pouring one, then two and three glasses. His hands were shaking. He could wait no longer. They must drink and get down to business. His business!

Margie reached out, tugging gently on the folds of his robe, the fire in her blue eyes giving way to a beguiling look of bedazzlement.

The Leader grabbed her hand, squeezing it with a power that scared her. He rubbed Margie's hand up and down his robe. It was all she could do to keep from fainting. The foreplay ploy was not working.

Her thoughts racing, she pictured, for the briefest of moments, the mannerisms of powerful men who imposed themselves. Yet who, she hoped, preferred a tasteful victory rather than a sordid rape. While rape was usually about power and control, she suspected that tender acquiescence to the man *himself* would be more appealing to his ego. She squeaked out a slight "Ow" as she looked downcast at her hand. She nodded to the bottle, moving her other hand to the Leader's robe with a caring caress.

The Leader caught himself. Forced subjugation and obsequious yielding were the same. Merely responses to imposed power. Would it not be so much sweeter—a reflection of his irresistible manhood—to have this woman care for him, to yield romantically? Nothing false. Any pig can rut. He would charm and seduce by his manly being.

He took a glass, carefully wiping its rim with a cloth napkin. Smiling at Margie, he patted her hand, tenderly dabbing her forehead with the cloth. Blinking out what he considered a most sincere look, he poured her a small portion of vodka, motioning to an ice bucket.

Margie answered sweetly, "No, thank you." Her fingers wrapped tenderly around his as she took the glass from his hand. Squinting as if to care, Margie nodded, then threw back her head and swallowed the vodka in one gulp. It obviously wasn't George's finest, causing her to bring her hand to her mouth, covering a slight cough. Holding the glass high, she gestured to the Leader to pour his own glass.

The Leader snorted, his eyes not leaving Margie's moistened lips. He poured his own large portion, spilling some. He held up the bottle to ask Margie if she wanted more. She nodded, "Yes."

She threw back her head, downing the second glass, dipping her head to suggest the Leader keep pace.

Without hesitating, his excitement provoked by her charm and beauty—her apparent warmth—he swilled down the entire glass. He smiled, victoriously.

Margie gestured that he refill his to the top, holding out her glass for a third and equal potion.

Their glasses full, she brushed her hand softly against his heaving chest and turned to sit back in her chair. Holding her glass high, she motioned the Leader sit back on the bed and take another drink. Margie was sure she had seen this scenario in a dozen movies. The difference was that this—as her only option, unlike those of Hollywood heroines—was infinitely more acute in real life. Smiling and raising her glass as if in toast, she said, taking a chance, "You are one fat pig." Her demure tone had the Leader gulping his drink. She pointed to the table and as he looked, his movements clumsily, she poured her drink into the back cushions of her chair. It worked, just like in the movies.

The Leader stood, staggering. As he lurched towards Margie, she braced herself, ready to fight him off. Ready to rush to the mirror across the room, break its glass to use on him, on herself. Raising her empty glass, she shoved it in his face. He stopped and caught himself leaning backwards, his feet splaying to the side. He focused on her glass, grabbed at it, and missed. Margie's heart skipped a beat. Was he really that drunk? He finally took hold of her glass and returned to the table to fill both glasses, spilling most of the vodka on the table and floor. He teetered back towards her, a pathetic glee in his eyes. She rose, taking the proffered glass and raising it in toast, hoping the Leader would take the earnest expression of her words in his own demented way. "Please, dear God. Please!" she whispered, smiling all the time. She walked to the bed, sitting on its edge and patting the quilt cover. She raised her glass in feigned celebration. The Leader stumbled, sitting next to her, trying to paw her with one hand as raised his glass in the other, seeking her acceptance as he drank. He emptied his glass, punctuated with a disgusting belch. He dropped his glass to the floor, let out a hideous sigh, and fell backwards on the bed, gurgling sounds emanating from his open mouth. One filled with lead fillings, she noticed, absently. She slapped herself. Time to act!

Timing was everything. Would the guards check on their leader? Were security cameras in this room? She had to assume so. She could take no chances. The threat avoidance training she had received in the first week of her presidency took over. For the possibility of cameras, she had to play to the Leader's expectations. She leaned over, caressing his sweaty forehead. His eyes were bleary, partially open. He moaned. She stroked his cheeks. Hiding her disgust, she pulled open his robe and rubbed his heaving belly. Margie took a pillow and holding it to her stomach, she let out a prolonged sigh for the benefit of any cameras.

She tiptoed behind an ornately-decorated dressing partition, praying it was secure from cameras. She found the clothes the Leader had been wearing, stacked neatly on top of the dresser. Opening a drawer, she found another robe. She quickly put on the Leader's clothes over hers, then the robe on top, hoping to appear ready to join the Leader in bed. Using the pillowcase as a sack, Margie filled it with some extra clothes and hats. She heard the Leader call out something, then grunt. Her heart raced as she tied the sack beneath the robe and returned to the bed. She carefully studied the room to get her bearings, then turned out the lights. Feeling her way through the dark, she went to the table, filling the sack with several plastic bottles of water, a bottle of liquor, and some fruit and snacks.

Listening to the snores and grunts of the Leader, she felt her way around the bed to the drapes. To the door. To freedom.

Once behind the drapes, Margie removed the robe as she peered through the door to the garden. Her luck held. Other than small floodlights washing the garden's walls, the garden was completely dark. She hunched over as Dong had suggested, staggering to the back of the garden, not sure what guards watching the security camera might see or think. She found the security pad and praying that by opening the gate some alarm would not sound, she entered the code and pushed down on the gate handle. It opened. Before her, in deep shadow, was a small meadow filled with tall grass and wildflowers, sloping down to the forest edge. In the fading dusk, she could not make out a path. Just the dark veneer of night absorbing the trees. "Just as well," she said to herself. No path meant hard going for her, but also it would be harder to be followed. Or, so she thought.

High in the sky to her left were spectral remnants of the sun. To her right, then, lay the east. She thought of the fields in Kansas that she had often roamed under a full moon. This was not Kansas, and there was no moon. The looming black wall of the forest seemed impassable.

Margie knelt in prayer. "Please, Father. Give me strength to use the gifts you have granted. Give me wisdom in this journey so that I may again be with my family. That I may reveal the person put in my place and return to lead a united America."

The night air frosty, she stood facing away from the setting sun towards the darkness of the forest, capped by the silhouette of distant mountains. With a determination grounded in thoughts of the many Americans who had gone before—who had sacrificed—Margaret Perserve, President of the United States, escaped into the forest and the greatest challenge of her life.

Escape? She was lost and alone in the wilds of a foreign, hostile nation.

CHAPTER 26

The Mountains

Margie was shrouded in complete darkness, the last vestiges of light taken by the departing sun. After fifteen minutes of walking into the forest, fending branches with her hands and arms, and jabbing her feet ahead to gauge the terrain and obstacles, Margie was beyond lost. Bruised and cut, she had fallen twice: once over a tree stump into brambles, and once down a shallow ravine.

She sat on the damp ground, her breathing heavy. She knew that she must not despair. That she *must* succeed. But navigating the forest at night seemed impossible. With no sense of direction, her dilemma was simple: to proceed, or not? She knew that the enemy behind—that man and his troops—was the far greater danger. She looked up, unable to distinguish the nearest branches of the trees from the dark sky. She felt around for any kind of walking stick. She found one about five feet in length. She tore off its small twigs. "What to do?" she asked her stick. It would not be the last time.

"If I continue at night, I could easily go in circles. I'd either end up back at that compound or be traveling farther from the coast," she said to her new friend. Margie threw her head back, her eyes tearing in the cold mountain air. It would so tempting to put on all the clothes in her sack and sleep on the mossy forest floor. So tempting. Her eyelids fell.

She woke abruptly, shivering, the crack of a nearby branch pulling her from a deep slumber. She stood quietly, peering into the dark void, holding her stick like a baseball bat. After waiting for what she guessed was five minutes, she crouched back to the ground. She wondered what wild animals inhabited this forest. With no further noise, she reached into her sack for an orange. The first juicy bite reminded her of the orange juice she relished at breakfast, back home. Home! She stood, trying to figure out some way to navigate in complete darkness without the aid of stars or moon.

"Oh, for GPS," she said to her stick as she reached out to a heavy shadow—a tree trunk. She felt around the trunk. About one-third of it was covered in moss. She knew that moss usually grew on the northern shady side of trees. Not always, but usually. She assumed the sun never penetrated this dense forest. Regardless, it was a chance she must take.

Using her stick, she swung it back and forth in the dank black of the forest, hoping to encounter a nearby tree. Her hand stung as the stick banged hard against another trunk. She felt around it to find its moss. Keeping her left hand on the mossy portion of the trunk, she swung her stick again, hitting another tree. Careful not to lose her bearings and keeping her stick in contact with the next tree, she walked directly to it. It had moss on the same side as the prior tree.

She repeated this process with three more trees. All had moss on the same side. With the mossy side of a tree trunk directly at her back, she estimated that east was on her right. She heard another noise.

Startled, she gasped. How long would the Leader stay passed out? How long before he loosed his guards and dogs? She must hurry. After a brief prayer, Margie continued her walk through the forest—much like a person without sight—using her stick to avoid obstacles and to find the next tree. As long as she launched ahead from the right side of a mossy trunk, she should be heading east. She didn't think about what would happen if she encountered trees with no moss. She didn't think about the dangers of animals or that horrible man. She made her decision and set her teeth just as she had done when she first drove her father's harvester years ago in Kansas. She was using her gifts.

Margie stumbled and fought her way up and down hill, through five miles of forest, before, ahead, she saw the sky turning pale gray. The clouds gone, the first rays of morning sunrise passed through the trees. She dropped to her knees, thanking God that her guesswork had been correct. She ate a banana and drank some water, unsure of how far she would have to go or how she should mete out the consumption of her scant supplies on her journey to the sea.

With the dawning light, she picked up the pace. A series of hills lay ahead. Margie realized that she needed to use the higher, snow-covered peaks—ahead and to the side—as reference points to maintain her easterly direction. Just as Dong had suggested. She thanked God for Dong. Where was she now? How severe a punishment did she face? A chill ran through Margie as she imagined how Dong would suffer. What had changed Dong and caused her to sacrifice?

The rising sun brought little warmth to the cloudless, crystalline sky. Margie half ran and half walked, striving to cover as much distance as possible. Her heart pounding in her chest, she knew she must not stop. Although exhausted from her ordeal, she felt invigorated by the cold breeze washing down from the mountain. The forest foliage had changed from the dense pines when she had first entered the forest to barren maple and elm trees surrounded by lush ferns. Nearby, a stream cascaded down the mountainside. "Are we on the western slope of the final mountain?" she asked, hopefully. She looked up the slope, wondering if she should attempt to go up or around. Kneeling at the edge of the stream, she splashed her face, the coolness providing a sense of renewal. How far she had come from the clutches of that fat pig?

"How far have we come?" she asked her stick, using it to poke the water. She figured no more than ten or fifteen miles. It could yet be hundreds of miles to the coast. "And what then?" Wouldn't she still be in this nation where people could easily spot her? Surely an alert had been sent nationwide. Margie exhaled a heavy sigh, watching the vapors of her breath twirl in the morning coolness. She needed to head more in a north-by-northeasterly direction towards China's border. China, with its handsome, pragmatic leader—who was cautiously embracing détente after the South China Sea catastrophe—was her best chance. She could not hope to make it to Russia. Nor would that be wise given that Russia's nationalistic mindset and its tall, fat Napoleonic leader— the one who continued to threaten NATO and its allies. No. China must be her goal. But how far to go?

Her head tilted against the wind, she gasped as a dog's bark carried across the spaces. She couldn't tell if the bark—now the excessive barking of several dogs—came from up the mountain, or behind her. Margie ran to a dense thicket of ferns, stilling her heart and trying to discern the direction of the dogs.

"Oh, no!" she whispered to her stick. "The dogs are coming from the west, from where I just was!" She knew there was no way to outrun them. Probably helicopters filled with troops were following the dogs and their handlers. She looked up the mountain. Too steep. Behind her, the dogs. To her left, just more sparse forest where she would be easy prey for the dogs. The dogs! A fearful vision unfolded: the dogs tearing at her, egged on by the amplified voice of the ego-damaged leader coming from one of the overhead helicopters. Only one way to go. Across the stream.

Before she realized she had reached a conclusion on what to do, she was in the middle of the twenty-foot-wide stream. The section where she stood, her feet and legs numbed by the freezing water, sloped slightly uphill. The stream's edges were thick with brambles and ferns, its bottom filled with small, slippery stones. Using her teeth, Margie managed to rip the top seam of the pillowcase. She tore the open end of the sack into two halves, tying them together to form a noose which she slipped over her neck to swing the sack onto her back. With both hands free, holding her stick, she rushed upstream against the current.

Margie stopped. She couldn't hear the dogs over the rush of the water. She scrambled to a shallow pool, turning her head downstream and listening intently. She heard the dogs, much closer now. Perhaps just a half mile away, maybe less. She turned upstream, vaguely realizing she did not hear any helicopters.

Around the next corner she saw large boulders. Her heart sank. There was no way she could escape through their clutter. Words unspoken entered her consciousness: the conviction that she must run as hard as she ever had. She must escape. Dear God, she must!

Using her hands and the stick to negotiate the boulders, she made slow headway, thinking she heard the dogs right behind her. She knew that their handlers—accompanied, she was sure, by soldiers, since she heard no helicopters—would search upstream and down, on both sides. She had four options in seeking her exit from the stream. If she was lucky, there'd be only two dogs. Two dogs with four options would buy her time. But was the outcome inevitable? That she'd go down under the dogs, or the pig? It was unimaginable. Mostly, she feared for

America. Her own life meant little other than releasing her beloved country from the grip of a bogus leader.

"No time for thinking," she said to her stick. "We must go till our last breath." She wondered about the strength of her stick; she was almost pole vaulting over the smaller boulders. Ahead she saw that the stream split, that it had two sources. A larger one to the right, coming from the right slope of the mountain, and a smaller one coming directly down the mountain. Decisions! Which fork to take? She imagined the handlers, upon reaching the banks on the left and right side of the stream, confronted with another decision. If there were just two dogs, again she was splitting their options. But more importantly, how would the handlers think? Would they guess she'd taken the smaller uphill tributary, or the larger one to the right, figuring she was heading around the mountain. That up the mountain was a dead end? She heard the barks, closer now.

Going against the obvious choice, Margie ran up the left, smaller fork. There were fewer boulders. The bottom was mainly mossy rocks over which her stick was saving her life. For the moment.

The small stream, shallower and ten feet wide, made running possible. She ran hard up it, avoiding any contact with the banks and the foliage. Around the next bend, off to the left through the trees, she saw a hut. She saw two men sitting in rough-hewn chairs at its entrance. An old woman appeared from the hut's door with plates of food. They were all looking out over their small plot of corn and thankfully did not see Margie as she rushed past. Beyond the hut Margie saw several cows and chickens. She prayed that when the handlers, the soldiers, arrived, these three would be able to say they had not seen her. It was a weak strategy among none that offered hope.

Margie kept running up the stream, its slope increasing. At some point she would need to leave the stream. Her shoes were torn, her legs numb. Off to the left she saw a wooded knoll. From that she could watch the little farm she had just passed. Her breathing came from her stomach, her leg muscles cramping. She knew that she had no choice. That she must exit the stream and accept the reality that her scent would give her away.

About to step out onto a large stone, hoping to avoid any telltale footprints, she had one last thought. She pulled the sack around to her chest. Reaching in, she pulled out the bottle of liquor. If she could walk backwards, slowly splashing the liquid behind her, would that mask her trail to the knoll? She thought for a brief moment. That was risky. One missed spot of scent, and it would be over. And a good dog was not thrown off by the smell of liquor. Something she remembered from her threat avoidance training. The only alternative she could think of was to remove her shoes, fill them with sand from the stream, and pour liquor into the sand. But wouldn't the dogs still pick up a trace from the soles of her shoes? Shoes muddied from her trek through the forest and covered with the same trail scents the dogs had been following?

She stood immobile, frozen in thought and by the cold water, the yelping and barking of the dogs rising above the gentle cresting of the water over the rocks.

CHAPTER 27

The Reprieve

Water and animals and scent. Margie saw tall stalks of red grain blowing in her imagination. She would never see them again. Never her family, her country. Oblivious to the sounds rising from the little farm, her weary mind crying to quit, a gunshot woke her from her exhaustion and fear. She knew that dogs smell like a human sees. She was toast. There was no way to thwart the dogs. She leaned on her stick, staring at the stream's water as it cascaded around the stick, forming small eddies in front of her freezing legs. Eddies? Eddie, her dear brother, killed in Iraq in 2014. "Oh, Eddie, where are you?" she asked her stick.

Three more gunshots echoed above the forest's mantle. The bush, next to the stone she was about to step on, moved. From it came a very large badger. It stopped, looking at her and depositing a large pile of scat just a foot from the bank. Margie watched, astonished, as the badger scampered off into the ferns. She looked closely at the bush. At its base were the remains of some forest animal. Its snout looked like that of a wild boar, perhaps a baby. Giant hornets, carnivores of the forest, covered the decaying body.

Margie used her stick to drag the badger's scat to the edge of the stream. Out of options, all she could think of was how to create some foul smell that would affect the dogs. Standing in the stream at its bank, leaning on her stick for balance, she removed her right shoe. Into the shoe she rubbed a large portion of the scat, inside and out. On top of that, she poured some liquor. Pushing out of the stream with the aid of her stick, she put only her right shoe on the stone. She stood on the stone and repeated the process with her left shoe. Stepping back onto grass, her shoes squishing, she used her stick to gingerly prod the decaying body out over the stone, effectively covering the area and the water where she had exited. The hornets kept eating.

Shouts from the farm had her panicking. With pronounced effort, walking flat-footed to squish the foul content out from her shoes, she climbed slowly up the knoll to see what was happening below.

She saw five soldiers holding restraints on three dogs. One of the soldiers was leaning over one of the men, who was prostrate on the ground. The soldiers were all gesturing up and down the stream, waving their rifles in the face of the old woman. Margie pulled the ferns around her. She stared at the man in the chair. Next to his chair, she saw makeshift crutches. One of the soldiers grabbed a crutch and prodded the man in the chair. Another soldier smashed the stock of his rifle against the man's shoulder, then hard against his left leg. Margie cringed as the man's scream carried across the spaces. He rolled to the ground. The soldiers all laughed until the one with the crutch, their apparent leader, shouted at them, throwing the crutch to the ground and motioning to search the hut and cow shed.

After a long delay, the leader waved his arm back towards the stream. He sent three of the men and two dogs back down the stream. Margie prayed that they were going to search back up the right fork of the stream. The leader and the remaining soldier started up the bank of the stream, on the same side as Margie. She bit her lip, shaking her head, sure she was now doomed. She wished that her stick, her faithful stick, had a pointed end she could use to impale herself.

She watched as the two men and their dog searched up the bank, nearing her place of exit from the stream. The dog pulled on its restraint. The leader yelled in a tone of victory as all three rushed forward. Margie lost sight of them for a minute. The dog was barking ferociously. Ten feet from the bush, the leader took off the restraint. The dog charged forward, the two men in close pursuit.

The resulting commotion was hideous. The hornets attacked the dog, and then the men. From what must have been a nearby hive, a dark swarm of more hornets descended on the writhing forms. Screams and yelping filled the air. The men stumbled into the stream as the dog tore off back down the stream. After scrambling downstream, slapping at the hornets, the men finally emerged below the little farm. The leader was yelling at the other man, shoving him, threatening with his rifle.

Margie lay exhausted among the ferns. The yells of the men and barking of the dog receded into the distance, downstream, as dusk fell. She pushed her face into the cold, mossy ground, stifling her sobs with her hands. Shaking uncontrollably, her adrenaline rush over, the stress subsiding, she finally took note of how cold it was. Margie pulled the few extra clothes from the sack. Shivering as she took off her wet clothes, she put on the dry ones and hung the wet clothing over a nearby branch. Night was falling fast. She had no other option than to tough it out, trying to sleep to regain her strength, to see what the morning would bring. Thinking of the badger and the boar, she kept her stick close. Her chaotic thoughts bounced with her chattering teeth to memories long ago, of camping out with Eddie and her friends down by the creek that bordered their farm. How, in spite of the cold, she had found warmth in the friendship and love of others. There was no such warmth now as she struggled to sleep.

After a miserable night, half sleeping, always shivering, Margie woke with a start, gasping as she recalled where she was. She arched her back, realizing she had slept on top of her stick, her only friend. Wiping her eyes with a muddy hand, she peered through the ferns to the farm. The old woman was tending to the man who had been pushed off the chair. He appeared to be younger—a teenager—and was writhing in pain. The other man—Margie saw now that he was older like the woman—was also kneeling next to the young man on the ground, trying to comfort him. Margie could see that the pants of the younger man were soiled and red. He was obviously injured. Had the soldiers shot him?

For more than fifteen minutes, Margie listened carefully for any sounds of the dogs. She heard no noise other than the intermittent wailing of the old woman. She wanted to ask the farmers for help. They obviously were no friends of the soldiers, but it was risky. Margie laughed quietly. Her whole journey had been fraught with risk. Risk or not, her only option was to approach the farmers.

Eating some fruit and drinking from the last bottle of water, she put her still-damp clothes in the sack. Parting the ferns, she moved diagonally to her right, using foliage and shrubs to maintain cover. She crawled down the knoll towards the back of the hut, keeping it between herself and the farmers at the front. Their grief was more apparent as she leaned against the back of the hut. She heard the cries of the old woman, punctuated by yells from what sounded like the older man.

Margie crept to the edge of the rough-hewn wood hut, peering around the corner. Off to the side by the cow shed, she saw two cows lying in the mud in a such a weird manner—one that she had never seen with the cows on her Kansas farm. They looked to have collapsed into sleep until she saw the blood from several ugly wounds. The shots from the soldiers. Her heart broke, not for the cows but for this small farming family, knowing how critical the cows were to their subsistence. Starvation was one form of control. Margie clinched her teeth as her eyes narrowed in anger at the evil that led this country. She looked more closely at the man on the ground. His left leg looked to be horribly broken, bent at an angle. His pant leg had been cut away, a tourniquet applied higher on the leg. Through the blood she could see the shinbone of his lower left leg protruding. Her mind raced. She realized that the young man must have had a broken leg when the soldiers arrived. That the soldier had caused the compound fracture when he smashed the young man's already-broken leg.

Margie debated. She could try to sneak into the hut from the back door, foraging for—stealing—food from this starving family before she tried to get to the coast on her own. Or she could present herself to this family, asking for their help. She was not sure they would aid an enemy of their nation, nor if they would be able to help. But she saw their anguish, and it meshed with her own. Lost causes on God's green earth. Lost to the brutal nature of man. The debate was easy to resolve. Like Dong had said, she had to trust. Mainly she had to trust God's hand to guide her. For a brief moment, she considered all the missionaries and innocent Christians throughout time who had trusted in God, yet, who, had often met with torture and violent deaths. Margie gazed up the mountain. It was magnificent: a painter's dream with whispery clouds uniting its rugged, white peaks and lush green forests. No other way. Trust and obey. Just like the song said. She cleared her throat.

"Hello," she said softly, as she rose to stand in full view of the family.

Up close, kneeling on the ground, the woman did not seem so old. Startled, looking up at Margie, she pushed off to stand, screaming. The old man grabbed a crutch, raising it, pulling the woman in behind him. The younger man on the ground twisted to look up at Margie.

Margie held both hands in the air, bowing and speaking softly in English. "Please, may I help this man? Please. Do not fear me. Please?"

The young man raised his arm, grabbing the old man's leg, shaking it, saying something. The tone of his voice was soothing, pleading.

The old man asked a question. Margie had no answer. He asked it again, raising his hand to his mouth. Margie shook her head, putting her hand to her ear, trying to express that she did not understand their language.

"Ah," the old man said, recognition crossing his face. He pointed to the stream.

Margie shook her head again, not sure of his meaning.

The old lady starting jabbering. She waved her hands, gesturing towards the stream and imitating the soldiers with rifles and dogs.

Margie, placing her hands together in supplication, bowed and said, "Yes."

The old man yelled, running at Margie, pulling her to the side of the hut, out of view of the stream.

The old woman followed, talking firmly in a scolding manner. She pointed to the stream and shook her head. She took Margie's arm, leading her to the man on the ground, the one Margie assumed was their son. The woman knelt next to her son. She touched the tourniquet and the bloody pants with the bone protruding lower down his calf. She raised her hands in desperate appeal. Can you help?

CHAPTER 28

The Farmers

Margie placed her hand on the woman's shoulder, kneeling next to her to examine the young man's leg. She put her hand to his filthy face, touching his cheek. Tears in her eyes, clinching her teeth, Margie nodded several times, thinking to herself, "This looks horrible. They've tied off the blood flow, but if we don't release the binding on his thigh, sepsis will kill him. But then, he'll bleed out."

The woman, gently pulling Margie's head around so they were eye to eye, asked what must have been, "Can you fix this?" The woman's eyes held such pain from life. They beseeched Margie to do something.

Margie did not want to offer false hope to this impoverished family; one that would probably starve if their son died. She closed her eyes, trying to remember the times the vet had visited their Kansas farm to set the leg on a cow or dog. But never a horse. Horses were put down. They would try to save a cow by putting it in a float tank to help it bear weight on an injured leg. The closest experience Margie had to what lay in front of her was when the vet had set the leg on her dog, Aksel, after first suggesting the dog's leg be removed. Margie knew that with this young man, amputation was not even a remote option. The only option was setting the leg best she could. With the compound, open break of the tibia, it seemed a hopeless situation. She gingerly pulled the torn pant leg to the side, looking more closely at the wound, his shinbone protruding through the ugly gash in his leg. He was a skinny boy. Perhaps, if he could bear the pain, and with the help of his mother and father, she could align the bone by feel.

The young man spoke softly, nodding at Margie. She took his words as confirmation, understanding that she should at least try to do her best. That he trusted her, regardless of the outcome. His eyes held a sad, fatalistic look: a determination to make the best of a life always lived in survival mode. "Has he ever experienced joy?" she wondered.

Margie felt tears of sorrow creep to the edge of her eyes. Sorrow for the plight of so many. Plight at the hands of others. With this young man before her, his plight was in her hands. Hands of love extending the grace of God. She knew no other thought.

"These people," she said to herself, "wake up each morning, as so many do, facing a day where their purpose is simply to survive until the next day. No joy—not usually—other than the birth of a baby. Even then, not always. Here is a family for whom, with guidance from above, I might restore some joy in the survival of their son. I must try, just as much as I must escape." It was who she was. Her dad had told her she had gifts from God. Here in this remote setting, alone with these people—prisoners in their own country—she was far from the medical miracles and excesses that defined American society. This family was no less worthy in God's eye than those in America. She must try!

The woman took hold of Margie's arm, asking by gesture if Margie could heal her son. A mother's appeal. Margie wanted to tell the mother—all of them—that she was no more capable than they.

The son spoke to the mother. His tone was urgent and overriding. He pointed to his leg, and with his hands implied that Margie must try to reconnect the bone.

Margie stood. She would try. She held out her filthy hands, gesturing at where to wash them. After returning from the stream, she directed the mother and father to lay the son on a clean blanket, in the hut. Pointing to herself, she said "Ma… Margie" as she looked at them, the mother's hands clasped in arthritic fear, the father's eyes sunken in lost hope. She pointed to the son.

He responded, slowly, "Yo-han."

Margie repeated the sound. All three nodded. She repeated his name, "Yo-han."

Smiling, the son repeated hers, "…M… Mercgy."

"Close enough," Margie gasped. She had the father open the door for more light. The mother added wood to the simple stove to boil water. She retrieved the liquor bottle from her sack, wondering once again why she had brought it. She would use the hot water to clean the wound and the liquor to sterilize it. Mimicking, with her fingers, sewing a thread to her shirt, Margie gestured to the mother. "Do you have sewing needle and thread?" Margie waited, hoping she would be able to pantomime all her communication with this family. Their often-shrill-sounding, rapid chatter was impossible to discern. She coughed briefly, stifling a laugh in appreciation at how foreign her own English must sound to them.

The mother's cheeks rose to pressure her eyes into a squint. After a brief moment, a smile of recognition had her eyes opening wide. She moved to a small bag on the floor, pulling out an old bent needle and a spool of thread. It would have to do. Margie dropped them into the boiling water.

Margie folded her hands, closed her eyes, and said a short prayer, asking God to be with them all. The three family members chanted while her eyes were closed. Whatever, and to whomever, their thoughts ran, she was encouraged by their simple faith. Simple, just like hers.

She took a towel, laying it next to the needle, thread, and liquor bottle. She took a deep breath, instructing the mother to sit behind the son and place her arms under his arms and clasp her hands together at his chest, her legs extending on both sides of his body with her feet at his waist. She instructed the father to sit, facing the son and mother. She put the father's right foot up against the son's crotch and the father's left foot up against the mother's right foot at the son's waist. Margie clasped her hands, gesturing a tugging of opposing forces, the father pulling the son's leg while the mother pulled back on her son's body. She saw the wiry arms of both parents: vein-streaked but strong. She smiled.

"Yo-han," Margie said, gritting her teeth, nodding her head. "Are you ready?"

The mother reached over to a nearby table, taking a wooden ladle which she placed in her son's mouth. She nodded, grunted and said something to the father as they both pulled hard. The son's eyes went wide, his teeth bearing down on the wooden handle, his eyes latched onto Margie's. "Go!" the eyes said. "And thank you."

Margie saw the broken tibia recede slightly below the skin of his leg. She poured hot water on her hands, and then the wound. The son groaned heavily, his body fighting against the pull of his parents. Margie wiped the wound with the towel and with both hands on his leg, by feel, she pushed the bone farther into the muscles, trying to align the broken halves end-to-end. The halves remained overlapped. The son looked close to fainting. "More!" Margie yelled, motioning with her hands that the parents should pull harder. "More, more!" she yelled again as she felt the overlap of the bones lessen. The grunts from the father and the crying of the mother told Margie this was their final effort. They could do no more. Margie clapped her hands, yelling, "Again!" As the parents struggled, she pushed and prodded the bones beneath the skin until ends of the tibia fell into place. She heard the ladle fall to the floor. The son had mercifully passed out. She massaged his leg, forcing the bone ends into a better alignment. It would have to do. He might have a permanent limp, but he would live.

Margie quickly poured liquor into the open wound. She took the threaded needle and poured liquor on it. Using mending skills her mother had taught her, she sewed up the wound, spacing the sutures closely. She asked for some sticks, and with strips of cloth, Margie attached a simple splint to the boy's leg.

The mother was still crying, holding her son in a rocking motion. The father knelt next to his son, his hand at the son's cheek, his eyes tear-filled as he nodded to Margie. She smiled back, her relief overwhelming. She, too, cried as she untied the tourniquet, checking the wound now that blood was flowing again. They all sighed deeply, crying and laughing in amazement and release. Margie poured some of the remaining hot water on her hands, wiping them on her pants. The mother made a sound and, opening the drawer of a makeshift dresser, brought out a most exquisite linen, holding it for Margie to use to dry her hands. Margie shook her head. The mother gestured again, insisting. Margie bowed, taking the linen. It felt delicate, like some she had at home, back in Kansas.

Margie held up the liquor bottle. Almost empty. She took a hard pull, draining the bottle in toast to her home and her dear family, so far away. Her thoughts flashed to that wonderful song, "So far away." She remained sitting on the floor, her arms wrapped around her knees. Exhausted.

The old woman stood before Margie, bowing at the waist, her hands clasped together as if in prayer. She was mumbling something that Margie took as thanks. The mother's tears fell on the rough planks, pooling at Margie's feet.

Overcome by a sense of humility that she had been able to help this family, and by a sense of humanity—sharing this ordeal with fellow humans no different from her in heart and soul—Margie stood up and put her arms gently around the mother in a loving embrace. Two mothers together. One whose son would live. One who might never seen her son again. As she embraced the mother, Margie could feel how thin she was. She looked over at the father whose head was down, his hands folded at his waist. He was repeating some mantra, some expression of faith and thanksgiving. She looked at the son. He lay exhausted on the floor, his chest heaving. His face broke into a smile as he looked over at Margie.

The mother pulled herself away, holding her hands out in question. She pointed in the direction of the stream, gesturing like the soldiers with their rifles.

"Yes," Margie answered, aware the word meant nothing to the family, but that perhaps her nod and tone might tell them the story. "America," she said, slowly, drawing it out. She repeated the word. The family looked on in confusion. Margie acted out the words. "The soldiers were chasing me. I was fearful and had to hide." She puffed up her chest trying to imitate the Leader. The family remained confused. Margie reached into her sack, pulling out the military hat she had taken from the Leader's dressing area.

The mother brought her hand to her chest, gasping. She stepped back from Margie, pointing repeatedly to the hat and then to Margie as if Margie was associated with the Leader.

"No, no," Margie said, shaking her head. "No, not at all!" She made a disgusted face, threw the hat to the floor and stepped on it to wipe her feet. "No," she repeated.

The father and mother rapidly talked back and forth, gesturing at Margie, the son's leg, and the hat. The father turned to Margie, making like having a rifle, thrusting it at her, then raising his hands in question.

"Yes!" Margie nodded, turning to kick the hat once more.

The mother brought her hands together, clapping in glee. She talked rapidly as she rushed to hug Margie.

After another lengthy embrace, Margie stood back, facing all three. "Do you have a map?"

Receiving only blank stares in reply, she mimicked writing.

The son said something and the parents both spoke, excitedly. The mother went to the little dresser and pulled out an old marking pen and a faded calendar.

Using the back page of the calendar, Margie drew a map, showing in outline form the nation's borders and proximity to the neighboring nation—one friendly to the United States. She stepped back, pointing to her drawing. "Do you recognize this?"

The son spoke, the mother leaning down to show him the map. He nodded and said what must have been, "I understand." All three started talking rapidly. The son pointed to himself, and then a spot on the map—the upper corner of the nation.

Margie took the map, put an X where the son had pointed. She drew a line from there to the border with the friendly nation. She was nodding vigorously. "Yes, yes! I must go there!" she said, repeatedly pointing to the border and then herself, motioning movement with her hand.

The mother stood back, a guttural tone in her voice as she said something, shaking her head, drawing a knife-like motion across her throat. She put her palm down on the line Margie had drawn, shaking her head to convey, "No!"

Margie held her hands together in supplication. "Please?" she asked.

The son yelled something to the mother, pointing at his leg. The two of them argued until the father stepped in. His voice firm, he put his hand on the mother's shoulder, gesturing to himself and to Margie.

The mother wailed, shaking her head, "No!" Clapping her hands in anguish, she collapsed on the floor next to her son. He put his arm around her, whispering something and pointing to Margie.

The father took the map. He pointed to the line Margie had drawn, then to himself, saying, "Kwang-Ju." He pointed at Margie and said, "Mercgy." He pointed to the line again. "Kwang-Ju... Mercgy."

Margie hugged him and, with extra tenderness, the mother. She bowed, repeating, "Oh, thank you, thank you!" She smiled with newfound hope. With Kwang-Ju her guide, a journey to safety and to home, now seemed possible.

Margie bowed her head in a quiet prayer. She knew many dangers remained for herself and for this caring family if she were caught.

The father called out instructions. The mother went to the dresser, fetching a headscarf and a coat for Margie.

The trek to safety had to begin immediately.

CHAPTER 29

The Call

The chilly, overcast day cast a pall of gloom through the windows of the First Lady's bedroom. At his desk, Roy leaned back in the custom *Eurotech* chair, chewing on the end of a straw. He thought of the hard times he had faced, the battles. All of which he had overcome with smarts, determination, courage, and stealth. He had always been determined not to be thwarted by hurdles or prejudice.

But now, he was thwarted by the mystery of his precious Margie. Something with which he had no experience. Sure, he could tell others, but if his suspicions were right, havoc would result. Not just for himself and his children, but much more importantly, for the nation. Roy shook his head, looking around the room, his mouth warped in frustration. He sighed heavily. The room's current decor, with the large cocktail table and plush sofa, might win awards for focal points. But what he wanted—really needed at the moment—was a private, secure control room. Not in the West Wing or here, in the White House. There were just too many prying eyes. A room where he could have private meetings, conduct online research, and have a clandestine staff. His dark eyes froze in concentration, boring a stare back at Theodore Roosevelt—solemn-faced and posing regally in the Sargent portrait across the room.

The ringing of the phone, his private line, thawed the focus of his eyes. Clearing his throat, pushing some papers to the side of his desk to reach the phone, he answered, "Yes?"

"Colonel Butcher?"

"Speaking," Roy replied, his voice edged with irritation at the interruption of his analysis of what could have happened to cause such a dramatic change in Margie's policies, behavior, and... her touch.

"Sir? This is Sergeant MacMahan. I met you at the New York VA a week ago. With a Major Evans."

Roy pulled the straw from his mouth. "Yes, Sergeant, I remember you. How'd you get this number?"

"Sir? You, ah... gave it to me. Do you remember our discussion?"

Roy leaned forward, his elbows on the desk, his eyes narrowing as he recalled that discussion in detail. It had to do with Margie. With the one concern that had Roy frantic. Was it a coincidence that this soldier was calling about his wife? After pausing to think through his response, Roy replied curtly, "I do. Are you calling because of what we discussed?"

"Yes, sir," Mac responded. He was nervous, memories fogging his mind. He felt the onset of the shoebox. Damn! He shouldn't have listened to Mindy, or Gloria and Blake. This call was a mistake. The last time he had talked with federal bureaucrats, it had been at the Commerce Department in D.C. regarding the D37 plot. He'd almost been blindsided by that. While Roy had been cordial enough in New York, what Mac was about to suggest might totally backfire. Not that the colonel could do anything to him as the D37 people did. But Mac liked Roy Butcher, and wanted to help.

His thoughts carried back to his last tour in Afghanistan, to that morning when he had to tell his squad about their being selected for an early-morning incursion in a valley known to be rimmed with insurgents. The burden of leadership—of having to put on a game face in front of those kids he loved—had almost broken him. However, Roy was a different audience, and life and death probably was not an issue. Even with that rationale, an overwhelming sense of responsibility had Mac choking: physically, and mentally. The damn shoebox was on the verge! How long had he paused? What had he been saying to Roy?

"Sergeant? I'm busy, so if you have something to say, please get on with it," Roy said, pleasantly enough after waiting for Mac.

Mac cleared his throat and his mind. "We discussed... and please forgive me, sir. I only want to help. What we discussed was... Okay! I'll just say it. What we discussed were possible changes in the president. You didn't deny it. I've thought of not much else since we talked."

Hoping to move this discussion towards closure, one that did not arouse suspicion, Roy said, attempting humor, "If I recall, Sergeant, you're still on your honeymoon. Yes? You telling me you're not thinking only about your new wife and how to please her?"

"That's just it," Mac replied, hesitant, his voice subdued. "It's my wife, sir, and some friends who've pushed me to make this call."

"What's that, soldier!" Roy shouted into the phone. "We agreed you could tell your wife. But no way anyone else! I had your promise!"

"Yes, I know, but I…"

"No buts!" Roy interrupted, thankful they were on a secure line, yet livid that MacMahan had been talking with others. Roy put the phone on mute and took a deep breath. He was, by nature, a person who always remained cool and objective, controlled his behavior and led his troops with conviction. Especially under fire. He exhaled through his nose, licking his lips as he took the phone off mute. "You say 'friends.' Please explain yourself. Are they there with you, listening?"

"No, sir. I'm alone in our house. My wife's out, trying to negotiate the snowy sidewalks." Mac attempted a laugh. "She knows I'm making this call, and that I need privacy to explain."

"This isn't your PTSD or CTE talking, is it?" Roy immediately regretted his words. If it was, MacMahan might not know how to recognize it.

"Sir. Please let me explain, from the top. Is that okay? Do you have ten minutes? What we've uncovered could be of critical importance."

Roy caught himself thinking that if the sergeant had some valid insight, whatever the hell that might be, he had all the time in the world. "Go ahead," Roy responded. "From the top."

Mac began, following the outline he had written down with Mindy, including the comments from Justin, Gloria, and Blake. He explained the project he had asked Justin to complete. At that stage, there was nothing untoward regarding the president. Justin was not suspicious. However, Justin had gone beyond the requested photo analysis by running recent videos of the president through a high-tech math filter. From this last effort, Justin discovered a shadow bracketing the president. A shadow and ripples. Not an issue, perhaps, until Justin ran older videos. Ones which showed no shadow or ripple.

Roy interrupted, "So you're saying, you believe this math filter-thing is valid. That it's not a virtual reality trick this guy Justin is using?"

"No, sir," Mac replied, thankful that Roy was asking sincere questions, his curiosity obviously piqued. "I understand your doubt. My wife and I, too, had to be convinced. So Justin came down from Boston with his laptop... down to our house. Ah, he was one of my students when I was teaching at the university. The other two, Blake and Gloria, were also my students. All three were instrumental in helping to crack the D37 case. Colonel, I would not have involved any of these kids if I didn't trust them implicitly. On my word, Colonel, you can trust them!"

"I'm baffled by what you're suggesting. Which is?"

"That there's an aura around the president that might be affecting her. We have no idea the source. To help pinpoint the issue for us, Justin ran other videos through his filter. Videos starting with the day of the inauguration right up through last week. The shadow and ripples began and became apparent, starting on February 15."

Roy couldn't help himself. "Oh, shit!" he gasped, thinking of that night, the 14th, in their bedroom when the alarm sounded and Margie had been escorted by the guard Sanchez. That from the next morning, the fifteenth, and since, Margie had been different, distant.

"Sir?" Mac asked, not sure he had heard Roy correctly.

"You say February 15, right? That up to that date, no aura. Right?

"Yes, sir."

"And that starting with the 15th, and ever since then, the math thing from Justin shows this shadow?" Roy asked, dumbfounded.

"That's why I'm calling, sir. We're confused. Mainly worried. It's why Mindy and the others said I needed to call you. I would have preferred to show you in person, but thought it urgent enough to call first. Justin is the only one who can run the filter."

"Mac? I recall you wanted me to call you Mac. Right?"

"Yes, sir. Colonel."

"I'd rather call you Professor... and don't argue!" Roy said when he heard Mac sucking air. "I will say only this over the phone, Mac. I think you guys may be on to something. I need to see it. Can you and your team come down to D.C.? Once I see your proof, if it's what you're suggesting, we'll get the FBI and CIA involved."

Mac put the phone to his forehead. He was excited that he had gained traction with Roy, yet scared that Roy was so serious and, more to the point, because of D37, he did not trust government agencies.

"Colonel, Justin is a true geek. Kinda weird in his own unique way. Basically, he's paranoid and convinced he found something really important. Bottom line, he's scared of leaving New York. As I said, he's the only one who knows how to run the videos through the filter."

"Why not run the videos on his computer's screen while doing the math-filter thing, and do a video screen capture?" Roy asked.

"Good idea, but we've already tried that. The shadow and ripples only show when the filter is applied to the original video."

"So we've got to meet, right?"

"Yes, sir. Here in New York City, with Justin," Mac answered, realizing that even with the stress of the moment, the shoebox was no longer an issue. Maybe it did take a crisis—action—to clear his head?

"I'll make the arrangement so we can meet in a safe house," Roy replied. "To keep things simple, but expedited, I'll send you, in open email, an invitation to a fashion show: where and when. Contact me *only* if that date does *not* work. Otherwise, see you in New York. Deal?"

"Yes, sir!" Mac replied, his voice filled with excitement. He was being helpful, and this was important. He couldn't wait to tell Mindy.

An agent of the Leader—hidden in a van in the construction yard next to the Washington Monument—aimed her ultra-sensitive telescoping microphone back and forth at the windows of the President's and First Lady's bedroom. She had been holed up for two days, fishing for a signal. About to quit, she noticed waveforms appearing on the device's display. She clapped her hands, remembering that line from Sun Yat-sen: the key to success is action and the essential in action is perseverance. By pure luck she was able to capture the entire conversation between Mac and Roy. She knew the Leader would be ecstatic as she transmitted the captured discussion to Building 666 for analysis.

CHAPTER 30

The Response

The Leader had processed numerous treats since the escape of his baggage four days ago. He couldn't remember how many treats, and didn't care. All that mattered was that he have a way to dispense his anger and expend his energy. This would steady his hand as he searched for that American woman.

He sat at his grand, executive-style desk looking out at the palace gardens. The windows were open, the curtains fluttering in the chilly breeze. A soft knock came from the office door. He put down the heavy combat pistol he was oiling.

"Yes!" he bellowed.

The orderly held onto the door handle as he stepped timidly inside the door. Bowing, he said, "Dear Father, I have an urgent message from your agent in Washington D.C. Decrypted by the Building 666 team for your eyes only."

"Bring it!" The Leader snapped his right hand at the orderly. "What is it now?" he asked himself. "Surely not that the president has already escaped all the way back to America?"

Bowing heavily, his eyes absorbing each stitch in the Persian rug that covered the office floor, the orderly placed the envelope on the Leader's desk. He walked backwards as he exited.

The Leader continued oiling the pistol's trigger mechanism. Finally, he wiped the unloaded gun and cocked back the hammer. Aiming at the envelope, he said quietly, "This had better be good news, or several generals will soon be shaking hands with this barrel." He pulled the trigger, laughing—somewhat laboriously—at an image of the generals, their faces blank plates filled with terror, obeying his death request. Nothing new. Especially in light of the forty or so soldiers and officers he had ordered executed for behaving like that American airline: allowing the escape—the loss—of his baggage. He had even considered shooting his longtime aide-de-camp for awakening him to announce that the president had escaped. It was his right as the nation's Leader. Fear was *always* the best method of control.

Placing the gun's barrel on the envelope, he drew it closer. It had the top-secret insignia of the D.C. agent. The Leader narrowed his eyes as he opened the envelope, removing and rapidly scanning its contents. His eyes opened wide as he nodded to the gun. "This is good news. Fortuitous that we know what this American husband has in mind. If I can thwart his plans, even him, then perhaps this will permanently establish our holohead as leader of the..." he laughed loudly to the gun, "...the free world. Yeah, *free*, on my terms!"

The Leader tossed the gun on the agent's report, rising to gaze out the window at his beautiful garden. He spoke to the fragrant breeze that washed his broad face, "With our holohead in place, our position at the Davos head table should become a reality! Yes. I must release Dong from the barracks. Exhausted or not, she will ensure that, with the holohead, I rule."

He envisioned himself on his throne as the minion leaders of the world bowed before him in unbridled allegiance, submitting to his every command. He imagined myriad treats from around the world lined up in a mile-long queue. His hand went to his chest with the vague thought of how his heart could handle such treasure. He sighed deeply. It was all coming together: the opportunity afforded him by Dong and that Doctor Juong. Perhaps he had been too harsh with her. She was, after all, critical to making this vision come true.

The Leader walked to his desk, buzzing his new assistant.

The door opened. A uniformed young man entered, clicking his heels as he approached the Leader's desk. "Sir?"

"Have you deployed the brigade to find that... woman? We know she is heading north by northeast. Have you?"

"Sir! Yes. Over three hundred troops have been deployed on the ground, and at least a dozen helicopters are canvassing that entire area. We have sealed all borders and ports in that sector. We will find her!"

"Make no mistake, Colonel. You are personally responsible for the success of this mission. You know what failure means? Do you recall the stories of Ivan the Terrible?"

"Yes, I do, dear Leader!" the assistant bellowed. "It is my honor to serve you and accept whatever outcome you deem correct."

"What a moron," the Leader thought, chuckling to himself. "Fear really does work so efficiently." Clearing his throat and pulling down on the edges of his suit jacket, he replied, "Bring me Director Dong. But... be sure she freshens up first."

As the assistant left, the Leader turned once again to his garden vista, the imagined hand of victory pinching his cheeks. He put his hands on the windowsill, closing his eyes. He imagined the rush of the wind in the garden trees being the roar of thousands of worshippers spread out before him.

A hard knock on his door stilled the roar.

"Yes?"

The door burst open as his assistant and the barracks commander ran in, both out of breath. They gestured back and forth as to whom should go first, knowing that the messenger was usually held responsible for the substance of the message.

"Well? What is this?" the Leader demanded.

The barracks commander, looking down, gesturing at the rug, said, "We have lost Dong. She has disappeared."

"What?" the Leader yelled.

"Yes, dear Father. She has been locked in with no way out. She was standing in the corner of the main room of the barracks. The soldier with her looked away for the briefest of seconds. When he turned back to her, all he saw was a pile of her clothes—there in the corner."

"What are you saying?" the Leader said, his eyes hammering his cheeks and chiseling away the pinch of victory. Without Dong and his "reclaimed" baggage—the president—all could be lost.

The assistant started, "I believe, Mighty One, what the commander means is that, in a flash, Dong evaporated."

"Evaporated! Is that what you mean, Commander?"

"Sir, there is no other explanation. The windows and doors to the room were shut, secure. I trust the soldier's explanation with my life."

The Leader, gritting his teeth, howled, "That is where this will lead unless you…" pointing to the commander, "and you, Colonel," as he pointed to his assistant, "find Dong and that American woman! Now, leave me, and report back within one day. Either with your success, or, the order for me to sign for your executions. Go!"

Both men tripped over themselves as they hurried from the office.

The Leader sat back at his desk, his forehead in his hands. "Why is fate being so cruel to me?" he moaned to the pistol. Puckering his lips, he recalled that Juong had claimed the holohead could not be traced back to their nation. That, without continuous teleported vectoring from the AI backend at Building 666, the holohead would disappear without a trace or trail, simply evaporate. "Wait! Evaporate? Is that what Juong said?" the Leader puzzled, pointing the pistol at a light fixture, his eyes wide with fear. "Is that what happened to Dong? What do we really know about her? And what about Juong? Will he be able to run 666 and control the holohead without Dong?" He pushed the buzzer, yelling, "Bring Juong to me immediately! And have the barracks staff executed!" He chewed his lips, shaking his head. "I am alone, surrounded by flunkies. Alone, to rule the world."

The Leader reached for his phone. "I must have a direct, secure line to our agent in D.C." he yelled. "I don't care that it's risky. I *must* have direct communication!" He thought of Elizabeth, Catherine the Great's predecessor. How Elizabeth had made it her duty to dispose of people who gave the slightest indication to not obey, or, who got in her way. This group of American geeks, led by that professor, *were* such people.

Five minutes later his assistant barged in carrying a phone. "This is a secure satellite phone that patches directly to your D.C. agent. She is waiting to talk with you, dear Leader."

The Leader tried to picture the agent. His motto—*hormones before duty*—had never failed him. He cleared his throat, commanding control of the discussion. "Comrade Jo? This is your Leader," he began, waiting to gauge her response.

"Dear Leader. My humble thanks! So very kind of you to contact me directly. I assume you were able to read my full report, the text of the conversation I intercepted from the White House?"

"Indeed. Why I am calling. You have done well. I will reward you, *personally*, when you return. You find that acceptable?"

Knowing the implication, yet also the penalty for showing anything other than a servile manner, she replied, "It would be my great honor to receive such a reward from you."

The Leader paused, snapping his fingers until his assistant showed him a picture of the agent. He smiled. "To business. It is imperative that we shut down and destroy that group of Americans that spoke with the president's husband."

"The whole team of geeks?"

"Yes, yes! If we can get rid of that team and any evidence they have—especially this mysterious math technology—then our holohead can continue in its service to our most wonderful nation. Do you understand? We must protect the holohead at all costs! And, if I may ask out of sincere concern, how is that family of yours. Your sister and parents?"

The phone static masked the agent's deep inhale. She paused. There were no options other than to obey. "I understand, Dear Leader."

The Leader, glancing at the transcript of the discussion between Mac and Roy, said, "The First Husband will be scheduling a meeting in New York City. He said he will use email to confirm the meeting. What a fool, not so? I want you to intercept his email and in its place send our own invitation. You can do that, yes?"

"Hacking his email will be easy," Jo replied.

"Invite them to a location where you can easily dispose of them. I must insist that it look natural so as to not raise suspicions. If that team is removed, the president's husband will, for sure, try to launch an investigation. So leave no evidence. Be thorough. Keep it simple. Your family requests that of you... that you succeed."

The agent, frantic with worry, asked, "How thorough? Do you want me to also remove the president's husband?"

"No. Emphatically, I say, no! With that team and the evidence gone, let that foolish, confused man blow all the tea-leaf steam he wants. Without evidence, he will sound a fool. We will vector our holohead to express sympathy for his condition in a manner that leaves no doubt that he is insane."

"Dear Leader, I will go immediately to New York. Please consider it done."

"I *will* consider it done."

The connection went dead.

CHAPTER 31

The Trap

The first day of spring in New York City—Friday, March 21— looked like anything but spring. Heavy, gray clouds boiled against the glassed-in towers of Wall Street. The Verrazano-Narrows Bridge was masked from the collective gaze of Street analysts striving to predict market reaction to the president's latest embrace of rogue nations. Crashing whitecaps broke over the decks of Staten Island ferries. The Columbus Circle webcam showed an ambulance skidding across icy lanes and through a stoplight. Horns blared. Pedestrians dodged cars as they negotiated Park Avenue intersections in the heavy, freezing rain.

Forty-two stories above the noise and clamor of Park Avenue, Agent Jo anxiously paced the halls of the large corner apartment. This was her nation's opulent safe house hiding in plain sight. Her concentration oscillated between strategies for isolating the geeks, her family's safety, and her trim figure reflected in the large windows backlit by a vista of Central Park. She had grown used to the freedoms and lifestyles available in America. So much in contrast with her own nation. Freedom versus subservience. Self-expression versus poverty of mind and means. If not for her family, she would seek asylum in this land of opportunity.

Finally, she decided. There was no out. She had to follow orders. It came down to the lives of her family versus those of six or seven people she didn't know. It was a decision she dreaded. She imagined that the Americans had families. Did her family matter more than any other? She was an intelligence officer, not a murderer. Jo moaned in anguish. She would have to bring up more agents from Washington D.C. Men. Strong, to execute the selected strategy. Weak, in humanity.

Returning to the desk in the apartment's library, she went online to *spacesavailable.com* to find listings of lofts, apartments, and commercial spaces. In addition to invoking a spoofed identity with private browsing, she loaded the details on over forty spaces. To obscure her focus on the three best prospects, she did screen captures. Totally anonymous. The three were lofts in the Lower West Side of the Tribeca neighborhood.

To reduce the possibility of escape by the geeks, her plan required a loft with as few windows as possible, a single entry point, and above the third floor. She found a perfect match on West Fifteenth Street. The fifth floor had two loft apartments serviced by a private elevator that descended to a loading dock at the rear of the building. She wasn't sure who occupied the other apartment, but she knew her agents would appear as ordinary renovation contractors, no questions asked. The fire escape was not an issue. Her agents from D.C. would seal the windows with *CryptoCoatSealer*, the clear, spray-on coating that made any surface impenetrable.

Agent Jo called her jeweler—one of her nation's shell-companies. She asked him to contact the rental agent to secure the loft apartment by tomorrow, Saturday. Jo's next task was to hack Mac's email and send the fake invitation. This took only fifteen minutes, using a hacking app available from *justaskme.ru*. She inserted a redirect function so that any further incoming email to Mac from Roy was sent to her secret account. She then hacked the email server of *GloryBeMe.com*, the popular fashion site, to email Mac an invitation to a fashion show at the loft address. For Monday evening at five o'clock.

Finally, she contacted her pool of agents, outlining what they needed to do in the loft by Sunday evening. Besides replacing the front door and sealing the windows, she instructed them where to mount the self-dissolving nanocams. Most importantly, how to alter the refrigerator's Freon system by overfilling the tank with carbon dioxide and attaching a nanovalve to leak the gas into the loft. Everything was to be tied to a radio-frequency initiation signal. There must be no trace of foul play. This was a direct order from the Leader, himself.

——— · ———

Mindy was stretched out on the sofa reading *Oblique*, the book that highlighted Mac's D37 near-crisis adventure. She was anxious to gain any insight into his behavior as a professor—anything that could help her help him suppress his shoebox.

Her cheeks pink from the warmth of the fire, Mindy ran her hand over her breasts and stomach to smooth out the causal blue tunic Mac had purchased for their two-month anniversary. He had been so excited over how the tunic brought out the blue of her eyes. She smiled, envisioning him at the store, fumbling with the decision on what to buy. Mac definitely was inept at certain things. Cocking her head towards the sounds of Mac typing away in the bedroom office, her expression was softly peaceful. Suddenly, Mac yelled, "I got it!" Mindy jumped, the book falling to the floor.

Leaning over to pick up the book, she called back, "What?"

Mac ran into the living room. "I got the email from Roy. The invitation to the fashion show. This means he's really on board with our investigation!"

"What did it say? Are you sure it's from him?"

"Had to be. Simply said the fashion show is Monday, at five in the afternoon."

"Who's the sender?"

"It was an invitation from a fashion design company showing the White House calendar that listed the fashion show along with other upcoming events. Like, the Easter Egg Roll next month and the president's kite-flying contest on the East Lawn. So he obfuscated the message to me within the calendar. Pretty clever, huh?"

Mindy rotated off the sofa, looking up as she placed the book on the coffee table. "Mac? This is horribly serious stuff. I was just reading about D37. That was close to life and death. This issue with Roy and the president surely is similar, at least in terms of danger. No?"

Mac brushed back his hair with his right hand, gesturing agitation with his left as a boy might when deprived of playing with his friends. "I gotta believe that Roy, the Colonel, knows what he's doing. That he'll have the safe house fully cleared and covered by the Secret Service."

"What does the email say about *where*? What if it's some dark alley?"

Mac laughed, sitting down next to Mindy, putting his arm around her. "You've read too many novels," he said, kissing her cheek. "Man, you're burning up." He stood, stretched, and walked towards the kitchen.

"Where is it?" Mindy insisted, watching Mac's cute butt disappear down the hall and thinking briefly that it was time for bed. She shook her head, laughing at herself.

Mac stopped at the kitchen door, taking hold of the doorframe as he looked back down the hall at Mindy. "That's the cool part. There was no address. An apparent goof. The only link on the email was to 'Deliveries.' I clicked on that, and the address came up in my browser window. It's over on Fifteenth Street, not very far from here. We can walk there from here. It's a loft on the top floor."

Mindy blew out her cheeks in exasperation. She walked down the hall, stopping briefly to adjust prints on the wall. Struggling to hide the amorous look painted across her face, she leaned in, pushing Mac against the doorframe. "So, Mister D37 survivor? You think we can just saunter over by ourselves. Like, a casual stroll. That the Secret Service will know who we are?"

"Yeah, I'm sure. Regardless, I'll do some recon on Sunday to check the place out. My guess is there'll be plenty of Secret Service coverage on Monday. We just won't know who."

"I don't like it. Why can't we have Roy come here?"

Mac gave Mindy a brief hug as he turned into the kitchen. He pulled some leftover pizza from the refrigerator. "If it'll make you feel better, I'll go with a team."

Mindy grabbed the pizza from Mac and took a bite, wiping her lips with an extended, sensuous display of her tongue. "What's this 'I'll go'? We'll both go!"

Mac took her face in his hands, squinting into her blue eyes. "Look, this is totally safe. But, on the off chance it does get serious, I'm going it alone!" His eyes held as stern a look as Mindy had seen. This was no namby-pamby shoebox indecision. He was telling her how it would be. Mac, the Sergeant.

"I don't care, Mac! I insist you take some backup with you."

Mac pushed one of the kitchen chairs up against the table. "Who do you have in mind? Of course, I have to take Justin. He's the only one who can run the concentric math filter."

Mindy came up behind him, putting her arms around his waist, her cheek against his shoulder. "I'm as adamant as you. I think you need to take the D37 team with you. Not just Justin, but Blake, Devon, and Gloria. They're all jocks. Strong. Could be important if anything happened."

"You *do* read too many novels!" Mac laughed. "What? Jocks against guns?"

"Guns!"

"Just saying," Mac replied, turning to embrace Mindy. "Look. All we're doing is showing Roy the *before* and *after* filtered videos. He'll decide where to go from there. So, I promise you there is no reason whatsoever to be worried."

Mindy pushed away, leaning against the kitchen counter. "In that case, I *am* coming with you. Period!"

Mac leaned down, slapping his knees, howling with laughter. "You should see yourself, right now. You're almost scary…"

Mindy rushed him, bending Mac back across the kitchen table in her embrace, chairs flying off to the side. "…and strong," he added as he picked her up and carried her to the bedroom.

Later that evening, a sated Mac called the core members of the D37 team: Blake and Gloria, Devon, and Justin. He asked them to meet at Mindy's house on Monday afternoon. He told them it was important to support Justin as he demonstrated his findings to 'the man' (Mac's vague reference to Roy.) Blake, Devon, and Gloria responded with excitement, although it meant missing classes and traveling down from Boston once again. But all agreed this was important.

Justin was harder to convince. Extremely nervous, he was sure they had stumbled across something that was, more than anything, dangerous.

—— . ——

On Monday evening, the IT team, along with Mindy, walked down Fifteenth Street. They went around the back of the building to the loading dock Mac had found on his recon visit the day before.

"There are two elevators. This one goes direct to the fifth floor. Guess it's a penthouse loft," Mac said, looking around at the people on the street and wondering which ones were Secret Service. He noticed, without thinking, that there were no cars in the parking lot.

"I'll go first," Blake, the linebacker said. "Devon, you cover our rear." The two football players laughed hard at their notion of being agents on a clandestine mission.

Gloria, joining in the role playing, took Mindy's hand. "I've got the president," she laughed.

Justin was having none of it. His beady eyes searched out the doors and windows on adjacent buildings. Entering the hall leading from the loading dock, as if for balance, he ran his hand along the wall. "Awful quiet around here, don't you think Mac? Where's the... protection the man's supposed to have?"

"All accounted for." The voice came through Agent Jo's earpiece from one of her spotters in the building next to the parking lot.

The IT team exited the elevator on the top floor. They were giddy with excitement, chatting about meeting the president's husband. All except Justin, whom Devon had to push off the elevator. Mac had his hand on Mindy's shoulder as he followed her up to the door marked "5A-Fashion Meeting." He looked across the hall, to the door marked 5B.

"This must be it," he said, pulling up on the door lever to 5A.

After a brief look around the interior of the loft, Mac noticed several binders marked 'White House, Eyes Only' on a nearby table.

"This is the place," he said, waving his arms to gather the team.

"All accounted for," Jo whispered, watching the nanocam feed from the loft's main room. "Stand by," she mumbled, devastated by what she was about to do.

Mindy noticed that Mac's grip on her hand was starting to hurt. She saw a look in his eyes that caused her heart to shudder: a fierceness she had never seen. "God help the shoebox if it ever encounters Mac in this mood," she thought, seeking to apply humor to what was becoming a tense situation.

Mac, his eyes frozen in situation assessment, growled, "Gloria, looks like there's just one other room. A kitchen? Check that out, would you? And Blake, look in the bathroom. I'm not sure where Roy is. I expected some entourage. At least some kind of security."

"I told you," Justin squealed as he edged back towards the open door. He could sense the rigidness in Mac's body.

"Listen up, guys," Mac commanded, putting his hand on Justin's shoulder. "I'm gonna check this out." He walked out to the elevator, closing the loft door behind him.

"Now!" Jo's agent yelled, holding his earpiece and hearing the door close. He prematurely pressed the button to throw the door lock and release the gas from the refrigerator.

"No! Wait!" Jo yelled, watching the loft's nanocam feed. "There's one out in the hall. You've sealed the door too soon!"

Justin, standing inside the loft next to the door, heard the large bang as the door sealed shut. He grabbed the door lever, jerking to open it. After a frantic few seconds, Justin screamed, "Blake! The door's been locked!" He banged hard on the door as Blake ran up.

Outside in the hall, Mac turned to the door. "What the shit!" he howled. He tugged on the door handle, hearing the faint banging from Justin. The door was thick, solid metal. His first thoughts were, "Ambush. Damn! I should have assessed the situation better!"

Mindy and Gloria joined Blake and Justin as they banged frantically on the door, jerking on the handle and checking the hinges. "Devon! Man, check the windows. Yeah, the one by the fire escape!" Blake yelled.

Devon ran to all the windows, stopping at the one with the fire escape and pulling hard on it. It wouldn't budge. "It's stuck, man! Help me try to bust through," Devon shouted back at Blake.

They took the table and, using it as a ram, ran at the fire escape window. "Watch for shattering glass," Devon yelled. Both wrenched their hands as the table bounced off the unbroken window.

"What the hell! We're trapped!" Blake shouted. "Everybody, try the windows. Throw anything you can at them. We don't need the fire escape." He motioned to Justin to help him toss the couch at a window.

Justin was panting. "Hard to breathe in here, yeah?"

"Me, too," Mindy screamed, watching the others sag to their knees.

"We're in trouble, deep trouble..." Blake whimpered, his mouth flopping open, his eyes unable to focus on his cell phone buttons. He stumbled back to the door, kicking and banging on it.

They were out of air. And time.

CHAPTER 32

The Execution

Blake's vision was fading. Through the haze he saw the others collapsing to the floor. With all his strength, he pulled Gloria to the fire escape window. Crawling, fighting not to faint, he also managed to drag the others to the window. With a final effort, propelled by the vague memory of the strength it took to play defense against a dominant offensive line, he pulled himself up to the windowsill. He could see people below, going about their lives without notice. He pounded his fist against the glass until the pounding of his heart began to fade.

Blake fell next to Gloria, the beautiful, wonderful woman he loved. Just a kid, really. Like all of them. Too young to die. His head on her chest, his right arm around her head, he shook her stilled body. He tried to give her mouth-to-mouth until, with some waning thought, he realized that he was blowing into her the same foul air that was killing them all.

He cried out to his mother. She had already lost her husband—his father—and her other son. And now, this. Blake's sobs rocked Gloria's body as he gulped for air. His ears rang with the pounding of his heart. He struggled to remember the goodness he had found with Gloria. With Mac, his mentor. Mac? Blake heard Mac's voice. It was high-pitched against the pounding sound. His heart? No, it was the door. The locked, solid door.

The agent's voice—tinged with a glee that had Jo seething—came through her earpiece. "They're going fast. We executed well, if you get my double meaning," he laughed.

Jo yelled back, no longer worried about stealth. "You idiot! There's still one outside. Our operation has failed. You have doomed us all with your anxiousness! Engage all the self-destruct mechanisms and vacate!

We must, at the very least, leave no evidence. Protect our dear Leader!" she yelled. "And… my family," she whispered.

On the outside of the door, Mac had no idea what was happening until he realized the banging from inside the door had ceased. Frantic, he thought of the fire escape. But it was not accessible from the hallway. He turned, banging on the door to apartment 5B. He heard someone coming to the door.

"What's with all the noise?" the young man asked as he opened the door. "Who are you guys, anyway?"

Mac, in full command, the shoebox a non-issue, rushed past the young man, yelling, "We have an emergency next door. People are dying in there! Call 9-1-1!"

"What the hell?"

Mac, picking up the phone, yelled, "I've no time to explain. There are people in 5A that we have to rescue!" He gave the 9-1-1 operator the address and said apartment 5A was on fire. He turned to the young man. "Who are you?"

"Martin Cortez, man. Who the hell are you?"

"I, we, are supposed to be meeting a… federal agent in 5A. Something has gone horribly wrong. No time to explain. Do you have a fire axe or something we can use to bust down that door?"

"No way, man. I saw the construction crew yesterday installing the heavy steel door. I was thinking that it looked impenetrable."

"How 'bout the fire escape?"

"Yeah, but we'd have to go down the elevator, then up the 5A fire escape. Which, by the way, doesn't have a ladder to the ground. I noticed them taking that away yesterday."

"We're wasting time," Mac yelled, taking a deep breath, engaging all his battle-hardened experience. With a flash of thought, he realized the shoebox was toast. He was needed to command. This was a battle he could not, must not, lose.

He looked around Martin's apartment. "You got no tools at all?" He looked up, seeing the skylight. "How does that open? Is there one in 5A?" he demanded.

"It opens with a switch by the door. Yeah, I think that unit has one."

"Can we use your fire escape to get to the roof!" Mac asked, frantic.

"Shit, no. Don't have one. The damn landlord doesn't have this building up to code yet. Why I'm paying sub-rent. She promised it would be installed…"

Mac interrupted Martin, waving his hands. "So how the hell do we get in there? We can't wait for the fire department! For all I know, they're already dead. We gotta move fast!"

Martin looked up at the skylight, fifteen feet above them. "I'm just back from the Adirondacks. Climbed Rogers Rock. I have ropes and a grabbling hook right here. We can climb through my skylight," he said, as he ran to switch open his skylight and grab his climbing belt.

Mac watched, amazed. Part of him couldn't help but admire Martin—his sheer talent and speed in tossing the hook through the skylight and securing it to something on the roof. Martin reminded Mac of Jaime, one of the soldiers he had loved, and lost, in Afghanistan.

Martin was up the rope in seconds. He turned to yell down to Mac. "Wow!" he roared, his eyes wide. Mac, the old, recovering veteran, had climbed up right behind him. "I'll bust open their skylight and drop in to open up the windows."

"Wait!" Mac shouted, as Martin pulled him over the skylight threshold. "There could be danger down there. I'll go."

Martin, with a fast appraising look at Mac, said, "Look, man, I'll be faster. I got my climbing hammer and some rock anchors I can use to wedge the windows, if needed. I can always climb back up the rope. You go over there," Martin pointed across the roof to the 5A fire escape. "Go down and bust in from there!"

Before Mac could respond, Martin was down the rope, into the poisoned air of unit 5A.

Mac was pissed, yet thankful. Thinking that Martin was, yes, the right man for the inside job, Mac ran to the fire escape and climbed down to the window. It was sealed tight. He kicked frantically. He tore up a slat from the old landing and started bashing the window. He could see the bodies inside. Finally, Martin was at the window, his face pale. He looked to be suffocating. Mac watched as Martin fought to pound and screw the rock anchors between the sill and window. Mac was yelling for Martin to hurry. He was torn between running back up to the roof and descending himself. But he knew he'd succumb just like Martin was. Their only chance was from the outside. He heard sirens in the distance as he watched Martin through the window, struggling, each stroke of his hammer less forceful.

Mac put his back to the railing and kicked the window with both legs, with all his might. Those were his troops inside. He'd never let them down. And Mindy! "Dear God," he yelled to the sky. "Please, help me!" he sobbed.

CHAPTER 33

The Evidence

Mac would forever remember the look on Martin's face. A brave smile—mournful—borne by acceptance of the outcome, the sacrifice. Martin nodded, his eyes holding Mac's as he struggled for his last breath. He had done his best.

Mac was screaming, throwing his body at the window. "No, No!" he yelled. "No! No, please no, dear God. Please…"

He looked up, about to go back up to the roof and into the unit. He could not bear life without Mindy. He could not accept the fate he had caused his team. He would join them. He looked down at the parking lot, the fire engines pulling in, too late.

With one last, mighty heave, Mac crashed his body into the damn window. A heave that would, thankfully, dispel the sealing capabilities of *CryptoCoatSealer*. The double-hung window popped open an inch, propelled mainly by pressure from Martin's rock anchors. Mac quickly picked up the slat and jammed it into the crack to lever the window. He pulled up hard. The slat broke. He grabbed the bottom of the window with his hands, pushing up with his legs with all the strength God had granted (or, so he would tell his grandchildren.)

The window squeaked higher. Mac pulled harder, screaming at the universe to free the window. The firefighters below on the ladder trucks, hearing him, swung a telescoping ladder up to the fire escape. Inch by painful inch, Mac pulled, his hands bleeding, his back breaking. After what seemed a lifetime, the window was open far enough. He crawled in and immediately brought the bodies closer to the open window. He saw the gray pallor of the faces he loved. He grabbed Mindy's body first, starting to shove it through the open slot. Mac could tell he was fading. There just was not enough fresh air! He fell to his knees, against the back of Mindy's legs, her body halfway out the window.

The next thing Mac felt was his face slamming against the inside wall below the window. Two firefighters had pulled Mindy out, immediately putting a respirator to her face.

"Stand back!" yelled one of the firefighters, swinging her fire axe hard at the window. It bounced off. "I need a jack!" she yelled down the ladder. The other firefighter took off his respirator, following it as he pushed it through the window. While alternating between putting his air mask on the ashen faces and then back on his own face, he managed to push Gloria through the window slot.

A third firefighter arrived up the ladder, carrying a hydraulic jack. "Watch out!" the woman firefighter shouted. "This platform is overloaded." She took the jack and placed it between the window and the sill. She heaved on the jack's lever. "Glass!" she yelled. The firefighter on the ladder jumped to the fire escape, throwing his body across Mindy and Gloria as the window burst under the pressure, spraying the rescuers in shards of glass. The firefighter inside the apartment had stood, his back to the window in an effort to protect the bodies. It worked for Mac and Blake and Justin, Devon and Martin. But not for the firefighter. The exploding glass pierced his reinforced thermal coat.

The firefighter who had covered Mindy and Gloria swept off the glass and started chest compressions. A second ladder swung up, a firefighter tethered to it, holding a rotary saw. He quickly cut seams through an adjacent window, kicking the glass in. He jumped into the apartment, followed by two more firefighters with extra air packs.

The last thing Agent Jo saw from the nanocam, before it melted, was that the entire IT team was alive. The first responders were cheering.

Walking slowly down Fifteenth, moving around the crowd of onlookers—fire trucks and ambulances—she said a prayer for her family. Her report to the Leader would beg for mercy. She would offer him anything, although she knew, in the end, she was dead. It was simply how he viewed life: a process of eliminating obstacles to achieve his glory.

A lieutenant from New York City's Special Operations Bureau was questioning Mindy as her gurney was about to be loaded into an ambulance. Mac, still coughing and weak, walked up with the assistance of a fire department captain. "Excuse me, officer," Mindy began as she reached out for Mac's heavily bandaged hands. "Have you figured out what we were breathing?"

"Looks like a defective refrigerator," the captain replied. "No traces of anything abnormal other than the Freon and what appears to be a high concentration of carbon dioxide. We're asking the FBI lab for help. Their team will be on site shortly."

"I'd like to stay and talk with them, if that's okay," Mac injected. He put his right hand gingerly on the lieutenant's shoulder, forcing down memories of the baton hit he'd taken from one of NYPD's finest. "Did you guys get any kind of read on the door? The fact that it locked on us seems bizarre. And the windows. They were sealed over. What's with that?"

"We're working on it," the lieutenant answered. "At first glance, seems like just some extra security built into that unit."

Mac shook his head. "Have you asked the neighbor from 5B? He saw contractors working on that unit yesterday."

"Yeah, we're working on that, too."

Without explaining to the police why they had been in the loft, Mac figured it best to fill Roy in with the details and let him take it from there. It was beyond a suspicious circumstance. Someone had definitely tried to kill them. Mac just wasn't sure whom he should trust: NYPD with their batons, or the Feds with shades of D37?

Martin walked up carrying a small oxygen cylinder, a mask on his face. "Hey, man! I never got to thank you for saving us," he said, putting his arm around Mac.

Mac turned to look Martin in the face. "It's because of you, Martin, that they're alive. You did it!" Mac pointed to Blake, Gloria, and Devon, all sitting on the step of the nearby fire engine, taking oxygen. And to Justin, on a nearby gurney, holding his laptop tightly. "It was amazing luck that someone with your skills and fast reactions was across the hall.

My guess is you saved us all, 'cause otherwise, I'd have somehow gotten into the unit, and died there. We can't thank you enough, man!"

Martin took a deep breath, squinting at Mac as he removed the oxygen mask. "I know you, man. You're the guy in the news last election, right?"

Mac shrugged.

Mindy answered for him. "Yes, this is Sergeant MacMahan."

"Sergeant? Thought I recognized you. Myself, I'm ex-Ranger," Martin said, snorting through his nose. "Hooah!"

Mac gave Martin a big hug. "Hooah, man! No wonder you can climb so well, huh?"

As Mac and Martin traded stories, the police lieutenant and fire captain walked back to the building. Mindy could tell that Mac was in his element. He had survived disaster and brought his team through. She held out her arms to Mac, asking for a hug.

Turning to the ambulance driver, Mac asked, "Where're you guys taking her and the others?"

"Lower Manhattan. Just routine. They seem fine."

"I'll follow you over," Mac whispered, leaning in to give Mindy a tender kiss. "You don't know hard I prayed, how I screamed for you and the others. I love you so!"

"I can see how hard you tried," Mindy replied, looking at his hands. "I love you, Mac!" She started to cry, the shock of the moment finally hitting her.

For some reason he couldn't explain, as Mac was kissing Mindy, Martin leaned over to embrace them both. "Hooah," he said, softly.

——— . ———

Roy had just finished showering after shooting baskets with Todd and Kari when the private phone rang.

"Butcher," he answered.

"Colonel, Mac here. There's been an incident."

"What?" Roy asked, sitting on the wet towel.

"We followed your instructions to meet at the fashion loft. You know, the safe house. Instead, we were attacked."

"Wait!" Roy exclaimed. "Our meeting is scheduled for tomorrow. You got my email, right? And... what's this about being attacked?"

"We were gassed! In the loft your email sent us to."

"Gassed! What do you mean? You okay?"

"Barely. Got lucky, I guess. Mindy says it was the hand of God. But whatever, it was real close."

"Mindy? Your wife was with you? Damn, Mac! This is terrible. Who's on the case? The police, FBI? Mac, you got it wrong! My email had us meeting at West Eighty-Fifth Street. A townhouse. Where'd you get the idea of a loft?"

"We went to a place on West Fifteenth, just like your... Wait!" Mac hissed. "We were hacked. Someone's on to us, Colonel! Gotta be that. All seven of us almost died. Didn't you see the news? It made this morning's *Times*."

"Soldier, I want you to take it from the top! Leave out no details."

"Sir? Is this line secure? Somehow, someone got hold of our plan. They... they had to have intercepted our last conversation. That was the only time we talked about meeting. We better say no more until we can meet in person."

"Understood," Roy replied, wiping his face with the towel. "I'll get up there immediately. Who's on this. NYPD, FBI?"

"Both, I think."

"I'll contact the Bureau to make sure someone's there to meet us. I'll meet you at the Manhattan Heliport near Wall Street, around 3 PM. Does that work?"

"Yes, sir. It does. See you then," Mac responded, about to hang up.

"Mac!" Roy shouted. "I'm truly thankful you're all okay. Was Justin with you?"

"Yes, sir. He survived. We'll pick him up. You'll be amazed at what he'll show us."

—— . ——

At 2 PM, Mac had a taxi pick up Mindy, Justin, and Gloria from the hospital, with instructions to take them back to Mindy's.

Mac used Uber to take Blake and Devon with him to the heliport. At 3:15 PM, Roy's helicopter landed. He exited with two Secret Service members. They walked over to two FBI agents standing by a large, black Suburban. As they left the heliport Roy spotted Mac standing at the heliport entrance. The driver pulled over to pick them up.

"Where to?" Roy asked after introductions had been made.

"Mindy's house. It's on a private alley, here in lower Manhattan. There's no way anyone knows about it."

"Sounds good," one of the FBI members replied. "We'll do a quick sweep, anyway." He looked out the back window, noting the intercept decoy from the Bureau directly behind.

Mac was worried about everyone fitting in Mindy's house. Worse, the Suburban reminded him of his hassles with the Pentagon and VA back during the D37 crisis. He had to stay intense to avoid the shoebox. "Colonel? Any more information on what hit us?" he asked.

The other FBI agent spoke up. "Turns out it was a faulty fridge, made so by some very intricate devices and primed with carbon dioxide. It was a death trap, for sure. The door, the window sealant—all point to a very sophisticated operation. Had to be state-sponsored."

"It's serious," Roy said, looking back from the front seat. "You've uncovered something big time, Sergeant. There's too much evidence. A state player, for sure. Well done."

None of which made Mac relax. Well done? He had been told that before, by his officers in Afghanistan. Even so, he had still lost brothers. The sooner this entire episode concluded, without involving Mindy or the others, the better.

He knew, however, that he would stay involved. To the end. If only to keep the shoebox away.

CHAPTER 34

The Guess

Mindy, on edge as the hostess, was reassured when Mac gathered everyone's coats, taking them to the bedroom. On the way back to the living room, he stopped to turn down the hall thermostat.

"I apologize for how hot it is," he said, as he rolled up his sleeves and sat on the sofa next to Roy. He glanced lovingly over at Mindy who raised her eyebrows.

Justin pushed some books aside to make room for his laptop on the coffee table. He squeezed between Roy and Mac. The Secret Service and FBI agents stood to the side, in the hall. Gloria and Mindy took the two wing chairs, with Blake and Devon standing behind them.

"Can I get anyone some water?" Mindy asked, looking around the packed room. Convinced everyone was overheated, she uttered a brief murmur when there were no takers.

"Thank you, Mrs. MacMahan, for opening your house to us. Say, O'Brien?" Roy looked up at the tall, flushed-face FBI agent who had just removed his suit coat and was smoothing down his ginger hair. "Sweep's clean?"

"Yes, sir. No issues. We have a car at the entrance to the alley and two over on Washington Square North. All good, sir," O'Brien replied, absently putting his hand on his sidearm as he stared at Mac.

"Thank you. Now that we're settled, let's get to it." Turning to address all four agents, Roy continued. "If you guys don't mind, I'm here to discuss a personal matter with these folks." Roy motioned around the room to the IT team members. Looking directly at O'Brien, he added, "Would you four please wait in the kitchen?"

"Do these kids have clearances?" O'Brien asked.

Roy nodded, acknowledging the appropriateness of the question. "We'll be discussing a hypothetical. Something personal."

Raising his eyebrows, pointing at Mac, O'Brien said, "Just asking."

Mac laughed, a little too loudly. He was still haunted by memories of how the FBI had treated him during D37. He suspected O'Brien was ex-military. Probably a junior officer. One who had never actually seen action. One who compensated by challenging those outside a perceived area of need-to-know. Mac was certain O'Brien had looked him up in the FBI database. "Sir," Mac began, his left arm extended towards O'Brien in a placating manner—one that revealed his horrible in-and-out-burger scar. "We're here to provide the colonel with information, not the other way around. No security concerns, if you get my drift?"

Mindy looked at Mac. Would this exchange bring on the shoebox? She held back the urge to remind O'Brien of what Roy had just said. After a tense pause, she gestured to the kitchen. "Please, follow me."

"Mrs. MacMahan, I'd like you to stay. You guys," pointing at the agents, "please give us ten minutes, alone," Roy said, firmly.

In spite of his uncertainty, O'Brien was a good solider. He nodded to Roy and motioned the other three to follow him.

"There's cold beer in the icebox," Mindy called out, immediately covering her mouth, realizing the inappropriateness of her comment.

Roy graciously injected, "We could all use a beer. Thanks, Mindy. May I call you Mindy?"

She nodded, starting to go to the kitchen.

Roy blurted, "No, no. Please, Mindy. Just kidding."

Mindy let out a sigh, pursing her lips in embarrassment while glancing over at Mac. His smiling expression held all the love she needed. She looked over at Gloria, whose dark eyes conveyed respect and honor. After smoothing her skirt, she sat, content.

Justin cleared his throat. "Mister... ah, what should I call you, sir?"

Looking down the hall towards the kitchen, Roy turned to Justin. "Roy's good. Justin, Mac says you have some kind of filter to compare my wife's behavior before and after Valentine's Day. Is that correct?"

Justin could feel sweat dripping from his armpits. "Well, that sort of describes..."

Mac interrupted. "Justin, you're doing a big service here. Roy knows the gist of what you've found. Go ahead and just take us through some filtered videos of before and after that date." Mac put his arm around Justin, giving him a hug for confidence.

Gloria and Mindy came around to the back of the sofa to look over Justin's shoulder.

Justin ran thirteen filtered videos: six from before Valentines Day, seven after. The shadow and ripples were very evident in the seven but nonexistent in the six.

After fifteen minutes, O'Brien came back into the living room.

"We need a little more time," Roy requested.

"Then, okay if we take a break outside?"

"Sure thing. Thanks for your patience and understanding," Roy replied. "Yeah, take ten outside." He sighed deeply. Gloria reached out, putting her hand on his shoulder. Without looking back, he put his hand back to hers, giving it a brief squeeze.

There was complete silence until Justin closed his laptop. He exhaled, taking a deep breath and sighing again. "What, to me," he began, "explains the shadows is, well, there must be some type of waveform impacting the president. The ripples, to me, signify a wave function. The shadow suggests a light wave."

"How is that possible?" Roy asked, incredulously.

Mac was wondering that, too. And how much NSA could benefit from someone like Justin. His attempt to hit on Mindy aside, Justin was the kind of brilliant geek the government needed.

"Justin?" Gloria asked. "What you've discovered is unbelievable. I wouldn't believe it if you hadn't shown us. But... how can you confirm it's some kind of wave? And from where?"

"Before we get to that," Roy stated, taking charge, "we need to confirm that some kind of signal or wave is being thrown at Margie... my wife. First, confirm she's subject to some kind of wave. Then we have to figure out how it is that the wave affects just her and not others around her..." Roy gasped, thinking of Kari and Todd.

"Then, we figure out from where. Right?" Blake injected, thinking of the many football games where the opposing offense had somehow read his team's defensive alignment and broadcast, from somewhere, an offensive adjustment without using signals from the sidelines.

Justin ran his hand over his long hair. Deep in thought, he popped his lips. "If we can isolate the president in a signal-free room, that could offer proof that some external wave is impacting her." Turning to Roy, he asked, "Are all communications monitored, like microwaves and any others, in and around the White House?"

Roy hesitated. The real answer involved national security. O'Brien would have him for lunch. But realistically, any high school kid could guess the correct answer. "Absolutely," he replied.

Mindy frowned, watching Justin rub his nose and wipe his hand on his pants. Her eyes tracked his hand as he pointed to the ceiling. "It's a simple series of binary tests," he said. "We run filtered videos on several cases, starting with the president in a room with someone else. We check the filter to see if the shadow appears on both of them. If so, it's a broadcast wave targeting the area, not the president. Then we isolate her in a room with interference mesh. We have someone else in there with her. If the concentric filter shows shadows for both, then it might be a broadcast wave. But… one at a frequency we don't understand because it shouldn't have penetrated the mesh. If not both, then it's something targeting just the president. And that's bad news. It would mean it's something beyond our understanding."

Mac spoke up. "Justin, what if it's not a wave at all? What if she has somehow been brainwashed. You know, like a behavior-mod method used in *Manchurian Candidate*?"

"What?" Justin replied, breaking away from his imagined analysis.

"That's absurd," Roy said, bitterly. "How would anyone get close enough to Margie to brainwash her? She's with someone twenty-four seven. It can't be that!"

"Colonel, we're all just trying to figure this out," Mac responded.

"Fair enough, Mac. Okay, sorry. It's more than the change in the president's behavior and her policy flipping. I'm hesitant to mention this, but it's important. She feels different. Plain and simple. We've been married for twenty years. So we're intimate. The suspicion that's been forming in my mind these past few weeks is that the woman who is president is different from my wife. I didn't want to mention it because it sounds crazy and I'm the only one who would know this.

We've not made love since Valentine's Day. Margie and I... Well anyway, two months is way too long a time. And this president knows none of the intimate signals that Margie and I have... or had! Damn! What am I saying? How the hell is this possible!" Roy bellowed.

Devon, anxious to contribute, blurted, "We're forgetting the close call we had in that loft. What if some group—I don't know, say a country or something like Bond's Spectre—has got ahold of the president and tried to kill us all to prevent being discovered?"

"What, you saying there's a crazy conspiracy, man?" Blake asked.

Justin stood, bumping the coffee table.

Mac had a flashback to when he'd found Mindy and Justin together. The pressure around his eyes was increasing. "Look, guys," he said, walking to stand by the fireplace. "If it's not President Perserve... whoever it is... is responding to waves. And if whoever is controlling those waves wants us dead, then for shit's sake, we need to bring in the FBI! Right, Roy?"

"Yeah, right Mac. But this all needs to be revealed carefully. You just don't blurt out that the president is some clone or some..."

Justin spun around, clapping his hands. He yelled, "Here's a possibility we haven't considered! What if the president..."

"Shh, shh," Roy whispered. "Keep it down."

Justin continued, quietly gesturing with his hands, "What if we're talking about some kind of clone?"

"That sci-fi shit, man," Devon sputtered.

"No, no! Think about it," Justin whispered, hushing the room. They were caught up in his imagination. "We know androids are science fiction. I mean, that is, until someone finally does create one. And this fits perfectly with the question we're trying to figure out. Who is the president, and what's controlling her?"

"Okay, Justin," Mac replied. "Let's go with your sci-fi angle. At least for a minute. If we find in your isolated-room scenario that the president remains this—whatever you want to call it—android, how is the controlling transmission being made?"

"If we prevented incoming transmission from its source and found that control of the president, as a receiver, continued independently...

Yeah, that's it! It would work if the receiver were a stand-alone data object. It would not involve frequencies or transmission of any sort. The answer would be *teleporting!*"

Roy rose from the sofa and slammed the wall. He looked up, facing the team. "Sorry Mindy. All this hypothetical talk leaves out, to me, the most important question. Where the hell is my wife?"

The front door opened. O'Brien ran in, looking around the room, at everyone seemingly frozen. Frozen by the outlandish scenario they were considering. "Everything okay, Colonel?" he demanded, his hand on his sidearm.

Roy went over, putting his hands on O'Brien's shoulders. "You're a good man, Patrick. Yeah, sorry if we alarmed you. I slipped and hit the wall. All's okay." Roy motioned around the room. The team, coming out of their stupor, nodded their assent. "Give us five more minutes, and then we're out of here."

"Yes, sir," O'Brien growled, giving Mac a prolonged stare, his hand still on his sidearm. "Five minutes. I'll alert the others."

As soon as the door closed, Roy ran up to Justin. "What's this teleporting? Is it real?"

"No, sir. At least, not yet far as I know. I would think some of your intelligence people would know for sure. Theoretically, it works. Just not sure it's ever been done in practice. The Chinese have attempted it."

"If this is what we're talking about, how in the hell would we know? And what the hell is teleporting?" Mac asked.

"It's just theory. But in theory, a... how to say..."

"Just say it, damn it!" Roy demanded.

"Yeah, in theory, a clone is a joined copy of a master photonic state. If that's the case, concentric math, with its unlimited number of interleaving derivative partitions, is probably the only way to detect an anomaly. That would be the copy—the clone—of the master. If we ran the math against the space the president—the clone—occupies, it would show that as the location of the joined copy, from which we might be able to, theoretically, find the master source.

"Is this bullshit, or for real?" Mac asked, his mind racing to understand what Justin had described.

"Doesn't matter, Mac. It's the best guess we have. I want Justin applying his filter at the White House," Roy demanded. "Let's move! There's no time to waste!"

CHAPTER 35

The Revelation

"No time to waste!" Roy's urgent yell had roused the IT team.

Roy called the four agents in from outside. He pulled over the lead Secret Service agent, Paul Hanover, along with FBI's O'Brien. He told them he had to be in D.C. as fast as possible. It would be five of them: himself, MacMahan, Justin Duddins—the long-haired surfer kid with the laptop—plus Hanover and his fellow Secret Service agent, Tristan Hayes. Hanover, a twenty-year veteran of the USSS, was all business. He told Roy that the time to get a helicopter, fly to Andrews, then motor back to the White House was longer than simply driving the Suburban down interstate I-95 with a trooper escort.

Roy's dark eyes lit up. He liked cutting to the chase. He turned to O'Brien. "Patrick, thanks for your understanding and help."

O'Brien replied, "My pleasure, sir. So this professor guy is going?"

"Doctor MacMahan? Yes, he's also a many-times decorated solider. Did two or three tours, as I recall. What about him? You concerned?"

O'Brien stepped back, his hand to his chin, casting a doubtful look at Mac. "Just wondering if he and that geek guy have the necessary clearances. This all sounds hush-hush."

"They have my say-so. That's good enough for right now. You should know. By the way, what's your clearance?"

O'Brien stiffened. "I was Q-level certified when at DOE. I'm section chief here in New York for sensitive compartmentalized information access specific to the White House. I'm Top Secret… TS-SCI, sir."

Roy frowned, looking at Hanover, who replied to the unstated question. "Colonel, that's about as high as it goes in terms of clearance and loyalty."

"I apologize, Patrick, if I'm a bit rough around the edges. But the issue I've been exploring with them…" as he pointed to Mac and Justin, "is extremely important. I can't say more because there are still unknowns. Please get in touch with whomever at your D.C. headquarters. I need a secure room there at Pennsylvania Avenue. And let me emphasize this! This meeting I just had with these kids, this whole enterprise, is ultra secret. No one at the White House, including the president, is to know about it. This is truly a national security issue. A need-to-know situation. Am I clear?"

O'Brien's eyes narrowed as he looked at Mac and Justin. "The president? Yes, sir," he replied, finally.

After Mindy's tearful good-bye to Mac, it was a rushed drive from New York City to Washington D.C. Driving the Suburban through the Holland Tunnel to I-95, Hanover did not speak other than mumbling to himself. His four passengers kept pulling their seatbelts snug, their hands on the overhead handles.

Tristan radioed the New Jersey State Trooper office in Trenton, requesting support for traffic clearance. As Paul brought the Suburban—sliding somewhat sideways—onto I-95 from Highway 78, there were three New Jersey state trooper Ford Victorias and two Ford Interceptors idling on the onramp.

"Go, go!" Paul yelled into the console speakerphone. It was already seventeen minutes since they had left Mindy's. He was starting to doubt his timeline. A direct helicopter might have been faster. The trooper vehicles pulled out, lights and sirens adding to the sense of urgency.

Justin, in the middle row of the Suburban, looked out through the windshield. "No way those utility trucks can keep up with the Vics," he announced. He was blinking rapidly, still trying to absorb all that had happened. That he, a geeky computer science major, would be involved in such a high-level emergency. He looked at Mac, sitting next to him.

Mac bit his lip, squinting back. "Big time, huh, Justin? You're in it now, and I'm glad it's you."

Justin felt his eyes suddenly mist. Inappropriate, but unavoidable. He had always wanted to be a team member. But his proclivity for continual submergence into geekdom had rendered few practical opportunities. Now this. He watched, amazed, as the Interceptors fell behind the Suburban and the three Vics paced themselves out ahead, their lights flashing. Taking a quick glance over Hanover's shoulder at the digital speedometer, he gasped. The Suburban was doing one hundred twelve miles per hour. He took a quick glance behind. The Interceptors were right on their tail.

"Clean up and support," Hanover growled, his eyes catching Justin's in the rearview mirror. "All these trooper units can do well over one hundred thirty. Just hang on and relax."

Right before Elkton, Maryland, the New Jersey troopers pulled over as Maryland state police units picked up the escort duties. District police took over at the National Arboretum.

"Two hours and thirteen minutes! Not bad," Hanover chimed as he brought the Suburban to an abrupt halt in front of the FBI Building on Pennsylvania Avenue.

"Hey, Paul. NASCAR, here you come!" Tristan joked.

"Yes, well done, Paul," Roy said, clapping Hanover on the back. "Now, let's get some dinner."

"What the... Colonel? So, what was the rush?"

"We'll eat as we work," Roy replied, looking over his shoulder as he jumped out, the others trying to keep up.

They burst through the doors to the FBI security station. "Eye scans!" the security officer called out, motioning them through the scanner.

"How do they know if it's me?" Justin yelped, thinking his techie adherence to the notion of convenience over privacy was now coming back to bite him.

Once through security, two FBI staff took the five up to a small room on the third floor. Justin ventured to a window, looking up at top floors of the JW Marriott hotel across Pennsylvania Avenue. "Anyone with a sound device can listen into this room, you know," he said, turning to Mac.

The FBI staff laughed. "We use an acoustic bounding mesh on all our windows. If someone is trying to listen in, all they'll hear is Willy gumming up the airwaves."

"Thank you!" Roy said, his voice firm as he looked at the door. The staff nodded, leaving water and sandwiches as they left.

"Okay," Roy began. "To business. First of all, Paul, you and Tristan are not up to speed on what we've discussed. Why all the rush. You guys have been my personal detail since Margie and I arrived in D.C. I need serious backup. I trust you guys. So, you're it. Yes or no?"

"With you, Chief," Paul answered, not hesitating. His admiration and loyalty to Roy went well beyond what duty required. They were brothers in heart, mind, and soul.

"Yes, sir. Colonel. As long as what you need doesn't go against my oath to serve and protect the president," Tristan added.

"In no way does what we're about to do violate your oath to serve and protect my wife. That's the nub of it. What you're about to hear will shock you. I'm still in shock! The question is, how do we confirm that the person acting as president is not my wife. That maybe she, or it… is some kind of clone? Justin, I think this is your department. Huh?"

"Excuse me, Colonel!" Tristan exclaimed. "And excuse my French. What the hell you talking about?"

Roy took a chair at the small table in the center of the room. He stared through Tristan, his dark eyes focused somewhere outside the building, towards the White House.

Justin opened his laptop.

"Tristan. What Mac and Justin have uncovered will blow your mind. It's okay to doubt what we're thinking because we doubt it. That's why this meeting is just us five. To ferret out reality. Yeah, that's the right word, because I'm still a little dizzy that what Justin has uncovered is, in fact, reality."

"You're the man, Justin," Mac said. "It's your show. Remember what I taught you last fall. Break down the *what* and the *how*."

"Can I have a Coke to wash down my sandwich? Yeah, and I need a bathroom," Justin replied, his sheepish grin breaking the tension.

They all laughed, nodding in agreement. All except Tristan. He sat heavily in his chair, unmoving, his arms draped to the side. Uneasy that he was involved, he wondered to whom he should report this meeting.

Justin was the first to return. He clicked his teeth, anxious if he could really do what Roy was asking of him. It was complex.

The last to enter as he closed the door, Roy pointed to Justin. "Well, son, do you have an answer?"

"Answer? No. But I've got a plan. Please, Colonel, it's just a wild guess!" Justin said with exasperation and in response to a collective moan from the others. "I'd like to show Mr. Hanover and Mr. Hayes why we think someone else is wearing the president's shoes."

Ten minutes later, Tristan was rubbing his forehead, shaking. "Are we on an acid trip, or something? This has got to be, excuse my German, total bullshit. Don't you think, Paul?"

Paul put his massive hands on the table. "Hmm," he said, his voice quiet. He thought back to discussions his family had had about the journey of Martin, Doctor King. About believing that present reality could be changed. That it would be painful, take time, but that it was possible. "Tristan, I gotta tell you, man," Paul began. "You not going to find a better man alive today than Colonel Butcher. He's lived Montgomery up through the ranks. He's backbone to the president. Helped shape her unity policies. Those policies are the only way to stomp out identity politics. To bring us together under the promises of the Constitution. That's why I love my job. We're at the hub of change. So, when Colonel Butcher says there's something weird going on, I don't ask what or how. I just stand ready. Make sense?"

Tristan went to the window, watching the flags above Freedom Plaza blow in the evening breeze. It was his duty to protect President Perserve—emblematic of that freedom. He turned to the table, all eyes upon him. "I'm all in. But..." he added, "I still think we're smoking dope or something."

"Good man!" Roy said, above the affirming murmur of the others. "Our challenge then, is to figure out how to get hard evidence that the president is not my wife."

"DNA?" Tristan asked.

"An obvious first step," Justin answered. "But, if this science fiction that we're chasing is real, and the president is a clone, then there has to be a way to generate its mass. And if whoever is behind this has figured out how to create and direct mass in the form of a human, I gotta believe they can replicate DNA. Think back, Colonel. Wouldn't you say there've been opportunities to publically collect her DNA? Like from hair samples off the back of a limo seat or saliva on a glass?"

"Justin? We're in never-never land," Mac interrupted. "This is too hard to accept. Not possible."

Roy responded. "Mac, what's impossible? I'm sure Margie's DNA has been left in many places. If those behind this have really innovated cloning, don't you think producing matching DNA would be easy?"

Mac shook his head. No. The shoebox was on the verge. Too much hypothetical. He needed action. "Justin, let's forget the DNA angle and go straight to solid proof. Something we can reveal to the Cabinet, the vice president, leaders in the Senate…whoever's in charge."

Justin tapped his Coke bottle against his teeth. "Solid proof? Things like family history, Roy's secret love exchanges… those could be defended as simple slips of memory. Like slipping on a surfboard."

"What in the world does that have to do with this?" Roy insisted, running his hand across his high forehead.

Justin took a long time to swallow his next hit on the Coke bottle. "It's like this. Slipping on a board is natural unless you use surf wax to grip your feet to the surface. Similarly, any aspect of her behavior has to be taken as natural. Like, who are we to say how or why she thinks, or anything about what she does? Her behavior may slip from what you, Roy, or others, expect. But that's not real proof. It gets us no closer to the source. My plan, you ask? If she is a clone controlled via teleporting, which happens to be our premise, we could use concentric math to isolate the patterns of her photonic state. We play the patterns back at her, ya know, *stick* them to her. Like, photon wax." He laughed.

Mac, walking around the table, said. "Look, Justin. I don't think any of us really followed you. And… let's *not* assume the president is not Roy's wife until we have proof. So cut the crude stick-it jokes. Put it in terms we understand."

Justin leaned into the table, burying his hands in his long hair. He looked at the door. Being a team member was getting hard.

Roy reached out, putting his hand on Justin's arm. "Son, if you think your idea will work, we'll try it. Just help us understand it better."

After emptying the Coke bottle, Justin chewed on his lower lip. "If we can isolate the president sitting in a chair, one which I have already positioned within a concentric math filter... call it a *zone*... Then the patterns of her... call it a *state*... can be isolated and mimicked. You know? Like played back within that zone. It'd be like putting her in an infinite loop. She'd repeat her behavior, continuously. While this is happening, we could extend the range of the zone to encompass different areas in the world. If we got lucky, we'd see—in the concentric math display—the source's repeated attempt to teleport its parallel state. Does that make sense?"

"It does to me," Tristan said, his enthusiasm reflecting that he truly understood. "It's brilliant, man!"

Roy and Mac exchanged looks. Mac sat back at the table, wiping imaginary dirt to the floor. "You're saying we put her in a trap, trap the incoming, and as she bangs her head continuously against the wall, we can track the source?"

"Oh, Mac," Justin replied, disappointed. "Yeah, it's like a trap, but she won't start to self-destruct. She'll just stay, in effect, in a frozen state."

"We're assuming she's not my wife. So what if she is my wife, just suffering from some mental issue? Will this harm her?" Roy groaned.

Justin took a deep breath, looking slowly around at the others. "This only would affect a mass, a data object, that exists via teleporting. If this is your real wife, she'll feel nothing, other than being imposed upon."

"Roy?" Mac asked. "Do you think you can get her to take this seat Justin describes?" Before Roy could reply, Mac turned to Justin. "How long does she have to sit in the chair? Can she move? Can we sedate her? Realistically, how do we pull this off?"

Justin scratched his eyebrow, frustrated that he was alone with Tristan in truly understanding the scenario. "You can't sedate her, probably. The source would see that she was not mimicking the master state. They'd shut down, and while we'd have proof that the president is not the president, we'd lose the source. They could try again, next time smarter."

Mac stood, again walking around the table, waving his arms. "Colonel? Say it turns out that she is a clone. This will be probably... No! Absolutely, it will be the biggest threat America's ever had! What are the steps? What do we do next?"

"We escalate, ASAP. This is way beyond me," Roy sighed.

CHAPTER 36

The Proof

At Roy's urgent request, Vice President Jacob Tandy agreed to skip dinner and come to the FBI Building to help with the meeting.

After showing Justin's evidence to Tandy, discussing Justin's plan, and asking for more water so the vice president could take his heart medicine, Roy got back to business.

"Jacob, I hope this has not been too great a shock. To be honest, we're all in shock! So, what does it take to isolate the president. I mean, to have you take her place without causing major upheaval?"

Jacob Tandy, former Constitutional professor at Vermont Law and ex-Marine, sat, staring at Roy. He adjusted his tie, smoothing back his thick, silver hair. "That would not be possible without approval from the Cabinet and National Security Committee. You could declare her unfit, per Section 4 of the 25th Amendment. But that would require a majority of sitting Cabinet secretaries to submit such an opinion, in writing, to the speaker of the House and the Senate's president pro tempore. At that juncture, I would become Acting President. A mess, at the least. And on what grounds would the Cabinet determine that President Perserve is unfit? That she's a clone?" His voice creaked. "No way to keep that out of the news. A disaster."

Roy slammed the table. "Disaster? Where the hell is my wife? That's the real disaster!" he shouted. "We think POTUS has been replaced. Who knows where she is? This could be the most egregious breach of national security we've ever seen. We must *not* tiptoe around this!"

"Excuse me, Colonel," Mac began. In his mind he saw this as a pending firefight, his area of expertise. "I think we should proceed with Justin's plan. We don't know the terrain... ah, if the president is a clone. We've got to do recon first!" He turned to Justin. "Does the president have to be sitting alone in the room, in the chair?"

"Not sure," Justin replied, rubbing his nose. "Theoretically, if the other person in the room remained still, and since they're not a clone with teleported reception, my guess is it would not interfere with the math display. But hey, shit, just a guess. Look at me! You're asking me about something with untold consequences. I'm just a student!"

Roy yawned heavily. Mostly nerves. "Tell you what, Justin. I have an friend at Carnegie Mellon. She's pioneered waveform research. I'll give her a call."

Roy left the room to find a secure outside line. He returned after ten minutes. "Professor Jenks told me that as seen throughout history, innovation is mankind's forever renewable frontier. Most innovation is for the benefit of mankind, but there will always be people who seek to create bad from good. She believes teleporting will be major innovation. Just a matter of time before it's perfected. That has her worried."

"Did you want to involve her in this?" Mac asked.

"I thought about it, sure. I was tempted," Roy admitted. "But, my take is we go with Justin. I asked her if she'd heard of concentric math. She wasn't sure. All I needed to know." He smiled, pointing at Justin.

Mac pushed back from the table. He walked around to Justin, putting his arm on Justin's shoulder. "Justin, there you are. I'd say your insight is on par with Roy's friend. You're much more than a student. You have God-given gifts. We all do. But... yours make you uniquely qualified for this. You can only try, Justin. We all accept that it's a huge gamble. But... man, you're our only option."

"Nothing like a bit of pressure, huh?" Tristan blurted. Absolute silence descended across the room until everyone started laughing, uncontrollably. At the insanity of what they were discussing. Justin laughed the hardest.

It was essential to maintain stealth, to involve no one else in their scheme. With Tandy providing security clearance to the White House and Paul Hanover the required Secret Service escort, Mac and Justin joined Roy in the First Lady's bedroom. The bedroom Roy now used. They used the connecting passage to enter the master bedroom—the President's Bedroom. Justin placed his laptop beneath Margie's favorite wing chair. The plan was to have Roy sit across from the president and discuss his concerns about Todd. Why wasn't he adjusting to life in the White House? There were issues at school. All false issues. But ones that would extend the time Roy was able to keep the president in her chair.

In the adjoining First Lady's bedroom, Justin set up his tablet to mirror control of his laptop's concentric math application. He ran a test with Mac in the master bedroom. No distortion. All looked good. Mac returned to the First Lady's bedroom as Paul Hanover joined them.

Roy left to have dinner with his family at the White House Mess. The plan was for him to ask the president to join him for a nightcap in her bedroom. Something they rarely did. Given the attempt to kill the IT team, they were aware that if the president was controlled by some outside force, she might have been cautioned to be on her guard.

Once Roy was talking with the president, if no ripples or shadows were detected, Paul would ring the master bedroom telephone twice, then immediately again once. Otherwise, Paul would knock on the master bedroom door after sufficient proof had been gathered.

After walking back to her bedroom accompanied by Roy, the president sighed as she kicked off her sandals and sat in the wing chair. "That was a ghoulish dinner. You've got to talk with Perkins about the food around here." She smoothed out her pant legs. "Why did you want to talk?" she asked, her tone bored, her eyes focused on the right-hand sleeve of her blouse.

"I'm concerned that Todd's teachers say he's been acting out in class, showing signs of frustration with his studies. They ask if he's getting time with us," Roy replied, leaning forward in his chair, his hands clasped, his concern evident.

"Todd and Kari both knew it would be stressful, didn't they?"

"Yes, but, well... how do I put it? In some ways we've become a single-parent family, like so many in America. The parenting is left to me. Not sure that's good."

"Like so many? Just shows we're normal," she answered, annoyed.

"Maybe, yeah, that's the new normal as the media and Hollywood like to remind us. But it dismisses the importance of the family unit. What I miss is our time together as a family, like we were in Kansas. The kids miss that, too. I know it."

"Family unit?" the president questioned.

In Building 666, Juong was frantically calling out orders to his staff to pull up advice on parenting in the culture of America. "Got it," a young woman yelled. "He's trying to be a rad dad with a wife who's a bitch! Got it direct from *undergroundparenting.com.*"

Shaking his head, his eyes flexed in frustration, Juong yelled into the control console, "Up six on sensitive exhaustion."

"Roy, let me be candid. I'm tired. Actually, I'm a bitch."

"No, no!" Juong screamed, shaking his finger at the young woman.

"What?" Roy asked, sensing that the president—if his wife or a clone—was struggling to make sense. "Bitch? No way, my dear Margie," he whispered, pouring on the charm, all the while his heart breaking at the dawning reality that he was not talking with *his* Margie. "Perhaps that's how the kids see you? How about we take a trip and get away? You've not left the country since your inauguration. It's time to see the world and have the world to see you. Air Force One stands at our beck and call. Why not be like those other presidents and use it to go shopping in Paris or playing golf in Florida?"

"Enough, not yet! Remember my exhaustion? That's why I don't fly?"

Juong knew the colloquialism: 'Enough, already.' What did she mean by, "Enough, not yet?" The holohead was obviously going off script. "Linguistics soften, persona three," he yelled, furious that Director Dong was not there to help with control.

Next door, in the First Lady's bedroom, Justin was recording the display on his tablet. The shadow and ripples around the president were significant. "Now!" he whispered, as he played back the ripples to the laptop underneath her chair. She started repeating herself and her movements. Every ten seconds she pointed to the window, saying, "Enough, not yet... Enough, not yet."

"Got it!" Justin whispered, pumping his fists. "Now, time for the source." He broadened the *zone* to ripple back over Europe, Africa, the Middle East, and finally Asia. A concentric node popped up. "There it is! We've got all the proof," he yelled, Mac rushing to clamp a hand over his mouth. It didn't matter. The holohead was looped and no longer listening.

Pushing hard against his control console, stomping his feet, Juong was breathing rapidly, lost without Dong. The holohead was running amok: lost in some kind of loop, not paralleling the master state, and not following teleported vectors.

"Get me the Leader," he yelled. Despondent, believing the entire mission had failed, he considered Escape Mode Two until Dong's admonitions came back to him. They had higher orders.

To answer the red emergency phone, the Leader had to pull himself out from under three treats. The phone was solely for state emergencies. He could not ignore it.

"Yes?" he growled, brushing one of the treats away.

"Dear Leader," Juong began. "We've lost control of the holohead."

"What?" screamed the Leader, kicking the remaining two treats from his bed. "What do you mean, Juong!"

Juong took a deep breath through his nose. It was the end of a grand effort. "The holohead is no longer reflecting the master state here at 666. Something has usurped control. We are trying all possible solutions. Nothing, yet. Perhaps it will come back. Perhaps, not..."

The Leader wiped his hand hard across his face several times. His dreams were dissolving. His vision of world domination replaced with mushroom clouds directly over his head. "This cannot be, Juong!" he howled. "Are you sure? How long *must* we wait until we're sure?"

"I'm not able to answer that with confidence. Director Dong would know, but she has disappeared. I assume she is under your protection. You must release her!"

"Fool!" the Leader yelled. "She has disappeared—evaporated as some of the barracks staff would tell you… if they could."

Juong was shocked. Dong had taken Mode Two. Why was he here left holding the proverbial bag? Why not bail as Dong had? "We must abort. No other choice. Perhaps the Americans have determined how to control the holohead. Perhaps, even, they have tracked it back to *you*."

"You devil idiot! You and Dong assured me that was not possible!" the Leader screamed into the phone line, the other end of which was dangling from Juong's console, above of a pile of clothes. Juong had left the building.

"What the hell!" Roy shouted as he fell backwards over his chair. The president had disappeared right before his eyes. All that was left were her clothes, settling on the wing chair.

CHAPTER 37

The Trek

Margie pulled the scarf tightly around her head, bending low and peering into the sad, deep-set eyes of the old woman. In them she saw the strength and fortitude of her own mother, bravely facing the cold easterly winds howling across their Kansas farm. She though of Todd, her cherished son, and how she would protect him with her life. Margie so wanted to tell this woman, this mother, that she understood. Language and culture could be such a barrier. But one message was universal: love. Margie tenderly took the woman's hand, kissing it. A heartfelt act of respect for the mother—for the gift of allowing Kwang-Ju to guide her out of this nation.

The woman gave a tiny shriek, tears welling in her eyes. She stood, bowing deeply to Margie. For a moment, their tears froze together in solace and in fear. The woman took Margie's hand, placing it to her cheek. She pulled it to her son's cheek. Margie knelt, deliberately staring into the young man's eyes. He could be any woman's son. The embodiment of God's creation. He was her surrogate Todd. The son's eyes perceptibly transitioned before her, from a thankful boy to a man convicted. He nodded. No more need be said.

Kwang-Ju spoke to the mother as he pulled on Margie's shoulder, handing her an old coat to keep out the cold in the journey east through the mountains.

Standing with Kwang-Ju on the knoll overlooking the little farm, Margie looked back, seeing what could have been a Rockwell painting. The smoke from the little house swirled, mixing the greens hues of the foliage with the good—the brown—earth. Margie turned back to the east. She looked up at the ragged peaks, dabbled with veins of green and crowned with mist and snow. A formidable barrier to her freedom.

Kwang-Ju made urgent gestures for her to take her sack and her stick and follow him closely. They followed the stream up into the hills.

Twice, they crossed the stream, Kwang-Ju not stopping to empty his shoes. Margie noticed there was no need; the holes worn in the sides provided sufficient drainage. Her feet sloshed in her own shoes. She made the decision as she tried to keep up with Kwang-Ju: she would not let her own pain, or any weakness, slow their journey. She would stand shoulder-to-shoulder with Kwang-Ju. She thought of her father and his endless hours working the farm, always exuding good cheer, speaking of her talents and gifts. Kansas was a universe removed from this remote jungle, but the dedication and love of parents was the same. Perhaps Kwang-Ju considered her like his daughter.

She held up her hand with a small grunt. Kwang-Ju stopped, turning, waving his arm that they must not stop. He let out a sigh as he took in the exhaustion evident in Margie's face. He motioned for her to sit and came back to her, kneeling to massage her legs. She smiled, her nose flaring to hold back the tears. She *was* his daughter. One he would protect with his life.

"Mercgy," he spoke, softly. He reached up to close her coat. His thin, drawn face smiled against a heritage of struggle.

It was at that moment, with Kwang-Ju's gaze upon her, that Margie closed her eyes. She prayed to God with thanksgiving. For the goodness of His people regardless of culture or nation. For the simple bond of faith that she earnestly prayed all of God's creation could embrace.

Kwang-Ju gasped and Margie's eyes popped open. He motioned her to lie down close to the ground under a bush. She heard something coming down the ravine. Kwang-Ju rose quickly, wading out into the stream. She peeked out. He was jabbing the water with his stick, as if fishing. From up the ravine she heard yelling and laughter. Two burly men came into view, pointing at Kwang-Ju, evidently laughing at his attempt to catch fish with a blunt walking stick. Kwang-Ju laughed back. They exchanged words. It seemed friendly enough until one of the men grabbed Kwang-Ju, shaking him. The man padded Kwang-Ju's cloak and pants, looking for something. Kwang-Ju held out his hand as if to say, "I have nothing." After a minute of frustration, the man pushed Kwang-Ju hard into the water. The two men continued down the stream, laughing.

Margie watched Kwang-Ju. He stayed sitting in the cold water until the men were out of sight. Slowly, he pushed himself up with his stick. He was soaked, freezing. He held up his hand. A signal not to move. He waded across to the far bank of the stream, standing to look back downstream. After what Margie thought was too long with Kwang-Ju standing there, shivering, he turned back up the stream, holding his hand to motion her ahead.

Margie ran across to him. She removed her coat as she pulled on his. It was then that she noticed the gash on his head. He had hit a rock on his fall in the stream. She pulled him around to a stop. She cried out at the fatalistic look in his eyes. Pulling him to the ground, she emptied her sack of the few odd clothes. Margie realized that if they were caught, the clothes and sack were an automatic giveaway. Her exhaustion had diminished her decision-making, her mind sliding on the skids of fatigue. She was, in spite of the insane journey she had been forced into, the President of the United States! Mistakes, big or small, were not allowed if she was to unify America against the petty identity politics that she had inherited. It was all so tiring.

She woke with a start, the dark cold of night washing across her face. She was on her side, lying on what felt like a bed of brush. Her backside warm, she felt Kwang-Ju's breath on her neck. Margie pushed up on her right elbow, feeling behind her the leaves and branches covering them. She dropped her head back to the bed of leaves. Sleep would make for a better day ahead. She thanked God for Kwang-Ju.

She imagined she had just fallen back to sleep when she felt Kwang-Ju move, pushing off the brush. Daylight was breaking. Margie stood as Kwang-Ju gathered the bed of branches and flung them into the trees. She noticed his head was wrapped in a dirty strip of cloth from the sack. As she raised her hands in question, Kwang-Ju pointed to a pile of nearby rocks. He made a motion of burying the sack and clothes.

Kwang-Ju pointed back through the trees to the stream, gesturing drinking water. He took bread from his satchel, putting it front of Margie. Finally, he grabbed some leaves, and smiling and bowing, he indicated what she could use the leaves for. He held up his hand, pointing to himself and then up the mountain, gesturing that he would be coming back.

"You are going to scout ahead, yes?" Margie asked, her eyes wide with the question.

Kwang-Ju repeated his gestures, nodding. He patted her head, turning back through the trees towards the stream.

Margie sat refreshed in the solitude of the forest. The continual, swaying music of the burbling stream was occasionally interrupted by birdsong. She lay back, peering up through the trees to the cold blue of the sky. She might as well be lying between empty stalks of corn on a cold autumn day. Back home, in Kansas.

The wind created a kaleidoscope with the sun high in the sky, shining through the tree boughs. "It must be noon or later," she said to the trees. She started, looking for her stick, her friend. "Where *is* Kwang-Ju?" she asked.

She walked out of the trees to the stream, taking another refreshing drink. She wondered what Kwang-Ju was scouting for. He must already know this area well. "Probably for other people," she told her stick. "More like those men yesterday." She shivered at the thought of those men capturing her. Biting her lower lip, understanding that she was still very much in danger, Margie walked back into the trees.

The sun was low in the west when Margie heard someone calling "Mercgy?" in a soft voice. She cautiously raised her head, parting the branches. She had moved from where Kwang-Ju had left her.

"Kwang-Ju," she whispered, her soul warmed by his loving smile as he came towards her. "Where have you been?" she asked, the gesture of her hands conveying the message.

Kwang-Ju pushed aside the leaves. In the dirt he drew a map. He drew the stream, and the mountains, its source. He drew a line around the mountains and said something, his eyes wide, his head shaking, "No." He then drew a line through the mountains, and on the other side he drew ripples.

"The coast?" Margie exclaimed. "Water, the ocean?" She gestured waves crashing.

Kwang-Ju nodded, smiling. Then he frowned, pointing to the line he had drawn through the mountains. He tightened his lips in serious contemplation, shaking his head.

Margie pointed to the line circumventing the mountains, going around.

Kwang-Ju shook his head, vehemently. He made like holding a rifle.

"Soldiers?" she asked.

He nodded, pointing again at the line through the mountains. The only way. He then pointed to the sun, holding up five fingers.

"Five hours more daylight," Margie asked, pointing to herself, to Kwang-Ju, and to their walking sticks.

He nodded, making gestures of eating, and had she used the leaves.

"I'm fine," Margie replied, hugging Kwang-Ju. She pointed to the line through the mountains, then raising her arm as the sweep of the sun. "How many days?"

Kwang-Ju shrugged, his eyes caught in calculation. He held up one finger.

"What!" Margie said, clamping her teeth so as not to shout. "One more day?" She repeated his gesture.

Kwang-Ju nodded, frowning again. He pointed to the mountain, then drew a snake in the dirt, and held his fingers to his face to suggest a wild boar. Again, he shook his head. Danger.

"Not out of the woods yet," Margie laughed sadly. "Just one more struggle. So close to the coast, across the mountains. Yet, so far. And… the coast will be fraught with danger."

Kwang-Ju stood, pulling Margie up with him. He made a gesture of exertion, flexing his legs. He looked at her questioningly.

"I'm ready," she nodded, gesturing that he lead the way. Looking upon his back as he stepped amongst the rocks and into the river, Margie imagined her own father, walking carefully amongst the rows of turkey red. She caught the gasp in her throat, her eyes tearing, her nostrils flared. Oh, how she missed her father. How he had always gently offered advice and extended steadfast love and care. With a start, she realized that she was imprinting her father onto Kwang-Ju. "At times like this, we all need a father," she spoke wistfully to the frail back.

Kwang-Ju led them back across the river, going up the left side of the ravine. They used their sticks to beat back the brush. Margie was concerned they were leaving an easy trail to follow. But she had no other choice than to follow.

The ravine steepened. The stream was off to the right, shrouded in trees and boulders. Kwang-Ju took them across a steep meadow, the grass slippery, their shoes sliding down a step for every three up. Margie was thankful for her stick, using it to wedge her way up in Kwang-Ju's trail. Once across the meadow, they entered a rock-strewn copse of gnarly trees. Margie's legs were cut and bruised. So were Kwang-Ju's. "If my father can do it, so can I," she repeated to herself. The mantra of the words 'So can I' helped set the cadence of her steps.

Twice, Kwang-Ju held up his hand to stop. Margie was thankful for the rest until he pointed to scat on the ground. He held his fingers up to his mouth as tusks. Wild boars.

They climbed for another hour, best as Margie could estimate. The sweat on her forehead was beginning to freeze, the sun close to setting far behind them. Up ahead, she noticed a narrow crevasse in the rock wall. It reminded her of New River Gorge in West Virginia—the rock climbers' stories of encountering venomous snakes. She was shivering. Was it the cold, the crevasse, or both? Hopefully, the cold meant the snakes were less active.

Kwang-Ju halted at the entrance to the crevasse. He pointed in. It was narrow, perhaps ten feet across at the base. There were pockets of snow hanging up against the almost vertical side walls. Margie, panting to catch her breath, held her palms open in question. She pointed to the sun.

Kwang-Ju clicked his tongue. He pointed to the ground, holding up two fingers and swiping his arm across the sky. He pointed in, holding up one finger as he again swept the sky.

"We stay here, it's two more nights, Yes? But only one night if we proceed?" she asked, holding up two fingers. "But how will we see in that chasm? It'd be like a mine shaft at night."

Kwang-Ju shook his head, not understanding Margie.

She moaned, exhausted and bruised. She reminded herself of the sacrifice Kwang-Ju was making. If she was angry, it should be solely at the insane leader of this country. She caught herself. Her situation was much more comfortable than that of the thousands he had imprisoned for no reason other than his ego and greed. She would press on, in the name of humanity. A human race, she figured that for some baffling reason, God had allowed to include people like that leader. Her thoughts wandering with her eyes, she collapsed on the ground. "God gave us free will. Some seed will not take and some will grow bad trees that bear bad fruit," she mumbled, thinking of Sunday School lessons long ago. "We live in a world today— heck, since forever—where man usurps the freedom and the lives of others. Nothing new. Not God's fault, just us people." She started weeping tears of futility.

Kwang-Ju leaned down, his hand on her shoulder. "Mercgy?" he asked. He pointed into the crevasse, then held up one finger and smiled. He held up two fingers and mimicked soldiers with rifles.

"I know, I *know*, Father," she said. "We must go on!"

He pulled her up, turning into the crevasse.

After fifteen minutes it was pitch black. She called out to Kwang-Ju. "Please stop. I can't see," she yelled, tripping over some rocks, her voice echoing off the walls. Kwang-Ju came back to her, took her hand, placed it on his shoulder, and started off again. He bounced his stick off the floor of the crevasse and off the walls, the tapping in rhythm to some tune he was humming. Margie, with no idea how he could see, found comfort in the feel of his sinewy shoulder.

She looked up, not seeing any stars. She shrieked several times at what she thought was a snake's rattle, not knowing if rattlesnakes lived in this impoverished land. Kwang-Ju kept humming.

After what Margie figured was every ten or fifteen minutes, Kwang-Ju would stop, turn to her, and by feel, put his forehead to hers. She would stroke his hair, making sure the tourniquet was in place on his head. And they would continue. After several of these stops it occurred to her that he was using the stops more as a cadence—a way to reduce the sense of overall effort and danger. "Your ways are simple, yet sufficient," she said to Kwang-Ju's back, squeezing his shoulder.

Margie's thoughts walked with her in the dark. Of times when she was unsure of what to do. Like, back in grammar school when the kids were playing a mean joke on someone and called her to join in. When she saw kids getting away with cheating on college exams. When she dated guys during her internship in D.C.—guys with one thing on their mind. How today that one thing was no longer a factor regarding character. The presidents preceding her had certainly helped deflect *any* notion of morality. Yet here she was. Being led through a dark passage by a total stranger. A fellow human who had discerned life's most important element: caring for and loving others. "I've got to survive, if only to tell the story of Kwang-Ju and his family," she said to herself.

Near exhaustion, after several dozen stops, Kwang-Ju finally halted, striking his stick against the walls. He held Margie's arms in the dark, motioning her to do the same with her stick. He made a "shh…shh," sound; one Margie took to represent snakes. They were warning snakes to keep clear. He pulled Margie to ground, his back against the wall. He had her sit between his legs and lean in against his chest. He brought his hand around to her face, gently closing her eyes.

Now that they had stopped, the cold wind tunneling through the crevasse had her shivering. Kwang-Ju put his arms around her, rocking her as he might a child. Her tears of joy and comfort rolled down her cheeks as she fell into a deep slumber.

"Mercgy?" She heard the words but did not want to open her eyes. She was asleep in safe embrace. He shook her again gently, repeating, "Mercgy?" She woke, stiff and sore, her eyes adjusting to take in the rock wall just yards away. She rolled to the side, looking at Kwang-Ju. He had not slept at all, keeping guard. She kissed his cheek.

Smiling, he raised his hand to stroke the warmth left on his cheek, his eyes shining in acknowledgement. Kwang-Ju stood, stretching.

Margie couldn't tell what direction was forward until she saw the sun's rays glancing off the walls ahead. And farther ahead, perhaps a mile or two, she saw the end to the walls. They were almost through the mountains. She thought she could smell salt air.

CHAPTER 38

The Decision

"Hey! What the hell just happened!" Roy clamored, grabbing the bedpost to pull himself up off the thick carpet.

Mac and Paul ran into the room, followed by Justin.

"Is it what I think it is, or was…" Roy asked, sitting on the bed, astonished, wiping the shock and doubt from his face.

Mac walked over to the chair, moving his arms over and to the side, as if trying to detect some aura, heat, or vibration. "She's gone, just like that," he uttered, amazed.

"Yeah, just like that," Justin repeated. "Makes total sense. The instant the master photonic state is turned off, the same happens to the teleported state. You know, the president—the version here. They've obviously shut down. That's good news because now we know that we—Roy—was dealing with a hologram version of President Perserve. And… the better news, we got a location on the source."

"Easy for you to say, Justin!" Roy shouted. "I mean, thank goodness we discovered this. But, shit! Where then, is my wife?" He sighed heavily. He knew that Margie's safety was, in reality, less an issue than eliminating the hologram-based android at the helm of America. He turned to Paul. "Get Vice President Tandy on the phone, right away. Tell him he needs to convene the National Security Council, the Cabinet, and our ever-wise Congressional leaders. Yeah, first things first. I'll be damned. Justin, you *are* the man! Without you, who knows where we'd end up?"

Justin knelt next to the chair, brushing back his long hair. He put his hand on the arm of the chair, bowing his head in homage to what they'd just experienced. "We have the proof! It also means that we've arrived at a new vista of science. Man! I can't believe what has happened. That it's real. I imagined this, but to be right here where…"

Roy cut him off. "Don't touch the clothes or chair. Let forensics have a go at everything."

"Sure, but they'll find nothing," Justin replied, standing. "What occupied those clothes was just a replicated state. There'll be no traces."

Mac put his hand on Roy's shoulder. "If that's the case, Colonel, I'm ready to help you find the president." He gave Roy's shoulder an extra squeeze. "Hooah!"

———— . ————

The next morning, Roy and Mac were seated opposite each other at the center of the long table. Sitting at the far end of the table, Justin connected his laptop to the overhead projector. His mumblings were drowned out by the overhead fans in the underground Emergency Operations Center.

Vice President Tandy, having called the emergency meeting, sat at the head of the table. He looked around at the assembled leaders of America: members of the Security Council, the Cabinet, the leaders of the House and Senate, Directors of Homeland Security, the FBI and the CIA, and the Chairman of the Joint Chiefs.

"Dear colleagues," he began, his humble tone drawing to attention the twenty-four men and women. "What we are about to show you will change your lives and your understanding of life on this earth—forever."

A noisy clattering of water glasses, pens, and the clearing of throats came from around the table.

Tandy stood, drawing to his full height, his face cast in stone. "We've all grown up in the nuclear age, with its Doomsday scenarios and fears. Probably, if you're like me, you figured the Doomsday Clock would never reach midnight. I know we've all prayed so. What we have not envisioned and never imagined was another insidious method for controlling—even destroying—the world. You've all heard the word *android* bandied about, even on product names. A reflection of how the techno-geeks of the world see the future. Mostly young folks. Us older types," he chuckled, "assigned such thinking to the realm of Buck

Rogers and science fiction. Well... I'm sad to say, the young geeks are right. The day of androids is upon us!"

The vice president leaned on the table, his voice deepening. "One such young man is Justin Duddins, there, at the end of the table. Because of Justin's efforts, along with those of Professor... ah, Sergeant MacMahan," Tandy paused, nervously wiping his hand across his mouth, "... and let me warn you here, it's going to be a shock... our president has been *kidnapped*. In her place, an exact replica—a hologram-based android—has been substituted!"

The stunned group remained in disbelief for several seconds until, from around the table, arose stupefied yells and shouts of incredulity. The vice president waved, nodding affirmation and trying to calm the astonished leaders.

As the uproar finally subsided, one question arose above all others: "How do we know it's an android, and where is President Perserve?"

"We're about to show you proof regarding the replica, the android. However, I'm sorry to report that we don't have an answer to President Perserve's whereabouts," Tandy said, his lips tight, gesturing towards Roy. "The purpose of this meeting is to bring you all up to date, and... to request that the members of the Cabinet submit immediately and as required, a written request to the speaker of the House and the Senate president pro tempore to have me serve as Acting President. We believe, and we pray that we can find President Perserve. So I am making this a temporary request. If, sadly, we cannot locate the president, these initial steps will at least ensure we make as smooth a transition as possible. We must keep America in the dark until we know for sure."

The Secretary of Defense, Regina Cameron, spoke out, raising her hand and addressing the vice president. "We, at the Pentagon, stand ready to find the president. Why have you delayed informing us?"

Tandy replied, "We received confirmation of this just last night. We had to collect evidence, the proof, before announcing our findings. Please, let's begin by showing you the proof. May I add, Secretary Cameron, that Colonel Butcher has requested that he and Sergeant MacMahan be involved in any recovery efforts. I think you can imagine why. But let's first see the evidence."

Justin showed the group the filtered videos, the zone rippling across the world to Asia, and the hidden video that Roy had asked him to set up in the President's Bedroom.

The group remained transfixed, letting out a collective gasp as the video showed the president disappearing.

"Some of our team," Justin continued, "used the word 'evaporated'. But that's incorrect. The state of the replica's existence was simply terminated."

"My God!" one of the Cabinet members yelled, "Huxley's *Brave New World* is upon us!"

"Not really," Tandy replied. "Shades of it, perhaps. Teleporting is not a new concept. Just not one that has been made practical until obviously, now. How the replica—the android—exists, though, is the baffling part. How to create an apparently living, flesh-like entity is beyond our thinking. Not so, Regina?"

The Secretary of Defense nodded, vigorously. "That tracks with what we know." She looked over at the DHS and the Chairman of Joint Chiefs.

After leaning over to whisper with the Senate Pro Tempore, the House Majority Leader cleared her throat. "Jacob, we've decided. Just as soon as the Cabinet gets the written request to us, we'll push for you as Acting. But, what do we tell the media? Like, where is the president?"

Roy raised his hand. "If I may. Why not connect, in the most positive way, the fluctuations we've seen in the president's behavior as being due to some health imbalance. Maybe, thyroid cancer. I know it sounds drastic, but it's got to be a solid story. So say that we have Margie sequestered to a ward at Johns Hopkins for recovery from her surgery."

"Not Reed?" Secretary Cameron asked.

"Too close to home," Roy replied. "Too many prying eyes. Plus, she's a civilian, and Hopkins provides some of the best oncology in the nation. We'll have to work this angle, but it should fly."

Secretary Cameron responded, "That'd work in the initial phase, but if we do find the president, you'd have to maintain the surgery story as part of her permanent history. Are you ready to do that?"

"Excuse me, Vice President," Mac injected. "There is no other option. If we find her," he looked firmly across at Roy, "and we will, you can deal with introducing the replica reality to the American public at your own pace. If we don't find her, she died during recovery."

"Excuse you?" Ashley Harper, the Secretary of Commerce yelled at Mac. "Just who the hell are you to so candidly define that outcome, that she died from surgery, right here, in front of her husband!"

Roy stood abruptly. "Thank you, Ashley, for your concern. But to all of you, I say this. Mac's correct. I had a tough night last night, not knowing if or where Margie is. Extremely tough! But I've come to grips with it. Soldiers do that. Mac... Sergeant MacMahan... knows firsthand the reality of a battle. We're in one now. Cool objectivity is what we need. Something all soldiers excel at." He smiled acknowledgment at the Chairman of the Joint Chiefs.

"I guess that pretty much sums things up," the vice president concluded, adding, "Let's pray for a smooth transition through all this. America needs it!"

—— . ——

That evening, Roy, Mac, and Jacob Tandy were having dinner in the White House Mess. Roy and Jacob laughed as Mac drained his second chocolate shake.

Looking across at Roy, "Shouldn't you be with Todd and Kari?" Mac asked, his face serious in spite of his chocolate mustache.

"After this morning's meeting, I spent three or four hours with them. We talked mainly about Margie. I kept debating if I should tell them the truth. It's horrible lying to your kids, especially mine. They're such wonders. Shit!"

"And, of course, you didn't mention a word, right?" Tandy asked, tapping his spoon against the side of his coffee cup.

Roy made a dumb-shit face. "What'ya you think, Jacob?"

They all laughed, releasing the tension of the day—of what had been learned and what lay ahead.

"Speaking of what a crazy day this has been," Tandy continued. "I heard from security that the White House guard, Sanchez, has also disappeared. Turns out her parents reported her missing to District police after all they found in her bed was her nightgown."

"You don't think?" Mac started.

Roy interrupted. "It's got to be! Somehow they replaced Sanchez with a replica, and then it helped to take away Margie. I hope the real Sanchez is okay…"

"But you doubt it, right?" Mac said, completing Roy's sentence. "The pragmatics say, destroy the evidence. What I'd do. Sorry, Roy."

"No so fast, Mac," Tandy rebutted. "We know the nation, although we don't know if it's their leader or some renegade group. Put yourself in their shoes. If your replica plan tanked, you'd still have POTUS. A huge negotiating chip. Perhaps poor Sanchez has met a harder fate, but I gotta believe Margie is being held for ransom, worst case." He took a long sip of coffee, his eyes searching Roy's face.

"That's my prayer, Jacob. Have to keep hope. I talked with Secretary Cameron at the end of this morning's meeting. She's up for the idea of Mac and me joining their special ops extraction team, if we're up for it. Mac?"

"I'm with you, Colonel. Totally in," Mac answered, signaling for another chocolate shake.

"You're going nowhere, Tubby, if you keep that up," Roy joked. "I'm going solo with the team if need be."

Jacob Tandy, the pending Acting president, issued his first order. "Sergeant, scrub the shake. Roy needs you. That's an order from your boss and trainer."

"I'm retired, sir." More laughter.

"So?" Roy responded, pushing back in his chair. "You want out?"

Mac stood, his emerald eyes glowing, his horrible facial scar picking up the reflection of the ceiling lights. "I said I'm in! We'll need input from Justin when en route and I'm the best liaison for that." Clearing his throat, Mac added, "And I have more time in-country, under fire, than you and the rest of the Marines. It is Marines, yes?"

"Roger that. It's an Army-Marine op. You and I are the Army."

Mac and Roy laughed so loudly that the waiters busing the other tables stopped, smiling.

Jacob studied Mac over the brim of his coffee cup. There was something about the man that made you want to depend on him with your life. There would be hell to pay if anything happened to Roy on this mission. He wanted Sergeant MacMahan there, on the team.

"More news," Jacob said, drawing another deep breath. "Your man Justin has been offered a job at NSA. The detection of androids, replicas, whatever, now has to be a top priority in our national security planning. It's one thing for NSA to have to authenticate all the technically-altered fake videos and audio streams saturating the air waves and Internet. But this whole notion of androids is just too unreal. Too spooky!"

"Agreed," Mac answered. "Justin's the perfect guy to help set up that capability. Yeah." He paused. "Regarding this special ops team. When and how soon?"

"Tomorrow, 0600, soldier," Roy answered, slapping Mac's back and laughing to soften the sudden reality.

"I know this new mission is urgent, but I need to say good-bye to Mindy. When I left New York, it was just short-term... to help you gather the proof. The evidence. That was the mission. Right?"

Roy reached out, his hand staying on Mac's shoulder. He felt for Mac. He had had hundreds of troops under his command. There had often been special requests, but on a mission, there was no room for special cases. "No can do, soldier. Call her. And please give her my best. Tell her that Margie and I are looking forward to the two of you staying with us at the White House. Hooah?"

Mac felt a pain in his heart at the loss of holding his Mindy. She would be devastated. She'd never had to ship him off before. And he'd never shipped out with someone to come home to. Yet, he smiled at the prospect of action. The shoebox would be toast.

He decided. "0600. Yes, sir!"

CHAPTER 39

The Goodbye

"Hey, it's me," Mac said softly, cradling the phone against his ear. He pictured Mindy in bed, the phone on the pillow next to her where he ought to be. He sighed into the phone, unable to hide the sense of dread enveloping his entire body.

"Where are you? I was expecting you home earlier tonight?"

Mac ran his fingers along the edge of the table between the hotel beds. "Still in D.C. At the JW. Something's come up. I needed to call," he replied, closing his eyes and imagining her breath on his cheek, her blue eyes boring into his, her hair draped across both their faces. The peace he found in her arms. Peace and comfort. Comfort for an old soldier. Now, a reminted soldier. Mac arched his neck back and forth. He imagined himself young again.

"What's that? Did the government people accept the proof? They'd have to be blind not to," Mindy said innocently, not aware of the turmoil in Mac's heart.

"They did, yeah. All that went well. The agenda moved on to finding President Perserve. That's where I come in."

"How so?" Mindy asked, pushing herself upright against the pillows and pulling the phone closer. "What do you mean?" She could hear Mac's heavy breathing. "Mac?"

"Do you remember the day we met?"

"Like it was this morning, today. Oh, Mac! What is it?"

"I remember that day, every day. How you called me after you started back to Manhattan. How my heart yearned to know you better. To find out if you felt the same way I did." He laughed softly, directly into the phone. "I remember each day since, with you. How the prayer in my heart has been answered by you."

Mindy coughed. "Mac, what're you saying?"

"Simply, how much I love you. Your tenderness, your respect for life, your belief in God. All of you."

"Mac! You're scaring me. Is something wrong? You okay?" The piercing tone of Mindy's voice echoed her heart's love for him.

"This is something I should be there to tell you. But... I can't."

Mindy's voice became a shout. "Now, I *am* scared!" She yanked the phone closer.

"I've been asked by Roy and others to help find the president."

"And, that means..."

"That we're going in."

"Damn it Mac! Stop talking in riddles. What do you mean?" Mindy knew what it meant. Images of loved ones kissing soldiers goodbye at dockside flowed through her thoughts as tears cascaded down her cheeks. She was going to be one of those loved ones. Without the dockside embrace. She started sobbing uncontrollably. In part, because she knew in her heart, that in his heart, Mac was a soldier. A soldier constantly under fire. It was who he was. Fighting his memories, mired in regret for losing his men, fogged in by a sense of destiny—and running from the shoebox and his PTSD.

"I'm to accompany a special ops team—Marines—with Colonel Butcher. We're going in-country, after the president."

"But... but, you're too old, damn you!" Mindy shouted, throwing off the blankets and turning to sit on the edge of the bed—the bed where they had so often made love, had shared love. "You can't do this. Not now!"

Mac's groan warmed her heart. She knew his love mirrored hers. They were connected by heartstrings. But those were only so good. She needed him there, beside her. She had news.

Her chin dropped to her chest, her sobs shaking the bed. "Mac, you can't go!" Mindy hesitated. This was not at all how she expected it to go. She was going to share the news over tonight's candles. Candles she had long since blown out. Mindy gathered her thoughts and emotions. Should she tell him? Would it give him more reason to be careful and come home? Or would it cause him worry, even bring on the shoebox at a moment when he needed to concentrate? The decision stormed in her heart.

"Dearest Mindy. I have to go. Call it duty, loyalty to Roy, to our country. To you, our future. I'm needed and I've got to go."

"Go? Needed? I need you here, more! Here with me and... and our baby!" she blurted.

"Oh, God, no." Mac's voice became a whisper.

She could hear him crying. Her soldier. "Mac?"

"Oh, shit! Damn! Oh, Mindy, Mindy! Oh..."

"Is... that, are you okay? You sound devastated!"

"It's the best news in the world!" he laughed through his tears. "Of course, it is! I just don't know what to do. I need to be there with you, for you. I *am* devastated because I'm not there! Really, our baby?"

Mindy fell back against the sheets. She pulled a pillow up to her chest, hugging it as in her mind she was hugging Mac. "Yes, our baby." She composed her thoughts. She had to be strong for Mac. He had to know she would be all right. "So now, you'll have two of us to come home to! Can't you get some leave before you go?"

"No, I don't think so. I've got to get down to Quantico this morning, and we fly out in a few days after we train and sort out the ahh... game plan. So it'll be an intense couple of days. Roy said so."

"Are you fit enough? Mac, you've been through so much already. Your wounds? What does it entail, or can't you say?"

"I feel strong. Yeah, good. And you guessed it. That's all I can say. That, and that I love you with all my heart, my entire being. I will be careful, trust me. For you, and our baby! I'd better go, now."

"Mac?"

"I know, Mindy. I do. I know how much you love me because it's how much I love you. You take care of yourself and *our* baby. Hopefully, we'll find the president in short order. I pray she's okay."

"Yes, I will pray that, too. I am yours, in heart and soul. Go with God's protection." She hung up, rolled over onto the pillow, and cried herself to sleep.

CHAPTER 40

The Storm

"Our team's name is Unity One," Roy said, as he threw his duffle onto the loading skid. "Tandy came up with that one. Sounds kinda candy-assed, but I know he was thinking of Margie."

"I bet, too, he was thinking of us working with the Marines," Mac laughed. "You know, Colonel, the Marines are good men—young and combat-ready. I've enjoyed these past three days. That Major Juarez, though. Man, he's a tiger! I woulda thought we'd have a higher-ranking officer leading."

"You forgot I'm a colonel?" Roy laughed.

"If you'll excuse me, sir. I said *lead*, not follow."

They both laughed. It had been a special few days. Mac had been given the handle 'Professor,' and Roy, 'The Man.' The bonding of the team, the Marine's 'Semper fi', had unified them solidly into one unit, with one purpose: find and rescue President Perserve.

"Justin's already on board at NSA. I hear he's been magnificent," Roy bellowed above the noise of the forklift taking the skid to the cargo door on the C-240 Stealthmaster.

"Magnificent? A geek?" Mac laughed back. He was excited, feeling strong. Pumped. He was the best shot on the entire team. He could rappel as good as any of them. It was the HALO jump that they had not had time to practice. He'd done well in the simulator. But the jump remained a question. Live fire always got Mac on edge, at his best. He knew he had to be at his best. Mindy and baby demanded it.

Once the Stealthmaster had lifted off from Andrews on its direct flight to an air base in the Shenyang Military Region of China, Major Juarez, 'Jock' to his men, went over the intel. "We have the coordinates of the teleporting source. It's in a remote area, up-country. The complex is a series of buildings. SATCOM imagery makes it look more like a lab than barracks. I guess we'll find out soon enough, hey?"

"Roger that, Jock," Roy answered, his eyes hard and firm.

"How is it we're flying out of China?" Mac asked.

Roy answered, "State contacted the vice chairman of the CPC. Their defense head. We got the green light to conduct an emergency search-and-rescue out of their facility. They don't know who or why, assuming they weren't in on this kidnapping. I doubt they are. They've been very cooperative these past few months."

"I find that curious," Jock injected. "President Perserve won as a staunch defender of American principles and economics. Not a pushover."

Roy replied, "China's cooperation will be viewed across the world as helping America and Margie's pursuit of unity. They know that and will play that message to the hilt. Nothing is for free. The only gamble the Chinese are taking is that we don't succeed in our mission. That they'll never have a story to tell the world press."

"Guys," Jock said, sweeping his arm across the team of twelve. "Let's catch some sleep. We've got a tough few days ahead."

———— . ————

Mac stood on the edge of the flight ramp, connected to the Go line, looking out into the dark void of night. Strapped to his back and chest he carried thirty-five pounds of survival gear, plus his M249 and three 200-round box magazines. In addition, there was the twenty-pound HALO rig, oxygen system, and thick jumpsuit. A digital chest-pack display provided all the navigation he needed. And need it, he would. The glide angle to the 666 complex had them jumping at 29,000 feet using TX-500 self-fly, propelled canopies.

They were seventeen miles from the complex when the jump light went green. Jock went first, followed by Roy and Mac and the nine other Marines.

The freezing air cut right through the jumpsuit. Mac no longer felt young. His goggles fogged briefly, bringing on a panic he'd never felt until the navigation display became visible again. He could see all the metrics needed. He was spot on the correct angle and direction. His display showed the status of the other eleven. "All go," he said into his helmet's headset as the team checked in.

Given the mountainous terrain and apparent lack of defenses around the complex, the decision had been made to use the complex's parking area as the landing zone. The team would descend to 500 feet and make the final drop to the ground together, almost canopy-to-canopy. Mac thought it sounded like the *Charge of the Light Brigade*, but the rational given was that below 500 feet, there were no alternative landing areas, and fighting from the ground was more effective than the team arriving serially, fighting from the air. He hoped the rationale was wise. It was one of those aspects of battle that dispelled the notion of 'take care of yourself.' There were just too many variables. He thought of Mindy, on the other side of the world. He thought and prayed.

In spite of his training with the jump simulator back at Quantico, his legs collapsed hard as he hit the pavement. He rolled to the side, his backpack taking most of the impact. He snapped off his flight harness and lay flat on the ground until he heard the signal from Jock. His navigation display showed all twelve were safely on the ground.

Following the plan, the team broke into two six-man squads. One to hold the perimeter of a building, the other to clear the building. Working methodically through the complex's four buildings, they found no one. An exhaustive search. No sign of the president.

The 666 complex had been abandoned per the Leader's emergency orders. He had been told two hours earlier of the penetration of their airspace, and one hour ago of objects descending from an airplane. His first impulse had been to destroy the complex, along with all the holohead technology. But even with Juong and Dong gone, he could not envision losing such a technological advantage: the holohead and its basis—Dong's control of the speed of light. All too astonishing. Perhaps he could find another Dong.

He had ordered a company of his crack Sentry scouts to deploy in pincer movement around the complex. Once the enemy had landed and cleared the buildings and determined the area abandoned, they would be easier to flank and capture. He needed more bargaining chips.

The hair on the back of Mac's head stood on end. This was too easy an operation. After clearing the buildings, the team had reassembled in groups of three, spread out, using the hilly edges of the parking area as parapets. "Jock," Mac whispered. "What d'ya think?"

"Looks like a bust, for sure," Jock replied. "My instructions are to gather intel from each building right before the STABO boys haul us out of here. My guess is they'll send in cruise ordnance once we evac."

"We gotta hurry on the intel, then. I sense it!" Mac yelled, holding his M249 close, energized by the strength he felt in his arms, his core. He was home where he belonged. With his brothers.

Dawn was breaking against the overhead clouds as two of the team set up SPIE harnesses for extraction. Three long-range Seahawks were due within five minutes from the carrier offshore. The men gathered, attaching their harness D-rings to three separate ropes. They would be pulled up in sets of four, strung together on a rope. One set per Seahawk. The plan had called for the president to be tethered to one of the Marines on the first rope. But with no trace of her, they were ready to evac. Most were already attached, waiting. Mac, the veteran with the most combat experience, felt sure that they were in a trap, being setup. That the enemy would storm out of the woods at any minute. He had no idea why their team had not encountered resistance. Perhaps, he guessed, they want some of us alive. He waited to attach his D-ring.

Just as the first Seahawk swept in over the south hill, the sun's early rays reflecting off its windows, the forest to the west erupted in gunfire. The Seahawk snagged the first string of the team, the four dangling in space, firing their weapons randomly into the woods. The crew member manning the Seahawk's left-door GAU-27/C gatling gun shredded the forest as the pilot flew off over the northern hill.

The hills had provided a stealth location for the complex. The hills also presented the Scout's commander with an opportunity for an elevated attack into the parking lot. However, in his anxiousness, he had kept his troops low on the flanking hills to execute a pincer movement. No one had told him such a strategy did not work from heavily treed cover that would hinder rapid troop maneuvering.

Jock and the remaining seven could see the enemy troops coming from the woods. Roy, the next priority after the president, had been shot in the chest. He was put on the second string. Jock radioed up to the next Seahawk to make a pass, blasting the hills with both side guns. The third Seahawk was to follow closely, benefiting from the covering fire. The second Seahawk would then be on its own to circle around and grab the final string of four. Jock's strategy worked. Roy and the two strings of four were now up and over the north hill. The ninth Marine was already hooked to the third rope, waiting for the final three.

The Scout's fire intensified. Jock spun to the ground, hit in the leg and shoulder. The Marine next to him went down, shot in the stomach. The third Seahawk was on approach.

"Professor!" Jock yelled, motioning Mac to hook up. He signaled that he, Jock, and the wounded Marine would stay and provide suppressing rear-guard fire.

"No way in hell, Jocko!" Mac yelled back, his eyes ablaze. He was in his element. He felt Jaime and Lenny and Bobby—his brothers—next to him. This is where he belonged. What he was made for: squad leader. Finishing the mission and getting his troops to safety.

The strap of the M249 was binding on his neck, a pile of spent 5.56mm shells trailing behind as he swept the charging Scouts. He ducked, falling twice as he raced to Jock. Mac pulled hard on Jock's SPIE harness and D-ring, rapidly fastening him and the wounded Marine to the third and fourth rings on the rope.

"No, no!" Jock yelled. "No!"

The last Seahawk swept in low, snagging the tethered rope and pulling the three Marines up. Mac's eyes met Jock's for the briefest of seconds—a look that conveyed all that need be said: "Semper fi, my brother. You've done well—things don't always work out. Godspeed."

"We can't leave him," Jock yelled into the swirling air. "We can't!" Jock did his best to fire at the Scout's as they advanced on Mac. The last he saw was the barrel of Mac's M249, glowing in the morning mist.

"No! Double shit, no!" Jock screamed.

It was too much like *Platoon*. It was all wrong.

CHAPTER 41

The Recovery

Roy, breathing hard against the trach tube in his throat, lay in his hospital bed, talking with Acting President Tandy. "We lost Margie, and Mac," he said, his words clipped.

Tandy looked out the window, across the parking lot of the Walter Reed Medical Center. "By some miracle, we had only three wounded. You and the two Marines," he replied, solemnly. "The good news, you'll all recover."

"Jacob, we shouldn't have left Mac. Damn it!" Roy retorted.

"That Seahawk pilot had her orders. Evac, stay low, and get to China," Tandy said softly, contemplating the cost of war. "She did the right thing, saving her crew and the last string. The Chinese were amazed she made it back, what with all the hits her ship took. Let's make no mistake about that aspect. The Chinese have been extremely helpful. They took tremendous care stabilizing you and Juarez, the other Marine. I have people at State working right now with their Chinese counterparts. At the least, from this tragedy, we might be able to improve relations. They've been informed that our mission did not retrieve our target. They've expressed a willingness to help."

"Still…" Roy replied. He was not one to cry. The racial overtones of life and his battle experience had taught him to check his emotions. To always move forward, keeping his eyes on the prize. But now, as the tears flowed, what he prized most, his Margie, seemed lost forever.

Margie sat in wonder, her legs dangling over the cliff edge as she looked back into the crevasse. "Kwang-Ju. The sun's rays against those ragged walls are so beautiful, painting purple, golden hues. Reminds me of Zane Grey's cowboys, seeing the Grand Canyon for the first time," she said, wistfully, thinking of the grandeur of America. Home. Would she ever see it again?

Kwang-Ju smiled, hearing her soft tone, the words unnecessary.

Below her feet, a three-hundred foot drop to the beach. To her left, a narrow animal track that seemed to disappear into the mountain side. She raised her face to the breeze, her ears to the crashing surf below. The smell of salt air was invigorating, the breeze scrubbing her memory of the rug in the closet, the hut, the look on that insane leader's face. She opened her eyes to take in the rugged, virgin coastline. No sign of humanity, just nature on its own. "Humanity?" She mouthed the words, thinking of Dong. What was it about Dong that had made her so fearsome, yet sensitive, with a curiosity and sacrifice that had saved Margie?

The wind was choppy and gusting. Margie filled her lungs with the sea breeze and her heart with thanksgiving. Whatever lay ahead, whatever the dangers, she knew she had survived against all odds. So far. She only wished that Roy and her children and her fellow Americans could share this rousing smell of freedom that cleansed her soul.

Kwang-Ju's urgent yell woke her from her reverie. He was pointing out to sea. A boat. It looked like a patrol boat. He began jabbering, gesturing to the left, along the narrow track. He was smiling.

"Are they friendly?" she yelled back, gulping the wind. She had no idea of what he was saying, but his actions said, "Yes."

He scurried to the left, down the narrow track. Margie hesitated. It was less than a foot wide ahead. She peered down at the beach. To come so far, only to slip to her death. "How ironic would that be?" she laughed at the wind. She took two calming breaths. She was giving birth to herself. "And," she said, "I've walked many a mile on narrower fence rails surrounding our Kansas farm. Cakewalk!" Her eyes focused with determination, her heart filled with release, she followed Kwang-Ju down the trail.

As she came around a blind turn, resolute to walk facing forward to maintain her balance—to not put her back against the sheer mountain side—she saw Kwang-Ju ahead, half on the trail and half over the edge.

"Kwang-Ju!" she shouted. "*My* father, hang on!" She stumbled over the same strewn rocks that had tripped him. Putting her right knee down on the outside edge of the trail, her left foot bent against it to pin her left arm to the rock wall, she grabbed his belt.

Kwang-Ju turned his face up to her. She saw his fatalistic look, painted with the briefest flicker of love.

"You're mine to save!" she yelled. "We," thinking the people of the earth, "… need you. Your courage, your simple expectations, your love!" With the word 'love' upon her lips, she found a crack in the rock wall with her left hand. Anchored, she pulled hard on Kwang-Ju's belt. "You *are* mine to save, for you have saved me!" she screamed as she tugged with all her might. For a second she felt as if they both were floating above the trail, in flight.

Kwang-Ju landed back on the trail, Margie on top of him, her left hand shredded but still pinioned in the crack. With her eyes closed, her breath hard upon his face, Kwang-Ju turned to kiss her cheek. She *was* his daughter.

Standing carefully, they took deep breaths and slowly continued down the track until they came to the ridge of a hill that went off to the right, down to the beach. Kwang-Ju motioned that they should stop. He inspected Margie's left hand. Her palm and three fingers were bleeding badly. He tore off the strip of filthy cloth from his head and wrapped her hand. Margie stared at the back of his head as he tended to her. The blood of his wound now covered hers. Her stomach heaved out and in, her chest unable to contain her emotions and her perception of life's rawness and beauty. "Oh," she thought. "To be alive with my fellow man."

——— . ———

They walked across beaches and bluffs until night brought chill winds and darkness. Margie and Kwang-Ju huddled together, half buried in the sand for warmth.

Rays of the rising sun drilled holes through the clouds. Margie woke with a sensation that a large wave was about to wash over them. She shook Kwang-Ju.

They walked for half a day until, over a ridge, she spied a small village. After gesturing that he knew someone in the village, Kwang-Ju cautioned her to stay in the brush while he ventured onto the main road. He seemed confident.

Margie stayed hidden the remainder of the day. She was hungry, dying for a drink of fresh water. She could smell herself. As evening came, she feared Kwang-Ju would not return. She had no idea where she was, or how close she was to any friendly nation.

She gasped as she heard footsteps approaching from behind her hiding place. "Mercgy?" came the whisper. She sighed with relief. "Kwang-Ju, I am here," she whispered back. He crept up. She could see his teeth in the dark. He took her hand, leading her to the beach. There were two men next to a small rowboat. They bowed, humbly, then rapidly picked her up and put her gently into the boat.

Kwang-Ju took her hand. He kissed it. His voice quaking, "Mercgy," he said. In the dark she could feel his tears falling on her hand. She pulled him to herself, over the boat's siding. They held the embrace until one of the men uttered a brief order. Kwang-Ju took Margie's hand and in the dark, traced the map she had drawn for his son.

"I don't understand?" she said, as Kwang-Ju repeatedly jabbed his finger into her hand.

"Ma...drin," one of the men said.

Margie repeated it. "Oh, Mandarin! China?"

The man grunted what she hoped was "Yes." She had no choice as they pushed the boat out into the breakers, Kwang-Ju's hand slipping from hers as his voice, "Mercgy... Mercgy!" slipped into the dark.

——— . ———

The men rowed for what seemed hours. Margie was faint from thirst. The sky filled with stars, the rhythmic lapping of the ocean swells turned her faintness to sleep.

She woke with a start. She heard an engine. Pulling herself up to the edge of the gunwale, she saw a patrol boat idling up to theirs. It had the red star of China on the side of its bridge, the flag of China furling from its stern.

"Chinese!" she yelled, coughing with emotion.

The men rowed closer to the patrol boat. A net ladder was lowered. Margie turned to the two men, their faces now visible in the breaking dawn light. They were gray-haired, hardened. Withered, but genuine, for their faces reflected the same joy they saw on Margie's. They hoisted her to the net as two sailors from the patrol boat descended to help her up. She turned to the two men in the boat as it drifted away. She made as if hugging them, her words, "God bless you, my friends," bringing out smiles more of understanding than comprehension. They waved back. The sailors put a blanket around her and guided her through a door to the bridge.

"Captain!" she said to the man standing next to the sailor at the helm. "I *am* Margaret Perserve, *President* of the United States!" She stood as straight as she could. Her father would be proud of her. Both her fathers. She had survived. Her heart was bursting as she fought to hold back her tears.

The officer shook his head, holding up one finger. He picked up the console microphone, speaking rapidly in Mandarin. After a brief exchange, he handed the microphone to Margie along with a set of earphones. The heavily accented voice came through the earphones. "Do you speak English?" it asked.

Margie described her identity and briefly her ordeal to the English-speaking Chinese woman. She was told she would be taken to a nearby port and flown to Beijing.

Still amazed that she had survived, she was taken to the captain's quarters, where she showered and was given a fresh officer's uniform. She was escorted to the patrol boat's small mess where she eagerly ate a meal and drank too much water, the sailors staring at her, whispering. She loved smiling at them. They bowed back.

The captain entered the mess, now fully aware of who his guest was. He approached Margie's table, bracing to his full height. Stiff yet respectful, he slowly saluted. It was at that moment that the fears and doubts—the longings and memory of the struggles—cascaded, let lose. Her fork in her hand, her body quaking, she sat firmly upright in her chair. Firmly to keep the tears from tumbling down her radiant face.

Margaret Perserve, the President of the United States of America—POTUS, the woman the Secret Service called "Unity"—pushed back from the table. She stood, bracing as the soldier she knew her brother Eddie had been, as her husband Roy Butcher was. She stood for all the men and women—the entire citizenry of the United States. Her chest heaved. In her imagination was the image of a harvester taking in wheat from a field so rich, provided by God. The field was America, the wheat its people. She been recovered so that she might serve.

Margie returned the captain's salute for, and on behalf of, America.

CHAPTER 42

The Aftermath

Alone at his executive desk, his humbleness garden no longer apropos to anything, the Leader debated giving the launch signal. Would his generals follow it? It meant annihilation. But America must be taught that it could not indiscriminately send cruise missiles like the ones that destroyed his Building 666 complex.

Pensively watching the pulsing veins in his arm, an arm full of blood—of life—he abandoned his Doomsday thoughts, deciding finally, to consult the pigs in his dreams. He hoped they would be merciful.

——— . ———

There had been much discussion in D.C. about how to verify that the woman so graciously assisted by China was in fact the real Margaret Perserve. Justin had been called in to run concentric tests. No ripples. It looked promising.

Not one to shirk from duty, Roy had volunteered to "check her out."

——— . ———

Margie rolled over, her elbow catching Roy's neck. "Oh!" she cried, touching his bandage. "Are you all right?"

Roy sat up in the large, comfy bed in the President's Bedroom. He felt his neck, laughing. "I'll survive, now that you're home."

He settled down next to his Margie, their legs intertwined. He felt her fingers on his chest, tapping out their love code.

She was home. They both were. America!

Epiloque

Questions

Mindy stood in front of her fireplace, holding hands with Gloria and President Margie Perserve.

Roy, Justin, Blake, and Devon stood with them, completing the circle.

Mindy prayed, "Dear God, we thank you for the safe return of our president. We pray for America, for continued unity. And I ask for a miracle. *Please*, dear Lord, bring Mac home to me and our baby."

She ended, asking the question on all their minds.

"*Mac! Where are you?*"

On a rocky outcrop overlooking endless barren mountain ridges, sat a man. His tears were for the others. The people of the world. He sighed, pressing hard the wrapper of his last MRE to his leaking chest. Behind his tears, he sketched a question across the heavens:

To the life I see inside of you,

I aim my love, I shall return.

Tis no greater wonder across this space,

The warmth I remember in your embrace.

And yet I fear man's greater quest

From hearts of love it seeks to wrest

The very essence of earnestness

The baby's soul of innocence.

Will creation itself suffer storm

As humanity innovates its own life form

In continual pursuit of the new

with little thought for the residue?

Is this what was intended, back in the beginning?

Made in the USA
San Bernardino, CA
11 September 2018